THEY WERE CAPTIVES IN STRIKING EAGLE'S CAMP,
AT THE MERCY OF HIS WILL . . .

McCall sat in the darkened tepee, with Striking Eagle
squatting across from him. To their side lay the buffalo
hunter Skinner, gasping and moaning, making no attempt
to hide his pain. Striking Eagle looked over at the moon-
faced man with disdain. Then he turned to McCall.

"Why have you fought with me, Crow Man?"

"I haven't fought with you. Your braves attacked me.
We've just been trying to make our load."

"You've been killing our brothers. Then you went too
far. You killed the white buffalo."

"We just wanted a few skins."

"Old Hoof says when the white buffalo are gone, the
Kiowa will go. That we will all die off as a people."

McCall didn't answer. He had heard such stories from
the Comanche, Cheyenne and Utes, and he could only
nod. Then, in his halting Kiowan, McCall replied, "I
didn't want to take all the hides, Striking Eagle. I tried to
stop the other hunters, but they wouldn't listen. To keep
me from interfering, they tied me up, just as you found
me."

For a long time Striking Eagle just looked at McCall as
if he could discover the truth with an unblinking gaze.
"You just want to save your life with this story," he
finally said. "But you are both to die making noises like
an animal who has no courage, not like men. . . ."

KIOWA FIRES

KIOWA FIRES

DONALD PORTER

A Dell/Banbury Book

Published by
Banbury Books, Inc.
37 West Avenue
Wayne, Pennsylvania 19087

Dell ® TM 681510, Dell Publishing Co., Inc.

ISBN: 0-440-04558-4

Printed in the United States of America

First printing—April 1983

Chapter 1

"Jesus, did you hear that?" Jack McCall asked Skinner.

"Hear what?" Skinner demanded, looking startled.

As he heard it again, McCall's heart turned over. "There, that noise."

"I don't hear nothing but the goddamn wind," whispered Skinner.

McCall's heart thumped. Lord, he prayed, don't let it be a herd of buffalo. A herd would crash through their wall tent like it was a holly bush.

"Listen," said McCall in a hush.

"I tell you I don't hear a goddamn thing," Skinner whispered.

The two buffalo hunters had been sitting in their tent for five days now waiting for the blizzard to blow itself out. Hearing the noise again, McCall, the taller and younger of the two, reached for his pistol with the cautious movements of a man keeping himself from alarming a nearby rattler.

Catching his drift, Skinner eased himself to his knees. So short, squat and bald that he looked like a turtle, Skinner felt around the canvas floor of the tent for his rifle.

"I know I heard something," breathed McCall.

"Only the goddamn wind," whispered Skinner.

"Then why you whispering?" asked McCall.

Then it rose again above the howl of the wind and this time they both heard it plainly. The keening moan instantly made the little hairs on the napes of their necks fly up. The sobs he heard made McCall envision an angry wounded creature from hell, bent on goring them before he died. Has to be a wounded buffalo, he thought. If they were lucky, just one, not a herd. From the power of the moans and the clear despair of the tones, the creature sounded no more than fifteen feet from the wall of their tent.

As they listened, staring at each other with glazed eyes, the keening grew louder and more desperate.

"What is it?" whispered Skinner.

"I told you," McCall hissed back.

Skinner cocked the hammer on his rifle. "Wolf?"

"Wounded buffalo," said McCall.

"Oh, Jesus," said Skinner with the tremor in his voice of a man who didn't often ask the son of God for help. "He may be looking for a place to scratch."

If so, it was enough to frighten anybody. McCall had seen log cabins against which a few buffalo had decided to alleviate the misery of the ticks that dug under their matted hair; all that remained of the cabins was a jumble of logs after a half dozen thousand-pound animals had rubbed against the house. Even a single buffalo would have their wall tent down in minutes if he rubbed against it. Though their little canvas dwelling had seemed snug for the last five days, McCall now was aware how fragile it really was compared to the blizzard and buffalo.

"If he mashes against the side," McCall said, "we'll shoot him. But let me shoot. I don't want to kill him."

"Don't want to kill him!" hissed Skinner. "What do you want to do? Invite him in for coffee?"

"If I kill him with my first shot, he may fall over onto the tent," said McCall. "I want to hurt him so he'll wander off."

Skinner looked so dubious McCall almost smiled. "Ain't that just going to rile him, Jack?" asked Skinner.

"Who's the shooter here?"

As if he had heard this argument before, Skinner sighed and said, "You are, Jack."

"Who knows the buffalo?"

Skinner refused to dignify this question with an answer, just nodded sourly. McCall noticed, however, that Skinner had pulled his rifle across his lap and was fingering the shells in his vest.

For a few minutes the moan of the wounded buffalo waned and then stopped. McCall felt relieved. He uncocked his pistol.

"He's wandered off," said McCall.

"Thank Jesus."

Then, startling the two, the buffalo started up again, louder and closer this time. Both cocked their guns and shoved them toward the buffalo's high moans, which clearly came through the south wall of the tent. The wind rose and shrieked but couldn't drown the sounds. Whaps of snow hit the tent, making it shudder.

McCall wondered what was about to happen. All the old stories he had heard since he was a boy filled his mind: wolves as big as houses with jaws the size of doors, mountain cats that traveled in packs of fifty, and buzzards so vicious they could tear off a dying man's hand with a flick of their beaks. Something angry and dangerous lurked just feet away from them out there, something about to walk through their tent.

But nothing happened. The animal's wounded cries rose and fell as the fire in their metal stove burned low. At McCall's instructions Skinner cautiously and silently re-filled it from the small pile of wood and buffalo chips. McCall noticed that his hands were slippery with sweat, despite the drafts and the chill in the air of the tent. One hand at a time, he dried them. He still held on to his pistol, although he had debated half a dozen times with himself whether the more powerful .44 rifle would be a better weapon. But he had visions of the tent around his ears like a net, and the long barrel of the rifle would be useless with the tent and an angry buffalo on top of him.

"What're we going to do?" hissed Skinner.

"Just wait," said McCall. "He may die soon. How long can he last?"

Jack McCall thought back, but he couldn't remember another situation just like this one in his twenty years of hunting buffalo. He had certainly been in tight spots before, but up to now he had known what he was facing: the sun, a winter storm, Indians, wolves, or thieves after his hides. Despite the tales of the Plains, he had never seen any giant wolves or monstrous buzzards, and what he hadn't seen, Jack McCall didn't much believe in. As he shifted uneasily in the gloom of the tent, he wondered what to do. If he could get the advantage with action, he ought to get on with it.

From the beginning, this trip hadn't panned out as they wanted. He and Skinner should have found a herd of buffalo by now, ten days out, and should have made their hides and been on their way back, but you could never tell about the buffalo. Maybe what the Indians said was true: that the buffalo came out of a hole in the ground in the spring to wander over the plains and then went back underground in the winter. Sometimes you could wander around for weeks without seeing a herd; other times it was all you could do to get out of their way.

When the storm hit, McCall had done what he always did, pulled in his horns and waited it out. He carried a little wood in the wagon, and a sack of buffalo chips just for such emergencies.

So he and Skinner had sat in here for five days now, waiting before they continued their hunt. Skinner Kincade was all right when McCall was killing buffalo, but he wasn't someone McCall enjoyed being cooped up with for days at a time. Skinner got more and more mean as he had less and less to do. Normally he was busy skinning the buffalo that McCall shot, but about all he could do when there weren't any buffalo was to sharpen that ten-inch skinning knife of his and complain about his lifetime streak of bad luck.

McCall didn't believe in bad luck. Somehow he had learned, maybe from the Cheyenne he had spent two years with as a boy, that luck came in two colors, good and bad, and that a fellow didn't get too much of one without some of the other. Of course, a fellow could get washed out by bad luck and have all his chips cashed in, but that was part of the luck of the draw. Skinner, on the other hand, expected to make their hides the first week out and seemed to take it as a personal affront that the buffalo weren't waiting around outside Hays City for McCall to gun them down. Well, McCall had been hunting buffalo long before it had become so popular—in Hays City some said it rivaled the '49 gold rush as a way to get rich fast—and he reckoned he would be hunting long after hard-tails like Skinner went on to mine silver or dig for some other treasure.

"I'm going out there," McCall announced to Skinner.

"What?"

"It ain't got no quieter, and if it's a buffalo, might as well put him out of his misery and get its hide after the storm lets up."

"You can't go five feet in that storm without getting lost," said Skinner.

"I'm going out on a rope. You hold one end."

"Suppose you don't come back," Skinner said. His face, as devoid of hair as his bald head, glistened madly in the lamplight. "I ain't coming out after you, Jack."

"I ain't asked you to."

"I'm just telling you," said Skinner.

"And I ain't asked you to."

"You're a damn fool to leave here."

McCall smiled. "I don't think I ever called you a damn fool, Skinner."

"I ain't never gone out in such weather. And it's dark too."

"You just hold on tight to the rope," McCall said. "If I yank it twice, pull me back in."

"Damn it, you don't know what that is out there!"

"Tie it around your waist, will you?" asked McCall.

"Around my waist?"

"Just like I'm doing, see? I don't want it getting away from you."

"Suppose it's a grizzly or something and he pulls me off with you?"

"Then we'll have to deal with Mr. Griz together, won't we?"

"Damn it, Jack."

"You untie that rope, Skinner-man, and grizzly or not, I'm going to scalp that bald head of yours when I get back."

Skinner nodded glumly as McCall tucked his pistol in his belt and reached for his buffalo greatcoat.

*   *   *

At the crest of the hill a powerful gust of wind and snow, like a maddened buffalo, smashed against the Kiowa hunter and knocked him off his feet into a four-foot snowdrift.

Panting from his efforts, Lone Wolf lay motionless in the snowdrift to catch his breath. How much easier to just remain here!

He would grow cold. Lone Wolf's feet would grow painful and freeze as hard as icicles. His fingers would become stiff and painful, but then he would grow warmer as the cold numbed his trunk. Gradually he would grow drowsy. He would drift off to that warmer world below, where his father and mother and all the people he had loved had gone when they died. To taste the promise of warm death, Lone Wolf sank back into the snowdrift. As he relaxed, cold fingers of snow worked their way around his buffalo coat's collar and tickled his neck, jerking him into a half-upright position.

No! Lone Wolf pushed himself up to his elbows. As a Kiowa warrior, he couldn't give way to that cold trickle, the finger of death. Angry at himself, he pulled himself to his feet, but he staggered as he struggled to regain his footing. As he rose, three more times the wind knocked him over. Finally he anchored his lance into the frozen ground and used it to steady himself. Now that he had reached the top of the hill, maybe he could see the Red Sand caves.

But no matter how hard he peered, all Lone Wolf saw was a swirling world of white snow. He had only a general idea in which direction lay the Red Sand caves. Panting, he leaned forward to see if he could make out any solid form.

Nothing. No matter how hard he peered through the

white gloom he saw no firm tree or rock to give him direction. Swirling about him in the wind, Lone Wolf saw the faces of white spirit-devils shriek and leer at him. As they whirled, they hooted with laughter, slapped him with their hard, icy tongues and made him shiver with dread, for he heard in their shrieks a yearning to crush him in their jaws. If he didn't find the caves, they would shortly carry him off.

Best to get off the top of the hill, he told himself, if I can't see anything. Using the lance to steady himself, Lone Wolf picked a path downward through the two-foot-high snow. His boots were wet all the way through. As if frozen, his toes creaked as they squished in puddles of melted snow. His deerskin leggings were soaked to above his knees. His breath came in shallow pants, as if his lungs didn't have the power to draw much air. Even if he got to a fire soon, as unlikely as that was, he would probably lose some toes or part of a foot. But something would turn up to save him, wouldn't it?

He couldn't even imagine what.

At the thought, rage as furious as the blizzard swept through him and Lone Wolf cursed himself. Damn women anyway!

On he trudged, fueled by his anger. Sweat dripped off his chest, while stabs of pain from his feet told him how severely the cold had attacked them. How much longer could they carry him? How much more strength did he have? Not much. The hill he had climbed had seemed like a mountain, and now even going down took a big effort. He couldn't march much farther.

In the middle of his anger at his helplessness, Lone Wolf still wanted to see his wife Onni again, even though she had caused all this. As well, it made him almost sob to think he wouldn't see his children Sun Boy and Little

8

Cloud again. Just once more, he begged the wolf powers, but the only answer was the shriek of the storm. He had known when he said good-bye that he might not see them again. Every warrior knew that whenever he left camp, but now Lone Wolf realized that he hadn't really known it when he had left camp this time.

He wanted desperately to convince Onni that he hadn't meant to hurt and embarrass her, and he wanted to make sure that Sun Boy was properly taught how to ride and shoot. Lone Wolf wanted to talk to his friend Left Hand to persuade him to educate the boy properly. And Little Cloud, that six-year-old flower—was he never to have her hot, wiggly legs and arms snuggling up to him and feel again her excited breath on his neck?

Lone Wolf wanted to cry out in rage, but the storm around him roared him down. His anger pushed him forward, giving him the fury he needed to push through the knee-high powder.

It had all started so simply. Late last summer Lone Wolf had gone out deer hunting with Left Hand. They had had a good time and good luck; each killed a deer. On the way back, at the top of Double Hill, both spotted Elk Woman, Eagle Beak's wife, out alone picking Juneberries.

"What's she doing out here alone?" asked Lone Wolf.

"Ho, ho! That one!" Left Hand said.

"One plumb morsel."

"I could go for her."

"I think I'll stop down there and do me a little other kind of deer hunting."

"Oh, no! That deer's mine," said Lone Wolf. "She's been giving me sweet looks for the past three months."

So the two friends had argued playfully over which of them would sidle up to this saucy woman, yet under the banter, the sharp edge of urgency showed, for each wanted her. After all, any fool could see she wasn't pleased with that worthless Eagle Beak. They finally agreed to match each other for the opportunity. Left Hand lost the toss and rode on to camp with a cooked-up story they both agreed to.

In the buzzing valley that hot August day, Lone Wolf thought Elk Woman fluttered in joy at seeing him. As well she might have; Lone Wolf might not be a Big Belly and sit in council all night, but he brought home many deer and buffalo and had three scalps to his credit. Everybody knew one day he would sit with the elders. He belonged to the Denoskin, the second-best war society. Her husband Eagle Beak might be an Onde, of the upper class, and the son of a great chief, but he had done nothing with the legacy his father had left him.

When he showed Elk Woman the deer he was bringing in, she complained about the poor game that Eagle Beak brought home. Seeing his opening, Lone Wolf complained about Onni, how she devoted herself to the children so much these days that she never had time for him.

Elk Woman responded that she would always have time for him if he was her husband. He replied that a real man needed a woman to be ready for him. Elk Woman giggled and said she was always ready for a real man. Lone Wolf complained that his wife never seemed ready. Onni must be the only woman in camp who had her monthly three times a month!

Elk Woman laughed at everything he said. She was a fine-looking woman, all right. Not thin and bony like Onni, Lone Wolf's wife, but with solid flesh on her strong frame. When Onni washed herself in the stream, it made Lone Wolf angry to look at how thin she was, as if she didn't eat what he brought home in order to shame him

10

with her bony looks. But this woman before him had full breasts and hips that swelled out like mountains. Her neck was thick and her head sat squarely on her shoulders, whereas Onni's was too long and angular. What had he ever seen in her? A man was a fool when he was young.

But Elk Woman—a man could sink into a big, firm woman like her, comforted by such strength the way the earth comforts the dead.

That August day it had been hot in the valley. As the afternoon grew hotter, Elk Woman loosened the top thongs of her deerskin tunic. Her bold eyes stared at him in a dreamy way while her fingers untied the thongs, which made Lone Wolf's heart pound, his stomach slosh with fire, his limbs weaken. He felt dizzy and lost within a swirl of hot, exciting confusion as they circled each other with gay banter and dancing eyes. That she smiled so roguishly and didn't bother to cover her half-exposed breasts clearly told him she was as willing as he.

Soon they were below the chest-high bushes together. That day Lone Wolf made love to Elk Woman three times, and what times they were! Over the next week they met alone four times, over the next month more than a dozen. Lone Wolf became as caught up in sliding around behind tepees with her as he had been when he chased girls at the age of eighteen.

Somehow they always managed to meet alone, although in the small camp of the Kiowa, with just two hundred lodges, such a feat continually amazed Lone Wolf. After three months, Lone Wolf not only couldn't but never wanted to stop. He hardly spoke to his wife Onni. He only came to the lodge to talk to the children every couple of days; nights he spent in his men's society tepee so he could sneak away without questions or dirty looks. He became comfortable with this way of life. True, Onni looked hurt whenever he saw her, and he didn't get much well-prepared food when he did come around, but things never were just the way you wanted them.

One day Elk Woman announced, "Let's get married, Wolf."

"How? You have a husband."

"I'll leave him."

"I don't know. Onni's not interested in my having another woman."

"Ha! Does she tell you everything you can and can't do?"

Lone Wolf flushed. "No, of course not."

"Maybe you don't want me."

"You know I do. But I don't have the rank Eagle Beak does."

"You will have. Being born Onde is the worst thing that can happen to a man, I think."

"It's true that everything I own I've had to take for myself."

"Eagle Beak's worthless. I need a real man."

He grinned with pleasure. "Me?"

"You—if you're not too frightened of your wife to take me."

"Of course I'm not frightened of her."

He had felt for a long time that his growing status with the tribe demanded that he take another wife, but when they were young and green he had foolishly promised Onni that he would never take a second or third wife. Now she held him to this promise. It wasn't fair. His Denoskin lodge brothers laughed at him. His best friend Left Hand had three wives, all sisters and all beauties, who treated him splendidly. At night when Left Hand came home to the lodge, they spread out his buffalo robe and vied for who should bring him his bowl of stew. They

12

were lovely to be with, those plump, giggling sisters. According to Left Hand they vied for his pleasure under the buffalo robe too. To hear his friend talk about it, nothing Left Hand wanted those girls to do under there was too much. Lone Wolf's best friend had everything a man could want. Why was Lone Wolf so cursed?

But if he could get Onni to see that it wasn't right to insist that he keep his youthful and foolish vow, he could take another wife—or even two. The poor gifts he and Onni gave away at gift givings embarrassed Lone Wolf. How could Onni think one woman could tan enough hides, decorate enough leggings, or sew enough tunics to bring honor to a warrior as important as he was becoming? Surely even a woman as stupid as she could understand this. As Left Hand said, Onni would get over it in a few months. Even a woman could figure out whose bow shot the deer she ate.

Elk Woman was just as fed up with Eagle Beak, so in the manner that the Kiowa divorce, she renounced her husband three times. She picked up her tepee and moved it to within twenty feet of Lone Wolf's.

Suddenly Lone Wolf's world turned upside down.

Onni wouldn't let Lone Wolf into the tepee at all. Eagle Beak hung around outside the flaps of Elk Woman's tepee screeching and carrying on in such a crazy fashion that after a week Old Hoof and the other Big Bellies had had to do something.

To Lone Wolf they looked like a bunch of slow prairie dogs hunched over, struggling to decide where to go next. They came and stood before the two tepees just listening while Eagle Beak shouted at them, accusing Lone Wolf and Elk Woman of being as evil as owls and bats. Lone Wolf stayed in the Denoskin lodge, where he and Left Hand and their cohorts peered out under the dewflaps

13

to watch it all with barely concealed mirth, only making sure their laughter wasn't heard by passers-by, who would have been angered by such callow mockery.

Old Hoof and the other Big Bellies held one of these all-night old men's ceremonies over what he had done. Lone Wolf wanted to go off hunting till the whole thing died down, but Old Hoof sent word that if he vanished for a week or so he might as well not come back to camp but stay out as an exile.

At this point Lone Wolf became worried. He said to Left Hand, "Go talk to them, brother."

"Aw, don't let those old men bother you!"

"Easy for you to say. Maybe that dumb Eagle Beak will cut off her nose or ears. I want to get him quiet."

"Will you give him some horses?"

Lone Wolf grinned. "I got a couple of spavined mares he can have."

"If you're not going to take this seriously there's no sense in my talking to them."

"I'll give him four horses, one a war horse."

"All right, then."

"He's got to leave her alone, though."

"It's his pride, brother."

"I know."

"He's Onde, you're Ondegupa," he said, referring to the aristocracy and the middle class of Kiowa society.

"I'll be an Onde one day."

"One day a bullfrog will get wings and fly, but not today."

Lone Wolf thought. "Six horses, then, but not a one more."

Both Left Hand and Lone Wolf were astounded when, through emissaries, Eagle Beak refused the offer, wouldn't make a counteroffer, and said he would kill Lone Wolf just as soon as he left the lodge of the Denoskin.

In fact, he challenged Lone Wolf to a knife duel, which made both of them groan and wonder if he had gone completely crazy.

The last knife duel between two bitter young men, both proud and spirited, had happened eighteen months ago. The two had quarreled for years and years over the Onde beauty Drema Deer Woman. When months of negotiation had become useless, the two determined to settle the matter once and forever.

All the men of the tribe had gathered out on a plain in a ring, with Old Hoof calling on *Wakan-Takan* to decide the contest. When their brothers brought the two naked contestants together in the center of the ring, their left arms, as far up as the elbow, were firmly lashed together with stout, thick cords of buffalo hide. They were bound so thoroughly that the possibility of their breaking away was beyond question.

Into the right hand of each was then placed a hunting knife with a heavy buckhorn handle and a blade about nine inches long, prepared for the occasion by having been sharpened to a keen edge on both sides. The brothers withdrew some twenty feet from the combatants, drawing from their belts similar knives, and when Hoof gave the signal, the fight began.

And lasted but moments.

In the sun the blades flashed up and down, up and down, and in seconds the men looked as if paunches of blood had been sloshed over them. Legs, arms and blades swirled through flying blood. Not two or three minutes went by before a mortal thrust by one was followed by a fierce blow from the other, gashing through the side of the first man's neck. His life spurted upward in a bright red arc, then both fell back lifeless to the ground.

Had either survived the conflict, according to the code of honor, it would have been the duty of his own brother to knife him to death.

The two were stretched out side by side on the spot where they had fallen, buried in the customary manner, and left to rest together in peace at last.

As if nothing had happened, Drema Deer Woman married one of the youths' cousins two months later and was now pregnant.

"No," said Lone Wolf. "None of that craziness for me."

"He's serious about it," said Left Hand. "Old Hoof has to take him seriously. He's not only an Onde, but a Denoskin lodge brother."

"Hoof! Nobody takes that old man's jumping around and singing seriously. That's for scaring children."

"I think he's a joke too, Cub," said Left Hand, "but you got to realize a lot of people don't."

"To hell with him."

"I don't know how you're ever going to get out of this tepee without meeting up with him."

"That goddamn woman!"

"They're nothing but trouble," agreed Left Hand with a weary sigh. "That's for sure."

Then to head off an inevitable blood bath Hoof and the other Big Bellies came up with another idea: that Lone Wolf give Eagle Beak all his property, agree not to meet with or speak to Elk Woman ever again, and go hunting for the hide of a white buffalo.

"All my horses!" exclaimed Lone Wolf. "No."

"Every one, bro," said Left Hand.

"Come on!"

16

"Take it, take it, take it. I'm telling you this stupid Eagle Beak is crazy."

"I knew that before. I'm happy enough not to speak to that woman, but there aren't any white buffalo out there for me to find."

"Don't you see? The old folks just want you out of the village for a couple of months."

"If I don't bring it back it doesn't mean I have to duel him or anything crazy?"

"Naw, don't be silly. I got it all fixed up. It just sounds like he's being rough on you."

"Taking all my horses and weapons *is* pretty rough. Will you hunt for Onni and the children while I'm gone?"

"You know I will, Cub," said Left Hand. "What's a best friend for?"

"Thanks. If I ever needed a friend, this is the time."

"So can I tell them yes?"

"Yeah, tell them yes."

"When will you leave?"

"Right now, if they want."

"They want."

The way things stood, not knowing whether any minute his wife was going to throw a bowl of hot soup in his face or Eagle Beak was going to knife him or Elk Woman was going to throw herself sexually on him in the middle of camp, it was just as well he leave for a while.

Loping out on Yawl, Left Hand's best hunting horse, Lone Wolf left camp in wry exasperation. Women! While this wasn't the first time he had gotten into trouble over a behind waggling itself at him, it certainly was the time that had caused him the most trouble. He struggled to accept this trip philosophically. He would be lonely out hunting by himself, but he saw no reason to run himself ragged looking for a creature that didn't exist—or if it did, there

17

hadn't ever been more than a half dozen of them in all of time. Certainly neither Lone Wolf nor anybody he had ever talked to had ever seen a live one, and the one white buffalo hide that the Ute shaman waved around in ceremonies looked more ash-grey than white, although perhaps once it had been lighter.

If this trip was just a means of Old Hoof's getting him out of camp till things cooled down, there was no reason for Lone Wolf to get himself into a sweat. After all, what sane hunter wanted to run into a white buffalo, even if they existed? If the stories told around winter campfires by old men were true, meeting a white buffalo would be too much like running into a combination of cyclone and angry summer sun all wrapped up in one blazing buffalo hide. The odds weren't great you would come out alive, and while it might be an honor to have a white buffalo present himself to you, it was an honor Lone Wolf, who had something of an easy nature, would just as soon forgo. He didn't expect to see one, anyway. Weren't white buffalo just stories old men and women made up to frighten children? The only man of the Kiowa who claimed to have actually seen one was Horse Leg, and what sensible person believed anything else that Horse Leg put out?

So Lone Wolf had decided he would wander around for a few weeks, stay out of the way of the Cheyenne and the white men that he had heard were hunting through the plains, and let things die down at home. Maybe by then Onni would realize that another woman in the lodge would do half the work, and if he did not choose Elk Woman, he could take another wife.

But then this storm had come up when he was two weeks out, catching Lone Wolf in the middle of a wide valley. At first it hadn't worried him. He had turned east and worked his way toward the Red Sand caves, but before he could reach safety the snow had become so thick he couldn't see his way.

When he reached the little slopes where the caves should have been, he found he was north, not east, and that there were no caves on this side of the valley. He had had to leave his horse, Yawl, then, for the animal had so exhausted itself that it couldn't get up. That was when Lone Wolf knew he was in trouble.

The first thing he would need would be fresh food. He had hesitated for more than an hour, but while the horse struggled to stand, it didn't have the strength. It hurt, but he plunged a knife into the beast's heart. Having killed Yawl, he cut off a part of his friend's haunch, wrapped his buffalo coat around himself more tightly against the blizzard, and set out eastward. He felt frightened now, but he would be safe if he reached the caves. With the coyote dung there he could build a fire.

Lone Wolf had set out with as fast a step as he could manage, about as fast as a buck with two broken legs. His feet felt wrapped in green buffalo hides and lifting each took a big effort. Every fourth or fifth step a gust of the wind would knock him to the side, making him use precious energy to right himself. Still he pushed on. Stopping meant death, although warm death began to look like an attractive alternative to the pain of pulling himself through the snow.

Now it seemed like hours that he had been pulling one leg up and pushing it forward, picking himself up out of yet another snowbank the buffeting wind had knocked him into and struggling to hold the heavy buffalo robe around himself. But Lone Wolf knew it had not been long, for he had started to count his footsteps when he set out from the north side of the valley, and he had only taken some four or five hundred steps.

19

Panting, he paused to look about himself. Somewhere here should be the little rocks that were scattered in front of the caves.

Nothing, just the swirl of snow. Lone Wolf pushed on another hundred steps. He peered through the white swirl looking for the rocks, but he saw only the white faces of the wind spirit shaking with hearty, jeering laughter. That wind had the face of the creature he was looking for, Lone Wolf reflected, the face of the white buffalo. I've found it, he said bitterly to himself, and it's the storm that will freeze me to death. He cursed Old Hoof for sending him on this stupid quest, and he cursed Onni for acting like a moonstruck puppy, and for good measure he cursed Eagle Beak for caring about one woman when with his Onde status he could have any girl in the village.

Then Lone Wolf tripped, which made him stop and rest once he had pulled himself again to his feet. Where was he now? Around him the wind howled and the snow whirled as if he stood in the midst of a waterfall. The wind and snow spirits were so cold themselves that they wanted to suck the warmth out of him. They longed to hug him to death in their freezing embrace. The thought made Lone Wolf shiver. But where was he? Where were the Red Sand caves?

Dimly he made out a firm shape to his right. Painfully he put himself into motion, using his lance to inch his way toward the shape. It couldn't be! His mind reeled. No! It was that old dead Yellow Hard tree he had started from this morning! Lone Wolf was back where he had set out from hours ago.

He felt so bleak inside at this realization that the wind seemed to howl through the spaces between his bones. Around him the wind's faces laughed more loudly. The buffalolike face of the snow creature bounced up and down in mirth at the joke he had played on him. How dare Lone Wolf think he could face them and beat them? they asked as they roared their laughter.

Lone Wolf sank to his haunches to rest for just a few moments. He would rest and then get up and start out again. He hadn't paid close enough attention and had veered to the left. His mind must have wandered when the wind had knocked him over, but this time he would make sure he kept his thoughts strictly on the direction.

Lone Wolf pulled his great buffalo coat around himself, making of it a little tepee that sheltered him from the wind while he rested. At first the wind tried to snatch it out of his hands, but after his enemy the snow had weighed it down, it was harder for the wind to take it. Lone Wolf laughed at how they had outsmarted each other.

Gradually he regained his breath and considered what to do. But no matter how he turned it in his head, he could see no way to escape. He had used all his strength. He might make it another fifty steps, but probably not even that. Just as Yawl had reached the end of his strength three hours ago, so had Lone Wolf. He couldn't make it now through this storm to the caves even if he had a rope to pull himself along and guide him.

His limbs trembled in helpless anger and twitched as he prepared to get back up. He would keep walking till he found shelter. He might be just twenty or thirty steps from the caves. He had seen men die a dozen feet from the tepee because they didn't know it was there. That wouldn't happen to him.

But his legs wouldn't obey. Five times he struggled to get to his feet, and each time his legs collapsed under him, aching with weariness. His chest felt cold and hollow from the hours of exertion. A stream of grief, as cold as rain, shot through his chest. He struggled against this as he realized the hopelessness of his situation. What was the use of making any struggle if every struggle was to end in death? He could stand, totter on and die, or he could stay here, keep as warm as possible for another few hours and die without any more painful expenditure of effort, the very thought of which caused him anguish.

He felt torn. If die he must, a part of him wanted to die struggling to escape his fate. Yet another part wanted to rest and to prepare himself for death, to look to see what life had meant to him, and to come to some peace with himself before the snow and wind crushed him.

Death? Death now? Within him fury rose. Suddenly he wanted to see Sun Boy, his eleven-year-old son, once more. The thought of never seeing Little Cloud, his six-year-old daughter, filled him with anguish. It wasn't fair! He hadn't really said good-bye to them, nor had he meant to leave them without him because of his fight with Onni. He had figured the fighting would ease and they would all be together at night in the tepee, happy again. This time with another jolly family member, Elk Woman.

But it wasn't to be. He was going to die because of his fooling around with Elk Woman. What a stupid thing! He wanted to wring Onni's neck at causing such a fuss over nothing. At the same time he wanted to hold her bony frame in his arms and hug her tight and tell her he still loved her as much as he did when they were courting. Then they had said wonderful things to each other and it had seemed as if no girl had ever met a youth like him, and that no youth had ever met a girl like her. Then she became pregnant. Lone Wolf couldn't believe that in her swelling belly lay a child, a person like himself, that he himself had planted there—he could do that!—and he had felt proud to be the father and husband of the family. He agreed to marry her at once, and they were happy. In those days he had brought home a lot of game. They had had jolly times around the fire. Then a couple of years ago it had turned sour. Onni hadn't seen that Lone Wolf was rising in the tribe. She found out about three of his escapades with other women and wasn't quick to forgive him the third time. He had steadily risen from his boyhood society, the Rabbits, to the Hawks, and now was in the Denoskins, the highest war society of all. Without being told, Lone Wolf knew that now that he was an important warrior and hunter of the tribe he was expected to give more game from his hunts to the poorer families and his lodge was to give more gifts at gift giving times.

As the storm raged, Lone Wolf felt the air getting close under the buffalo coat tepee. It was completely black in here. His feet felt as hard as blocks whenever he reached down to touch them. Shortly the cold would rise to his knees, locking them. A part of him sobbed with grief over losing his feet; another part wondered what it would feel like not to be able to move his frozen knee joints. He felt frightened. To allow himself to breathe, he poked his unstrung bow up through the top of the cone of buffalo coat around him to make an air hole.

He couldn't get up and move now even if he wanted to. He knew that. He knew what would happen now. He would grow sleepy and drowsy, and the pain in his legs and fingers would increase and finally lessen as each part of him died.

He didn't have much time. He had to get ready. He had to sing the chant that Little Robe had taught him so many years ago, the one to sing when he knew his time was up.

Grandfather! Grandfather!
Hear me! Accept me!
Old wolf, make a place

For your grandson, who comes
To join you.

I've acted in ways I shouldn't have.
I haven't acted in ways I should.
My heart isn't clean.
Grandfather, grandfather!
Help me to clean myself,
To purge myself of my bad acts,
So that I'm worthy of living with you.

Grandfather! Grandfather!
Hear me! Accept me!
Old wolf, make a place
For your grandson, who comes
To join you.

The chant went on for another twenty verses, and as he sang, Lone Wolf felt better. Some of the weight he hadn't realized he had been carrying since he left camp seemed to lift off. He *had* done things he shouldn't have. He should have dealt with Onni before he started courting Elk Woman, and he shouldn't have allowed his head to become so scrambled over spending so much time with Elk Woman that he couldn't act like a man and do the right thing. The sexuality of her had almost bewitched him.

With these realizations came a sense that he hadn't sung his death chant right. When he touched his legs and feet they felt more numb and hard than ever. Lone Wolf pushed away his grief and started his death chant again, struggling this time to put more of his whole self into it, so that when death came he would be ready. He wanted to mean what he sang with every part of himself, and he sensed that part of him had held back the first time. He wanted to mean it when he said that he was ready to die, that a wolf died and yet his pack lived on, and that a man who clung foolishly to life had no more dignity than a prairie dog.

By keeping his mind completely focused, this time Lone Wolf sang it with a still higher voice and with more of his being in the words and music.

Singing in this way made him feel more satisfied, and now, warmer. If this was the worst of it, death wasn't so bad. He understood now why so many seemed to smile mysteriously as they died: they saw that being dead was to be much less of a struggle than living, and that if you had to go—why, it was a pleasure after all the effort that life took. This thought made Lone Wolf laugh heartily, and in a peculiarly cheerful frame of mind he started his death song for a third time, eager now to put every bit of his remaining strength into it.

His whole being focused on singing properly. He lost count of the number of times he sang. He seemed to have entered a long passageway, dark as a cave but with a shining fire at its end, which he realized with a warm sort of satisfaction was the way to death. He floated forward, feeling no pain, only a kind of lilting joyfulness at understanding that he was part of everything and thus could come to no harm, in the way that nothing could happen to a rock except to be busted into sand—the rock still existed, just in a different form. He moved forward into the cave.

At the back end of the cave he saw it wasn't a light there but a glowing man, all in white, who had brought him a piece of the sun and who waited for him with outstretched arms. The man smiled in welcome to Lone Wolf, who laughed uproariously at his grandfather—but a grandfather as young as he! What good times they would have, he and his young grandfather! Maybe when his father came too, they would all be the same age. Maybe all their grandfathers would be young and hunt as a pack of wolves hunted together, and over the years of good hunting to come their grandsons would join them.

Lone Wolf rushed forward to throw himself into his grandfather's outstretched arms. As he reached them the pleasure he felt rose to a thin, high frenzy. He abandoned himself to a swoon of ecstasy.

With a final shudder he let go. Finally he had arrived home.

Chapter 2

After McCall had bundled up in his buffalo coat, pulled on his buffalo-hide gauntlets and protected his head with a helmet made of buffalo skin, he made his way out into the dim light of dusk, braving the storm and carrying a tin lantern with a single glass eye.

Outside, the rushing of the wind by his head made it harder for him to hear the creature's bellowing. He had a hard time keeping his footing, and twice he fell over in the snow as the coat acted like a sail in the wind. Then he heard it again, and he turned in its direction. McCall almost tripped over the little cone-shaped hill in front of him before he realized that the moaning was coming from it, rising and falling in hard rhythms. He almost laughed.

An Indian was in there! One dumb solitary Indian, and the poor idiot, figuring there wasn't another soul in fifty miles, was singing his way to paradise.

The wind shook his coat, rattling McCall. Continuing to sing as he did, the Indian didn't know he was out here or he would be begging for coffee, if McCall knew Indians. Probably best to yank the rope attached to his waist the two times and have Skinner haul him in without saying a word, as they had no way to care for a half-frozen Injun.

McCall picked up the slack rope and held it for a few seconds. The wind rushed by him, flakes lashed his cheek, and his coat flapped like a shirt in a hurricane. Damn it, he just couldn't. He sighed. Damn Indian would be nothing but trouble, but he guessed one Indian wasn't going to hurt them. Besides, if they were lucky, he might have seen buffalo around here, so that when the storm was over they would know in which direction to strike out.

As soon as McCall reached up under the Indian's buffalo robe, the fellow collapsed. As he slid his hands up under the Indian, the man felt stiff as a log. He probably won't live, McCall said to himself as he picked up the brave in his arms. Probably I'll take him back and he'll shiver himself to death by morning. In the gale winds he just barely managed to hold on to the fellow and give the rope around his waist a couple of yanks.

"What's that?" were Skinner's first words.

McCall staggered on into the tent, bowing under the Indian's weight and keeping his head from bumping into one of the tent's two poles.

"Injun."

"Hell, I see that."

"Kiowa. See how his hair's cut short on the right side? Every Kiowa brave cuts it like that." McCall eased himself to his knees and lay the Indian down by the little stove. "Get me all our buffalo robes," he said to Skinner.

Skinner's mouth dropped open in amazement. "Our sleeping robes? What for?"

"For him. He's about to die of the cold."

"I ain't wrapping no Injun up in what I sleep in," said Skinner.

Shaking his head over Skinner's reply, McCall scrambled about on his knees getting together six blankets and

28

quickly covered the unconscious Indian's form. "Build up the fire, Skinner, and don't give me no argument."

"Hey, Jack," said Skinner. "I don't like this. Let's shoot him and dump him outside. You was the one said we had to ration our firewood."

"Well, I've changed my mind, Kincade," said McCall as he pulled off the Indian's boots.

"Better to shoot him, Jack," said Skinner. "Supposing he comes to?"

"Giving his condition, I wouldn't bet on it."

"He'll attack us."

"You know, his friends might not be more than five hundred yards away out there," said McCall as he massaged the feet so frozen just touching them made him wince. "He might have gotten lost going out for firewood. A shot might bring thirty of them over here."

"Yeah, I hadn't thought of that," Skinner said. He held up his knife. "I'll give his throat a close shave. They can't hear my knife."

"We ain't killing him," said McCall. "They find him killed near a spot where we camped, we're as good as dead."

"Then just put him back out there! He's done stopped that howling he was doing."

"This is the man who can find us buffalo, brother Kincade," said McCall. "Ever think of that?"

"Find us buffalo?"

"Who knows where buffalo are better than an Indian?" asked McCall. "And ain't he going to have some gratefulness to them that saved his life?"

Skinner hesitated and looked around the tent. "I don't know. He looks mighty big and mean to me."

The Indian was large, as tall as McCall but much broader in the chest and jaw. McCall judged him to be in his early thirties, and from the calluses on his hand, not one of the snooty Ondes of that bunch, either. Given that hair style and the well-decorated coat he wore, this was a no-nonsense hunter. Skinner certainly had a point, but if anybody of that tribe knew where to find buffalo, Chief Big Jaw here likely did. At present, frozen and near dead as he was, he might look big, but he certainly wasn't mean. Before he regained his strength, McCall could decide what to do with him.

"Build up the damn fire, Skinner. Last I heard, this outfit still belonged to me, and you come along for the ride."

"I'm here as a partner, was our agreement, Jack."

"Junior partner, as I remember."

Skinner looked down thoughtfully at the skinning knife in his hand. "But you didn't say you was taking on no Indian as a partner with me."

"I ain't. I'm just trying to earn a little gratitude. Now, get busy, will you? I'm getting cold."

Skinner paused to consider it. "All right, but I don't like it."

"I know you don't like it. How about just doing it?"

So in a slow, sullen manner Skinner built up the fire while McCall set out to rouse the Indian and save his frozen limbs. He wrapped the man in blankets and struggled to get a few sips of hot coffee down his throat. He massaged his frozen fingers and feet, making the man groan when he moved the frozen joints. Shortly, the tent warmed up so much that McCall took off his buffalo greatcoat and spread it on top of the blankets over the Indian.

He saw that Skinner, while obeying his orders to keep the fire built up, made coffee and provided him with boiling water. He was still sour about it. McCall's partner had strapped on his .38 pistol and had stuck his skinning knife in his belt as if he expected any moment to be the object of a vicious redskin attack.

He smiled at Skinner's precautions. From the Indian's feeble responses to his treatment, McCall would be surprised if the brave lived till morning.

Lone Wolf was falling over a long cliff at night. Around him the air rushed.

A roaring, then heat. Pain, more pain, and then a long darkness and more shooting pain. He groaned loudly, which startled himself into silence. A man didn't groan with pain. With that thought he realized he was awake, although it was still dark. He lay in a cave. In the gloom he saw a couple of figures moving around.

Lone Wolf was in a cave. His grandfather and his grandfather's father were tending to him, putting him back together after his painful journey from the other world. He remembered now: he had been in the storm, he had frozen, and these grandfathers were warming him up. When he was well they would all go out hunting buffalo, but on a plain where it never dried up like in high summer or grew cold with a blizzard.

"This poor child thanks you, Grandfather," said Lone Wolf, using the most elaborate honorific he could think of in order to get off on the right foot with these spirits. The two grandfathers jumped around to stare at him.

He stared back. Dimly he was aware that they had a piece of hot metal, doubtless ripped from the sun, standing near his side to warm him, and that they had given him a thick layer of blankets while wrapping none around themselves.

"I should wait on you, not you on me," he said to them in his humblest tone.

31

One of them leaned forward with a cup, and Lone Wolf saw he was meant to drink the potion, which looked as black and bitter as night. Shuddering, for who knew what the grandfather's potion would transform him into, he made his heart brave, raised his head and submitted to the drink. Bitter, sweet and hot, it warmed his stomach and made him shudder. He might now suddenly become a hawk or a flea, depending on what they had in store for him.

The grandfathers murmured together in their strange tongue. The cave swam around him. Lone Wolf drifted off again into a world of frigid black mouths with breaths of snow and teeth of ice. In these dreams he flew over the earth, and below rumbled herd after herd of buffalo. If they murmured in another tongue, how was he to understand his grandfathers? The herds of buffalo shook the air as their hooves pranced against the hard earth. Besides, the grandfathers' hair wasn't cut properly. Grandfather Turtle Shiny Head had no hair. Grandfather Crow had long hair, long on *both* sides. No Kiowa grandfather wore his hair so long.

With a start Lone Wolf woke up. He opened his eyes to see the two strange-looking men staring at him.

They weren't grandfathers—but white men! He was trapped by white men who would shortly kill him. He swallowed his fear of their magic. A man didn't allow his enemy to see that he was afraid.

Lone Wolf had seen only a few dozen white men before in his life, and them at a distance as his tribe lived over the mountains from where the whites camped. But he had heard plenty about them. They hated any Indians. Shortly they would kill him unless he ran. But how could he escape from this cave? Then he saw the dim light coming through the skin of the lodge, and he realized that he was in the white man's tepee. Maybe he could rush backward, surprising them, knock down the tepee and escape in the resulting confusion.

Then the tall white man who looked like a crow signed to him: Rest, friend. Want to eat? Want to drink?

Lone Wolf recognized the choppy style of these hand signs. This white crow must have learned to sign from the Comanche. Behind him, a knife in his hand, the Bald Turtle hopped from foot to foot in a little dance preparatory to falling on Lone Wolf, held back only by the Long Crow Man's other and more evil plans for him.

It would be useless to try to escape, Lone Wolf saw that. His fear rose again, but again he did as Hoof had taught him: he steeled himself and made himself swallow the fear. They could kill him any time they wished. He had to accept that and look to escape at a better moment than now. Outside the tepee the wind still howled; judging from how the tepee shook, the storm still raged. Lone Wolf would need a coat and weapons if he was to survive. Better to play like a docile captive. After all, if they were going to kill him, wouldn't they have done it already? Could they plan to take him back to the women, to let them torture him the way it was said the Sioux did in the north?

Lone Wolf saw how wise it would be to deal cautiously with these powerful creatures. With slow movements, not to alarm them, he signed back that he would like to eat and to drink.

He would do his best not to startle them, and when neither was looking or both were asleep, he would gather enough gear to protect himself from the storm and escape.

"He hasn't ever seen socks," said McCall as he and Skinner watched Lone Wolf push one on and off his hand, marveling at its cut and flexibility.

"He ain't never seen soap in his life," growled Skinner. "God, he smells!"

McCall laughed. "I doubt if we smell so great either, pard. Look at us—neither you or me has washed in three weeks, and once we start killing buffalo, why we'll smell like animals till we get back."

"That's different," Skinner said. "That's good clean dirt. An Injun's smells, now—it's more like a skunk that died a couple of weeks ago in a closet and you just opened the door."

McCall laughed again to make light of Skinner's hatred of the wounded Indian. In the three days since he had rescued Lone Wolf, McCall had not only managed to save the Indian's life but had begun to bring back the savage's frozen limbs. The right leg worried both McCall and Lone Wolf, for its lower part was now blackened in spots and yellowish in others. Both recognized these as the early signs of gangrene, potentially fatal. Still, Lone Wolf didn't seem to have too much fever.

In an attempt to make friends with the redskin, McCall had passed the time talking to him with sign language and learning a few dozen words of Kiowan. Skinner looked up sourly any time he heard McCall say anything in English, which was frequently, for McCall found Lone Wolf bright and eager to learn his language, which surprised him, for in twenty years on the plains, he could only recall a few other Indians out of the hundreds he had known who had shown a similar interest.

He didn't let Skinner's sourness irritate him. The bald Skinner would just have to learn that he ran this little expedition, and that if he said they needed an Indian guide, then they damn well needed one.

"Boy, the two of you are having a high old time,"

groused Skinner the fourth day, during a fit of laughter between McCall and his patient.

"We got to jawing," said McCall. "Lone Wolf here don't believe that the world is round."

"I don't either," said Skinner. "I heard that. Any fool can see it's flat."

"He says folks would fall off the other side if it was round," McCall commented.

McCall saw Skinner glance over at Lone Wolf with new respect. "Maybe he ain't so dumb after all. What does he say about finding us some buffalo?"

"I ain't got that far yet," answered McCall. "I figured we ought to get to be friends first."

"Well, I wish you'd hurry up," said Skinner.

"Some of these Indians are touchy about it. Lone Wolf here belongs to the Kiowa, and they haven't had much experience with the new buffalo hunter."

"Sleeping in the same tent with him don't just offend my sense of smell, but also my idea of sensible ways of keeping alive." He peered at McCall with his hardest stare. "Every time I fall asleep I expect to wake up just in time to see him sticking a knife in me. It's got so I can't catch a wink of sleep at night."

"What bull!" McCall exclaimed. "Your head no sooner hits that blanket than you start whistling and snoring like you was sawing down an oak."

"Like hell I do!"

"Like hell you don't!"

Skinner smiled sheepishly, as if he had heard this complaint before, then said, "I don't sleep good."

"Partner, you damn sure don't show it."

Skinner shifted uneasily and flipped into his right hand the skinning knife McCall had noticed hardly left his hand since Lone Wolf had arrived. That knife moved restlessly from hand to hand most of the day, as if Skinner were unsure what to do with it.

Skinner was something of a curiosity in Hays City, a city filled with those who didn't fit into society back east. To hear him tell it, although nobody in Hays City could say they had seen him without clothes—not even the "up-stairs girls" at Moar's Hide & Skull—Skinner didn't have a hair on his body and had never grown one. He didn't shave because he didn't grow a beard, he didn't have even the sign of a hair on his head, and even his eyebrows were missing, giving him the appearance of having been skinned. This smooth-shaven look had given him his name, not his trade of skinning buffalo, which had been his work only over the last year since he had arrived in Hays City. At forty-five, Skinner looked about himself like a large turtle peering suspiciously at a world he was certain was filled with boot heels about to crush his shell.

Jack McCall had spent fifteen years hunting alone on the Plains till the buffalo hunters had come in droves two years ago. While he much preferred working alone, the offers from outfits to find and shoot buffalo had been too tempting. He saw how well the hunt masters had done when they sold their hides in Dodge and Hays City. Tired of working for wages, he had put together this hunting outfit and come out to hunt for his own account. Skinner was his accommodation to the shooter's need for help in skinning and hauling hides.

Unable to pay cash wages after buying the wagon and its equipment, McCall had to make a partnership deal with Skinner. The hard, squat man was willing to put in hours of hard work in return for one fifth of the profits of this trip, but McCall had had to throw into the bargain that he would teach Skinner how to shoot buffalo, which was where all the money was.

Generally speaking, McCall knew that Skinner's fear of Lone Wolf wasn't dumb. Far from it. By 1871 virtually every warrior band of Kiowa, Comanche, Ute and Pawnee on the Kansas and Texas plains were furious at the number of white hunters with long-range heavy rifles out slaughtering buffalo. As recently as three years ago there had been so few white men hunting buffalo that McCall had known every white buffalo hunter in both states, and they didn't number more than a hundred, all told. Today there had to be several thousand, and that number grew daily. Three years ago McCall and his fellow hunters would have thought two hundred hides a hunter for a season was a triumphant success; today these new outfits might bring down a hundred buffalo a day, in a season several thousand. Sooner or later he figured it had to make a difference how many buffalo were left on the plains.

Certainly millions of buffalo were left now, but such furious slaughter made McCall uneasy. It seemed against the natural order of things, although he too had taken to using the Sharps .50-caliber rifles with their heavy slugs to bring down more buffalo per hour of shooting.

McCall recognized that even the buffalo were changing. He could remember that only two years ago, half the time a man could walk up to a herd and shoot the two or three cows he needed; now herds were skittish and you had to be careful to approach them downwind. Whenever the Indian bands could, they attacked and killed the white hunters, stealing the grub, stoves, wagons, horses, mules, guns, shells and hides the men had accumulated. The tribes' anger over the past year had made the hunters wary of all Indians, but with all their caution, hunting parties were wiped out by Indian attacks. Among others, George Winston, his six buffalo hands and two wagons had been spread across ten miles of prairie last year, and McCall

37

knew if it could happen to George, it could damn well happen to anybody.

Still, one Indian wasn't a pack, and even a savage could be grateful for their saving his life. Lone Wolf might well give them information about the buffalo if he were approached the right way after McCall had made friends with him.

"I don't like the looks of his leg," McCall said to Skinner the next day.

"I don't like the smell of it," said Skinner. "What's he doing out here anyway? I thought Injuns liked to hole up in the winter?"

"He's out here looking for buffalo—some sort of sacred buffalo if I get it right."

"Injuns!" snorted Skinner. "Sacred buffalo!"

"I think I got it straight," said McCall, "but he don't understand much Comanche and I don't understand much Kiowa."

Skinner snorted again. "What's the difference between one buffalo and another? They're all dirty, smelly, filled with ticks and lice, and got about as much sense as that stove over there."

"Says his head man sent him out, but he doesn't want to talk about it much."

"He don't know whether he's coming or going, just like all Injuns," said Skinner. "If they wasn't around, this country would be a fitting place to live in."

Not wanting to get into an argument, McCall said, "I'm going to change the dressing again."

"You just changed it last night," said Skinner. "I don't see how you can go to all this trouble for an Indian. I honestly don't. A horse, now, that I could see. But all this Injun's going to do—mark my words, Jack McCall—is stick a knife between your ribs one of these nights."

"You told me that before, Skinner."

"I'm saying it again, Jack."

"I've heard it enough."

Tired of Skinner's continual belligerence over Lone Wolf, who had spent almost every minute of the last five days resting and sleeping, McCall stared down Skinner. Finally Skinner turned away and seemed to draw his neck back into his shell, a turtle plotting his next move, but his eyes had glistened over with something McCall couldn't quite read: fear or hate.

"All right," Skinner muttered. "I guess it's your rig."

"Yeah, it is," said McCall. "And let's not forget it."

So McCall changed the bandage, with Skinner peering over his shoulder out of curiosity, and all three of them saw that the wounds on the lower right leg had reddened still more and were again filled with pus.

"God, don't that look nasty!" said Skinner.

"Smells worse, too," said McCall.

"What you going to do?" asked Skinner.

"Soak it in some more whiskey, I guess."

"Aw, Jack! We ain't got but half a dozen bottles left."

"That or cut it off."

"You! Cut it off?"

"It's that or die, right, Chief?"

Lone Wolf looked up with what McCall thought was the supplicating appeal of a child. McCall had lived with and around Indians enough during his life to feel for the redskin. He had learned that Lone Wolf had a wife and a couple of kids he missed, as well as a woman he had been fooling around with, but both of them knew that with this gangrenous leg it was doubtful if Lone Wolf would ever see any of his tribe again. Shortly the poison would start to spread, red streaks would run up his leg toward his torso, in a matter of days they would hit his heart, and then he would die in hours.

In the best of circumstances it wasn't the sort of message McCall or anybody else liked to deliver, but he steeled himself and used the pidgin Kiowan he knew to tell Lone Wolf that he either had to cut off the leg or he figured that Lone Wolf was a goner from gangrene.

After the Indian had answered, McCall said to Skinner, "He says no. He doesn't want to go below with just one leg."

"Go below?"

"It's where he goes when he dies."

Lone Wolf said something else. Puzzled, McCall asked him to elaborate and gradually pieced it together.

"Now what?" asked Skinner.

"He wants me to burn his leg," said McCall.

"Burn it?" asked Skinner.

"Says he knows how to heal a burn, not how to heal this oozing sickness."

"Burn it, though! You want to do that?"

"Not really. If it'll help him, though, I can't say no."

"Hell, I wouldn't help the son of a bitch. It's like helping a rattler with a broken fang."

"You don't never give up on him, do you?"

"I've seen what they done to folks."

McCall laughed. "And I got to give him tea from this dried plant before I start," he said, holding up a little pouch which he opened and from which he shook out a handful of greenish-grey powder. He leaned forward to sniff it. "Rattlesnake weed powder. Big medicine."

"How do you know?"

"Can't you look at it and tell?" joshed McCall.

"Is that pouch made out of what I think it is?" asked Skinner.

McCall grinned. "I think so. The pouch is a part of the power of this stuff—buffalo scrotum."

"There ain't nothing crazier than an Indian. You ain't going to do it, are you?"

"*You* want to cut off his leg?"

"*Me?*"

"When he don't want you to?"

"Me," said Skinner, "I'm for shoving him out the door or sticking a knife in him before he does it to us or just shooting him in the head like you do a lame horse."

"Well, he don't want me to shoot him or cut off his leg—he wants me to burn it good with a brand from the fire."

"Count me out," said Skinner with a shudder. "I may go sit out in the snow for a while. Last thing I want to hear is him yell—before I hear you yell when he forgets he told you to burn hell out of him and jumps your butt."

"I don't know the Kiowa all that well," said McCall, "but if they're like any other Indians, I bet he don't make a sound when I burn him."

Knowing how it would smell, McCall gritted his teeth, got a grip on his stomach and put some of the rattlesnake weed powder on the fire, which made the tent stink. He made tea from the powder too, and Lone Wolf insisted that he be given about two quarts of it to drink before the burning. He told McCall that he might yell and talk out of his head, but he wasn't to let it alarm him, that many powerful spirits would come into the tepee when he drank the tea, and that if it looked as if he was getting too rambunctious, McCall was simply to tie him up while telling him over and over that this would pass.

41

For McCall, then came the hard part. Gritting his teeth and clenching his stomach still more strongly, he took his sharp skinning knife and sliced a neat cut into Lone Wolf's suppurating leg. Pus and blood oozed out, making McCall feel faint, but he held on to himself. On the other side of the tent, Skinner mended his second saddle, acting as if nothing of interest was going on.

McCall had built up the fire and set out the brands just as Lone Wolf had told him. Taking up the first firebrand, he held it near the open sores of Lone Wolf's leg, close enough so that after a few minutes the moisture in the wound began to steam. As instructed by Lone Wolf, he kept the brand close enough to cause the pus and blood to boil, but not so close it blackened the flesh, although, as Lone Wolf had said, it wasn't an easy distance to find and if a choice was to be made, better he be burned than lose the leg or his life.

Feeling faint most of the time, McCall didn't like the task, and several times he thought he would get sick himself. From time to time he sat back to rest. Skinner made some comment about the foul smell of burnt rattle-snake weed, burning flesh and pus, and left the tent, saying he figured he would work on the wagon since the weather was so much warmer.

Going back to his task, McCall kept the brand about four inches away from the bubbling sores. Lone Wolf had said nothing. His face was glazed over with sweat, his eyes held as firm as marbles in his head, and his limbs were rigid with tension. Twice Lone Wolf had had McCall give him another quart of that terrible-smelling tea, and finally the Indian said that ought to do it. McCall reckoned he had held the hot brand near the wound for more than an hour. He found that his shirt was drenched in sweat.

"How do you know it's enough?" he asked Lone Wolf.

"I feel better."

"I'll wrap it up."

"No, better for it to breathe."

"How often does this work?"

"Sometimes good, sometimes not."

"And this time?"

"They're fighting over me," said Lone Wolf.

"They?"

Lone Wolf grinned feebly as he looked toward the ceiling. "You don't see them?"

"See who?"

"Eagle there, and that beaver-looking devil with the arrowhead on the end of his tail and fangs?"

A shiver went up McCall's back. Unable to stop himself, he looked up. He saw only the tent rippling from the passage of the wind.

"No, I don't see anything."

"The tea gives a man eyes," said Lone Wolf. "You can't see much of what's real without it."

Even before McCall had brought the Indian into their tent, McCall had bothered Skinner. The man just rarely had a word to say to him, as if the shooter were traveling with a block of wood. Sometimes days went by without a word passing between them—which wasn't all that bad—and then McCall would give him a couple of brief orders. Most of the time Skinner got the feeling he hardly existed for McCall. He knew McCall's reputation, for he had asked around the Drum Saloon and the Hide & Skull before he agreed to come. The man was a loner, kept his own council, and rarely had much to say to anyone else.

He played a strong but quiet game of stud poker, drank quietly and by himself, and didn't throw his money around on the whores at the Hide & Skull. A solid, dependable sort, Skinner had been told, if not the friendliest fellow in the world.

But now Skinner saw that McCall had started messing with him. Probably McCall wanted to hire on the Indian cheaper than him and the two of them would murder Skinner, but that wouldn't work. The Indian wasn't as sick now that McCall had brought down the festered-up leg by burning it. Too many times Skinner had awakened in the night to shiver with dread when from the soft glow thrown by the Dutch oven he saw the Indian's hard bright eyes glaring lidlessly at him.

Dumb savage didn't even know enough to blink, Skinner said to himself. Well, damned if he was going to lay here till the redskin knifed him in his sleep. That bull of McCall's about his sleeping at night, too. Skinner ought to know if he slept or not, and he knew damn well that he didn't, and now McCall was getting the Indian to back up his claim that he slept through the night, treating it like a joke. What bull! Skinner hadn't closed his eyes in almost a week, and he was so exhausted from the strain of living in the same tent with a smelly killer that he was ready to shoot the two of them.

McCall was the problem, him and his treating a fellow like he was a block of wood. McCall might be the world's best buffalo hunter, but he was definitely the world's biggest pain when he got his head stuck on something, and he definitely had his head stuck on the idea that this smelly savage was going to up and tell them where to find a big herd of buffalo. Any damn fool knew that no Indian liked a white man enough to tell him where he could find his private stock of buffalo. And that same damn fool knew that all Indians wanted to kill the white men who hunted buffalo. The only sensible thing a white man could do was to kill any Indian before he killed you. Every damn fool back in the Hide & Skull would tell you that, but this goddamn fool McCall, he had to be different.

As he worked around the wagon, struggling to make the cracked rear axle stronger, Skinner puzzled out what he might do. He could put his foot down with McCall, tell him that it had to be the Indian or himself, never mind if the savage died out here in the cold. Trouble was, Skinner figured that was what McCall wanted, for him to up and leave. If Skinner left, McCall and his new stinky friend got to share all the buffalo hides, and McCall probably figured he could pay the redskin a damn sight less than he had promised Skinner. No, sir, Mr. McCall, Skinner told himself, you don't get rid of me that easy.

He could reason with McCall, but he had tried that. The bastard didn't listen to anybody. And never had, if what Skinner had heard around the Hide & Skull was right. For instance, Skinner figured they would be safer with the Indian tied up, which he had suggested to McCall, who had only grunted no. The son of a bitch, sighed Skinner. He don't leave a man no choice. Skinner didn't know what was going to happen, but he knew something would. The Indian's foot and leg were almost healed, and just as soon as they were—watch out! The three of them would go to sleep one night and there wouldn't be but one of them that would wake up. The Indian would laugh all the way back to his tribe driving their wagons filled with their guns and grub.

Skinner figured he was going to have to take his fate in his own hands. Finally, after thinking it over for three whole days, he decided to do that thing that he didn't want to: get old Jack McCall mad, but make damn sure the Indian didn't knife them in the night. Skinner would do it to him first.

That night Skinner decided to act as if he wasn't planning anything, so he offered to cook and clean up. He even went so far as to give the Indian seconds, and after supper they had a right good time drinking up the last half bottle of their whiskey, although no matter how much you downed you couldn't forget that smell of Indian in the tent. It came from how they lived in those tepees with dogs wandering in and out urinating on the floor and on their buffalo rugs. The Indians just rolled up in them and went to sleep, thinking nothing of it. So Skinner acted friendly that night, and figured he had done a right good job of it. That night he lay in bed, his eyes closed, his skinning knife next to him, as usual, his pistol up under his bedroll—nothing to make Jack McCall suspicious later on. He would lay awake till it got real quiet, then he would get things back to normal around here. After a half-hour, he reckoned he better play like he was asleep, so he started to imitate his own snoring, hoping it sounded real.

Skinner woke with a start. Except for the breathing of the other two, the tent was cold and quiet. He felt frightened. Christ! The Indian could have stuck a knife in him just as easy as you please. He listened to the soft breathing of the other two, struggling to figure out if they were really asleep. For a few moments he considered just going back to sleep and forgetting his plan. Killing the Indian was going to rile up Jack McCall good. He was going to have to make this look just right if he was going to keep McCall off his back, but if he didn't do it, he knew damn well he was going to wake up one morning at the pearly gates trying to sweet-talk St. Pete into letting him in.

Here goes, he said to himself as he quietly eased a leg out of his bedroll.

He planned to roll over onto all fours, crawl over as quiet as a cat after a frog the five paces to where the Indian slept, grab him and pull him back over on top of Skinner's bedroll, and while he and the redskin were wrestling there, stick the knife in between his ribs. McCall would see that the Indian had snuck over to kill him, after Skinner had given him a nice supper, letting him have seconds even, and that luckily Skinner would awaken, so that before first light both McCall and Skinner would have been knocking at St. Pete's door if not for his alertness.

Skinner inched on out of his bedroll. He stopped to listen. The breathing of the other two hadn't changed. Quietly he rolled himself over onto his hands and knees. He stuck the knife in his belt, changed his mind and placed it between his teeth. The Indian was strong and he didn't want to chance the savage's getting the best of him. Maybe it would be better to stick him first where he lay sleeping, Skinner thought, then grab him and pull him up in the air back on top of him onto his bedroll. Yeah, that's better, he told himself. I wouldn't want to get beat at wrestling with this son of a bitch.

He took several minutes to crawl the few paces that separated them. Better to take the time now and be able to sleep soundly for the rest of tonight.

Finally he had reached the bedroll of the Indian. Skinner took the knife from his mouth. He peered down. Yep, that was his chest there. He would have to make it quick, he knew. Stick it in and pull him over to my side of the tent, he told himself.

Skinner reared back and plunged the knife at him. The clatter and the shouts woke up McCall at once. He grabbed his pistol and got to his knees. In the weak light he saw the other two wrestling on top of Lone Wolf's bedroll. He fired the pistol in the air and the two fell apart, gasping for breath.

"What the hell?" McCall asked.

"He done tried to kill me!" shouted Skinner.

Lone Wolf was backed over against the wall of the tent. In the feeble light from the Dutch oven, McCall saw the Indian was poised to wrestle off another attack. The Indian's hands were empty, in Skinner's his skinning knife was poised for attack.

"Tried to kill you?" asked McCall.

"Point that gun somewheres else, Jack," said Skinner. "He was going to kill both of us. Stick a knife in us and make off with everything we own, just like any Injun would."

"He was?"

"Yeah. Let's finish him off, Jack. I can't take it no more."

"Stick what into us?"

"This here knife, Jack."

"That's your knife, Skinner."

"He done snuck it from me while we was sleeping."

"Yeah? So just how did you wind up on his side of the tent with the knife in your hand?" asked McCall.

"Hey, whose side are you on?"

"In fact, just how did he get you to come over and give him your knife?"

"Jack, don't act the fool," said Skinner. "This here's serious. Damned if I'm going to live in a tent with a crazy savage that's just waiting for a chance to stab me."

"He don't want to kill you, Skinner," said McCall. "I done told you that about twenty times."

48

"You been lying to me, Jack," said Skinner. "You and him been planning to find them buffalo together. You want all the hides for yourself. I know your plan."

"We planned it?"

"Yeah."

"What are we waiting for, then?"

"Huh?"

"If we're going on without you, what're we waiting for? Why didn't we kill you a week ago? Or day before yesterday?"

McCall watched Skinner think this one over. Dumb bastard, he said to himself. I ought to kill him. How're we going to trust Lone Wolf now that he's seen Skinner wants to kill him? He surely will want to get us before Skinner gets him.

"Come on." McCall pushed his partner. "Ain't you got no answer?"

"I guess you waited to make sure he wasn't going to die on you," said Skinner. "Otherwise you wouldn't have had nobody to skin your buffalo for you."

"You dumb, dumb bastard," said McCall. "No Indian knows how to skin buffalo right. Or fast enough. He'd run off the first day. No Indian works steady like a white man."

"He was going to kill me, *that* I know."

"Skinhead, he's grateful we saved his life. He was going to show us to a buffalo herd he knows."

"He was, huh?"

"He says according to everyone he's talked to, they ought to be right about here right now."

"Hogwash. Either you or him is lying."

"He wants to help us. Or did. I expect he'll be gone by morning."

49

"That's all right by me, Jack."

"It ain't by me, and last I heard, this is still my rig."

"You can push that crap just so far."

"I'm pushing it this far, Skinner," said McCall. "You can't live with him, leave now. I've found buffalo for fifteen years by getting along with Injuns, and if you're going to hunt with me you better get used to it."

"I ain't no Indian lover."

"Then you better not be an Indian hater, cause I'm warning you, you have another go at him, you better have one at me too."

Skinner dipped his head around in that hard, feisty way he had and gave McCall a sullen look. "Now, why's that?"

"Because I wake up and find him dead and I'm going to find you dead real quick."

"You wouldn't kill me over some dumb Injun."

"I done told you. I ain't one to go back on my word."

McCall watched Skinner absorb this, obviously a bitter point.

"No, you ain't joshing, are you?" said Skinner. "But what am I to do if he jumps me one night, like I know he's waiting to do, and I kill him? You going to shoot me then?"

"You heard me."

"That ain't fair, Jack. I'm going to defend myself."

"You ain't doing right to jump my friend in the middle of the night."

"Friend! *Friend!*"

"Yeah, friend."

"But how can I keep your friend from jumping me?"

"You best make friends with him yourself, Skinner-man."

"How come you care so much for one dumb redskin?"

"Him and me been signing and talking, Skinner," said McCall. "I told you, but you can't hear. We're friends. You just don't stick a knife into a friend of yours that's sleeping, that's all. It ain't right."

"The hell it ain't, when it's a redskin."

Feeling something shake him in his sleep, Lone Wolf had instinctively pushed Turtle Shiny Head back violently. He had sprung back against the wall of the tent, his heart beating wildly, furious at the attack. He would have sprung forward, but Long Crow Man's gun held firmly on them both.

From the stove, a crack of light spilled into the air of the tent. Long Crow Man and the Turtle talked. As Lone Wolf realized that the Crow aimed to keep the Turtle from attacking him, he gradually calmed and became aware that something hurt under his left arm. Feeling there, he discovered a stream of blood.

Opening his tunic, Lone Wolf found that the hairless Turtle had slashed him, but that his knife had been bent away from its purpose by his hard buffalo robe and only gashed his side a bit. As he watched the two white men argue in their strange tongue, he struggled to figure how to escape, but the Crow had his gun pointed right between the both of them. Lone Wolf wouldn't get under the flaps before that gun would knock a hole in him.

Lone Wolf then noticed that Crow had the gun pointed mostly at Turtle Shiny Head, not at him, which surprised him. What was this about? He had thought that Long Crow Man was his friend and could control the other, that he was the chief of the two, but now he wasn't so sure. The

51

two argued in that choppy tongue of theirs, sounding like a couple of dogs growling and barking at each other.

"I'll leave," Lone Wolf announced in the combination sign language and Kiowan he and Crow had adopted together.

"No, your leg ain't ready," said Crow. "Did he cut you?"

"It's not much," said Lone Wolf. "The bleeding has already stopped. He'll kill me."

"I've told him not to," said Crow, sounding as if he could be trusted. "I've told him if he does that he has to kill me too."

For a moment or two, Lone Wolf couldn't grasp this, then said, "Why, then he will."

"I don't think he's dumb enough to try that."

Lone Wolf sighed. "What do I do about him, friend Crow?"

"What do you want to do about him?"

"I don't want to worry about him," Lone Wolf said. "I want to sleep without expecting to get stuck with a knife."

"Can't say as I blame you," said Crow. "I think I can solve that for you."

"You want what?" roared Skinner.

"You heard me," said McCall. "Every damn thing you can hurt him with."

"Not my pistol and my skinning knife!" said Skinner. "They wasn't furnished by you. They're mine."

"No sir, they're going in the box."

"Like hell!"

"Like hell."

"I ain't going to do it."

"Skinner, I ain't funning with you," McCall told him. "I'll round them up myself with this cocked pistol on you."

"Go right ahead."

"It goes off it's going to leave a mighty big hole."

"But what am I going to sleep with?"

"Not a goddamn thing."

"He's going to have his knives and arrows, and I ain't to have nothing?"

"I'll take his too," said McCall.

In the end Skinner figured he was better off to do the moving around rather than have McCall nervously picking his way around the tent.

McCall saw that Skinner was seething, but he no longer cared how the other felt. McCall was out here to get buffalo, and no Missouri river rat was going to get in his way. He considered simply shooing one or the other of them off, the chief or Skinner, but that wouldn't work well either, as he needed one to find the buffalo and the other to skin and haul them. Besides, he liked the Indian. In a bunch of ways he was a lot better company than Skinner, reminding McCall of carefree days of hunting ten years ago.

When Skinner reached for the chief's weapons, the Indian pulled them back suspiciously. Even when McCall explained he was locking them all up, the Indian's reaction was just as bad as Skinner's.

McCall decided he was beyond caring what either of them thought. He put all their knives, guns, arrows, and even the redskin's war lance into his locker and gun bag and locked them. While the two continued to glower at each other over the next few days, at least McCall had pulled their claws.

Lone Wolf's leg healed and he practiced walking on it every day even though the weather hadn't cleared. Gradually it strengthened so that he could spend a couple of hours on it at a time.

Finally a few days later a morning arrived so clear that McCall and the other two judged that the storm had blown over.

"We've sat on our behinds long enough, Jack," said Skinner. "Let's get us some buffalo."

"Let's see if our friend will help us."

Skinner spat in disgust. "Help us! He'll lead us into a war party. That Injun's going to be the death of us, Jack McCall. You mark my words."

"That Injun's going to make us rich, Mr. Kincade, if you but had the patience to see it."

"That Indian don't no more know where buffalo are than my mother knew where Adam hung his hat."

"Let's find out."

So with Skinner watching from a polite distance, McCall hunkered down with Lone Wolf.

He explained that they were out looking for a big herd of buffalo. Lone Wolf repeated that he too was out looking for buffalo, which still puzzled McCall, for he knew that Indians didn't hunt much in weather like this. But, as they were both looking for the same thing, it seemed better to ask no questions and ally forces.

"Where should we go to find a good-sized herd?" asked McCall.

"Go? Why go?" asked Lone Wolf.

Confused, McCall repeated his wish. "We want to find a herd of buffalo. You want to find a herd, too. We'll travel together. You'll find them and we'll shoot them with these guns."

When Lone Wolf again looked puzzled, McCall started in once more with his explanation, but he was interrupted with a hand sign by Lone Wolf.

If he got it right, McCall thought Lone Wolf was saying that buffalo were here, in this valley. Well, if they were, they damn sure couldn't be seen, because the men could see from one side of the valley to the other this morning. Or was this the place where the Indians believed the buffalo came out of the ground in the spring?

"What's he saying?" asked Skinner.

"The buffalo are here," said McCall. "Same thing he told us the other day."

"Are where?"

"Maybe I didn't understand him rightly."

"That's the sign for buffalo, all right," said Skinner as Lone Wolf repeated the sign. "Even I know that. And I guess that means 'here,' all right. What's that with the two hands at the side of his head?"

"He's surprised we're asking."

Skinner made a long, exasperated sigh, then sprang back to the side of the tent as Lone Wolf quickly lowered himself to the ground cloth. For long moments he lay there, his ear to the ground.

"Now what?" asked Skinner.

"He's listening," said McCall.

"Shhhh!" Lone Wolf demanded. After a while he turned his head over and put his other ear to the ground.

"He can't remember what's his good ear," said Skinner, laughing.

As McCall threw him a scornful look, Lone Wolf jumped to his feet and rushed outside.

"Come on," said McCall as he and Skinner followed the Indian out.

55

The sky was bluer than McCall could ever remember seeing it. The sun's flame lit up the miles of snow around them so brightly it was all he could do to keep his eyes open. The dunes of snow receded in waves to the distant mountains. The air felt warmer, and the snow on the top of the wagon had begun to melt, dripping water into little puddles at their feet.

"Another couple days and the ground is going to be nothing but mush out here," Skinner judged.

Lone Wolf had climbed up on the wagon's tailgate and was peering around at the horizon.

"What the hell's he doing?" asked McCall.

Lone Wolf pointed north and shouted excitedly.

"What's he saying?" asked Skinner.

Then McCall saw it. "Look yonder." He pointed to the blue haze on the horizon.

"What?"

"Buffalo haze."

"What's that?"

"From their breath. Rises from the herd."

"That's great!"

"Pack up!" shouted McCall, breaking into a run for the tent. "We got to get out of here."

"Pack up? Let's shoot us some buffalo."

At the flap of the tent McCall whipped around. "Shoot? You don't understand. It's a stampede and it's headed this way."

"Jesus!" breathed Skinner, and he looked again to the north.

Against the white of the snow, not two miles distant, he saw the blue haze. Below it, accompanied by what was now a faint rumble, a long line of wavering brown stretched from one side of the valley to the other, and as he watched, Skinner saw it grow faintly larger.

"A stampede!" Skinner shouted. "We're done for!"

"Easy," said McCall. "We'll outrun them. Throw the stuff in the wagon."

In a panic, Skinner shouted, "What? Forget the wagon and let's just ride the horses!"

"Leave all I own?" asked McCall. "No! Throw our stuff in the wagon."

And as Skinner watched, speechless, McCall disappeared into the tent.

Chapter 3

Skinner caught McCall tossing pots, pans, plates and cartridges into the trunks. As he came up, McCall pushed the gun bag into his arms. "Put this into the wagon."

"Come on, Jack," Skinner pleaded. "If they can knock over a railroad train, I don't think no wagon is going to make it."

"I know it's not much of a chance, but let's take it. Just hurry," said McCall.

"Let's run for it on the mules."

"No, they'll run them down. The wagon's our best chance."

Skinner wavered. McCall was supposed to know what he was doing. "You sure?"

"Hell, yes. Get moving, man!"

They ran from tent to wagon with boxes and implements. The Dutch oven was too hot to take, but they carried it out so they could ball up the tent. Now the faint rumble had become a steady roar. As McCall passed Lone Wolf, he put his hand on his friend's arm. "Put this in the wagon," he said, handing the Indian the box of flour and beans.

"No good," said Lone Wolf in English, gesturing toward the buffalo. "Bring guns."

59

Annoyed that the Indian thought their guns could stop the herd, McCall shouted at Lone Wolf to help them pack, but the Indian wouldn't stop pulling at McCall's sleeve. He kept signing that McCall should shoot the buffalo.

"Our guns won't kill enough," McCall told Lone Wolf, and then realized he was talking in English and in such a rush he couldn't think of the right Kiowa words. "Let's try the wagon."

"Get him to help us pack!" shouted Skinner as he flew past. "They'll be on us in minutes."

"He wants us to shoot them," said McCall. "Cut it out, damn it!"

Lone Wolf had pulled him down to the earth into a squatting position and was making a drawing in the snow with his finger. He put buffalo chips where the herd was, and others where they should shoot from.

"Like a rock in the water," said McCall as he looked at the drawing. "Maybe, maybe so." He looked up to find his partner. "Come on, Skinner, let's shoot buffalo."

"What?"

McCall ran to the wagon and grabbed the gun bag. "Bring the shells, Skinner."

"What for?"

"Hurry! Let's try something different!"

"Tarnation!" Skinner exclaimed, dropping the box of horse tackle he was carrying and turning to the wagon.

McCall set down the gun bag about twenty yards toward the advancing line of buffalo, which by now had become easily visible, but Lone Wolf tugged his sleeve again and pulled him farther on toward the advancing herd till he was at a spot about fifty yards from camp.

"Jack!" shouted Skinner, arriving breathlessly. "What's going on?"

"Come here and get a gun. Shoot the buffalo heading

60

toward us when they close,'' said McCall. "We're supposed to make a barrier between them and us. We might save the wagon as well as our necks.''

"What? A barrier?''

"Like a rock in the water, the dead buffalo will part the herd and keep them from running over us.''

"He says so?'' Skinner asked, pointing at Lone Wolf.

McCall was busy rooting around in the cartridge box and filling his pouch with handfuls of shells. "Yep.''

"That's crazy! Let's run for it. You can't trust no redskin.''

"Don't shoot till they're within a hundred yards,'' said McCall, stuffing shells into the rifle. "No use wasting shells or heating up your gun.'' He knelt in the snow, steadying his gun with an elbow on his knee.

Lone Wolf said something that Skinner couldn't understand, and he turned to look at the Indian, who was gesturing toward the gun bag.

"He's making signs like *he* wants to shoot,'' said Skinner.

"Think he can?'' asked McCall.

"I think he can shoot us in the back.''

"We need all the firepower we can get,'' McCall said. "He's going to get run over just like us.''

So McCall pulled out his old .40-caliber Henry and showed Lone Wolf how to operate it, but they didn't have much time, for the herd was almost upon them.

Skinner fired the first shot, hitting a young bull in the leg, which didn't stop him, and he came charging right at them.

Skinner and McCall opened up on him, firing as fast as they could pump shells into the Sharps. Suddenly realizing that this panicky shooting wouldn't work, McCall steadied himself, took careful aim and squeezed off a shot.

But the young bull continued to bear down, only twenty yards away.

Around him he heard the other two guns bam and roar. Again McCall shot at the animal, aiming for the heart, which the charging animal obscured with its lowered head. It headed right for the opening between Skinner and McCall, never slowing. McCall shot again, still not knowing if he was hitting him or not, yet when the charging buffalo was ten yards in front of them, it staggered, fell to its knees, rose to wander in confusion in front of them. McCall aimed for the heart. The buffalo fell over five yards in front of them.

McCall didn't like shooting headfirst at buffalo. Normally he shot at them from the side, where he could get a good bead on their heart and lungs. From the front, not only did he have a poor target, but he reckoned he had hit the charging animal on the horn or head plate and the ball had bounced harmlessly off.

"Come on!" yelled McCall, and he picked up his shell pouch and headed for the stricken buffalo. "We can rest our guns on him."

To their side now ran the first few buffalo, the leaders of the herd, who lurched from side to side as they ran past. Hearing a crash, McCall looked back briefly to see a buffalo bounce off the wagon, stagger about in a stunned way, then continue on.

With buffalo streaming by him and with the dead bull under him for support, McCall settled down into the snow to shoot. They had to make sure no line of buffalo started streaming over their position; once buffalo started through a spot, little could stop them.

Keeping his nerves steady, McCall aimed as he never had before in his life, trying to place every shot in the left shoulder blade of the onrushing beasts where the ball would reach the heart. Maybe a third of the time he was successful, for then the animals would lurch forward to their knees and tumble into the snow. Those behind would veer away from the unexpected obstacle, and those behind them would follow this new direction. This was typical of buffalo, who forever played follow the leader and were timid about striking out on their own in any direction.

Neither the sight of the men nor the noise of the guns fazed the onrushing herd of two-thousand-pound animals, for behind them came more tens of thousands of buffalo, crowding them forward. Stampeding herds, a force of nature as blind and powerful as cyclones and hurricanes, had knocked over entire railroad trains.

McCall fired slowly, endeavoring to give his gun barrel twenty seconds between shots to cool. It if became overheated, he couldn't touch it and it would start to lose its accuracy.

He stopped several times to slow down the firing of Skinner and Lone Wolf, who otherwise seemed to be doing well. In front of them now lay an obstacle course of fifteen to twenty buffalo, around which the herd veered, just as they would have stepped around rocks or tree stumps. Still, the dead buffalo in front of them didn't keep every buffalo away. Several times they had to dodge some twelve-hundred-pound cow who ran right at them and jumped over three dead bulls they crouched behind at the last moment, followed seconds later by a two-hundred-pound calf who would have broken an arm if he landed on it.

But Lone Wolf's strategy was working. The herd had opened up to go around the dead buffalo before them. The more they shot, the higher the barrier protecting them grew and the less the chances were that their position would be overrun.

McCall turned to Lone Wolf, shouted, and raised his fist in triumph.

"Lots of meat," Lone Wolf said. "We'll eat good."

"Damn right!"

Eager to see what was going on now that the buffalo presented almost no danger, McCall stood. On both sides of them streamed a brown flood of buffalo. Skinner and Lone Wolf stood by him.

"How big is this herd, Jack?" asked Skinner.

"Stand up on this one and see," said McCall. He helped Skinner steady himself as the shiny-headed man climbed on top of the dead beasts, which gave him an extra three feet of height.

Peering around, Skinner said, "I don't see nothing but brown."

"How many more are coming?" asked McCall.

"Nothing but brown all the way back to the mountains," answered Skinner. "Hey, give me that gun."

McCall handed him his Sharps. "What is it?"

Skinner looked down to give him a huge grin, one larger than McCall had ever seen on Skinner's moon face. "Wait till you see what I'm going to get!"

Skinner aimed his rifle at the advancing animals, leading some individual beast that neither Lone Wolf nor he could see from where they stood. Then the repeating Sharps bammed out three shots.

An animal out of McCall's sight bleated and groaned loudly. Then veering out of the herd toward them came a sight that amazed McCall: a white buffalo, its red eyes reflecting the late morning's sunlight, trying to escape the wound in its lungs by clambering over its dead brothers.

"Jesus!" shouted McCall. Skinner shot three more times and the animal collapsed. McCall had only seen such an animal once before, although he had heard Indians talk about them many times with awe in their voices.

"Ohhh," moaned Lone Wolf, cowering to the ground as if to escape a danger. "White buffalo. *Wakan-Takan*."

"I got him!" shouted Skinner. "I got him!"

He dashed off the dead bull and ran forward.

Behind him McCall only watched. "Damn fool," he muttered. "He'll get out there in the wrong place and they'll stomp him into the ground."

"Look," said Lone Wolf, pointing to the right.

In the maelstrom passing by them like a river of brown hides, McCall and Lone Wolf saw a herd of dozens of the rare white buffalo. Many of them were larger than their brown brothers. McCall stared open-mouthed at the sight. He thought the bulls might weigh as much as twenty-five hundred pounds, they were so large. He counted them and got to fifty before he stopped. Then, as suddenly as they had appeared, they were gone. Lone Wolf and McCall turned to look at each other, their faces filled with awe.

"*Wakan-Takan* here," said Lone Wolf.

"A heap of *Wakan-Takan*, friend."

Lone Wolf shivered all over as if a blast of frigid air had struck him.

"I've never heard of more than one or two being spotted," said McCall. "Not ever."

Lone Wolf shuddered again, as if to throw off his chill.

"What's the matter?" asked McCall, even though he had some idea why Lone Wolf was behaving this way. When he was with the Comanche, even a boy who possessed a white buffalo robe commanded more respect than a veteran warrior with many enemy dead to his credit, and he supposed the same was true for Kiowa as was true for Comanche, Cheyenne and Ute. According to Comanche legend, the power of the white buffalo could be traced back to earlier times when a certain warrior, assisted only by a white buffalo, had distinguished himself by massacring single-handedly a horde of invading Sioux. The creature had appeared to him in a vision, an unusually large buffalo with red horns and red eyes, granting that warrior the power to transform himself into the great white in time of need. The visit of a single white to any tribe impressed them enormously; they regarded it as the sacred leader of all herds. Some tribes believed that the man who succeeded in killing a white received a special blessing from the mysterious powers who guided the world, collectively known as *Wakan-Takan.*

"Dangerous place," Lone Wolf said. "So much *Wakan-Takan* here. The ground could open up and take us."

"Yeah, but not before we skin our buffalo," said McCall. "Hey, Skinner, how about doing some more shooting?"

Skinner was coming back to them now. His grin spread from ear to ear. McCall saw that Lone Wolf looked at Skinner with new respect.

"He's a beaut," Skinner said to McCall. "How much you reckon we can get for his hide? He's got big red eyes like a big fat hog."

"Let's shoot some more buffalo, hoss, while we still can."

Skinner began to reload his Sharps rifle. "How much, Jack, sure enough? Three hundred dollars? Four hundred dollars?"

"I heard Myron Jackson got close to seven hundred for his'n he shot two years ago."

"Seven hundred! One hide?"

McCall grinned. "You missed all the others."

"What others?"

"The others me and the chief here saw when you was out chasing your'n."

"You seen more of them whites?"

Enjoying Skinner's discomfort, McCall nodded.

"Did you hit any, McCall?"

"Didn't shoot," said McCall.

"How come you didn't shoot?"

"Cause you got one."

"Seven hundred dollars a robe and you didn't shoot!"

"Come on, Skinner, get a rifle and let's shoot buffalo. Either that or get out there and skin some."

"Damn, McCall! Sometimes you're the most ornery man I've ever met."

So Skinner and McCall continued to shoot buffalo. It took till midafternoon for the herd to pass, leaving the valley quiet in an unsettling way after the rumble. Around the three men lay well over one hundred fifty buffalo.

"How many you think we can skin today?" asked McCall.

"As many as we can," said Skinner. "I'll go get the horse. Start cutting the skins of the big ones."

McCall too felt the urgency. While the buffalo were still warm, it was easy enough with the horses to drag off the buffalo hides; by tomorrow they would be frozen to the animals and Skinner would have to skin them inch by painful inch.

McCall went to the nearest dead buffalo, drew his skinning knife and lifted the animal's shaggy head to cut a deep incision around its neck, sawing through the gristle where he had to. Then he lifted the animal's front foot and sawed a long incision down the buffalo's underside, right to his tail. That done, he made similar cuts so that the hide was entirely loosened underneath.

As he finished, Skinner came back carrying an iron spike and a hammer and leading the largest mule, which was dragging a singletree and a trace chain.

As McCall took the iron stake and the mallet, he looked around to see Lone Wolf, bundled now in his buffalo coat, looking intently at them.

"I guess he ain't never seen white men skin a buffalo," said McCall.

"He's going to see it done the right way, then," said Skinner, who led the mule around to the back of the buffalo, dropped the reins, and picked up the trace chain and carried its end to the bunched-up skin on the back of the buffalo's neck. With a heave, McCall drove the three-foot iron spike through the buffalo's nose down into the earth. The spike wouldn't penetrate far because the ground was frozen. Rearing back and swinging the mallet, he drove the stake as far as he could into the hard ground.

Skinner proceeded to tie the length of chain to the nape of the buffalo's skin.

"Ready, Jack?" he said finally.

"Try it," said McCall, breathing heavily. "But go slow. I don't want no torn hides."

Geeing and hawing the mule, Skinner had him pull away from the buffalo. The animal, pinned to the ground by the stake driven through its snout, had its hide ripped off it in a few minutes. The process produced a noise like a giant sail tearing. It came off whole, although this didn't always happen. They would tear one out of twenty hides so severely that they would have to leave them, but this method would save Skinner days of skinning the animals by hand.

Lone Wolf watched them skin five buffalo. In Kiowan and through hand signs, Lone Wolf asked McCall if he might skin the dead white buffalo. McCall told him sure, but to take care that he didn't rip the skin. Lone Wolf said something that McCall didn't entirely catch about it being a job a man had to do carefully, but Skinner was ready to pull, so McCall didn't have time to study on it. The sun hung halfway down the afternoon sky, and they needed to work quickly if they were going to skin many more buffalo today.

"Where's he going?" asked Skinner.

"Wants to skin the big white for us."

"He ain't going to ruin him, is he?"

"You want to rip the hide off him with the mule?"

"Hell, no—might tear."

"Then let him do it for us."

"At least he turned out good for something," said Skinner. "He shot pretty good too."

As they went back to work, McCall felt tired yet satisfied. They had come out here to get buffalo, and he had begun to think he might have to go back to Hays City with an empty wagon, which would have been a disaster. McCall had never before been out with his own rig and he had everything he owned right here, and a good bit of it was being eaten up every day by himself, Skinner and the chief.

"Hey, he ain't going to think that bull's his, is he, Jack?" asked Skinner, standing motionless and gazing at Lone Wolf, who stood off from the big white a bit, bowed forward, as if asking the dead animal something.

"Naw," answered McCall.

"'Cause we shot him."

"He knows that."

"He better."

"We saved his life, Skinner. The man figures he owes us something."

They went back to work as Lone Wolf took a couple

of tentative steps and went back into his hunched-forward stance again.

"Goddamn crazy savages," said Skinner as he shouted at the mule.

Until now, McCall had always hunted as an employee on other men's rigs, but the last four times out he had grown so irritated at seeing others make big money off the hides he found and shot for them that he had saved his money and bought his own hunting outfit.

On this, his first time out, he couldn't afford more than one helper, and that one on shares, whereas the most profitable way was to pay your men per hide skinned and to have three men with you, but he wouldn't be able to do that till maybe next trip. That was all right. A man didn't get there in a day, and a decent load this time would insure that he could get himself a crew and maybe an extra wagon and not have to pay a Skinner so much of his profits next time out.

McCall and Skinner had been together on several trips before, and Skinner had handled himself well and worked hard. Back in Hays City the two had talked. Both had an urgent desire, like every man in Hays, to make some real money. McCall had seen how hard Skinner would work when he got thirty-five cents to skin a hide, and he reckoned that if the man got a share of the profits, he would work that much harder.

The afternoon proved to McCall he had been right. By nightfall, working at almost breakneck speed, they had skinned fifty of the buffalo.

After going back to the wall tent, which had been trampled into the snow by the herd, and getting his skinning knife, Lone Wolf trudged back to the white buffalo with mounting dread in his heart.

Skinning such a beast wasn't a task a man took on lightly. On top of the physical difficulties that one man had in skinning an animal that weighed over a ton, Lone Wolf had to be triply careful not to be disrespectful. Maybe Old Hoof could just tackle the job with his bare hands, but Lone Wolf knew that if he touched the *Wakan* creature with his naked flesh he could get burned by the fire of the white.

The closer he came to the huge animal, the more frightened he became and the slower he walked. When he was twenty feet away he stopped. Something kept him from going forward, as if a force wouldn't let him approach, and he decided to chant his wolf power song to see if his namesake would help him.

Hai! Hai! Hai!
Hear me, Father Wolf.
Come to my aid,
Mother Dog.

Hai! Come to my aid,
Fill my heart with wolf courage,
Fill my stomach with wolf growls,
Fill my sight with the power of wolf eyes,
And protect me from this white.

Hai! Hai! Hai!
Hear me, Father Wolf,
Come to my aid,
Mother Dog.

He chanted this for several minutes until he felt the wolf power softening the air around him that was hard with danger.

He approached the dead white then, feeling the white buffalo power pushing him back, but he continued to chant to make this place less frightening. He kept his eyes averted, afraid to look brazenly on such power.

It took him nearly a quarter of an hour to go the last twenty feet. The big white lay on its side. Its pelt looked more cream-colored than white. It had fallen when it was clambering over another dead buffalo, so that it was half raised in the air, which would make skinning it easier. One red eye glared fiercely at Lone Wolf, sending a bolt of dread into his chest. He steeled himself, for the arrival of the herd and the white buffalo this morning had signaled clearly to him that Old Hoof, as he always had when Lone Wolf had been a boy, knew what he was about. Old Hoof had sent him on a quest for a white buffalo, one had appeared, and it was his task now to take the pelt. If in the taking of it the power of the white destroyed him, Hoof and the rest of the tribe would shake their heads sadly and murmur how justice had meted itself out.

Why had he ever chased Elk Woman around the village, arousing her lust for him? Not even a Comanche in battle was worse than this fate. He would touch this white creature, even with something to protect his hands, and fire would leap from this animal and burn them. He would thrash around till the fire ate him up entirely. What power did a wolf have compared to a buffalo, anyway?

Old Hoof's voice, from his boyhood days, sprang into his mind. "Right there, Young One, that's fear. Mark it well. Fear goes with the warrior everywhere. Recognize it, and when you see it, deal with it or you can't do those things a man must."

Yes, he was afraid. He used the remedy Old Hoof had taught him: he chanted louder and kept his mind full of the chant. Gradually his fear receded, crouched in his mind like a mountain cat ready to attack.

To further calm himself he walked around the two buffalo. What a large animal was the white! It looked as big as four horses, but other than its cream-colored pelt and red eyes, *Wakan-Takan* had fashioned it much like its brown brothers: same matted hair around the neck, narrow withers, skinny tail with the switch at the end, paunch and hump, and dainty hooves. The thought of sticking a knife into the creature squeezed his insides. *Wakan-Takan*, in the shape of a white buffalo, had made the world, and this creature contained all the power that *Wakan-Takan* had used. Why, he could stick his knife in this white and lightning might travel right up the blade and blast him, just as it had struck Moon Face two years ago and left him nothing but a mess of bloody, twisted flesh.

But it had to be done. If he didn't stick the knife into the flesh, he couldn't skin the white, and if he didn't skin him, he couldn't return to his camp, and if he didn't return to his camp—why, he might as well have perished in the storm. Nothing was left to him without a family and a tribe to come back to; he would be like some mangy wolf who had been exiled from the pack, creeping around men and hoping to be killed because he was so miserable. No, Lone Wolf had to be strong and skin the animal.

But first he needed to protect his hands, and he sat on the rump of the dead brown buffalo and took off his boots. The little shoes the white man wore inside his boots would do fine. Thin, they would give his hands freedom of movement.

It took Lone Wolf close to two hours to skin the white, and he only touched the dead white directly five times. The burns weren't as bad as he had thought. Touching the animal had felt like resting your hands on a hot

73

kettle without realizing it: first it was cool, then painful. Afterward a blister rose where you had touched it.

He wrapped the white's hide into his coat and dragged it back to the camp, where he spread it out and pegged it down on a piece of canvas to dry. The hide was so full of blood that it was too heavy for a man to carry far.

That done, he examined his hands and arms, which had five great blisters where he had touched the skin directly and dozens of minor blisters where he must have touched the hide without realizing it, perhaps caused by white hairs that had stuck through the white man's feet-gloves and touched his flesh. He melted some snow and washed his hands thoroughly, feeling lucky that the damage was so slight.

Maybe he was more a *Wakan* warrior than he thought, he said to himself. Maybe wolf power was strong enough to handle white buffalo power, but even as he thought it he felt ashamed at such a prideful thought, knowing it wasn't true.

But skinning the white without being harmed was a major event in his life, of that Lone Wolf was certain. Only the most *Wakan* of men and the most virtuous of women could perform even the smallest task on the hide of a great white. Till now he had rather confidently thought such creatures were nothing more than old men's stories. The spirit of the white must have a path to show him.

That thought sobered his moments of triumph.

That night Skinner, McCall and Lone Wolf slept soundly, worn out by the work of the day after having been idle for the last two weeks.

The two white men felt as fulfilled as Lone Wolf. They had slain one hundred thirteen buffalo and had taken one hundred and eight complete hides. They brought all one hundred thirteen frozen tongues because they could get twenty-five cents apiece for them as long as the weather was cold enough to ship them back East and keep them frozen.

At first Skinner was grateful for the care that Lone Wolf displayed in caring for the big white's hide, and Lone Wolf showed him more respect as the man who had brought down the big white.

After all, Skinner told McCall, the Indian had skinned the animal himself the first day, managing to pull it over without any help from them, although God knew a horse would have made that job easier, and then he had dragged the hide back to camp, where he staked it out to dry over the next few days. The Indian then built a nearby fire and kept the hide heated so that it would dry. He knew that nobody could prepare a robe like an Indian who took his time. He realized that having an Indian fix up the white hide would make it that much more valuable.

Both he and McCall often admired the hide as they ate their beans and johnnycakes. Once or twice Skinner hadn't liked the look in the Indian's face when he went to touch the hide, as if the Indian thought he owned the damn thing, but then Skinner had to laugh at what McCall told him by way of explanation: that the Indian had told him he had been worried that lightning might strike any of them just for touching the hide.

"I still think we better pack away some of these hides and mosey on," Skinner said to McCall as they neared the end of their skinning operation. "I don't like the way the chief's been hanging on to the big white."

"I wanted to talk to you about that," said McCall.

"Packing up?"

"The big white. The chief wants to keep it."

"Well, that's too bad."

"I want to give it to him."

"Give it to him! What for?"

"He says that's the hide he was sent out here by his head man to bring back."

Shocked, Skinner snorted. "Like hell! That's the hide I was sent out here by my pocketbook to sell to Johnny Moar."

"We wouldn't have a single one of these hides if it wasn't for our red friend here. In fact, I'm not sure we'd even be here."

"I don't care. We shot it—hell, *I* shot the damn thing—and I want to sell it. Besides, what shooter in Hays is going to believe we got a white buffalo if we don't bring back his skin?"

"I don't care what they think," said McCall.

"Well, Jack McCall, you care about your pocketbook. I done heard you talk enough about it."

"He's going to help us find buffalo."

"You're supposed to be the best buffalo finder in Hays. We don't need him."

Skinner didn't like the exasperation that passed over McCall's face. "Well, I *want* to give it to him."

"Well, I don't. I'm the one that shot it."

"So what? Are those I shot all mine?"

"No, I get a fifth."

"And ain't this my rig?"

"Yeah, but we're partners."

"I'll give you hides to make up for it."

"No, I want the white hide. Back in Hays I can get work as a shooter on the strength of it."

"It ain't all yours, you've already said that."

"I want my part of it."

"You want to cut it?"

"Cut it? That'd just ruin it."

"You get a fifth share with me, Skinner," said McCall, "but it's my rig and my outfit. The man saved our lives in that stampede and we owe him something. I make the decision, and I'm deciding the chief gets the robe. You get extra hides to make up for it. Hell, getting off with your life, I think you made a good bargain."

"This ain't right, Mr. McCall," said Skinner.

"Maybe not, but it's how it's going to be, Mr. Kincade."

While the white man who resembled Crow—whom he now called Jack—told him he could have the white robe the Turtle had shot, Lone Wolf saw that the Turtle wasn't happy about it.

Shiny Head would stand near where Lone Wolf worked on the hide, making angry words in that harsh language of theirs and looking as if he wanted to take the hide back. Clearly, the cream-colored hide fascinated him, for his eyes were fixed on it rather than on Lone Wolf. The man's possessive look bothered Lone Wolf. In order to keep the white man from stealing it, he rolled it up at night and dragged it to the outside tent wall near where he slept, where he would undo the tent flaps. He pushed it inside, where it spent the night behind his head.

There was one thing Lone Wolf didn't understand. The two white men worked hard for almost four days skinning the buffalo and taking their tongues, then did nothing with the rest of the animals. At first Lone Wolf figured they were resting and perhaps communing with their buffalo spirits at this part in their buffalo-taking ceremony, but when he hesitantly asked if this were so, McCall told him no, that they didn't intend to take any of the meat.

"What will you do with all these hides?" asked Lone Wolf.

McCall said they would be sent on an iron horse to a place near the edge of a big water where, as he pointed to his own dress, they would be made into boots, belts, hats and coats.

"What will you do with the meat?"

"You can have it."

"My women are far from here. It will lay here and rot. Take such a gift back to your women."

His new friend laughed in a strange way. "We can't manage it. How would we get all those buffalo humps into our wagon?"

Of course, Lone Wolf saw that. But the answer confused and frightened him all the same. Why, then, had they shot so many buffalo? Surely not just for the pelts and tongues. How had they dared to rip the fabric that *Wakan-Takan* wove as he made the world by destroying so many of his creatures without purpose?

Lone Wolf trembled each of the many times he considered this. The white men had strong powers, just as did witches and warlocks. Without thinking, he had assumed that more wagons would come and take away the buffalo meat. On the other side of the Humpback Mountains, he and his tribe had heard vague stories that white men sometimes left buffalo meat to rot on the ground, but he hadn't paid much attention to them; who would be such a fool? But now this flaunting of buffalo power made him reel with fear.

He had to get away from these two evil warlocks. His stomach churned at the idea of their having killed—bad enough that anyone had to kill *Wakan-Takan's* most powerful creature to live—and then throwing the results of the hunt back into the buffalo powers' eyes, as if what these men had been given by those powers wasn't enough. It made Lone Wolf tremble with shame as well as fear. For everyone in his tribe, the buffalo, like all the animals, were brothers and sisters, fathers and mothers, grandfathers and grandmothers. Men had been born to move among them, to take what they needed, and to do the will of *Wakan-Takan*, but not to wreck his works.

Even though he would have liked to have stayed to work more on the white hide, Lone Wolf decided that he had to leave. But how was he to get the heavy white hide back to his tribe, now that he had it? It weighed nearly one hundred pounds. While he could carry it for miles on his back, carrying it the seventy-five miles to his camp would take more than two weeks, and he might get caught in another storm.

The only thing to do, although he didn't like asking such people for anything, was to ask to borrow a horse or mule, with the understanding he would bring the horse back to Jack McCall once he had delivered the hide.

That night after supper, when McCall heard Lone Wolf's request, McCall was tempted to say yes, for Skinner had whined about losing the hide to the "greasy savage" several times a day since McCall had put his foot down. McCall figured that once the thing was gone, Skinner might shut up and put more effort into the skinning. He had started to slack off.

Still, McCall had to think ahead of how loaning an animal to Lone Wolf would work, so he answered, "A horse? No sir. We've only got eight, four mules to pull the wagon, two spare mules, and two horses to ride. Can't let any of them go."

"What does he want?" asked Skinner.

"A horse to get that heavy hide back," said McCall.

79

Skinner snorted and threw him a hard look. "I can solve that problem," said Skinner. "He can leave the hide with us till he comes back with his own horse."

"That's not a bad idea," said McCall.

But when he told Lone Wolf this, the Indian protested. Lone Wolf said he knew how to track and find an Indian who had made such a promise concerning a white hide, but not whites.

"I been studying on this thing, anyway," put in Skinner. "The long and short of it, McCall, is that I want that damn hide."

"Now we been all over this, and at least half a dozen times. I'm sick to death of hearing about it. It's finished."

"Naw, it ain't. Not for me," said Skinner. "I'm riled up over being treated worse than this greasy savage here. I want to ride back into Hays City with that thing. I want folks to know I'm something as a shooter."

McCall sighed. "Skinner, I'm tired of fighting with you. We got to get along if we're going to finish this trip without killing each other. What do you want?"

"I done told you, damn it. I want *my* hide."

"If you just got to have it, take the damn thing."

"I did shoot it, you know," said Skinner. "It ain't even the money, although I'm so broke I don't know why I'm talking this way. It's what's right. I don't want no savage to walk off with something that's mine."

Skinner moved over to the side of the tent where Lone Wolf had been watching this with large eyes. "I'm taking the white hide, Chief. We done decided."

Lone Wolf pretended not to understand the Turtle, although inwardly he cursed himself for not leaving last night when the hide still lay in the little space between his head and the tent wall.

After a while, though, he had to admit he knew what the shiny-headed white was talking about, for Turtle Head had drawn his gun and held it on Lone Wolf while he went into the corner, grabbed the end of the bundle containing the white hide and pulled it out into the middle of the tent.

McCall told Lone Wolf that the white man could not bear to part with such a beautiful thing, that to keep the peace in his own camp he was reversing himself, and that the Turtle would get much gold for it back in their village.

Lone Wolf struggled for an hour to make his friend understand that *Wakan-Takan* resided in the hide. A warrior didn't just let such a thing leave his possession. Besides, he had been sent here to get the hide by Old Hoof, who most of the time knew what he was doing, and as this was obviously the hide Lone Wolf had been sent to get, what was the use of flouting the will of *Wakan-Takan*? Surely even the shiny-headed white could see such a thing?

"He's my partner," answered McCall. "I got to live with him. We got to finish out this trip together. If he really wants it that bad, I got to give it to him."

That night the shiny-headed man moved around the lodge with his gun in his belt, clearly hoping that Lone Wolf would reach for the white hide, which sat in its bundle in the middle of the floor. Lone Wolf constantly felt drawn toward it, as if it were begging him to carry it away.

Over and over he saw himself pick up the bundle and walk away from the camp, and over and over he saw the shiny man point the gun at him and shoot him in the back. No matter how much the bundle pulled at him, he knew it was better not to act as if he wanted it. With great difficulty, Lone Wolf refused to allow himself to even look at the bundle.

81

After they ate, it looked as if Shiny Head was disappointed that Lone Wolf hadn't gone for the bundle. Giving Lone Wolf a look as sly as a dog sneaking away a bone he knew he shouldn't have, he dragged the hide behind his sleeping roll and put it next to the wall just the way Lone Wolf had arranged it.

Jack said that they were going to pull out tomorrow to find another herd. Did Lone Wolf want to work with them? Help them find herds?

Lone Wolf told him no, that he would leave tomorrow. Now that his leg was better and he had regained his strength, he wanted to see his family and his tribe, he said. A man shouldn't be away in the winter. Spring and summer were the times for hunting.

It took everything Lone Wolf could muster to act as if tonight were nothing but another night. He lay down the same way he had on other nights, and he put his things by the head of his bed the way he had always done, but his mind was running as fast as a fish darts through the water.

He suspected that Shiny Head expected him to steal the hide tonight, for the man had gotten into his bedroll with his gun in his hand and that same crazy gleam in his eye. Lone Wolf knew the sort of night breathing he usually made as he slept, and after a half-hour, he began his regular pattern.

Between their snorts and wheezes, he strained to hear the other two. It took forty-five minutes for McCall to fall asleep, and it wasn't till well after midnight that Shiny Head dropped off. As excited as this made him, Lone Wolf forced himself to wait another half-hour before moving, and when he did, it took him more than a half-hour to leave the tent, so slowly and stealthily did he creep outside.

The air there was freezing. Putting his pouch of belongings on his back, Lone Wolf slowly crept around to Turtle's side of the tent to see what he could do to rescue the white pelt.

When he reached that spot where he thought Skinner slept, he crouched next to the wall and listened, and through the fabric of the tent he heard the two men's gasps and snores. Was the Turtle faking sleep? Lone Wolf didn't think so, but he couldn't be sure.

He took out his knife and slowly sawed through the three tent peg ropes nearest Skinner's position, and then still more slowly lifted the loosened tent flap till he felt the bundle containing the white hide. Just getting his hand on it had taken ten minutes.

Once he had his hand on the bundle came the hard part: he had to get it out of the tent without making enough noise to wake Skinner, whose ear wasn't more than a foot from him. Lone Wolf hunkered down into a crouch, put both hands under the bundle and slowly lifted and pulled it toward him a tiny distance. He held his breath, expecting the roar of the pistol any moment. Extending his body forward into the tent, he closed his two hands on the package more firmly and lifted. As he had almost no leverage, he could only move it another tiny distance. Inch by inch, he drew the bundle toward him, each time managing to move it silently.

Gradually it came forward, making almost no sound, and then it had cleared the tent!

Checking his relief and excitement—by no means was he out of danger—Lone Wolf stood and looked about.

Overhead the stars shone as if they smiled on what he had done. A surge of energy rose through him. He was doing the right thing—taking the white robe to Hoof as he had been commanded.

Carrying the heavy bundle, he crept to the front of the tent where the wagon and the line of picketed horses and mules stood. Of course, the two men would be after him as soon as they found him gone.

While to steal a horse meant the added risk of waking one of them up, he didn't stand a chance carrying this heavy bundle himself.

And if they caught up with him, what was he to do? He put down the bundle and stepped back to the tent, again going into that close air and the smell of whites, which he hated. He carefully felt around and found McCall's rifle. He took it, along with the little pouch McCall wore that carried the shells.

He put the rifle and the pouch of shells on top of the bundle and stealthily unhooked a horse from the picket line. He had spent every spare minute of the last few days making friends with the horses, often giving them bread he had secreted when the three men ate. Now that paid off.

By dawn he had ridden for three hours. They might come after him, but at least he had a lead and a mount.

"My hide's missing!" roared Skinner. "That son of a bitch stole my hide!"

Roused by the shout, McCall jumped out of his bedroll, reaching for his rifle. With a sinking feeling, he knew what had happened. Without saying anything to Skinner, he pulled on his boots and walked out to the picket line. Yep, his best horse, a black mare called Nicky, was missing. Damn, damn, damn!

He looked west and saw horse tracks leading over the bleak snowscape. The wind blew weakly across the grey dawn as his anger mounted. Why had he been so generous to a thieving redskin? Skinner had been right, but he was damned if he was going to tell him so.

"See! Your softheadedness got us into this," Skinner shouted behind him. Irritated, McCall turned as Skinner continued, "My hide's missing. Your horse's gone, and you couldn't find your Sharps .50, could you?"

He had no answer. He didn't mind the Indian making off with the white hide, indeed felt he had it coming. McCall didn't own much that he really cared about, but he cared about Nicky and that rifle. He felt as bleak as the drab dawn.

Skinner pushed on. "We can catch him. That horse's worth two hundred dollars, your rifle ninety-five dollars, and that hide five hundred dollars and maybe a thousand."

"Ah, let him go," said McCall. "I'd just as soon let him have the hide."

"Let him go!"

"We owed him something, didn't we, Skinner?"

"No, he owed us for taking him in when he was about to shiver to death."

"Let him have the hide."

"Hell, no, I won't," said Skinner. "You going to let him get away with stealing your horse and your Sharps?"

McCall had a harder time swallowing that, so for a few moments he chewed on it.

Skinner pressed on. "No, you ain't. Not if you got any self-respect. He was a stinking, thieving redskin when you found him, we should have done away with him then, and that's what he is now and we ought to get our stuff back. You coming with me?"

Taken aback, McCall asked, "Where you going?"

"I'm riding after my hide. Ain't you coming after your horse and rifle?"

"On what?"

"On a mule, if you have to."

"We'll never catch him."

"Like hell," said Skinner. "He's got to leave tracks in this snow, and he had to wait till we was both asleep before he left, which couldn't have been more'n three, four hours ago. If we ride hard we'll catch him. He'll be afraid to ride too hard, afraid of wearing out his horse."

"You got a point. That damn hide is heavy too," said McCall.

"Right."

"Suppose somebody comes along and steals my rig?" McCall speculated, looking around the little camp composed of tent and wagon.

"What he's got of ours is worth more'n everything in this camp put together," said Skinner. "I tell you that damn white hide's worth close to a thousand dollars. All the hides in the wagon ain't worth more'n three hundred to four hundred."

McCall could see that, particularly when he added in what he had paid for the Sharps and Nicky.

They packed some cold roast buffalo, filled two canteens each and saddled up. McCall didn't like riding Jenny, the lead mule, but she was a damn sight better than walking. Besides, the more he turned it over, the more he was riled over the loss of his rifle and horse. The hide, that he could understand. He knew what a white meant to any Indian. But he had saved up for six months to buy the Sharps, specifying the size of the barrel and breech from the factory so he could safely fire cartridges with a double powder load. He had bought his horse Nicky a year ago from Santana, a mount that had been trained to take Santana's huge bulk easily, so that it was particularly well suited to McCall's lanky frame.

Angry at himself for being so wrong about his so-called friend, McCall uncharacteristically allowed Skinner

86

to lead him. Following Nicky's hoofprints, they rode for six hours, hardly speaking, till they reached the edge of the valley, climbed the narrow path through the rocks of the surrounding mountains, and spotted a figure on a horse from the top of the range picking his way across the next valley.

McCall pulled out his telescope and said it was the Indian.

"Has he got the hide?"

"Looks like it. He's got something tied behind himself."

"That's it, all right." Skinner pulled out his own Sharps .44.

"You can't get him from here."

"Like hell I can't," said Skinner. "You seen me hit that white, didn't you?" Before McCall could stop him, Skinner raised the rifle and took aim.

"Don't," said McCall. "It'll just warn him."

But the admonition came just as Skinner pulled the trigger.

The sound of the shot mushroomed to fill the valley, and then echoed back half a dozen times as they watched the tiny figure on the distant horse turn, look at them, and spur his horse forward.

McCall and Skinner urged their horses forward.

"Damn it, Skinner, don't you shoot my horse!"

"How else are we going to stop him?" asked Skinner over his shoulder. His horse was making better time than McCall's mule.

"We'll catch up to him," answered McCall. "Carrying that hide has got to slow him down."

As they reached the bottom of the slope, they saw Lone Wolf's silhouette pass over the ridge above them out of sight.

"We're gaining on him," said Skinner.

It took them most of an hour to gain the top of the next ridge, where they saw that Lone Wolf had increased the distance.

"What the hell!" said Skinner.

McCall pulled out his telescope and looked. "The hide," he said. "It ain't there."

"What do you mean, ain't there?"

"It was a brown bundle sitting behind when he crossed the ridge an hour ago."

"You sure?"

"I'd swear it."

"He's stashed it, expecting to come back for it," said Skinner with a grin. "We done beat him and he knows it."

"Looks that way."

"So what do you say—look around for the hide, or catch him?"

McCall looked up at the afternoon sky, which had started to darken. "We don't know where his blood brothers are."

"You mean they could be over the next hill?"

"Yeah, and we're eight hours away from camp ourselves. He's got that rifle, he ain't that bad a shot, and if he ain't got the hide, I'm not too keen on getting too close."

"Well, this is the best shot we've had all day," said Skinner, again pulling his rifle out of its scabbard. He peered down its long barrel, but just as he pulled the trigger, McCall pushed the barrel harmlessly up into the air.

"What the hell!" shouted Skinner. "What'd you do that for?"

"He saved our lives, damn it. All I want's our stuff. If we can find that hide around here, that's enough."

Lone Wolf's mount broke into a faster gait.

"I could have got him!"

"You probably would have killed Nicky."

"Then we'd have got him. He'd be on foot. Sometimes you act the fool, McCall. If I'd known you was going to be so damn crazy for Injuns, damn if I'd have come out here with you."

"I ain't crazy for Injuns," said McCall. "He stole it because I don't think he could help himself—a white hide is powerful magic to him. It would be like putting you in a tent with ten pounds of gold—wouldn't you steal it if you could get away with it?"

Skinner twisted his face into a crafty grin, showing stumps of tobacco-stained teeth set in his moonlike face. "I ain't out nothing, McCall. It's your horse and gun, and we'll let them go if you want. Let's look around for that hide, which is partly mine."

"It's got to be near the trail."

"We'll see his tracks in this snow. He's crazy if he thinks we won't find it."

"He may just want to slow us down."

"As long as I get my hide, I'm as good as slowed."

"Let's hurry. We can't take more'n a couple of hours if we're going to get back to camp tonight."

"We got to get back," said Skinner. "We didn't bring any bedrolls."

McCall kicked his mule forward and Skinner followed.

They took three hours, but could find nothing. Even though they assumed that Lone Wolf couldn't have gotten off the trail to cache the hide without making tracks, they discovered none.

Finally the darkening landscape forced them to return to camp, although it took them most of the night to do so. Neither had much to say to the other.

In fact, once they had returned, they didn't feel like talking to each other at all, and over the next week, while they had no trouble finding buffalo, hardly ten words passed between them as they did their work. That suited both of them, both reckoning that if the same number passed between them the rest of their time out here, that would be another ten words too many.

Chapter 4

"You've actually brought in a white hide, young Wolf?" asked Hoof, the old shaman.

"Yes sir," answered Lone Wolf.

"You're sure?"

"See for yourself, grandfather."

"This isn't one of your tricks, is it?"

"Trick?"

"An elk hide with white clay smeared over it, perhaps?"

"No! A real hide from a large white bull."

"You have time to change your mind if this is a story, son."

"I have no mind to change, grandfather."

The old man nodded and said to his aged assistant, Stomach Wind, "He thinks he can pass off a rabbit skin on me because I'm so old."

"Come see for yourself," said Lone Wolf.

Stomach Wind, who hadn't disagreed with Old Hoof in fifty years, said, "These boys get more unruly every year, Plum. Conjure some worms to gnaw out his gut. Then he'll show some respect."

God, he sometimes hated these old men, Lone Wolf

thought. Had he been through all he had over the past weeks just to hear them mock him? All he wanted to do was to give the *Wakan* hide to the *Wakan* man and sleep for three days, for he felt as much dead as alive from his ordeal and the hard ride back. Of course, it would be nice to have a pat on the back for bringing in the only white buffalo pelt anybody alive had ever brought in, but he certainly didn't deserve sharp looks and the accusation of playing a trick on the old man.

Hoof had been like a wise uncle to Lone Wolf as a youth, looking out for him in councils, teaching him some of the old wolf chants, and making charms for his shield and lances in exchange for portions of the game he killed. Now Hoof had become old and, in Lone Wolf's and Left Hand's view, a bit touched in the head. His stories had become longer than usual and you never knew when he made you a charm whether it would have any power, or if indeed it might actually be a weakness.

Hoof nodded agreeably at Stomach Wind's suggestion in a way that showed how weary he was of the foolishness of youngsters.

As if just getting to his feet were painful, the old man gave his hand to Lone Wolf so the younger man could pull him up. Holding on to each other for support, Hoof and Stomach Wind tottered outside, followed by Lone Wolf.

In a circle around the white man's exhausted horse were a group of Kiowa, a dozen children, a half dozen women, and two or three men, all looking at the thin horse and the bundle strapped to its back.

Like so many old men Lone Wolf knew, Hoof just stopped and looked at the horse before doing anything. Cautious, always cautious. May *Wakan-Takan* grant me an early death, Lone Wolf prayed, preferably one on the battlefield, and not this living death of the old. Here the old man had sent him out to get the damn thing, and now he didn't want to admit that Lone Wolf had completed such a hard task.

"Well, aren't you going to open it and look at it?" asked Lone Wolf.

"You're sure it's a white hide in there?" asked Hoof.

"I told you so."

"From the white buffalo?"

"No, from a white squirrel."

"Son, don't joke about such matters!"

The old man's tone sent shivers down Lone Wolf's back and brought him to attention. Sometimes the old man knew what he was about, but after all, Lone Wolf had traveled with the hide for a week now and little untoward had happened to him. He couldn't think of any answer that wasn't disrespectful, so he said nothing.

"Cow or bull?" asked Hoof.

"Bull."

"Bull," mused Hoof, looking into the December sky as if the meaning of this were written there.

Hoof reached out to take Lone Wolf's hands in his, turned them over, pulled them to within inches of his face and peered at them. His old eyes were steady in his crosshatched face. "Where did you get these blisters?" Hoof asked finally. "And these warts?" He was referring to the large black warts that had appeared inside Lone Wolf's palms and along the outer ridges of his wrists.

"From it," answered Lone Wolf.

"The white hide?" asked Hoof. "You touched it? Directly?"

"Yes sir."

Holding Lone Wolf's hands in his, Hoof raised his ancient yellowed eyes to stare directly into Lone Wolf's eyes, which made the younger man squirm a bit. Still, he

93

wasn't going to back down from some dried-up old man who half the time couldn't remember what ceremony he was performing, not after having brought back such a powerful bundle. Let the old man go through his fiddle-faddle.

"Maybe so, then," murmured Hoof, "maybe so."

That he felt relieved by the old man's absorbed tone made Lone Wolf irritated with himself.

Then what made Lone Wolf feel full of pride was the old man's holding off doing anything until one of the criers had run through the village with the news to call in the warriors of the Kanasa society, the bravest and most valorous fighters of the entire Kiowa. Under Hoof's supervision, four Kanasa carefully unstrapped the bundle from the horse and took it, with Hoof insisting they each keep a hand on it, into their society's lodge. They were as careful as men carrying a sleeping bobcat in their arms.

It made Lone Wolf chuckle—but under his breath—to hear the tremor in Hoof's voice as he gave the four Kanasa orders, for he had handled this bundle alone for the past week. Lone Wolf found it typical of the arrogance of shamans that the old man wouldn't stoop to ask him what chants he had sung to keep the white buffalo spirit at bay. Like all shamans, he was sure he knew everything about spirits. Then it made him feel still more proud, if a bit anxious, when the old man ordered him to come into the Kanasa lodge with them. Lone Wolf had never been inside it, since it was above his own men's society lodge, the Denoskin, in rank.

Inside the large tepee Lone Wolf saw a buffalo altar, a circle of stones, a hollow for a fire, and many rich buffalo robes around the outer edge. On the inner wall of the tepee, hanging at the height of a man's head, glared a circle of twenty stuffed buffalo heads, their *Wakan* eyes staring fixedly at Lone Wolf.

Only five Kanasa were now in the tepee, but even as they carried the bundle toward the buffalo-skull altar under Hoof's sharp orders and warnings, Lone Wolf saw others come in behind them. He felt proud that they should handle what he had brought back in so carefully, but knew he shouldn't grin and act the fool. The time would come for him to tell them the story of his adventure.

For the first time he realized who he was now, and would always be: the warrior who had brought back the only white hide his tribe had ever had. In doing so he had had to brave a blizzard, nearly losing his leg and his life from gangrene, and a buffalo stampede, which when he told the story might bring him praise and maybe even a spot in the Kanasa lodge. That thought made his heart skip a couple of times. To be a Kanasa! It would mean others thinking he was one of the bravest in the tribe. He would have a new set of friends and comrades, and perhaps in time not one but two new wives! New rituals, much respect, and a seat on the council—all things he had dreamed of, but never thought he might accomplish. He might even be seen as now having quasi-Onde status, a sort of junior member of the aristocracy. After all, had he ever heard of anybody but a Kanasa entering their lodge? Maybe with Hoof's telling him to enter, he had taken the first step in becoming one.

Hoof lowered himself to his hands and knees in front of the bundle of old skin that held the white hide. Hesitantly he reached his hand toward the rawhide strip that tied it together.

Lone Wolf knew what the trouble was: like any sane Kiowa, Hoof was afraid the white hide would destroy him.

He almost came forward to open the bundle for the old man, as Lone Wolf had handled the hide dozens of times. Of course, Lone Wolf had always handled the hide with the feet-gloves the white men had given him. He knew how to handle it safely, but he also knew it would be politic to let Hoof direct matters from here on out.

Everybody in the lodge—even Lone Wolf, who had seen the white pelt many times—leaned forward with his breath held. They all knew the dangers. Unless Lone Wolf was lying, out of that bundle could come charging a giant white buffalo bull who would tear up the tepee as he gored and trampled them all to death. On the other hand, if the force in the bundle was controlled and contained, it would mean a source of good luck and fat hunts for years to come, as well as a shield to keep them safe from attacks of the Comanche and the white men.

Then, withdrawing his hand from the unopened bundle, Hoof pulled back and sat on his heels. "I cannot," he said, folding his hands together in front of his chest. "One here is impure." Hoof then turned to stare at Lone Wolf, as did the dozen Kanasa who now filled the lodge.

"Me?" asked Lone Wolf, disappointed that he hadn't opened the bundle to show the others his trophy. "How?"

"I don't know, but you must take a sweat bath and cleanse yourself with chanting and prayer."

"Sweat bath!"

"The white buffalo mustn't be made angry."

"I haven't had much to eat the last few days. When I rode in, I came right to your lodge."

"And you did right, son. Danger lurks around this lodge now like demons who walk the night."

Lone Wolf looked about the Kanasa lodge, but saw no helpful looks from the warriors there. More than anything, he wanted sleep. He did not want to go through a sweat bath, with its rigors of fasting, wakefulness, and endless songs and prayers.

"As well," said Hoof. "You must not lie with a woman for two weeks."

"Two weeks!"

"Otherwise this bundle is poisoned and we might as well burn it."

"Burn it!" exclaimed Lone Wolf.

"Burn it," said the old man firmly. "This is such an important matter, I myself will take charge of your purification."

So, to Lone Wolf's chagrin, the bundle was left just as he had brought it in, all tied up, before the buffalo-skull altar of the Kanasa.

A sweat tepee was quickly erected. Buffalo paunches of water were brought into it, and hot rocks were dropped into the water, filling it with steam. Before he entered, Lone Wolf asked Hoof if he might eat, for he hadn't eaten in three days. The withering look the old man gave him was his only answer.

Inside, to his discomfort, Lone Wolf was forced to strip naked and to sit on a low log while Hoof led him in chant after chant. Quickly he became yet more exhausted, wanting only rest, a hot meal, and Onni making cooing noises over him. But from the few words from Hoof, and from his stern gestures, he gathered that what was going on here was more important than his mere comfort.

The steam, the chants, the sweat dripping off his body, and his hunger and thirst combined to make him woozy. Hoof poked him in the ribs whenever he failed to sit up straight and shouted at him whenever his voice flagged. If it weren't for the honor, Lone Wolf told himself wearily, he would just as soon do without this.

When the Kanasa tepee got too hot for Hoof, others

from the Kanasa society took his place in leading Lone Wolf in chants and keeping the lodge filled with steam, and whenever they needed a rest, still other Kanasa spelled them. The only person who wasn't spelled was Lone Wolf, who sat and chanted, prayed and sang, for the rest of the day and then all night, without food and without saying a word to his family or even seeing them, although he was told that his three children had come and gone from the front of the tepee. His wife Onni had not come, he was led to understand; no one had seen her in front of the Kanasa tepee. Although it wasn't explicitly said, the hints and nods Lone Wolf was given led him to believe that Onni was still as furious with him as a disturbed rattler.

While he didn't want to sit here without anything to eat or drink, sweating and praying and wishing to see his children and his wife, it was such a great honor to have the Kanasa attend to you like this that he decided to put up with it. In addition, he had the sense that Old Hoof, foolish as he might be at times, was in no mood to take no for an answer, that this gain of a white pelt was close to the most important thing that had ever happened while Hoof was the tribe's shaman.

As he chanted and endured the hours of steam that made him weaker and weaker, Lone Wolf marveled at what an important thing he must have done. He had known it was important, but *how* important he hadn't been able to appreciate out there alone on his horse and while in the white man's tepee with Shiny Head and Long Crow. But now that he was back in camp, he realized that he had brought his people a priceless gift. Nobody else had ever done it before, but he had. From now on the other tribesmen, including Hoof and the Kanasa and the Big Bellies, would have to treat him with more respect. He also sensed that such respect contained a responsibility too, such as this one to just sit here for weary hours and chant, even though what he really longed to do was sit and eat with his family before sleeping for a couple of days.

For close to two months now he had been away from his family and the tribe, and he had missed everything that made camp life worth living. He had missed the evening meals with other Denoskin brothers in one of their tepees. He had missed playing with the children at night, hunting with Left Hand, and the long stories they all told each other night after night. He longed to race a horse, although he would have to go on a raid to get some before he could do much racing and gambling. But going out on a raid with his Denoskin brothers was one more thing he had missed. He had missed sleeping with his wife and with Elk Woman, and if he wasn't to get Elk Woman permanently, then he wanted to find himself a second wife. He didn't want to sit in this sweat lodge, no matter how important it was to Hoof. But no matter how he figured, he wound up thinking it was best to stay on the good side of the old man, or some of the reasons he had been sent out on the quest might be brought back up. That he didn't need at all.

He just hoped Hoof got through all this soon. Lone Wolf was afraid that, even though it wouldn't look so good, he might pass out from exhaustion if they kept this up.

"Hey, brother," said the Kanasa who was in charge. "You've stopped chanting."

Lone Wolf nodded vigorously and picked up the chant, shaking his head as he did so to shake the sleep out of his eyes. How hard to remember what chant they were doing! If only this ended shortly!

"Not me," said Onni to her sister, Willow.

"Onni, you have to."

"No, I don't."

99

"Think how it'll look."

"I don't care."

"Oh, Onni."

"Don't give me that. Look what he did to me."

"They'll talk about you."

"I don't care."

"It's an honor."

"He hasn't said he's sorry—not once."

"Why should he?"

"Willow! I thought you were my friend."

Willow sighed with what Onni thought was exasperation. Onni had been asked to work with the other wives of the great warriors in tanning and decorating the white hide that Lone Wolf had brought back, but on top of not wanting to have anything to do with him till he had apologized, she didn't like working with the senior women of the tribe. Just as her mother had, they would look down their noses and criticize the way she held the knife or what beads she chose.

"If I wasn't your friend, I wouldn't be talking to you this way, Onni."

"Then you should understand."

"I understand you aren't giving him a chance."

"Did he come to me when he rode in?" asked Onni.

"He had to go to Old Hoof's! Onni, you're not seeing straight."

The two sat in Onni's tepee scraping a hide together. In many ways Onni didn't like to discuss her marriage with Willow, who didn't have trouble with men and never would. While only seventeen, Willow treated her half dozen suitors casually, which made them all the more eager to bring her gifts and play the flute for her. Now Onni and Willow were alone, but not for long, as shortly the children would be coming back for the evening meal.

Shocked by her sister's response, Onni stopped pulling her tanning knife across the buffalo hide. "I'm your sister. We've talked about it. You know what he did with me—seeing that witch! How can you take his side?"

"Maybe you should look at what *you're* doing."

"Me? *Me!*"

"Yes," said Willow. "Lone Wolf's becoming an important man. They might make him a Kanasa! Why shouldn't he have more than a single wife? Sure, he was seeing that woman. Because you wouldn't let him take another wife."

Inside, Onni shriveled, for she had sensed that Lone Wolf's feat in bringing back a white hide had tipped the tribe's sympathies in his favor. She said, "I thought you were on *my* side?"

"I am, Onni, I am," Willow responded. "You know I am. It's just that you've got this idea in your head that won't let you see straight."

"Why don't I feel like you're on my side?"

"Because a prairie dog's kicked sand in your eyes. Because a blind man can't see. Because you think what happened to Momma has to happen to every first wife."

Onni had no answer, for she had run out of energy. She hated this tugging within her own family. She was thin, small-busted, serious, and quick as a rabbit. Ever since late last summer, when she had discovered that Lone Wolf was seeing Elk Woman on the sly, she had grown even thinner, more serious, and jerkier in her movements.

At twenty-nine, Onni had three children, a large tepee she and Willow had made together, and what she had figured was a settled future. When Lone Wolf had courted her ten years earlier, she had gotten a promise from him that he would never take another wife, as did maybe half the Kiowa men. She had seen what that had done to her mother, and if it meant not marrying, she wasn't having anything to do with a second or third woman in her lodge, even if it made the burden of work easier. Of course, now Willow often helped her with her work, a big help, but shortly Willow would marry. It made Onni uneasy when she thought of how she was going to keep up with all the hides she would be expected to tan and decorate, leggings and moccasins she would have to sew, and belts and quivers she would want to make as the wife of a Kanasa. After all, it did seem Lone Wolf was to become one, a status that would demand that her husband dispense many gifts.

As a girl Onni had never been like other Kiowa girls, and as a woman she wasn't a lot like Kiowa women. Thus, where most girls quit playing with boys between ten and twelve, she never had. While she had never allowed boys to lie down with her—they knew better than to try if they didn't want a knee in the groin or a poke in the stomach— she had gone on rabbit hunts with them, played buffalo and braves, and made bows and arrows till she was fifteen or so, when her mother had insisted that she give up running around with young men if she ever expected to marry one. This was a paradox Onni had never fathomed.

Onni had resisted her mother's injunctions, but the combined pressure of her mother, her aunts, the other women of the village, and the looks and jeers of almost everyone else in camp finally convinced her. But still, married, even with three children, Onni didn't feel she belonged with the women. She never had, and she didn't believe she ever would. Where other women had big, soft hips, she was sharp and bony. Where other women had plump breasts and ample waists, she had little more than skin covering her. Other women smiled, jeered, giggled a lot, and when they were angry they had loud, raucous voices; Onni seemed serious most of the time and spoke quietly. Other women seemed to loll and roll their way to the spring, almost inviting men and boys to stare at their great hips and full breasts, their eyes darting to the side to see who was watching them. Onni went with her water paunches and did everything quickly, with a hard, fast intent that was more like a man's than a woman's.

Getting Lone Wolf to marry her had been the one great joy and accomplishment of her life. To her, he was a large man with a thick chest and a gentle nature, more a bear of a man than the wolf of his name. She felt safe with him, felt he could protect her and the children. But to have another woman in her own tepee! Someone plump and jolly, someone lolling about, giggling all the time, some woman who didn't poke Lone Wolf with the sharpness of her hipbones—the thought pierced her heart with pain. In this situation, Lone Wolf would never pay attention to her. He would ignore her and take up with this other woman, perhaps several, relegating her to second or third wife.

Just finding out last year that her husband had lain with Elk Woman—a creature with plump curves, flashing eyes and a lascivious, pointed tongue—had hit Onni like a fist in the stomach, for she had believed till then that after so many years the bond between her and Lone Wolf was firm.

Now she sighed. Why couldn't some spirit help women? They were never safe from a man's roving eye, never safe till men were too old to be men. But even then the old men sat toothlessly in front of their sons' tepees and would watch younger women going by, and you saw them talk and laugh among themselves, and you could just imagine their wishing to each other that they were young enough to still chase them. Men! Damn men!

"I want him to say he's sorry," Onni told her sister.

"Say he's sorry! For what?"

"For breaking his promise."

"He made it years ago, Onni."

"He knows how I feel."

"But do you know how he feels?"

Onni felt congested. She didn't like Willow pushing her on like this. "Let's get the meal ready for the children."

"No, you listen to me," said Willow. "There's some things you need to hear. Now, you can't treat your husband this way. Here's a man who's been out for weeks on this crazy chase, came back with that white hide when there hasn't been anybody who ever did anything like that before, and he's being made a Kanasa at an age when hardly anybody of the low status he started out with has ever been made one, and you act as if you can treat him like a lovesick boy who's courting you. You're acting crazy, sister."

"But Hoof sent him out as punishment—"

"No, stop, you just *listen* to me. I've been listening to you for weeks. I've heard everything you have to say. He comes back, more dead than alive, and that loony old man pens him up in the Kanasa lodge and sweats him still more to death, and when he was allowed to come over here after a week, all you did was what? Served him up burnt food."

"That wasn't my fault! I didn't know he was coming home that night."

"You should have borrowed something from another lodge," said Willow. "Now he's eating over at Left Hand's almost every night, and you know how his wives feel about Lone Wolf."

Onni knew indeed. It wasn't that she didn't like Left Hand—nobody who knew him could help but like such a jolly man—but he had *three* wives who were like sisters with each other. In fact, two *were* sisters. The three women got along wonderfully, spoiling Left Hand—and Lone Wolf too, whenever he came by for a meal.

"You don't see how serious this is, do you?" Willow continued. "Do you want him to renounce you and take up with Elk Woman?"

"But I'm the one who was wronged, Willow. Can't anybody see that? So what if he brought back that stupid hide?"

"Shhhh! Be quiet! If the buffalo hears you, he'll run through this lodge."

Frightened by the truth of this, Onni nodded, for she had said a foolish thing.

"Sister, I'm going to tell you something," said Willow, "but you have to promise me something first."

"What is it?"

"You have to promise first."

"Promise what?"

"That no matter what I tell you, you'll treat Lone Wolf right."

Wary, Onni looked at Willow. The two sisters got along well, but from time to time Onni resented Willow. What came hard to Onni came easily to Willow. Willow had four or five boys running after her, but unlike Onni at her age, she was in no hurry to take one. She wanted to make sure that their father got plenty of horses when she married so the boy would value her, and that the man she did marry would go a long way in the tribe. As Willow said when Onni pushed her, she didn't want to be camped in the outer circle of the tepees. Rather, she wanted to be in the choice inner ring of camp, in one of the largest lodges. Willow had a cool head, something Onni wished she had, but not such a cool head that she couldn't enjoy life. She made the combination of falling in love and getting for herself what she wanted look easy, and Onni knew her sister would always be happier than she was.

Bewildered, Onni asked, "How can I promise that?"

"If you can't, I can't tell you."

Onni knew Willow meant it. Even at eighteen, she was tough. If she said she wouldn't, no matter how juicy the gossip or how much she might long to speak, she wouldn't. Willow knew what she wanted and she knew how to trade for it. After they had argued about it for a few minutes, Onni finally gave in, longing to hear what her sister had to say.

"I saw them together," said Willow.

She didn't have to explain. With a clenching in her stomach, Onni knew she meant Lone Wolf and Elk Woman. "No!"

"Out past the spring," said Willow.

"What were they—"

"Talking. Laughing. She touched him and he smiled at her."

Onni's heart was in a rage. "Did they see you?"

"I was in a bush."

"How *could* he!"

"Calm down. You promised."

"What?"

"That you'd treat him right," said Willow. "Can't you see? He's looking for a woman. He's been away for weeks. If you aren't that woman, then he'll go somewhere else."

But Onni's head spun and her stomach felt cramped, as if someone were squeezing her rib cage so hard that she couldn't take a deep breath. Treat him right! Make *him* feel good? What about her? Who was going to make *her* feel good? How could Willow expect her to cook and sew and clean his gear when he was out in the bushes with that witch? "I'll kill him."

"Onni, you have to face the truth."

"He was punished once for this by the Big Bellies. They'll do it again."

"No, he's different now. They probably expect a man of his rank to take another wife."

"Then I'll punish him."

"No, Onni, no."

"I will."

"You're in the wrong now."

"I won't let him get away with this."

Finally Hoof and the leaders of the Kanasa decided that Lone Wolf had to have something to eat or they were likely to kill him.

They brought him roast strip of buffalo hump, and after another few days, Hoof reckoned Lone Wolf had become cleansed enough that they could open the bundle.

Lone Wolf watched the unraveling closely, and he saw that Hoof only allowed the bravest Kanasa to handle the pelt, which really was beautiful—huge, cream-colored, rich with deep thick winter fur, and without a tear in it.

They all chanted over it and prayed for another couple of days, while Hoof had the women build a special tepee just for working on the white hide. Then, after the old man felt that everything had been purified—Lone Wolf, himself, the Kanasa tepee and the rest of the tribe—he started purifying the new tepee and the women who had built it. He insisted that the women decorate the hide properly.

As the wife of a soon-to-be Kanasa, Onni was to be one of the women to dress the hide, an honor that made Lone Wolf feel proud. Maybe that would make her ease up on him, he said to himself. She never felt she was as good as the other women. Maybe this would make her feel better about herself. He had hoped that after being gone so long she would forgive him and they could go back to the same relationship they had had for the past ten years. Those years had been somewhat stormy, but they were filled with stretches of time in which she'd fixed his favorite meals, worked hard to make a comfortable lodge for him and the children, and at night given him energetic loving that left him satisfied.

But the first night he was back in their lodge, she burned the food, and in a huff he had gone over to see Left Hand. Not that he could have lain with her, for Hoof had been sharp about this point, telling him that he would dirty himself if he slept with a woman before the white-buffalo hide singing was done.

All evening Left Hand's women had treated him right, insisting that he tell the story of how he got the white hide three times and asking lots of interested questions. It made Lone Wolf still more jealous of Left Hand to see how the three women scrambled around the tepee to do what he wanted, and from the hints and winks he got from his jolly friend and his own knowledge of Left Hand, Lone Wolf knew that he would have a terrific time under the blankets with one of them tonight. Lone Wolf went back to the dreary, cold lodge that the angry Onni had made for him. Damn her. Why couldn't she act more the way a woman ought to?

The second time that Hoof had let him go out, Lone Wolf had run across Elk Woman on the way to his tepee. She had a water paunch in her hand, obviously on her way to the well, and while she didn't say a word, she didn't have to. A single sweep of her eyes across Lone Wolf's body, a toss of her head and a curl of her lips said it all:

"Why don't you swing around in a wide circle, fine big man, and meet me? It's been too long."

With difficulty, Lone Wolf averted his eyes and struggled not to look at her or smile. She was a fine woman and seemed spirited and full of fun compared to that wasp of a woman in his tepee. About thirty, Elk Woman was full-figured, and her flesh rippled invitingly as she moved. Her eyes were filled with a smoky sultriness that spoke of a deep love of what a man could do with a woman. He imagined easing himself into the comfort of her rounded, soft flesh. He sighed. He couldn't. Hoof had been explicit on this point, and gossip about the two of them would sweep through the camp in minutes. Just talking to her was dangerous. He would banter and play with her for a couple of minutes and move on. Why shouldn't he have a little bit of fun after all that praying and sweating and then the anger he got at home?

Because she had turned his life into turmoil last year good and proper, he answered himself. But maybe, he argued with himself, he could have a good time with her just once more, something to make up for doing without a woman on his trip and since he had returned to the village a week ago. After all, if he could get some comfort from a woman, why shouldn't he take it? He couldn't get it at home. Onni might have stopped the angry words, but she hadn't stopped giving him hard looks. A man needed something from a woman besides scolding.

Why had he made such a foolish vow when he was a youth? One wife! What Kanasa had one wife? How could a *Kanasa* have just one? Who would do all the work around such an important man's lodge?

But on this occasion Lone Wolf had simply passed by Elk Woman and resisted the impulse to follow her, feeling that he was doing the right thing. The last time he had gotten involved with this plump woman, it had brought ruin. He didn't need that again.

One day when he went out to check his horse herd, he had to go alone, for his sturdy younger brother, who took care of his herd for him, had a bad toothache.

On his way back, as Lone Wolf trudged through the January snow, he saw a buffalo cow pass over a hill to his left. He chased after it, for his lodge was short of fresh meat, but when he went over the ridge, all he found was a little green meadow set in a grove where no snow had fallen. And there stood Elk Woman, who laughed at him in surprise.

"What are you doing here?" he asked.

"You've been dodging me, pretty man."

Taken aback by her bold stare, he laughed. "Where's the buffalo I was chasing? Where's the snow?"

"Forget that buffalo," she said. "Forget the snow. I'm here instead."

He felt uneasy. How could that buffalo have just disappeared? And how could grass grow in the middle of winter? And it be so warm and like spring? "No, I've had enough trouble, Elk."

"Trouble? There doesn't have to be any trouble."

Beaming, her eyes narrow and intent on his face, Elk Woman moved forward and touched him on the chest with several fingers. She rubbed him there in a pattern that made him dizzy. He had to get away. Hoof would be furious, and if Onni found out, he would never be able to explain this to her. Even as he thought these things, though, he felt himself churn from a fire that surged up out of his stomach.

She laughed heartily. "Ah, you do like that. Have you forgotten how good I make you feel?"

"No, Elk, I've had enough trouble."

"No more trouble," she answered.

"Right. It's over."

She laughed in an amused way and touched him again on his chest, this time with both hands spread flat. He wanted to move back, but his feet felt rooted to the ground.

She said, "It doesn't seem over."

"Yes," he said. He felt confused and dizzy. Today was uncharacteristically warm. The sun beat down hotly, and his head spun. "I mean, no."

"You enjoyed us."

"Yes, but I don't want to take another man's wife," he said, struggling to get his feet and hands to obey his mind's orders to back away from her. But nothing obeyed.

"I don't think you could say I'm still really married to Eagle Beak," she said. "He doesn't really want me. I don't want him."

Confused by the heady feeling her fingers made on his stomach and chest, he only said, "I see."

Elk Woman snuggled up to him, pressing her body to his. She took off one of two amulets on rawhide thongs from her neck, each of which looked to be little knots the size of a thumb, made of buffalo-tail hair. She put the amulet over Lone Wolf's head.

"What's that?" he asked. He looked around fearfully, for his head roared as if he were standing in the middle of a waterfall.

"Something to protect us."

"Protect us? From what?"

"From others' eyes. Promise me you won't take it off."

He touched the little knot of hair that now hung down on his throat. "What is it?"

"Just a little love knot for old time's sake," she

111

answered. "We each have one." She clasped hers and his in her fists. "Promise not to take it off?"

He still felt dizzy, as if he had eaten too many chokeberries and might be sick. He nodded, she smiled back, and gradually he felt better. The waterfall that roared in his ear had quieted.

"You and me, we're going to have a good time," she said. Her laughter calmed him and promised everything he had needed for the past two months—soft comfort, the release of hungry tension, respect, and the satisfaction of thrusting into her with all the power he could muster.

"Yes," he said, reaching for her. She came to him willingly, with a fierceness in her mouth and hands that fed as well as satisfied his hunger for a woman.

The sun had warmed his skin, and he pulled her toward the bushes a few steps away. Once more wouldn't hurt Onni. How could she find out if he was so far away from the village? The same went for Old Hoof. A man needed a woman, and what stupidity not to have what you needed.

In a few minutes they had shed most of their clothes. He took her once, fast, both of them eager, and then, after he had rested, he turned her over and took her again, the way a horse takes a mare, mounting her triumphantly.

Before they parted, they made a time to meet the next day. But when that time came, Hoof told Lone Wolf he had another set of chants he had to sing for most of the afternoon, so he couldn't meet her.

The day after that, Lone Wolf had to climb up Raven Hill with Hoof and most of the Kanasa as they took the now-decorated white hide to the top of that small mountain. There the hide was spread out on a little rack they made as an offering to *Wakan-Takan*, an offering of the most valuable thing the tribe owned.

As the man who had brought the tribe such a piece of good fortune, Lone Wolf led the singing and praying. Half a dozen times he lost his place, drawing angry stares from Hoof. He knew he should concentrate harder on the chanting that went on throughout most of the cold night they spent up there, but he simply couldn't. His mind was too filled with Elk Woman's moist, hot flesh, the sensuous way she opened herself to allow him to sink into her, and her eagerness for him to experiment and explore her body with his sex. How lucky to have her! She appreciated his power as a man. He should have married a woman like her. If only she didn't have a husband, Eagle Beak, he would take her for his at once, never mind what that bean-thin Onni had to say about it. He had put up with enough. As far as Lone Wolf was concerned, Onni could pack up and go back to her mother.

Not having an agreed-upon place or time, Lone Wolf didn't meet Elk Woman the next day, nor the one after that, nor could he figure out how to get word to her where to meet. If he was seen in camp talking to her, he knew the outcome. First, Onni would hear about it, and second, Hoof would jump on him, for from the first day of cleansing Hoof had made him promise not to sleep with any women till the buffalo spirits had accepted Lone Wolf as a recipient of their power. Reluctantly Lone Wolf had agreed, and Left Hand and his wives had made fun of him for it. His friend said, in fact, he didn't see that it was any great honor to be a Kanasa if you had to promise not to mount your wives, a statement that produced shrieks of merriment from his three women.

With the hide up on Raven Hill, Hoof let up some. For a few days Lone Wolf kept to himself. He wanted to go out to tend the horses, but his brother felt bad that he had let such a rising member of the family down and insisted that he do his own job.

Eagle Beak's tepee was up in the front circle, as he was an Onde, one of the aristocrats making up a tenth of the tribe, so that Lone Wolf spotted Elk Woman whenever he came to the Kanasa tepee to chant or just sit around with his new society. Much of him longed to go back to his old society, but a man who wanted to move up in the tribe just didn't say no to the Kanasa.

Seeing Elk Woman did him little good, for both of them had the sense to keep their eyes averted from each other. On top of that, Eagle Beak was not only of the aristocratic Onde class but a Kanasa too, and he watched Lone Wolf with hard eyes whenever his rival was present, obviously still resentful over Lone Wolf's having stolen his wife last year. Any sign that something was shuttling between the two would have given Eagle Beak the opportunity to whack Lone Wolf from behind and nobody would have thought the worse of him because of what had happened the year before.

The fourth day after his first meeting with Elk Woman, Lone Wolf was walking back to his tent from the Kanasa tepee at dusk when he seemed to blink and suddenly found himself not in the camp, but in a grove of oak saplings as green and warm as late spring, although it was still the dead of winter.

Startled, he turned around in the gloom of dusk and saw not only no tepees but not a soul, whereas a moment before he had been in the center of a hundred lodges, dozens of cooking fires, racks of drying meat, and the shouts of children and barks of dogs.

"Over here," called a familiar voice.

He whipped around as his heart leapt. He peered into

a green thicket, and there he saw Elk Woman, smiling, coming forward toward him.

"Where am I?" he asked.

He felt a bit frightened, for the shift between this place and the camp had happened too fast for a man not to recognize a sort of magic was at work.

"Don't you recognize it?" she asked.

He looked around. "Where we were the other day," he said. "That same grove."

As Elk Woman neared him, she smiled still more deeply. "Yes. And we can keep coming back—as long as you wear the twin of this amulet." With a smile, she touched the buffalo-hair knot at her throat.

"The amulet!"

"Yes."

Her hand caressed the hair knot at her throat as his went to his own. The amulet there felt hot to his touch, as if it had been near a fire. Now he felt frightened. Something wasn't right.

"How did I get here?" he asked.

"We can meet any time we want," she answered.

"What power is this?"

"Have you come here to ask questions?"

"Elk, where did you get such magic?"

Near enough to touch him, she drew a hot palm along his cheek. "Hold me," she said. "We don't have much time."

He felt something turn over in him as his fear gave way to delight. As before, her eyes promised ecstasies.

"No one's around?" he asked, taking her in his arms.

"Everybody's in camp making the meal or waiting to eat," she said.

He leaned down and kissed the tip of her nose, which shot a shiver of pleasure through him. She then kissed his cheeks and his neck and his ears, and he shuddered in pleasure as he surrendered to her lips. He ran his hands all the way down her back and sighed. God, how good it was to feel her firm, full body!

Afterward, no stars shone in the clear night.

"Where is this place?" he asked.

"So many questions!"

"But I don't see the stars."

"Let the stars take care of themselves. We have other business."

"I have to get back," he said. "Which way is camp?"

"Not yet!" she cried.

He smiled in the darkness. Apparently he had aroused her hunger for him as much as she aroused him.

"I must get back."

"No, not yet."

"Yes. Which way?"

Finally he got her to point, but he could hardly see the hand with which she pointed.

"Can we get away again?" he asked.

"Oh, yes," she breathed, then laughed. "Any time we want to. All we want to."

"How did you do this?"

"I bought the amulets with nine of Eagle Beak's horses."

The number made Lone Wolf reel. Just so they could be together? The poverty of his youth rose up to protest, "Nine! *Nine,* woman?"

"It's well worth it."

What a sum! But what power! "You really want to be with me, don't you?" he asked.

In the darkness, her rich chuckle thrilled him. "How can you doubt that?" she asked.

His own chuckle answered hers and he gave her a

hard squeeze. Onni would never be so resourceful. How his luck had shifted over the last few weeks! He had always wanted to move up in rank and status, and now he had really begun to. The daughter of a great chief, the wife of an Onde, wanted him and had even paid nine horses to make sure they could be alone together. He had become a Kanasa. Hoof worked over him, chanting and praying many hours a day, as if he would someday be a leader of the tribe. Never had things looked so good for Lone Wolf.

Walking in the direction she pointed, he reached camp an hour later. In no time he had a furious argument with Onni over where he had been. He wound up eating with Left Hand again that night, something that was happening more and more now.

Late that night he crept back into his tepee, but he didn't sleep well. All night long he dreamed of his disappearing and reappearing all over camp in different tepees and startling the owners. Each time they became angry and drove him out as if he were a demon, but he would exercise a mysterious dream power and disappear himself away from their blows, an experience both satisfying and disturbing.

The next day, exhausted and weary, he was on his way to the Kanasa tepee early, for Hoof wanted him to go through the third series of induction chants to the Kanasa society again. He had told Lone Wolf that they had not been done well. Lone Wolf wished the tribe had a younger *Wakan* man; Hoof was far too fussy about these things. He seemed to blink, looked around himself, and found he was back in the little grove he had left last night.

He groaned. He was in for it now. Hoof had been very clear about his showing up this morning before the sun was halfway up the side of the sky, and now here he was an hour away from camp. Elk Woman would expect him to make love to her, yet even if he set out right now, he wouldn't arrive at the Kanasa lodge till almost noon.

"Can you catch me?" came a shout from the thick grove of saplings, and through the foliage Lone Wolf caught the flash of a bare buttock and the jiggle of an uncovered breast. She was naked there! A rush of heat hit him as fast and hard as hot oil bubbling through his innards as the thought seized him of chasing her through the saplings like a buck after a deer.

Whatever Hoof had in mind was forgotten at the thought of what he would do to her. Lone Wolf grinned as he trotted through the hot sun toward the thicket. The sun was as warm today as it had been every other time he had been in this strange meadow.

When he reached the thicket, he saw her naked flesh flash again behind a shrub twenty yards farther on.

"Come catch me, slowpoke. If you can."

He laughed and broke into a harder trot. He could catch her in a minute if he really tried, but that would take the fun out of this. But once he did catch her, he would show her who was playing games.

He didn't catch her till she had plunged into Yellow Creek, where he stripped, plunged in and grabbed for her. Like the meadow, this portion of the stream was warm. She felt slippery and hard to hold, but her wet flesh aroused a storm of power within him. He knew now how a stallion felt as it neighed and rose, pawing the air before mounting his mare.

He took her once in the water, a fierce coupling more like a fight than mating, once on the bank, and again, much more lazily, on the grass under the shrubs.

The sun stood straight overhead, a giant, lidless eye roaring like a fire at them. Why wasn't it tilted to the south? he wondered. Then he groaned as he realized he had to go. Old Hoof would be furious. He was hours late.

But before he left, Lone Wolf told Elk Woman not to do what she had done this morning in dragging him out of camp. "I had some business for the Kanasa."

"But I wanted you. And I knew you wanted me." Her brazen eyes danced. "You loved it. You didn't want to sit around with those dried up old men."

She was so right it made him grin. He had loved it. "Yes, but I have to fulfill my new lodge's obligations. Just don't jerk me away like that. We'll make a time."

They decided on tomorrow night at dusk.

Indeed, when Lone Wolf showed up in midafternoon, Hoof was angry. They started the chants anyway, but Hoof stopped an hour later, shaking his head and grumbling that something wasn't right and that they would do them again tonight.

"What's the matter with you?" Hoof asked.

"Nothing, grandfather."

"You're not concentrating. It's not just the words, son. You have to put your heart into the words."

"I know."

"It's not a woman, is it?"

"Sir?"

"I told you, no women. A man can't concentrate with his mind on women."

"No, no women."

"You're sure."

"Yes."

"Tell me if there is, now."

What did this old fool suspect? Telling him would just cause trouble. "No. It's just I'm still weak from all that stumbling around in the snow."

"You come back tonight, hear me, son?"

Lone Wolf was glad to get away, although he knew that Hoof was capable of insisting that he chant the next twenty-four hours through. Still, what a day he had had with her!

The next day at noon, Lone Wolf was out with Left Hand and his brother in the north meadow breaking a horse when he seemed to blink and was back again in the sun-drenched grove.

This time he was angry with Elk Woman and bawled her out. She was contrite. Agreeing they shouldn't waste the opportunity, again they made love.

The next day, about to enter the Kanasa lodge, he blinked and again found himself in the grove. This time he was so angry that he stalked off without even touching her, but he no sooner got to the edge of the camp than he seemed to blink and found himself back next to her.

"Don't ever walk away from me," she scolded. "That was mean."

"You dragged me here."

Furious, for she looked evil, hard and angry, he reached to his neck to pull off the buffalo-hair amulet in one snatch, but his hand was powerless to touch it, as if it were sheathed by dozens of layers of invisible buffalo hide. Three times he struggled to break through the force that kept his hand away from the little knot of hair, but he couldn't summon up the strength.

His heart was hammering and he found himself trembling in fear and anger. "What have you done to me?"

"Done? Nothing," she said. "Just arranged a way for us to meet. Isn't that what you want?"

"You've bewitched me. Let me go."

She only grinned, her eyes dancing as boldly as flames.

"I like being with you. You like being with me. We can be together all we want."

"I'm leaving," he said. "And don't bring me back here if you don't want to get a good whacking across that broad behind of yours."

Before long, in a series of similar encounters, Lone Wolf found himself captured by Elk Woman. Whacking her broad behind was out of the question; in some perverse reversal, any blow that landed on her seemed to rebound to himself and throw him to the ground. He struggled to remove the amulet, but to no effect. Not only couldn't he touch it, but when he asked Left Hand to remove it for him, his friend looked at him as if he were crazy and said Lone Wolf didn't have anything around his neck. Yielding to Lone Wolf's craziness, Left Hand even grasped where he was told to grasp, but pulled away nothing from around Lone Wolf's neck but air.

Over the next week Lone Wolf was dragged away from every part of his life at all hours of the day and night. While some of the times were pleasurable, many embarrassed him. When he remonstrated her, Elk Woman protested that she had to see him, and didn't he want to see her? He certainly had a good time, she insisted. He had to agree to this, for hardly ever had he not made love to her once he arrived in the grove. But the dread of not knowing just when he would arrive there rattled him and put him off his feed and his sleep.

He cursed the days last summer when he had admired the waggle of Elk Woman's hips as she walked through the village under a load of water or wood. Now, as then, he grew tired of hearing her complain about her husband Eagle Beak. In fact, these days she seemed yet more scornful about him: Eagle Beak was lazy, played around with other women—particularly younger women—and dodged leadership on war parties so that she recognized he would never sit on the council of Big Bellies. While his being an Onde was a great honor, it didn't mean that an Onde husband was much of a man. She cursed herself for ever marrying him. As a girl she hadn't understood these things; now that she was a woman, Elk Woman knew more and valued Lone Wolf. Eagle Beak had never done anything that made the village look up to him as they looked up to Lone Wolf for bringing the pelt of the white buffalo. That had showed everybody what a powerful person Lone Wolf was and how far he would go with the tribe.

All that might be true and at some other time might have made Lone Wolf feel terrific about himself, but what concerned him more was finding himself hurled across the distance from the village to the grove at least once a day now, sometimes more, on a trip that rattled him more each time he made it. He pleaded with Elk Woman not to drag him here any longer, and each time she petulantly agreed. But then she would only keep her agreement for a day or so before unexpectedly, perhaps in the middle of talking to Left Hand about a deer hunt, Lone Wolf would find himself back in the now-familiar grove. It infuriated and mystified Lone Wolf that Left Hand would notice very little amiss.

Cautiously, Lone Wolf questioned whoever he was with when he was flown to the grove. That person would say that Lone Wolf had gotten up, said he would be right back, and dipped around behind the tepee or tree or bush, presumably to relieve himself, and then hadn't come back. Yes, this had been perplexing to Lone Wolf's companions, but as Left Hand put it with a raucous laugh, "I figured you'd found something more important than me to pat on the rump, huh, friend?" His old friend would then wink and leer. Obviously Lone Wolf's failure to deny this only embedded it more deeply in Left Hand's mind.

In the weeks that had passed since Lone Wolf's return, he hadn't made, or really wanted to make, peace with Onni. He now slept most nights in Left Hand's tepee, the nights he wasn't going through the training required of an initiate to the Kanasa society.

Hoof wasn't pleased with the way this initiate absorbed the training, and he insisted that Lone Wolf sleep more and more nights in the Kanasa lodge.

"Something about your innards is still not clean," Hoof put it.

"What makes you think that, grandfather?" asked Lone Wolf.

"You talk too much in your sleep, for one thing," said the old man, who peered at him with suspicious eyes.

"And the other?"

"You only chant with half yourself. You're not concentrating properly."

"You always say that. Ever since I was a boy I never heard of any initiate in anything you didn't complain about."

The old man grinned like a dog caught pulling at the meat rack, and Lone Wolf laughed, hoping he had joked away the old man's probes.

Indeed, Lone Wolf didn't sleep well, but he didn't want to tell the old medicine man what the problem was. His dreams—more nightmares, really—were about flying buffalo, white men who could toss rocks as big as a man's head with great speed, angry women chasing him, and white buffalo as large as clouds racing across the skies. He dreaded going to sleep and put it off for hours, knowing each night he would flee across an angry landscape and barely escape a dozen horrors.

123

One day, Hoof, Stomach Wind and the three other elderly men who assisted Hoof in his *Wakan* duties sat Lone Wolf down in the hot, deserted tepee of the Kanasa. Lone Wolf wanted to leave, but he saw how serious they were.

"What's the matter?" he asked.

"My son, your soul is troubled," said Old Hoof.

"I had a hard trip," said Lone Wolf, looking around at the faces of the assistants of Old Hoof, who only looked at him impassively.

"I've worked with you since your return," said Hoof.

"I know. Thank you, grandfather."

"It had been difficult to make the white buffalo spirit easy so we could decorate his hide, and we weren't able to keep it. He insisted that we sacrifice it on the hill."

"Yes, grandfather." Maybe if he just agreed, the old man would leave him alone.

"All the chants and prayers we've tried since your return haven't quieted your troubled soul," said Hoof, and he looked around at the others, several of whom nodded.

"I'll be all right," said Lone Wolf. The last thing he wanted was more treatment.

"We've talked about it," said Hoof. "The Kanasa have talked to us. They want you in their lodge, but none of us wants someone with such a troubled soul in such an important lodge."

"Not even in camp," said Stomach Wind.

Nobody said anything, just waited for something to happen, which was often the way of these old men. Lone Wolf thought furiously, wondering about himself, What *was* wrong with him? It was Elk Woman's shooting him all around the camp, that was the problem. It had rattled him, as well it might, but he couldn't tell these old men this. Not only would Grandfather Hoof be angry that he had disobeyed and slept with a woman, the old men would turn both Elk Woman and Lone Wolf out of camp at once, branding them witches.

He just had to play dumb and hope it all blew over. The only good thing that Lone Wolf saw about Hoof's spending so much time inducting him into the Kanasa was that apparently the little buffalo-hair knot didn't work in the Kanasa tepee, as if its power was weaker than that of this power society's tepee. At least he had a rest from the bouncing urgency of Elk Woman's loins when he was in here. Sometimes she never needed rest.

"We have thought and counseled together, grandson," said Hoof. "We want you to go on a peyote journey for us."

Peyote journey! While Lone Wolf didn't say anything, inwardly he reeled. He wasn't even sure what peyote was, as it stayed hidden in the sacred grandmother bundles that the *Wakan* men such as Hoof carried. He only knew that two years before, the tribe had encountered the Apache who lived like them, known as the Kiowa-Apache, and their *Wakan* man had given Hoof, in exchange for twenty horses, a bundle said to contain the most powerful spirit any man had ever known—peyote, a substance that sent a man into the next world to travel with its spirits. Rumor had it that the Kiowa-Apache only sent their most respected leaders on such a journey, and only in the direst times, as no man knew the consequences of consorting with the makers of the world.

So while Lone Wolf kept his face impassive, inwardly he quaked. What was this all about? How had getting inducted into the Kanasa been raised to this?

No one in the tribe had ever taken a peyote journey, and the only knowledge Lone Wolf had of it came from some hazy talk of Kiowa-Apache warriors he had overheard two years ago. According to them, the peyote journey summoned up all the spirits of the world into one tepee to surround the traveler. There they fought over the soul of the man who was undergoing the journey. In a single night, otherworldly titans clashed, as if an entire skyful of thunderstorm were locked into a single tepee. It took a powerful man to eat the peyote substance, draw forth the clash, and endure such a battle, as well as a powerful shaman to guide the journey so that its outcome was constructive to the chief participant and the tribe. Why they called it a "journey" as well as a "clash" made as little sense to Lone Wolf as any of the stories.

Lone Wolf didn't want to go on such a journey, but he would look like a coward if he said so. He looked everywhere in his mind for good reasons to refuse such an honorable torture.

"Surely we haven't much peyote in the grandmother bundle," he said. "It would be wasted on me."

"On the man who brought back the white buffalo hide?" asked Stomach Wind.

"I only need rest," said Lone Wolf. "This chanting for day after day, night after night . . ."

"You've been resting for weeks," said Hoof. "You haven't hunted even once."

"Yes, I'd better go on a hunt."

"Don't jest with us," said Hoof. "Your work is here."

"I am not made of what Kanasa are made of," Lone Wolf said, preferring to withdraw from the society if it meant tangling with demons as large as hills, as dark as night and as powerful as the thunder. "I'll return to my own lodge."

"But *Wakan-Takan* gave you the white hide," said Hoof.

"I'm not ready for such an honor."

"You're acting the foolish boy," said Stomach Wind. "You'll gain in knowledge and strength by being with Kanasa. You'll gain in wisdom and courage by wrestling with spirits. Such a journey will strengthen you. In my youth we wanted the strongest and most favored men in the Kanasa lodge. Today it's the same."

"Yes, but no one of our tribe has ever eaten peyote," said Lone Wolf. "It's worked very well for us with your just carrying it around in your grandmother bundle. Eating it—that's just talk of the foolish Kiowa-Apache."

"Nobody in our tribe ever had the strength to hunt down the white bull, either," said Hoof. "I have struggled to induct you into the Kanasa, but a large obstacle prevents you from connecting to that worthy lodge."

"A large obstacle?" asked Lone Wolf.

"I've put this off and put this off," the old man said. "It grieves me to take this step, for none of us have taken it before. But the tribe cannot have the man who has gone to the white bull and returned in such a troubled state."

"I'm not in a troubled state."

"That you don't know you are is the saddest part, son," Hoof said.

For another couple of hours, Lone Wolf sat before the old men, who certainly weren't in any hurry, casting about for more objections, He couldn't put his heart into his answers after this last speech of Hoof's. The old man was onto something about him, and he saw he couldn't escape. As he realized how firm they were in their intention, gradually a chill of dread settled over him. He knew them well: when they wanted something they would sit quietly and counter whatever anyone else said till they had their way. They hadn't become the *Wakan* leaders of the tribe by being weak-willed. They might look old and thin and enfeebled, but underneath their thin chests and yellowed eyes lay spirits that had concentrated for days on chants, had endured vision quests for weeks, and had gone without food and sleep till the spirit they sought came to them.

Did Hoof know what he was doing? He had made mistakes in the past. In a lot of ways, Lone Wolf didn't like having anything to do with shamans. You never quite knew what was going to happen with their ceremonies and magic. Hoof had prayed over Teeth Bite for days before the Ten Dance Battle with the Comanche, and had even made a shield especially for Bite to carry, and what had happened? The first arrow shot had hit Teeth Bite in the eye, killing him before he fell off his horse. In years past, Hoof had used the rattlesnake as his power animal till one had bitten a childless woman who had paid him four horses to cure her barren womb. She had died two days later and Hoof swore off snakes, saying that the woman had been too evil-minded for him to help. Rumor had it that he had forgotten two entire verses from the proper chants to control snakes, and the fact that he returned the four horses to the husband confirmed the gossip.

Lone Wolf knew enough about such powerful events to realize that if, after a couple of years, Hoof had forgotten one or two of the directions or the words of the chants, the spirits who were aroused might twist his head off in their anger or exuberance.

But he could think of no way out. No honorable way, even though he could just bolt and live in the wild for a few weeks or months, returning after this had blown over. But he couldn't do that. He had never expected to become a Kanasa, but now that he was on the verge of accomplishing it, he liked the respect he was shown by the others in the tribe. Besides, his father hadn't raised him to be someone who ran away from his problems. He couldn't return afterward to be just one of those lower-class lay-abouts on the fringes of the tribe.

For the most part, Lone Wolf had done what he could for the good of his family and his tribe, but not too much in addition to what was expected. He never expected to be much more than simply another warrior. He didn't have the ambition to lead like some of the boys he had grown up with.

But he could see no way out of this. As far as he was concerned, for an ordinary mortal to come before the presence of so much *Wakan* as was summoned up by the peyote was like entering a cave filled with dozens of angry bear: Lone Wolf wasn't sure of the outcome, but he was certain it would be a terrible ordeal.

"Well, when did you think of my taking this peyote journey?" he asked Hoof.

"Many Legs is preparing the bundle now," said Hoof. "As soon as you have your sweat bath."

"Now? No."

"The sooner the better," said Hoof, turning as the flap of the tepee opened. "Here's Many Legs now with the peyote bundle."

Chapter 5

Now that eight buzzards, each the size of a boy, had flapped their way into the tepee and eyed him hungrily, Lone Wolf felt his strength shrivel. He had beaten off the dozens of snakes that had crawled after him under the dewcloth of the tepee, he had chased away the dog-sized spiders that had dropped on him from the smoke hole, and he had endured his flesh changing colors, from copper to black to grey, as if he might melt, all the while struggling to maintain a brave front to show Hoof, Stomach Wind and the other shamans that he was worthy of being a Kanasa. But the four-foot-high buzzards, their red necks and filth-covered beaks pecking toward him robbed him of courage.

"No, get them back!" he shouted at Hoof.

He found he couldn't move. Around him Hoof and the other shamans' faces receded. The buzzards pranced in a circle before him. Alarmed, he looked at his arm, where his flesh was now turning green. As he watched his arm, it yellowed and then became blue before becoming black. Such decay happened to buffalo and other animals who lay dead on the prairie. With a rising sob of grief, he realized he was dying and that Hoof and the others didn't care. His flesh dripped off his bones, and the buzzards with their red eyes and redder necks snatched it off the dirt floor of the tepee, their faces bright with relish. If only he could get away. But every struggle to move only rotted his muscles all the faster.

Hoof's mouth was open and he was saying something to Lone Wolf, but Lone Wolf could not understand him, for the old man's mouth was full of sparrows and roaches. Every time the old man spoke, more sparrows and roaches fell out into his lap before flying off or crawling away. Lone Wolf gave up trying to tell him to talk without all those creatures in his mouth. Every time Lone Wolf himself spoke, his own words became grey bird feathers that filled up his mouth with so much fluff that he could hardly breathe. He had to remain quite still and not speak, or he would choke to death.

So now Lone Wolf was reduced to quietly watching the four largest buzzards strut toward him, having pecked up all his blackened flesh that had run off onto the floor of the lodge. Their faces blazed with cruel hunger. Each leered as if he would enjoy tearing Lone Wolf into such little pieces that when he arrived in the next world he would be nothing but a pile of stripped bones, unable to go hunting with his grandfathers, probably unable even to talk with them. Lone Wolf was speechless with terror, and he could do nothing. For all time, till the sun itself went out, Lone Wolf would lie on the desert of the other world, a pile of bones, a victim of these black-feathered, dirt-covered, lice-ridden eaters of death.

Unable to stop himself as the buzzards neared, he shouted, "Get back!" But again his mouth filled with the feathers, this time black ones like those covering the buzzards, tipped with hard shafts and crawling with iridescent

132

lice who glanced up at his face in an amused way before
they jumped off to feast on his rotting flesh.

He shut up. His breathing was as labored as the wind
struggling to escape the trees. He felt as if he would
shortly drown in feelings of shame, unworthiness, helplessness and anger. What had happened? He remembered
taking six of the mushroom caps, and then he had been
sick. Later, not long after, storms gathered in the tepee
and lightning flashed from cloud to cloud. When the storms
left, the animals started to come in under the dewcloth,
through the entrance hole and down the smokehole. First
in ones and twos, then by the dozens—bats, owls, snakes,
wild dogs, wolves, rabbits, spiders, ticks, flies, gophers,
rats, fleas—almost every animal and insect and bird he
knew of ran through the tepee of the Kanasa.

He took deep breaths now as the biggest buzzard put
his filthy beak to within inches of Lone Wolf's face. The
mean-looking beak quivered, and a thin, active tongue
darted out. Lone Wolf was terrified that the buzzard would
go for his eyes, for he had seen buzzards eat enough
rotting buffalo and deer to know that they fought over the
eyes of the dead as a delicacy. But he was afraid to cover
his eyes, even to blink, for fear of alerting this demon that
he cared. He could tell from the buzzard's hungry look
that this eater of the dead wanted to find out what would
dismay Lone Wolf the most and eat that. He had to sit still
and hope the buzzards would cease to see him, a strategy
he realized was foolish but was all he could think of. As
he watched out of the corner of his eye, Lone Wolf saw
his thigh flesh suppurate into yellow and black, and then
slide off the bone. Like a turkey after corn, the next largest
buzzard hopped forward to gobble up the flesh.

The largest buzzard, his face gazing at Lone Wolf's,
didn't come nearer, just stared at him. Lone Wolf stared

back, anxiously waiting for the moment of attack. If only he had his knife, his bow, or his lance! But he was here in this Kanasa lodge, naked, with the old men. It was clear they couldn't see these attackers, to judge from the calm way they had sat about since the creatures had filled the tepee.

Lone Wolf felt tears forming. They frightened him, for if his words were feathers, he expected his tears to be urine or excrement or the pus and green that flowed out of three-week-dead corpses. But he couldn't stop them, nor did he want to any longer. He had pushed and fought all these animals and his own feelings of shame and unworthiness, and he didn't want to fight anymore. They could have him. He was a child and frightened and they could know it. He had kept up a brave front, only occasionally screaming when some squirrel or spider took an unexpected bite from his hand or chest, but now he would surrender to his tears. Of course, only children—not warriors or Kanasa—cried, but he had held himself back long enough. If only his mother could hold him now, cradle him against that large bosom as she had so often when he hurt himself as a child! From his eyes came scalding tears, which fed his feelings of unworthiness and summoned up still more sobs.

The filthy buzzard looked at him quizzically, cocking his beak and eyes this way and that, as if inquiring what the problem was.

Sobbing, Lone Wolf decided not to answer, fearful that the feathers would again come out of his mouth. But he would command his tears to talk for him. He made them say, "I'm sick of living. I'm sick of dying."

"Then why are you holding on?" the buzzard asked. "Can't you see you've made us come here?"

"No," he made his tears answer. "I want you to go away."

The buzzard cackled. "But that's what made us come. You've done that all your life."

Suddenly Lone Wolf could look back and see his entire life, which stretched before his eyes like a long strand of rawhide, a knot in it for each day. His experiences danced along the strand like ants on a buffalo hide. He saw there that he had turned his head away from much of the unpleasantness. . . . No! That word "unpleasant" was itself a turning away! Away from the decay, the loss, the filth, the pain, the unbearable agony, from the death that was in life, from all that in fact made life what it was. Near the end of the rawhide strip of his life sat the six mushroom caps, which showed him that the power of the peyote mushroom was to display before him all of his life, that which he acknowledged and that which he had evaded.

"I shut my eyes to you," Lone Wolf made his tears say to the buzzard, and then he felt his tears flow faster, shouting that sentence over and over: "I shut my eyes to you!"

When the buzzard had first entered the Kanasa tepee, he had eyed Lone Wolf with eager hatred, but now the creature's eyes seemed filled with a sadness that agreed with Lone Wolf. In a desperate wish to undo this wrong that seemed so shameful, Lone Wolf reached out to the giant bird's stiff, stalky neck and pulled the buzzard's head to him. Surprisingly light, the bird seemed to float toward Lone Wolf, who had trouble keeping the bird from floating upward to the tepee's smoke hole. But by hugging the filthy creature more tightly, he kept him from escaping.

The tighter he held on to the giant buzzard's head and neck, the better he felt. He felt the bird's giant mouth reach for his shoulder, and out of the corner of his eye he saw the bird take out a large piece of his blackened flesh. The bird chewed on it with satisfaction.

"Yes," he said with his tears. "Yes, yes, yes." He loosened his grip on the bird enough to offer him his hand, which the bird calmly bit off. At his feet were another couple of buzzards, these only half the size of the giant bird now poised between his legs. He lifted up his feet, black as soot and covered with pus-filled sores. The two smaller buzzards cawed in a manic way before pecking at his rotting flesh, pulling great shreds of it off.

He let go. He would accept whatever it all was. He let go and lay back to allow them to finish him, uncovering himself from the crouch he was in. There now seemed to be dozens of birds coming in under the dewcloth, through the entrance, and down through the smokehole. He felt their beaks all over his body, cold beaks sliding along his bones, lifting off all his rotting flesh.

But no pain. It was strange, no pain. He felt both sad and joyous. Sad to be giving up his life, joyous not to be fearfully clinging to it any longer. What a burden it had been! He relaxed still more. Through his tears, he insisted that the birds eat. He felt better, almost happy, as he felt the beaks ripping flesh off his entire body. Strangely, their pulls were now more like caresses than bites. Soon he would be devoid of flesh, nothing but a pile of white bones. With his tears he called for a giant buffalo to come chew them.

Giant buffalo! he exclaimed to himself. Where had that wish come from?

He opened his eyes in time to see the large buzzard's beak not inches from his eyes, and he tried not to flinch as the buzzard plucked them out. He could still see, but without eyes in his head. His spirit was perched up near the smoke hole, resting on the lodgepoles, as if he were a small bird, and he saw a giant white buffalo push his way into the lodge through the entrance hole. Amazingly, Hoof, Stomach Wind and the others didn't see him, or they acted as if they didn't see him. Just as Lone Wolf had asked, the white buffalo pranced over to the lines of bones, all that remained of Lone Wolf. With his jaws, the buffalo picked up the scattered bones to make a neat stack, all in a row with the skull on the top. Then the buffalo stretched his mouth wide open. Amazingly, the pile of bones rose and flew into the buffalo's mouth, where the massive teeth crunched down on them.

That crunch of his bones freed him. Lone Wolf found himself flying up through the tepee's smoke hole as if he were actually smoke. He flew through the night air in a rush, the wind whistling past him.

Over the land he flew, across rivers and mountains, able to see from horizon to horizon by starlight. How thrilling to fly like a bird! How much better than lurching about on land! Rushing on over the world, he finally caught the sun. This made him laugh, for the sun was now but a small fire far below him.

Spread out before him lay the vast expanse of the world. To his left yawned the giant hole in the ground from which the buffalo sprang each spring, to his right camped all the tribes of the Kiowa, and in a hundred places he saw other tribes of Indians, while in many tall caves by the water he saw the white men.

From this vantage point, he saw that the whites who stayed in the caves lived one way, and that his people, the buffalo people of the meadows and woods, lived so differently as to comprise two different species. One fact stood out clearly to him: the two peoples couldn't live in the same place.

As if in a dream, he watched the whites come from

the caves at the edge of the world by the giant body of water. They spread across the buffalo country. Where they spread, the buffalo died—not some of them, but all of them, even the yearlings and newborn calves. They killed buffalo by the thousands and tens of thousands, and entire herds that had migrated north to south and back for hundreds of years had been slaughtered to within a few thousand head of extinction. The skins of these animals were packed on iron wagons of death and run on an iron road to giant caves, where they were ripped into clothes, belts, coats and shoes. Many skins then were placed on giant canoes and sent toward the middle of the water, although why this was done escaped Lone Wolf.

Then, with a shock that sent him hurtling hundreds of yards through the air, Lone Wolf saw that the intention of the white people was to rid the world of buffalo, while *Wakan-Takan* had put the Kiowa and all the other buffalo people on the land to live with and guard the buffalo, a great wonder of his creation. Buffalo people had been put on the earth for a purpose, and were allowed to take buffalo only insofar as they served *Wakan-Takan's* purpose, which was for them to protect his creation. But this was no dream, he realized as he hung above the earth. The two white men Shiny Head and Long Crow were but two of the many whites who came to the country of the buffalo with nothing but death in their hearts.

Having seen so much and feeling an urgency to get back, Lone Wolf, alarmed and frightened, wheeled away from the delights of flying and flew down to the Kanasa lodge. How he would have liked to remain a bird! But he had to warn his people.

For a delightful few minutes he raced along with the sun. When he arrived back at camp, he flew down the smoke hole and shouted at Hoof, the other old *Wakan* men, and the Kanasa, who had all gathered there while he was flying across the world.

"Grandfather!" he shouted. "We are to protect the buffalo! The whites want to destroy him!"

Some of the old men scooted back from him, and they all stared at him open-mouthed.

Old Hoof held up the gourd rattle as if to protect himself from Lone Wolf, demanding in a frightened voice, "Who are you?"

"Grandfather, it's me! Lone Wolf!"

All around him sunlight spilled into the tepee, lighting up the dirt on the floor and the air under the raised dewflaps. The morning was as clean as the water in a falls, and the air delicious to taste.

Lone Wolf laughed at their sleepy faces and slow minds. "Wake up," he said to them, but as he said it, he realized that the spirit of the peyote had made him so fast that his mind flew about as quickly as a bird.

"You don't look like Lone Wolf," said Hoof, turning to the other men for confirmation.

"You gave me the peyote last night. I was eaten by death and flew around the world, and I have come back with a message."

The more he talked, the less frightened they seemed, as if they had to become used to a stranger who had just thrust himself into camp. With Hoof drawing him out and getting him to linger over parts of the tale of his journey last night, Lone Wolf described his experience.

After he had finished, Hoof passed around two pipes to settle the air in the Kanasa lodge before he spoke. "It is clear that *Wakan-Takan* has spoken to us through our brother, Lone Wolf here. Indeed, it is even clear that this brother of ours is not only to be the messenger from the sun, but someone to show us the way of the sun."

Lone Wolf wondered what the old man was talking about. They had to save the buffalo, and they ought to get their ponies together and leave today to stop the white man.

"It is also clear that this is not the same man who walked into this tepee last night," said Hoof. "That man died. Lone Wolf is dead and we have a new man who has come to fight with us—a man who flies through the air like a hawk and stands ready to fight like an eagle—Striking Eagle."

The others murmured approval. Amazed, Lone Wolf looked from face to face, confused and wondering why they were talking about him in this way. He wasn't Striking Eagle, he was Lone Wolf. He was about to say so when the chants, led by Hoof, stopped him.

He joined in the chants, which were praise and thanks to *Wakan-Takan* for visiting them and sending them a new tribal leader.

Leader? thought Lone Wolf. I may become a Kanasa, but I'm no Big Belly or member of the council. He started to protest, but it seemed to flout the strong feeling of the gathering to interrupt. As soon as they paused, he would set them straight. He was only a messenger and a warrior, nothing more.

When the chants ended, he was amazed to hear himself say, "I'm preparing a war party. I will attack the whites who are laying waste to the buffalo. I leave tomorrow morning."

He had never announced a raiding party before, although he had gone on many that others had led. Immediately all the Kanasa who were young enough to fight shouted that they would join him.

* * *

By nightfall, thirty-five out of the camp's one hundred twenty able men were preparing their ponies and weapons to ride out the next morning. Ten teen-age boys had begged to come and eight had been chosen.

Striking Eagle, he repeated to himself most of that day. I am Striking Eagle, he would muse. At first, through most of the morning and the early part of the afternoon, he laughed at such a new name, but in the midafternoon, in the midst of the frenzy of a major war party preparing itself and with braves and boys asking his advice, he found that he knew the answers without hesitation, and he was forced to realize that he was indeed, through some power he did not understand, Striking Eagle, a new leader of the tribe. Lone Wolf had died.

One other event convinced him. As he sat behind his tepee putting together his war kit, arrows for his quiver, the two mock-orange bows, and the rifle and cartridges he had taken from the Crow, Elk Woman appeared before him. For a moment he was afraid of her, but something in him rose, something full of power. She seemed fearful and her face was lined, as if she had been drained by illness. He laughed and simply stared at her in an amused way.

"You didn't come," she said.

"What?"

"I pulled at you six or seven times. You didn't come. You look different. What's happened?"

He realized he not only hadn't thought of her or Onni all night or day, but he also hadn't been shot across the fields and streams to the grove in two days. He reached up to his neck. This time he easily grasped the buffalo-hair ball and tore it away.

"Here," he said, handing the amulet to her. "I've been given too much power by *Wakan-Takan* for such a small bit of magic to affect me. You won't fly me around anymore."

She took it with a sullen gesture. "You'll come back to me, won't you?"

She looked haggard and frightened and a part of him wanted to comfort her. He had a hard time staying angry at Elk Woman; she had pulled him to the grove against his wishes only because she wanted him too much.

"Woman, I have something to do, something more important than lying around with you in the bushes."

"What happened last night?" she asked.

He told her a short version of his adventure.

"You're going to be important in the tribe," she said. "Just as I knew. You need more than one wife." She looked at him coyly and smiled. "I want to be your next wife so much—Eagle."

Eagle, he said to himself as he smiled at her. He liked the sound of his new name.

"When I get back, we'll see. But you have a husband. If I take another wife, it's not right that she already has a husband."

Elk Woman looked lost. "But I *want* you!"

"I have a lot to do, Elk Woman," he said. "We Kanasa leave at dawn."

"Is Eagle Beak going too?"

"He didn't tell you?"

"We don't talk much."

She looked drawn, sulky, and full of plump good things all at the same time. He wanted to slap the smirk off her face and drag her into the bushes and make love to her till all of her sassy energy was spent. With a weary sigh, he dragged himself back to the task of getting himself ready to ride on this war raid.

"No, Beak's not going," he said. "I don't think he'll ever ride under my command."

"Just you remember," she told him. "I'll be here when you come back. We can start all over where we stopped yesterday."

"It's over, Elk. I have duties to take care of."

"No, I'm not giving you up. More than ever, you're who I want."

"No, Elk."

"Yes!"

"You have a good man. Fly him around the countryside. I can't deflect my energy from what I have to do."

"You can't do this to me."

"I'm not doing anything to you. Find yourself another fellow."

"I don't want another. I'll never give you up!"

After five days of hard riding through the mud and rain, the war party found the trail of Long Crow and Shiny Head, tracked them for four days and then caught up with them one chilly dusk.

Leaving his men tending their weary horses, an excited Striking Eagle and Left Hand crawled forward to the edge of the ridge to observe their enemies.

Below them they saw the two hunters and a herd of buffalo. The Crow lay on his belly about one hundred fifty yards away from the herd, his gun nestled in a forked stick, shooting once every few moments at the herd, some fifty of whom lay about the prairie, dead.

As Striking Eagle knew, Long Crow would lie there, with Shiny Head changing guns and feeding him ammunition, until they had killed every buffalo that their powerful rifles could bring down.

"The Crow and Shiny Head," said Striking Eagle as he pulled back from the edge of the ridge.

"You know them?"

"They're the ones I stayed with."

"Who killed the white buffalo?"

"Shiny Head, there." Left Hand nodded slowly as he peered intently at the two, struggling to see the great power of Shiny Head, the great power he must possess to have killed the white bull.

A leader of the milling, unsettled herd was moving a few yards east, obviously preparing to lead them away from this bloody-smelling place, when the Crow's rifle barked and the leader of the buffalo slumped forward on his knees before pitching over.

"Aaah," said Left Hand in a little cry of agony. "He'll kill them all!"

"We have to keep away from those guns."

Another shot rang out, another buffalo teetered and then slumped over, obviously dead or dying.

"At such a distance!" said Left Hand.

"They'll kill us just as easily."

"What's your plan, Eagle?"

"Lemme shoot now," said Skinner eagerly.

"Not yet," said McCall, letting off another shot.

He felt a cramp in his right shoulder. The .50-caliber Sharps had one hell of a wallop, knocking his shoulder back each time. But he didn't want to complain, because Skinner would then insist on shooting.

He aimed again carefully at the big cow to the south of the herd who looked as if she might take charge. Knowing which animal to go for was what separated a good hunter from the man who came back to Hays with next to nothing. A great shooter could shoot at a herd all day and the animals would never move off the spot they stood on. It all depended on knowing buffalo, knowing which ones were likely, once the obvious leaders had been killed, to take charge. If you killed them, the herd couldn't move, for then it had no leaders. Guess wrong and you lost the herd. Of course, it was important not to shoot so rapidly that your gun barrel heated up and you lost the temper of the metal, yet the all-important thing was to keep knocking down the leaders before they led off the other buffalo. Once they started off in a direction, your stand was over. What a Skinner didn't recognize was that knowing the buffalo wasn't something you picked up in ten minutes, hardly could pick up in ten years. But you couldn't tell a fellow like him that he didn't know something. He just wouldn't listen.

McCall reckoned he had about forty-five to fifty-five head down. Not a bad couple hours of work by a long shot, but of course nothing like his record—seventy-eight last year at Hawk Pass. It was these new Sharps rifles that allowed a hunter to make such a big stand. Back when it had been just McCall and maybe a dozen others out in Kansas hunting buffalo and there wasn't a high demand for the hides they brought in, he shot a .36 Spencer, and while it had downed its share of buffalo, it didn't have the Sharps' range and accuracy.

"I'll take over if you want," said Skinner.

"I'm all right."

"That thing packs a wallop, don't it?"

"I'm fine."

"Which one you aiming at now?"

"Shhhh!" McCall demanded, squeezing off his shot.

The cow quavered, took another three steps forward, then wobbled. The herd had turned to follow her and quickly caught up as she went down on her front knees.

145

Her calf, irritated at his mother's balkiness, knelt to get to the udder. For a few seconds she held there.

"Put another shot in her," said Skinner.

"Too many around her," replied McCall. That was the trouble with Skinner. No judgment. McCall didn't want a gun in his hands at a time like this. "I don't have a clear shot. If I wound one and he runs off, the others will follow."

"She's getting up!"

Besides, my barrel will be cooler, thought McCall as he drew a bead on the cow, who had indeed stood and looked about fretfully.

"Shoot!"

"Wait till she picks a direction and gets clear of the others," said McCall.

But McCall didn't have to shoot, saving himself about twenty-five cents, he figured. The cow's hind legs gave way and she sat. Still she struggled to get her hind legs back under her, but her strength was ebbing. McCall figured he had caught her in the lungs. She toppled over onto her side.

Six other buffalo cautiously leaned their shaggy necks forward to sniff her. Her calf butted her side repeatedly, obviously irritated at his mother.

McCall drew a bead on the heart of the largest bull nearest him, a shaggy creature he reckoned to be more than a ton in weight, and slowly squeezed the trigger.

At that moment from somewhere else—nearby!—a shot rang from another rifle. A bullet hit the ground in front of them and knocked dirt in their faces.

At McCall's side, Skinner jumped over on his back and shouted, "Hey, who's that?"

Startled, McCall's gun jerked to the right and went off. As if in a dream, he saw the bullet travel not at the bull he was aiming at but at a two-year-old heifer, who was hit right where the tail joined the rump. The large-grained slug tore such a slice out of her rump that she bellowed from the pain and charged forward, head down, into the herd. She moved with such strength that buffalo scattered in every direction out of her way.

Cursing, for that heifer would stampede the herd into running off, McCall rolled over toward Skinner, who had moved behind a large rock to their right. He shouted, "What the hell was that?"

Skinner had the other rifle on top of the rock and was peering around through its sights at the surrounding hills. "Somebody shot at us."

"Didn't that sound like a Sharps?"

"I can't tell."

"That's what it was." McCall looked around at the silent hills and saw nothing. "You were supposed to be watching."

"I *was* watching," Skinner protested. He then snapped off three shots, filling the canyon with their echoes.

"What are you shooting at?"

"Nothing," said Skinner. "Wanted to see if I could stir them up."

"I pay for them shells," said McCall. "Don't shoot unless you see something to hit."

Still they saw nobody.

"If they're not showing themselves, must be Indians," said McCall.

Skinner snorted derisively and said, "Bull, if that was a buffalo gun. Ain't no Injun got a Sharps .50-caliber—"

He stopped and they both stared at each other. McCall knew they were thinking the same thought. The only Indian in all of Kansas with an expensive Sharps buffalo gun would be Lone Wolf, the Indian McCall had nursed back to health, who had stolen the gun from him.

"Naw," said McCall. "Couldn't be him. Not even a Kiowa has so much meanness as to come back and rob the men who saved his life."

Skinner broke into a ranting curse that damned every man, woman and child who was red, along with their parentage and ancestry, and ended with a plea that the entire species should roast in hell for as long as hell existed.

"Our camp!" McCall exclaimed. "They have us penned down here with that big gun. Meanwhile they're going to attack the camp."

"Shoot! You're right," said Skinner.

"They may have captured Phil and Joe by now," McCall said, referring to the two haulers and skinners he had been able to hire on since his last trip.

"I ain't heard nothing."

"Kiowa don't have many guns."

"Arrows!"

"Yeah. Keep us penned down here with that cannon while they overrun our camp."

"What're we going to do?"

"The question is," said McCall, "is that the only gun they have up there?"

McCall thought back over the last few weeks. Since Lone Wolf had ridden off with their white buffalo hide weeks before, McCall and Skinner had fared well. In the next two weeks they had filled their wagon with flint hides—the dried, untanned hides that the market was so hot for—and had driven back to Hays City.

After a few days of rest there, McCall had bought another wagon with his profits and had hired on another couple of skinners from the crowd of hard-drinking idlers that hung around the town's two saloons. While he wasn't all that happy with the man's company, Skinner Kincade did work hard, and he wanted to make a profit as badly as McCall. Better the devil you knew than the one you didn't, McCall told himself, and being a sweet talker didn't have much to do with making a go of a buffalo hunt.

So two weeks before, the four of them had set out with two wagons. The agreement was to share the profits the same way as before, four parts to McCall, a fifth to Skinner, providing that Skinner would make sure that the two helpers, who were paid by the number of buffalo they skinned, kept up with McCall's shooting, and that Skinner would only shoot when the skinning was caught up. Both acknowledged that on a good stand it was foolish for any but the best shooter to fire, as only a superb shot could place balls into the buffalo in such a fashion that the herd wasn't spooked. It was almost an art, and a man didn't learn it overnight, but McCall promised, as part of Skinner's end of the hunt, to teach him what he could.

They had done pretty well on this trip, and McCall himself, having seen no Indians, had even relaxed his guard. They would be finished up in a few days, two wagons full of flint hides, eight hundred hides in all at three dollars each, twenty-four hundred dollars worth of hides before expenses. The sum made McCall, a man who had rarely seen one hundred dollars in one place before this past year's orgy of buffalo slaughter, dizzy with disbelief. That he should clear some twelve hundred dollars in the space of a month seemed like a miracle.

But now he had to protect that miracle.

"We got to get back to camp, but not so they can see us," said McCall.

"Keep them from seeing us? They got us pinned here."

"Maybe, maybe not." As he spoke, a series of shots rang out.

"What's that!" shouted Skinner.

"Listen."

"We have to get back! They'll steal our hides."

"Damn it, shut up and listen."

Skinner started to protest, but McCall scowled at him. Concentrating, McCall could differentiate three guns from the shots. One was a .36-.06, the repeater. That would be Little Phil. The boom would be the stolen Sharps. He could recognize the sound of his favorite gun anywhere. And that other sound was Joe Mates' shotgun.

"They're up on the hill to the south of the camp," said McCall. "Little Phil and Joe are holding them off."

"Now how the hell do you know that?" asked Skinner.

"I can hear it."

"And that's your stolen Sharps?"

"Yep."

Skinner sighed with exasperation. "Shooting at us with our own gun. Goddamn! I should have stuck that Injun when I had the chance."

"Get ready to move."

"Where?" asked Skinner. "Sneak along this wash, break into camp, and help Phil and Joe?"

"That's what they expect. We do, and if they're on the south hill, when we break for it they'll have a clear shot at us for a hundred yards."

"Hell, he couldn't hit us down here when we wasn't moving," said Skinner. "How's he going to hit us running for camp?"

"I don't want that Sharps shooting at me no matter who's holding it."

Skinner saw the wisdom of that and said so, then asked, "So what do we do?"

"Go the opposite direction and sneak around to camp from the other side."

"That'll take too long."

"Yeah, but it'll get us there. They may even think we've run off."

They crept back away from the rock that was shielding them. Just as they dropped into the wash, McCall saw four Indians come over the rim of the hill.

"Kiowa, all right," he said as they hit the bottom of the gully.

Turning back, Skinner saw them, stopped, and said, "Lemme shoot one!"

McCall grabbed him. "No, they'll pin us down here. They want to keep us away from our camp. They know you and I are the best shots."

Constantly urging Skinner along, crouching to keep from being seen, McCall moved down the wash the opposite way from camp. He knew that, with any luck, when the Kiowa didn't see them, they would think they had gone toward camp and rush to head them off. Meanwhile, McCall and Skinner would sneak around to come up on whoever was shooting on Little Phil and Joe from that south hill.

During the half-hour of anxious running along the gully, over the ridge and along the other side, they didn't see an Indian or get shot at, although they still heard occasional gunfire from the direction in which they were running. The gunfire lifted their spirits. Once the Kiowa overran camp, they wouldn't waste ammunition, difficult as it was for an Indian to get.

Both of them ran and climbed as if their lives depended on it, for if the Kiowa overran their camp while they were maneuvering, they might never make it back to Hays City. Climbing over the series of little ridges behind the hill winded them, but finally the two were in sight of the back of the hill to the south of camp.

Some four hundred yards away, poised at the rim of the hill, they saw a dozen Indians on their stomachs peering down at their camp in the late-afternoon sun.

"Goddamn sons of bitches," said Skinner. "Lying up there like they was knocking down a stand of buffalo."

"Get down," said McCall. "Don't want them to see us. They might turn and pin us down."

They crouched behind a fallen gnarled pine that crossed over a pile of large grey rocks. "Make sure you're loaded up," said McCall as he checked his .50-caliber rifle's load.

Skinner leaned so close that McCall smelled the coffee on his breath. "What is it you want to do, now?"

"Discourage them," said McCall.

"Discourage! Let's wipe them out."

"We'd bring the whole tribe down on us. We just want to run them off."

"Goddamnit, Jack."

"Let me do the shooting unless I say for you to shoot."

"Aw, come on. Don't start that. I aim on getting me a couple."

"Keep down. Shells cost money, and I don't want them to spot us as long as I can help it," said McCall.

While he took careful aim, striving to place his shots within five yards of the group and not hit them, McCall found that at six hundred yards a group of Indians were far from a herd of buffalo. His first shot went so far wide of the mark that he couldn't even see where the bullet had gone, but it did stir up the Kiowa. The knot on the hill immediately scattered, heading off in what looked like a dozen different directions, with Skinner snapping off shot after shot of twenty-five-cent ammunition after them till McCall ordered him to quit.

"I think I got one!"

"Damn it, it's my money pays for them shells," said McCall.

"Then I'll take five bucks' worth!" shouted Skinner, his face blazing with excitement.

"And I told you we just want to scare them off, not start a war with them."

"Damn it, they're shooting at us."

"We ain't found out why yet."

"What's *why* got to do with it?"

"Because not even an Indian, Kincade, shoots without a reason."

"I'm shooting to bag me one or two."

But there weren't any more Kiowa to shoot. Moving forward cautiously but still rapidly, McCall and Skinner ran around the hill and down into camp where Little Phil and Joe Mates were delighted to see them.

"We figured you two for goners," said Joe, a weary-looking scarecrow of a man with a scraggly beard and tired, sad eyes.

"No such luck," said Skinner. "Nobody's getting my share of these hides but me."

The only damage was a mule they had to shoot and an arrowhead embedded in the right calf of Little Phil Compton. With Skinner and Joe standing guard, McCall cut the arrowhead out and dressed the wound. Little Phil had been a gambler on Mississippi riverboats till he cheated a captain one night. Since then it had seemed safer to seek his fortunes farther west. Just now he worried whether the arrow had poison on it. He cursed Indians, wagons, dirt,

Kansas and buffalo in an unsuccessful effort to ignore the pain. He declared that he hadn't gone west far enough.

After the afternoon had worn on without further attacks, McCall told them to pack up camp while they still had some light, that they would sleep and be ready to pull out at first light. Skinner protested, saying that they hadn't skinned the fifty or sixty buffalo that McCall shot today.

"We ain't going to skin them," said McCall. "Our company will be back."

"But we can't just leave them," said Skinner. "That's twenty-five dollars of my money laying around out there."

"I tell you what," said McCall. "You want them, you go skin them and you can have every one you bring back."

"You mean that?"

"I said it."

"Phil, Joe—come with me. We'll rip the hides off all those buffalo before dark."

The other two looked uneasy. Looking more mournful than usual, Joe asked, "Jack, them Injuns coming back?"

"I'd say before dark, certainly tomorrow morning."

"How the hell do you know?" asked Skinner. "Don't let him fool you."

While tempted by the extra money, Joe and Phil chose not to go, fearful that McCall, who was supposed to know more about Indians than anybody who hung around Hays City, did know what he was talking about.

McCall proved right. As the afternoon hobbled into night, the Kiowa attacked twice more, both attacks from a distance, but still deadly, for not only did arrows rain down but also the occasional bullet came into camp from the big stolen gun of McCall's.

As sunset neared, McCall commented about Lone

Wolf, "He's afraid to shoot too much. He only has those few shots I had in that pouch he stole."

"How many was in it?" asked Skinner.

"No more'n twenty or twenty-five."

"He must have shot at us a dozen times."

"Nope, nine," said McCall.

That night, McCall wouldn't let them build a fire, afraid it would make them targets and blind them to an attack, although buffalo country wisdom had it that Indians didn't attack at night.

Still, during the night somebody sneaked up on them and made off with three of their fifteen horses and mules, a feat that made the four realize the skill of their attackers.

The accuracy and power of the buffalo rifles had shaken Striking Eagle's men, which alarmed him. He had to infuse the war party with new courage, for the guns had made even Left Hand, as brave a rider as the Kiowa could mount, waver in his resolve to follow him. Striking Eagle wandered away from camp to think. What would Hoof do in a situation like this? he wondered. Have some dumb ceremony that would exasperate me, he answered himself. But maybe such a ceremony made sense, if it gave the men the confidence to press the attack.

While it was still light, he had Left Hand and three of the boys cut the hearts out of half a dozen of the buffalo that Long Crow had shot, and he insisted that each man gather around the fire that night to prepare for tomorrow's fighting.

First he had each man follow him in feasting on several strips of roast buffalo heart. Afterward, Striking Eagle insisted that every warrior relate his bravest deeds to the rest of the company, a powerful way of raising the men's spirits and imbuing them with their fullest courage while keeping them from thinking about the power of the enemy.

They got so roused that they put forward many plans for dealing with the whites. Striking Eagle approved of Left Hand's and Cactus Back's idea of stealing some horses, never a bad idea, and they set out before first light. Success in a small raid would certainly make his men bolder.

Their success raised the men's spirits still higher. When the bottommost rim of the sun cleared the mountains, Striking Eagle and his riders came whooping up the gully from the east in an attack that, backed by the sun, would blind the white men's aim.

The riders reached the camp before the white men could get off many shots. They galloped through the camp, shielded from the big guns by their horses when they weren't tossing lances and shooting arrows at the four buffalo hunters. But the steady firing of the guns, the loss of three horses, and two casualties stopped any more passes, for Striking Eagle saw he would lose too many warriors with more attacks like this one.

Several of the braves wanted to pull out of the war party after this, grumbling that *Wakan-Takan* wasn't with them. But Striking Eagle said that they had just misjudged the firepower of the whites' rifles. They would surround the little camp, stay well back but keep the pressure on the enemy, and maybe something would fall their way.

The siege went on for three days.

Pinned down and unable to move away, all McCall, Skinner, Phil and Joe could do was stay under the two wagons and fire an occasional shot to keep the Kiowa at bay. They passed from fear to anger at the nearly invisible Kiowa, and on the third day entered a kind of weariness in which they simply fought for their survival. Luckily they had a full water barrel, and they ate the rest of the cold meat and beans for two days until Skinner rigged up the Dutch oven under a wagon to bake more bread.

It surprised McCall that the Kiowa were so tenacious. Normally, what an Indian couldn't get easily, he gave up on. McCall reckoned there were thirty to forty warriors, but at least their buffalo rifles' firepower was a match for the single rifle and the bows of the Indians. If he ran out of ammunition, it would be another story, but they had come out here with kegs of powder and pounds of shot, and as they had repacked their spent shells every day, once they got a fire going and some lead melted, they were in no danger of running low.

By the fourth day, McCall and his crew had begun to doubt that the Indians would ever leave. The water in the keg was two-thirds gone, and the Kiowa had managed to set one wagon afire the night before by sneaking up on it while other attackers kept the whites engaged. McCall and Skinner were just able to put out the fire by beating it with blankets while Joe and Little Phil kept the Indians at a distance with rapid firing. While not all its contents were burned, the wagon was too damaged to travel, a loss that infuriated McCall. Skinner had had a slice taken out of his arm by the Big Fifty Sharps rifle that the Kiowa used, although they reckoned that nearly all its shells had been expended.

By this time, Striking Eagle was having his problems too.

He had three wounded, two men and a boy. And there were two dead men, Red Belly and One Beaver. These were about all the losses a war leader could absorb and still lead effectively. Their deaths weighed on him, for his visions of saving the buffalo hadn't included the deaths of friends. Having rendered one wagon useless, his men now wanted to call it a victory and go whooping back to the village. This certainly tempted Striking Eagle, but he didn't want to quit the attack till he had killed these men who had wantonly destroyed so many buffalo.

During the fourth day, he was approached five separate times by warriors who urged that he abandon the fight. Three months ago, as Lone Wolf, he might have agreed. But now, while he found it difficult, he refused their entreaties. He hadn't finished with these whites.

Leading warriors was a wearisome job. All through this raid he had had to convince and reconvince those with him to continue to fight, as they owed him nothing but the allegiance he commanded with his personality. His respect for the leaders of war parties grew as he found out how difficult the task was.

Even his closest friend Left Hand sidled up to him to say, "Come on, Eagle. You've shown what a strong leader you are. If you lose any more men, people will be afraid to ride with you. Stop now. This is a wonderful beginning for a war chief."

"If we leave now, they'll just go back to shooting buffalo."

"But we can't get closer because of those guns."

"I'm going to try something," said Striking Eagle. "Are you brave?"

"Am I brave?" repeated Left Hand, puffing up a bit. "Hey, brother, you know me. I'll do anything that has to be done."

"Will you follow me tonight?"

Although no Kiowa liked to be in the open after dark because of the demons that prowled the night, Left Hand rose to his bait. "Right into the mouth of a grizzly, Eagle—if you're walking with me."

For days now, Striking Eagle had felt stretched thin, and yet it was pleasurable to stretch himself to make happen what he felt was right. Throughout these four days of the attack, he felt the way he imagined an eagle must feel as it soars. He was on the ground leading his men, but in his mind he also soared above the battle and looked down on it from a great height. From this vantage point, he saw that he should let some of these white men go free, not killing more than one or two, so that they would tell the others and make them fearful. It was *Wakan-Takan's* wish that the white men be afraid to kill buffalo. If they didn't send these men back with that message, the other whites wouldn't receive it. But they weren't afraid yet. His plan was to render the white men powerless and at the same time increase the size of his horse herd.

That night he set himself to wake up a couple of hours before dawn. He quickly woke Left Hand, who rolled out of his blanket. Only a couple of other warriors stirred.

Shivering, they gathered their weapons and walked to the top of the hill overlooking the whites' camp, all the while keeping a fearful eye out for night demons.

"What do you want to do?" asked Left Hand softly.

"We want their horses," answered Striking Eagle.

"That's fine, but *now*? In the dark?"

Fearful, they both looked around in the darkness, where Striking Eagle saw the dark outlines of the night's leering demons. A man exposed his soul to their biting when he wandered around in the dark.

"Yes, now. You said you'd go into a bear's mouth with me. Are you ready?"

159

He heard nervousness in Left Hand's voice as he agreed to come.

They crept down the hill toward the whites' camp. Left Hand stopped him once to ask what spirits prowled in the whites' camp at night, and Striking Eagle had to calm him by describing a couple of innocuous fire imps he had seen.

They reached the whites' camp an hour before dawn. A hint of grey showed about them. In front of the burnt wagon, the tall white sat, his head slumped on his chest, obviously left on guard duty but sleeping. Left Hand signed that he wanted to shoot the man with an arrow, but Striking Eagle wouldn't let him. Just the whump of arrow striking a body might be enough to arouse Long Crow and Shiny Head to come out shooting.

Slowly they moved forward, and in minutes they had sneaked through the entire line of horses and loosened their ropes. They made sure they worked so deftly that the horses and mules didn't run off at once, for hoofbeats would awaken their sleeping enemies.

Via hand signs, Striking Eagle gave his friend orders. As soon as the entire herd was loosened, Left Hand swung himself up on a horse and drove the animals west through the draw. Striking Eagle hid himself in a clump of mesquite he had spotted yesterday, not fifty feet from the camp. There he waited.

As he figured, the hoofbeats brought the whites out running. Not a shot was fired at Left Hand till he had gone a hundred yards. Keeping his head and torso down near his mount's back for fear that the whites could see even in this grey light, Left Hand urged the herd on faster.

As he drove the horses into camp, the war party jumped to its feet. Following Striking Eagle's instructions,

Left Hand ordered them to strike camp and move toward their homes. Close behind him came the whites with their deadly guns, for they needed the horses for survival.

"Just one mule," said Joe for the sixth time. "They didn't leave us but one mule. One mule can't pull the wagon."

"We'll just have to walk it, boys," said McCall.

"How far is it?" asked Joe.

"Sixty, seventy miles."

"Tarnation!"

"Damn!"

"They come back, and we're going to be in tough shape," McCall noted.

"Let's get on out of here then," said Phil, looking around the quiet prairie fearfully.

"I hate leaving them wagons," said McCall. "Not all the hides burned through. Those wagons are all I got in the world."

"You ain't got nothing, then," barked Skinner. "And nobody to blame but yourself."

McCall just nodded, hardly interested in hearing again from Skinner how he had engineered his own disaster. In the midmorning light, they surveyed the remains of their camp. They had chased the Kiowa on foot, but their legs were no match for the mounted Indians. In the dawn, the four discouraged men had trudged back to camp only to find the two wagons on fire, victims of their chase to get back the horses.

They were left with little. Each man had a pistol, a rifle, and maybe fifty rounds of ammunition. They had managed to catch one mule. From the five burnt wagons, they looked to salvage what they could. They found two canteens, a half-charred sack of flour and an undamaged sack of beans, a couple of ropes, three ponchos and a half dozen skinning knives.

Apparently the Indians had called it quits when they got the horses, for not an Indian had been seen in two hours.

"How long you reckon it'll take us to get to Hays?" asked Phil.

"A week," McCall replied.

"Mind if I ride that mule?" Phil asked.

"You got the stuck leg," said McCall. "But you might have to let one of us rest on him every now and then."

For the next couple of days, McCall noticed that Skinner had little to say and walked a fair distance away from him. Skinner never had much to say, but by now McCall had learned to read his moods. From his sour silence and the way he snapped at Little Phil and Joe over nothing, McCall sensed that Skinner's anger at him was mounting to the boiling point.

Hour after hour they trudged through the prairie in silence. The March wind whipped at them, giving them chills, and at midday the sun roasted them. They seemed to have been walking forever. Luckily the Indians hadn't gotten their hats, or the sun would have fried their brains. They grew sick of the endless countryside they slogged through: scrub mesquite, buffalo grass, distant mountains and an endless blue sky. Three times in those first few days they came upon small buffalo herds, herds that, had they had empty wagons, they would have shot. At night, having posted a guard, they ate a mush composed of the dried beans and flour without benefit of cooking. They were afraid to light a fire for fear that the smoke in the day or the flame at night would alert marauding bands of Indians.

On the fourth day, Skinner began a loud series of complaints to Little Phil and Joe. "Injuns wouldn't have robbed us if big man here hadn't helped him out."

McCall let the remark go without comment.

Later, Skinner said, "An Injun thinks you're nice to him because you're afraid of him. If a white man has any sense, he gets rid of the Injun."

Again McCall let the comment go. After all, he too was burned up over his losses.

"It's our own damn fault, boys," Skinner went on. "We never should have hired on with a man who makes friends with the Injun."

Phil and Joe just grunted and shot McCall glances from under the brims of their wide felt hats. Like McCall, they saw a gathering storm, and they didn't want to get in the middle of it. As they walked on, these two men fell behind, keeping themselves and the mule well away from McCall and Skinner, who walked on in front, although separated by twenty yards.

While angered by Skinner's remarks, McCall showed little irritation. By nature a quiet man, McCall had no wish to involve himself in a useless quarrel with his junior partner, expecting his anger to blow over as Skinner accepted his loss. But Skinner spoke more and more boldly about McCall's mistakes with the Indians and his general fearfulness of them, so that one morning, just before they were about to leave their makeshift camp, McCall said, "You've run your mouth a lot the last couple of days, Skinner. I think you've run all this into the ground."

Clearly worried by the sober tone in McCall's voice, Phil and Joe glanced at each other and drew back. McCall watched Skinner closely. He didn't know what had stuck in Skinner's craw so hard, but the baldheaded man clearly was spoiling for a fight.

"You owe me something, McCall," said Skinner. "Your foolishness has cost me plenty."

"I don't owe you nothin'," McCall answered.

Skinner lowered his rifle from his shoulder to his cradled arms as if preparing to use it.

Phil said, "You fellows cut this out. We got enough trouble without y'all fighting."

Without taking his eyes off McCall, Skinner said, "Just shut up! This ain't your business."

Skinner stepped forward toward McCall and swung the rifle barrel to point at him. McCall found himself looking at the muzzle hole of the .36 Spencer with Skinner's voice ringing over it, "You done robbed me of my share of the hides, McCall, and I want you to pay me for them."

"I don't owe you nothing, Skinner. This is just the breaks of hunting. Don't point that gun at me."

"I say you owe me."

"I say I don't. You hired on with me to get a fifth of what we got, and we didn't get nothing."

"Yeah, but we would have—we even had some—but you let your friend take it away."

"I fought him off as hard as any of us."

"But if you had let me do him in when I told you to, none of this would have happened."

"We didn't know that."

"I knew that, and I told you so." The barrel of the buffalo rifle jabbed forward. "Now, Jack, what I want to know is this. Are you going to make good on what of mine you lost or not?"

"Make good? I don't owe you nothing."

"Then I'm going to take what I'm owed off you."

"I ain't got nothing on me."

164

"I'll take what I can get. Or you'll promise to give me what you owe me when we get back to Hays."

"I don't owe you, and I'm wiped out, Skinner."

"I see a gun. And that's your mule, there. And I wouldn't be surprised if you didn't have some gold notes in that fancy wallet you carry."

"I'm not giving you nothing."

"Then I'm taking."

"You going to shoot me down?" asked McCall. "Right in front of those two?" He jerked his head toward Little Phil and Joe.

"Hey, don't bring us into this," said Joe. "This ain't our fight."

"Yeah," said Phil. "You two settle your accounts without us."

Closing the distance between them, Skinner poked the rifle smack up against McCall's chest and said, "They see I'm right, Jack. Now pull out that fancy wallet of yours or I take it off your carcass after I blow a hole in you."

He cocked the rifle.

Chapter 6

"I'm not giving you my goddamn wallet," said McCall.

"Yes you are, Jack."

"How was I to know that Injun would come back?"

"Cut the stalling and hand me that wallet."

McCall sighed and sagged as he said, "All right. Lemme get it out."

"Real easylike, Jack," said Skinner, grinning. "I wouldn't want to blow a hole in your chest by mistake."

Cautiously, McCall reached for his back pocket and pulled the wallet out with elaborate care. Holding it out to the right of his body so Skinner could see it easily, he let it go. It slapped gently against the hard ground. For the brief moment that Skinner's eyes followed the black wallet, McCall ducked down and to the left, coming up under the gun, his right fist traveling as fast as he could push a punch. His fist hit Skinner in the gut the way a mule's kick might sink into a sack of flour.

Making a noise like a man with the heaves, Skinner collapsed backward onto the ground. The rifle fired, Little Phil and Joe hit the ground, and McCall followed through by pulling the gun away, casting it aside and throwing himself on top of Skinner.

McCall didn't think it would be much of a fight, figuring his first punch would start and end it, but Skinner surprised him by gathering his strength, pushing him off and coming at him with his head lowered just as McCall got to his feet.

He hit McCall in the stomach, his bald head seeming as hard as a cannonball. A little dazed, McCall pulled himself together and ran forward to Skinner, who was lurching his way toward the rifle that lay between Joe and Little Phil. Quickly, Joe and Little Phil moved back from the fight. As Skinner leaned over to pick the rifle up, McCall hit him with the running force of his whole body, throwing Skinner forward to crash onto his face. McCall landed on top of Skinner's broad back, pummeling him with punches.

That ended it.

"Enough!" shouted Skinner.

McCall didn't get up. As he looked around, he saw Phil holding his wallet, its flap open.

"Something in there you want?" McCall asked.

Phil started and put on a nervous smile. "Naw, Jack. I was just seeing if anything fell out."

Breathing heavily, McCall reached out his hand and said, "Give it to me."

"Lemme up," whined Skinner. "You're hurting my back."

"Wasn't you the man going to blow a hole in me?" shouted McCall.

"I just wanted what was mine, Jack," said Skinner. "Get up. You're killing my back."

"Now why the hell should I let you up if you aim to put a hole in me?"

"I won't no more."

"How do I know that?"

"It's over, Jack."

"It will be if I cut your throat."

"I'm finished. No fooling."

"I don't know, Skinner," said McCall. "I don't want you putting no knife in me one night."

"I ain't going to."

McCall sighed and looked up at Joe and Little Phil, who gazed at the two of them with the rapt looks of men watching a particularly interesting bit of theater.

"I didn't get much help from you two."

At almost the same moment they both shrugged without a flicker of change in their expressions. McCall knew what they were thinking: Skinner could kill all the Jack McCalls he wanted to as long as he left the two of them alone. He didn't like the low-lifes that buffalo hunting drew, all misfits who couldn't make it back to the East.

McCall finally let Skinner up after he swore the fight was completely over, but he took the precaution of removing the shells from Skinner's gun and the man's two skinning knives from their sheaths.

"I told you I ain't at you no more, Jack," said Skinner.

"I know you ain't, Skinner, but if I got your teeth in my pocket, you can't bite."

"I need my shells and knives."

"Yeah, you'll get them too, when I'm sure you ain't going to bite me, turtle."

That's how it stood. McCall stashed Skinner's shells and knives in the saddlebags and they continued their trudge toward Hays City. A wary anger settled between the two, with McCall keeping plenty of distance between himself and Skinner.

McCall felt discouraged, for he had had high hopes that these two loads of hides would get his buffalo hunting business on its feet and subsequent hunts would enable him to put together a large enough stake to quit the business. The past year's work in putting a rig together was all for nothing, for even if Skinner had raided his wallet, he wouldn't have gotten more than two hundred dollars, hardly enough to buy a wagon and equipment.

McCall had been hunting in the Kansas Territory since he was eighteen, and now that he was thirty-three, he had grown weary of it. Now that buffalo hunting had become rampant across the Kansas plains, McCall felt the easygoing life he had loved for fifteen years drawing to an end. This attack by Lone Wolf might be the beginning of a war between the white hunters who had recently crowded into the territory and its half dozen tribes, a war many of the old-timers like McCall felt had become inevitable.

While he had said little to Little Phil, Joe and Skinner, in all his years on the plains he had never known an Indian to repay a man who had saved his life with an attack. That Lone Wolf had attacked them in such strength showed McCall how much the thousands of low-life buffalo hunters who had crowded into the territory had spooked the Indians.

McCall didn't know what to do now. Having had his own rig, he particularly didn't want to go back to working for someone else. That was no way to get enough money to leave Kansas and set himself up somewhere else like the Northwest Territory, which they said wasn't crowded.

Somehow he had to find a way to get enough scratch for his own rig. When they got back to Hays, he would see if he couldn't borrow the money.

His heart pounding with excitement, Robby held the bow back as far as he could pull it, the arrow notched in his fingers the way Uncle John had showed him, sighting for the buffalo calf's heart.

At the age of eleven it was hard for him to pull back such a powerful bow, but his excitement gave him strength, for not fifteen yards away grazed a buffalo calf and its mother. He had done just as he had heard the men around the hotel describe: he had crept up downwind on the pair.

Following them and keeping himself hidden, the two had led him on a chase across rocks and gullies that had lasted two hours. The buffalo cow and the calf weren't rushing about in efforts to find their herd, but obviously they were lost and looking for their companions. Robby knew he had to bring down his game, the calf, before they found the herd, or he would lose this rare opportunity.

His excitement had mounted when the pair had led him into the mouth of High Fork Draw, for there he had the two of them trapped. Crouched in the rocks above them, all he needed now was for neither to move for the next few seconds.

He let the arrow go, and it hit the calf in the neck, causing it to bellow in a low bleating sound and run in a circle before running into its mother.

Elation shot through him. He had hit his first game! Fumbling with his makeshift quiver, Robby quickly notched another arrow and crept forward. The calf was wounded, and if the buffalo hunters in the saloon were right, now his real prowess as a hunter would come out. If you wounded on the first shot, you had to move quickly to get in the second or you lost your buffalo.

The calf struggled to get up under his mother to suckle. About four months old, he bleated as he pressed against her side, for the arrow in his neck wouldn't let him get to her udder without hurting him. She turned to see what was wrong, licked the calf a couple of times, then turned back to graze, waiting for him to feed. When he didn't, she turned in a circle to her calf and pushed her head against him in a puzzled way.

Having shot a trifle too quickly the second time, Robby's arrow veered off course, missed the calf and caught the cow in the rump, lodging there at a depth of two inches, more an irritant to the fifteen-hundred-pound animal than a threat to her life.

She snorted, made a couple of angry bellows, pawed the earth and switched her tail vigorously. Pushing her calf before her, she moved toward the mouth of the canyon, and Robby suddenly realized he was losing his prey.

By the time they got to the mouth of the draw, the calf was wobbling. The cow slowed and looked around, and Robby froze. They said if you didn't move, a buffalo couldn't see you. It must have been true, for she looked directly at him for a while and then back down to her calf, who was on the ground now, heaving and panting in pain.

Robby scampered up a couple of rocks to get a better angle on the two animals. For a moment the sight of the calf's convulsions caused a wave of pity to sweep over him and he regretted shooting the calf; then his pride reasserted itself. He was proving he was as tough as any buffalo hunter. He had tracked down the animals and made his kill, even though the calf's mother looked the size of a locomotive.

The cow now swaggered around angrily. Robby hoped the calf would die soon. She would leave, he would use his pocketknife to skin the calf, take the hide back to Uncle John and see if he could sell it. He knew most of the hides brought from two and a half to three dollars. Maybe Uncle John would give him a dollar for it.

That would show his mother. She might not allow him to hunt, but a man shouldn't listen to what women had to say, not if he was going to stop the men in the saloon from teasing him about being a momma's boy. This would show them all. When they saw he could bring in the game, they might even take him with them on a hunt, which Robby wanted more than anything he could think of.

He had been tracking the two buffalo since noontime, and judging from the position of the sun, it was now late afternoon. Now that the most thrilling part of the hunt was over—the shooting of his first buffalo—he wanted to get back to Hays City. He knew his mother would already be wondering where he was and would be worried about him, and if he didn't get back soon she would scold him terribly for days and days. He knew it would take him an hour to skin the calf and another hour to walk back to town, and here the calf hadn't even died yet. He had another four arrows in his quiver. Did it make sense to get closer and kill the calf so he could finish this before dark? He wasn't all that frightened of being out past dark, but as Uncle John put it, his mother would "have a duck" if he got home much past late afternoon.

He decided to inch forward through the rocks to get closer to the two. They stood now to the side of the mouth of the draw, which was only about twenty feet across. He would have to pick his way carefully along large granite boulders if he was to get closer without their seeing him.

Each time he passed a rock, he peered around. Unfortunately, on the third one the cow saw him. On the fourth, she was coming over to see what he was. According to the stories he heard in the saloon, buffalo were nothing if not curious. With a start, he realized as well that he was now upwind, a cardinal mistake, and that she could smell him. Uncle John and Seesaw said a buffalo couldn't see, but it damn sure could smell as accurately as a crow could eye you.

He ducked below the rocks and scrambled up the side of the draw, sure that if she could get to him, she would mash him against the side of a rock for what he had done to her calf.

He peered around again when he was about twenty-five feet above the bottom of the draw. He saw that the cow had returned to her calf, her muzzle pointed to the smaller buffalo who lay there with its head stretched out in an unnatural fashion. She butted the calf in an attempt to rouse him. Was he dead? Dying? Or just wounded? Robby was thirsty, hot and tired. He wanted this over with.

He notched another arrow. He had been practicing—without his mother's knowing about it, of course—for weeks with his other bow, the weak one. He figured he could hit the calf again from this distance. Once more a surge of pity rose in him over wounding the calf, but again he shook the feeling off. A man had to bring home game or his family didn't eat. Of course, in his case this wasn't true. With his momma working for Uncle John, the one thing they had enough of was buffalo steak. But still, he wanted to show her and all the men, especially those in the bar who laughed at him and teased him, that he was a man and not a boy.

He felt pride at how accurately his arrow flew: it sunk into the ribs so solidly that the calf never quivered. Two shots only! His first kill!

But something was wrong. The cow nuzzled the new arrow and again poked her dead calf in an effort to get him up. When that didn't work, she tried it again, this time with more force. She raised her snout in the air and gave a long bellow of pain and anguish. Once again he felt a sharp spasm of grief and wished he hadn't shot the calf, no matter how much it proved he wasn't a momma's boy. With a pang of regret, he realized there wasn't any way for him to undo the death of the calf. No matter what happened, he couldn't make the calf come back again. He wanted to declare to God that he had been playing, only trying to see how brave he was and how powerful was his bow. God could now bring the calf back, and he, Robby, could chalk this up to experience. He was ready to forget the hide and the praise from Uncle John, Seesaw and the men in the saloon. But while he felt better about considering the situation this way, he had the sinking feeling that even God couldn't bring the calf back.

Under the baking sun, on the rough granite on which he sat, thirsty and tired, in an effort to grasp what he had done, he told himself several times that the calf was forever and ever dead, and that he, Robby Rawls, had killed it. A new sense of his ability, including the power to do things that could make another part of him cringe, washed over and rattled him.

Now that her calf was dead, why didn't the stupid cow go away? Robby wanted to go home.

But over the next two hours, the cow didn't leave the side of her calf. The calf was dead. Of that Robby was sure, for since the second arrow, he hadn't moved, and no matter how much the cow butted him, he didn't get up.

The sun hung no more than an hour from the rim of the world when Robby realized that she might spend the night here, preventing him from skinning his kill till morning, if then. He had to leave. It would get cold out here at night, and he hadn't had anything to eat or drink since noon. Indians were all around these parts, and if they caught him, they would roast him first and scalp him next. Suddenly he wished it were this morning again and that none of today had happened.

He decided to sneak around the cow and walk back to Hays City. First he moved backward and went up the side of the draw. He crossed it much farther back, hoping that the cow couldn't see several hundred feet up the draw through the long late-afternoon shadows. He crept along the other side of the canyon, the shady side, toward the mouth. But as he popped up his head to see from time to time, the cow was moving in his direction and farther and farther away from the black shadow that was her dead calf. Robby then tried to time his dashes when she was looking another way. Why didn't the stupid cow stay with her calf if she wanted to hang around this canyon?

And when he came around a large rock near the mouth of the canyon, he saw a broad brown face not five feet from his. He scrambled back, heard a clatter of hooves behind him, and half-climbed and half-pulled his way up the side of the rocky draw. From the noises of her breathing and the crunch of loose rocks behind him, he knew she was no more than a few yards behind him. She might have no horns, but her head had looked half the size of his body, and he figured she would mash him into the side of a rock and trample him with her hooves if she got the chance.

Winded, he finally got so high up the ever-steeper slope that the cow didn't seem able to follow. Sitting atop a round granite boulder, he looked down into the cow's determined face fifteen feet below. For a long moment the two stared at each other.

"Go on," shouted Robby. "He's dead. Can't you understand that, you stupid cow!"

The cow didn't move, just watched him steadily.

"I didn't mean it," he shouted. "Go away."

She pawed the ground.

"You can have another calf."

She raised her nose in the air then and gave a trumpet of a bellow, frightening him.

"I really really really didn't mean to. Honest."

The cow daintily moved forward, picking her way between the rocks surprisingly well for an animal of such bulk. To Robby, she looked as large as an angry wagon.

After staring at him atop the rock for what seemed like forever, she turned and picked her way down the slope to her calf.

Over the hour before sundown, she went back and forth between Robby and the calf five times. He kept trying to sneak from rock to rock, to clamber along the side of the steep cliff so he could pass over the two of them and on out of the draw. But the cow seemed wise to his plan, and whenever he moved forward, she ran up the slope after him, causing him to scamper farther back up out of her reach. He had heard men at the Hide & Skull say buffalo could climb like mountain goats, but he could hardly believe such an ungainly-looking beast could pick her way so rapidly between rocks on such a steep incline.

As night approached, he put his pride in his pocket and shouted for help, but only his echo answered him. He felt the chill of night falling. It would freeze tonight, might even snow, and he didn't want to turn into a block of ice the way the men said you did if you were caught in a blizzard.

Desperate to escape, he climbed farther up the walls of the draw in an effort to get so high that the cow couldn't follow him. Up here there were fewer large rocks and more loose dirt, and several times he almost fell, till he decided to cache his bow and arrows. They hampered his firmly gripping the walls of the canyon as he climbed. With a pang, he tucked them behind a rock.

Higher and higher he climbed, and when he looked down, he saw the cow had followed him up till she was only forty feet below him. In order to go around her, he began to make his way foot by treacherous foot along the steep slope toward the mouth of the draw, yet several times he had to descend toward her in order to escape a patch of loose, clodlike earth that wouldn't support his handholds and feet.

On one of these swings downward, Robby again saw the cow picking her way up through the rocks toward him. She came with such speed and adroitness—as if a wagon were picking its way between the boulders—that his tired legs and arms suddenly betrayed him by turning cold and weak.

At the same time, the rock he was holding on to came out of the wall and he felt himself falling. He screamed. He hit the ground and rolled downward over and over.

In flashes he saw the cow bearing down on him as he struggled to stop his end-over-end fall. As he spun down the slope, blows from the rocks and dirt hit him, yet they felt nothing like the imaginary spikes of the cow's hooves and teeth as they sank into him.

Robby put out his arms and hands to stop his fall, and gradually he pulled himself to a stop. On toward him charged the cow, head down.

He struggled to get to his feet, but his feet couldn't get a purchase on the incline's rock chips. On his back like a struggling turtle, he pushed his way up the slope till he bumped against a rock. Pushing himself to the left, he got into a crevice just as the cow arrived. She slammed into the large boulder so hard that he felt it shake, but he seemed much safer in the fissure. The cow switched about, bellowed, then looked for him. Finally she stuck her head into the crevice.

As he cringed farther into the tight slit, he smelled her foul breath. He stared into her angry, crossed eyes. Her head moved from side to side against the walls of the crevice as if trying to shove apart the rocks to get at him.

She pushed her head forward. Robby screamed, for she was pushing her way into the crevice, when out of her mouth blood gushed into his lap.

He screamed again, struggling to push the blood back with his breath, but she pushed toward him again, heaved once more, and again a bucket of blood gushed over Robby.

"Help! Help!" he shouted. "Help me, please!"

"No luck?" Sally asked Seesaw.

"No, ma'am. I'm sorry."

"Could you look through the hide sheds again?"

"We've looked three times, Miz Sally."

"But he has to be somewhere."

"Yes'm."

"You're not quitting, are you, Seesaw?"

"It's getting dark now."

"But you can use lanterns."

"Miz Sally, we done looked in every corner of town, and not once but three and four and five times. He just ain't in Hays City."

"But he has to be!"

Standing in the saloon of the Hide & Skull, Seesaw, an aged, hunched-over buffalo hunter, nodded in agreement, but it didn't soothe her. She knew he couldn't bear to bring her such terrible news, news that her son had disappeared.

"Will you go back and keep looking?"

Seesaw didn't say anything, obviously preferring silence to saying no to her.

"Have a drink on the house and go back again, will you, Seesaw, for me?"

"Yes'm, I will." He started for the bar and stopped. "I sure is sorry, Miz Sally."

She nodded vaguely. He moved to stand near the murmuring group of men huddled at the bar, and Sally sat down at a table in the half-empty saloon by herself. A part of her longed to empty herself of grief through tears, but she seemed unable to, as if another part had given up on crying when Dave had died last year.

Now that night had fallen, so had all her hopes. Sally Rawls knew her son Robby was dead.

No eleven-year-old could disappear for an entire day in a town the size of Hays City without something serious happening to him. A town of only one thousand people, Hays City was too small. The men had searched every one of the five stores, the three saloons, the two hundred fifty tents, the dozens of bunkhouses, ten woodsheds, two stables and their haylofts, the blacksmith's shop, the cooper's shed and, in case he'd been sleeping or injured there, even on top of and along the hundreds of feet of buffalo-hide sheds. But no one among the one hundred twenty-five men who searched had found a trace of the boy.

Robby had disappeared, and Sally thought she knew why. Her boss, John Moar, had given Robby a new bow and arrows yesterday, something one of his buffalo hunters had picked up out on the godforsaken prairie of this godforsaken country. The boy had been shooting it all over town this morning and he must have strayed out into the brush near town where some wandering Indians had found him and taken him off.

Of course, John dismissed her theory that his present had caused Robby's disappearance, but he had marshaled every able-bodied man in Hays to look for him.

If Dave were still alive, it would be a different story. Dave would know what to do. But she had had to plead with these rough men all afternoon to keep up the search, and to get John to set up more whiskey for them, for it seemed that only by wetting their whistles could the men be induced to keep looking through the already looked-through town.

Was it possible that Robby lay dead out on the plains somewhere? Scalped? Or tied astride a pony, terrified as he was taken hundreds of miles away from his people?

Oh, why, why had the Lord taken her Dave? And why did he want her only other man? What was he trying to do to her? Most days she was too busy working to brood about her loss, but now, faced with her loss of Robby, all she had been through over the past months swept over her. While her grief was so real that she could almost touch it, she couldn't cry. That surprised her. Last year, when she had first come to Hays and wanted to put on a brave front, she had cried every time she remembered Dave. She understood nothing of all this. Tell me, Lord God, what you want of me! she shouted inside. But she got no answer.

Because of her muffled grief, the few men around her in the bar who weren't out looking for Robby talked in hushed tones. Normally at this hour, the Hide & Skull overflowed with shouts and the high gabble of excited men. She knew John Moar wouldn't like the day's figures from the bar and the restaurant. On top of her having given away a lot of whiskey, not much money would have passed hands because most of the men had been either searching for the boy or hiding out in their competitor's saloon, the Drum, across the street.

Sally dared, just dared, John Moar to say one word to her. After all, it was he who had given Robby that blasted bow and arrows, and she was certain it had had everything to do with the boy's disappearance. Works of Satan, all such implements of violence. Dave had refused to carry a weapon, the gentle lamb. Sally sighed and shivered at the thought of her dead husband. She almost asked Bob for a drink, for her father had said it was good for frayed nerves, but she knew now wasn't the time for such a remedy. She had to remain alert and ready to deal with the men when they wanted to quit the search because of dark. Indeed, she had pleaded with them at dusk to go back out beyond the borders of Hays, but none would go, citing the uselessness of searching at night. But she knew the real reason they wouldn't go. They were afraid of the Indians, which was what, if they were real men, they should have been doing—rescuing her son from the savages who had captured him.

Sally got up from her table and walked to the door of the saloon. Looking over the swinging doors at the main street, she noticed how quiet it was—like the night before a funeral. Strange shadows played on the dirt street from the lamplit windows, as if grinning demons from below the earth were preparing to step above ground to snatch her. She watched them as if spellbound. Was she going crazy?

Maybe, she mused, when the Indians attacked the wagon train last year, they killed me. I am dead and actually living in hell. Satan is taking away those I love one by one. First Dave, now Robby, and next Eva, and then I shall spend eternity here alone with these ruffians, Satan's laborers.

From the first moment she had laid eyes on Hays City, Sally had hated it. Something seemed wrong with everything in the town: every building either sagged, stunk, or looked jerrybuilt. Its dilapidated stores and houses, its dirt streets, the long, stinking hide sheds, the dust, the saloons with their foul smell of buffalo hunters' sweat, stale breath, cigar smoke and buffalo ordure all conspired to make her loathe Hays City. If she had to spend eternity in hell, what had she done as a sin for God to make it such an abomination of a dwelling?

She and Dave had started out from Missouri with such high hopes—was it just *nine* months ago? She hadn't wanted to go, preferring the terribly hard times Missouri was experiencing to the rigors of the unexplored.

But just as she had trusted the Reverend Douglas Carter, her father, she trusted Dave Rawls, her childhood sweetheart. She had never really known any other men but these two, and no sooner had her father stopped exercising the influence of his decisions over her when her new husband Dave stepped in. After considerable soul-searching and praying, Dave decided they should head west, and she put her misgivings aside, throwing herself into the journey to make it work for all four of them. It had all seemed right and inevitable up to that terrible morning just nine months ago.

Then the Indians attacked. Confused and panicked, she had pulled the two children into their wagon and hidden herself and the two of them under the tarpaulin there while Dave, as a preacher and farmer unaccustomed to using a rifle, helped the men fend off the whooping savages.

Dave died that morning, she lived.

That sentence, repeated to herself hundreds of times, defined all her new existence.

Dave died that morning, she lived.

A hundred times she wished it had been the other way around. Their wagon had been destroyed too, by fire, but she and the children had lived. Without goods or money, the wagon master brought them on to the next town, Hays City, Kansas—buffalo hide capital of the world. While they were embarrassed to say no, none of the others in the wagon train had the room or provisions to take them on farther west, although through her grief, all Sally wanted was to continue on to San Francisco, her and her husband's original dream.

And to finish out that journey was all she wanted now for herself and the two children, a new start in a decent place. But she didn't have nearly enough money for passage on the Kansas Pacific Railroad.

Upon Sally's arrival in Hays City, with just fifty dollars in cash and four trunks of household goods, for the first time in her life she had needed work. Of course, she had worked twelve and fourteen hours a day on the farm with her parents and with her husband Dave on their place, but she had never held a job for pay. A proper woman didn't, a woman with decent menfolk. She had suddenly found that what worked with her father and Dave—hard work, piety, sweetness and loyalty—put her at a disadvantage in Hays. Her piety had no value and was thought of as priggishness, her sweetness was taken advantage of, her hard work was paid next to nothing, and her loyalty was seen as stupidity. What the rough hunters valued were her youthful good looks and sexuality. She had not learned to value either and the power of both frightened her.

As the initial weeks wore on, she found that respectable employment for a decent woman was something impossible to find in a town composed of a thousand buffalo hunters, nine whores, and one other woman, Buffalo Falla, half buffalo hunter and half veterinarian.

Of course, she was offered all sorts of opportunities by the buffalo hunters. Most of these opportunities were so indecent that she wouldn't even listen to the men finish their proposals, and most of the other jobs she turned down as not fit—such things as cooking for a hunters' bunkhouse or doing hunters' laundry, with of course the implication that sooner or later she would gratify their lusts.

For weeks she had lived at the Hide & Skull, the town's only hotel, and watched the rough hunters come and go as her bill mounted. The few buffalo robes she had seen back on the farm community in Pearl, Missouri, had been romantic, involving stories of mammoth herds of millions of animals on the prairies, but Sally had come to loathe everything about the great, shaggy animals, particularly the men who hunted them.

To her, the average buffalo hunter was a failure at half a dozen endeavors, a failure who had come to Kansas to pick up easy money. He dressed in ripped and patched buckskins that were perpetually covered in ordure—dried blood, excrement and offal from skinning buffalo, caked mud from crawling along ridges to sight the creatures, and fleas, lice and ticks from rarely bathing. They smelled like a walking slaughterhouse, and they swore the air purple at the least provocation. They drank lye-hot whiskey whenever they could get it: in the evening to carouse, in the morning to ease the pain of the previous night's carousing, and at noon to wash down the dust that had settled on their dinners. They frightened her, although she hid her fear well. Shaggy, unkempt men with long, tangled locks and wild beards constantly stared at her like crazy demons, their red-rimmed eyes locking on her as if to punch holes of lust through her, eyes behind which she saw cruelty, loneliness and insanity. These men knew nothing of the gentleness and kindness that could exist between people, nor anything about raising a family. They only wanted to satisfy a beastial lust. The sight of them often made her shudder.

Not that Sally considered herself some pale slip of a lady like some of the belles from the large farms she had known back in Missouri. At twenty-eight she regarded herself as a robust woman on the border between East Coast civilization and the wilderness, thrown into a situation that was over her head.

The entire United States was in the midst of hard times. Just last year, 1870, business all over the country had slumped so much that nobody was putting any money into any business, and from what she could gather, the buffalo hide business was the only booming thing across the entire continent. Some said it was a second gold rush. It would have to be, she mused, for so many men to be lured to such a desolate region across which raided hostile bands of Utes, Apache, Sioux, Comanche and Kiowa. Few wagon trains could be tempted to come through here— she had attempted to join three and failed—but almost daily, desperate-looking men arrived in town looking for just enough of a stake with which to buy the camping gear and expensive rifles that John Moar sold in his general store in order to go out on the range and make their fortune.

While a few of these men had the skills to make a fortune, fewer kept it. Only a tiny few, six, had approached her, hat in hand, to ask her to marry them. Not more than two or three of those rough-looking men had been warm and decent enough to tempt her, and it had turned out they weren't offering real marriage. Dave hadn't wanted her only for her sexuality, which was the lone desire of these men. Dave had also wanted her for her gentleness and the love she could bring their family. Occasionally, she realized that she was still so much in love with her late husband that she couldn't put her heart into marrying anyone else, no matter what his motives, which didn't

186

seem the most sensible attitude for a woman in her situation to cling to. Much of the time, holding herself back as
she did made her feel vaguely guilty that she wasn't doing
right by Eva and Robby, but she didn't like the sense that
she had to use her sexuality and shrewdness in order to
survive. Surely it wasn't right for a person to use such
tools of the Devil to manipulate others?

Stranded in Hays, without kin or prospects, having
sold everything including her wedding ring, the family
Bible, and her silver hairbrushes, and with no one left
back home to write to for money, Sally had felt forced
after two months to take the job John Moar had offered her
as manager of the hotel he owned, the Hide & Skull. It
involved not only running the hotel and the bar/restaurant,
but also supervising the cleaning staff and the "upstairs
girls," as the town called them, who lived in the tiny
rooms in the attic.

At first Sally had refused to have anything to do with
them, but John told her that if they weren't part of what
she handled at the Hide & Skull, then she didn't have a
job. It took her two weeks to work this part of the job out
for herself, for Dave certainly wouldn't have approved of
her working in a place with prostitutes. Sally saw clearly
that she couldn't depend on any man in Hays City for what
she and the children needed. Working it out meant giving
up her priggishness about the upstairs girls, seeing them as
down on their luck and doing their best to survive and not
having had her advantages. Keeping her revulsion at bay,
she threw herself into the work and used her friendliness
and natural sunniness to win the women over.

Shortly, she agreed to handle every aspect of the
hotel: the bar, the saloon and the upstairs girls. But only if
she was given a free hand.

John Moar, busy with his property acquisition, the

general store, and his booming hide business readily agreed. She had tackled the problems in her own way, organizing all the help, and had done a good job with the girls, insisting that they bathe every day, not drink if it was their day to work, and have the doctor inspect them once a week. Those girls who became pregnant she wouldn't allow to work. The girls thought this was fine, but John Moar thought it was a waste of money. She had it out with him and decency prevailed.

As she stood in the doorway of the saloon waiting for the men to bring her word of Robby's death, down the street she heard shouts and commotion. Her heart stopped, started, and seemed to shake within her chest. They had found Robby, dead. In seconds it would be over. They would burst through the door and Robby would be lying limp in some man's arms. She would bury him in this quiet, dry country and cry herself to death. She raced toward the doors. A sob tore from her throat, though she tried to push it back. Outside, the commotion became greater. The men standing at the bar now stared nakedly at her.

The doors were flung open and there stood a buffalo hunter, the tall, quiet one they called Jack McCall, covered in dung, mud and blood, holding in his arms Robby, also drenched in blood, his face pale and slack and his eyes closed.

Her heart fluttered against her ribs like a dying bird with a broken wing.

"Robby!" she cried as she rushed forward.

The boy's eyes opened to stare at her limply and with confusion—but he was *alive*!

To one of the men alongside, she shouted, "Get the doctor, quick." To the hunter carrying Robby, she said, "Give him to me."

As the tall man opened his mouth to protest, she snatched the boy from his arms. The living warmth of her son's body struck her so hard it made her faint. Staggering as she turned, Sally lurched forward to one of the round card tables. The men sitting there scraped their chairs back. For a moment she didn't think she was going to make it, that from Robby's weight and the shock that she was going to actually pass out. But she felt a strong pair of hands support her waist as she gently placed the boy on the table. Looking around, she saw the hands were those of the tall man who had been carrying Robby.

"What did you do to him?" she shouted. "Did you think teaching him to shoot buffalo would make him one of you?"

McCall looked at her in a dazed way and started to answer, but she cut him off with, "Killing's not the only way to live."

"He's not all that hurt," the tall man protested.

But Sally saw from his confusion and awkwardness that it had been he who had lured Robby off this morning. He had gone along with the boy's pleading to learn to hunt buffalo, had taken him out, and now this!

"He's covered in blood!"

"Just buffalo blood."

"Get out!" she shouted. "And don't come back—not ever!"

The man looked at her with such a guilty, queasy expression that she knew she had struck the heart of the matter.

"Just git—now!"

As McCall shrunk back, behind him she saw the doctor arrive. She dismissed the hunter from her mind as the doctor hurried toward Robby.

*   *   *

"A broken leg," the doctor said. "That seems all."

Relieved, Sally had the boy carried upstairs and ordered the cooks to boil water so they could bathe off the filthy, caked blood.

Upstairs in his bed, the boy looked frightened of her, and she wanted to hug him and shower him with kisses. But she also wanted him to know how angry she was. Not till eleven o'clock, after the boy's leg was in a splint, he'd had a bed bath and a hot supper, did she get the story out of him.

No sooner had Robby told her of his day than she realized with a pang of guilt how wrong she had been with McCall—the man hadn't lured Robby out, the boy had gone on his own. Now that she thought about it, she hadn't seen McCall around for a couple of weeks, not since she had heard he had come in with a large load of hides. She cringed inside at what she had said to him. It hadn't been right. The man had saved her son's life, if Robby's explanation was correct, and she had ordered the man out of the hotel.

She slumped by the boy's bedside. He was sleeping now, thank God, and she turned down the lamp and crept out.

Under the flickering light from the two lanterns in the hallway, she considered what to do. She decided she had to apologize to Mr. McCall first thing in the morning. She turned to the stairs to go up to her room, but something stopped her. Agitated, she couldn't figure out what it was, and then she realized that she kept seeing McCall's face in her mind as he struggled to explain to her. The man had been trying to tell her what had happened, but in her anger she had cut off and pushed away the man who had saved her son's life. She sighed, knowing herself only too well; she would feel so guilty that she wouldn't be able to sleep for having wronged this man who had gone out of his way to save her son.

She went downstairs to the bar. There she asked Bob to come with her. He left Shorty in charge and they went outside.

"I've made a fool of myself, Bob," she confessed.

"I thought you flew off the handle there," said the barkeep.

"He says Jack McCall saved him, shot the buffalo that had him cornered."

"That's what I been hearing."

"Who is he, Bob?"

"Who, Jack McCall?"

"Yes."

"Just another buffalo shooter, Miz Rawls, but a real old-timer. Jack was hunting buffalo fifteen years before there was a Hays City and buffalo hunting was big business. Lost his rig this last trip out. Him and his crew were walking in when they come on Robby."

"Lost his rig?"

"Injuns burnt the wagons he had just bought and almost got the four of them. I hear he's down on his luck, needs another stake."

"Where would McCall be?"

"You told him not to come in here, didn't you? Over to the Drum, I reckon," said Bob, talking about the only real competitor to the Hide & Skull, but one without the upstairs girls to attract customers. This was a real disadvantage, but the owner, Hanrahan, didn't have a hotel attached to the saloon as did John Moar.

"Come with me?" she asked.

"To the Drum? I can't be gone too long," Bob said. "You know how Mr. Moar is."

"I'll take the responsibility."

They found McCall, bathed and in fresh clothes, sitting in on a poker game at the Drum. As she and Bob made their way through the dim, smoky room, the clatter of voices gradually ceased. Probably hadn't been a woman in here in—well, maybe ever, Sally reckoned.

The six men at McCall's table looked up at her as she and Bob approached and stopped at McCall's place.

McCall rose, towering over her.

"Ma'am?" he asked.

"May I talk to you, Mr. McCall?"

"Yes'm."

"Alone. Maybe outside."

Again, in that confused way of his, he looked at the poker table, at the cards in his hand, and back at her, although he wouldn't look at her full in the face like so many of these men, as if he might see something there that either would embarrass or frighten him.

"Yes'm."

He followed her and Bob back out front. Feeling the eyes of dozens of men rake across her figure, Sally stiffened her posture and looked straight ahead. She knew that more than half of these rough men, given a lonely spot, would have forced themselves upon her. That knowledge made her shoulder blades shake as they walked back out through the Drum's swinging doors.

Outside, the night was cold. Thank God he had found Robby; the boy would have frozen before morning. Mannerly as always, Bob stood well away from the two of them, and with a sense of relief she stopped on the dimly lit porch and apologized for her behavior, excusing herself by saying how worked up she had been about her son.

McCall silently nodded and said it was all right. She thanked him for saving her son's life, and asked what she could do for him.

McCall looked at her then, his eyes staring easily into hers, and he said she didn't owe him anything. He and his men had heard the boy's cries on their way into town, came over to find out what was going on, and shot the buffalo. Wasn't nothing to it.

"Still, I'd like to do something for you."

"Well, thank you, ma'am," McCall said. Something in the way he said this pushed her in a peculiar way.

While she liked the man's natural modesty, which so few men in Hays had, he was so self-sufficient that it irritated her. Buffalo men! He didn't need or want anything from anybody. He would have shot the buffalo no matter whose son it had been, and having done it for his own reasons, he didn't want anything from her. The man was hardly civilized. In addition to satisfying her urge to thank him, she wanted to show him that life was about more than just taking care of yourself.

"Perhaps you'd like to take some dinners at the hotel," she said. "Or even a room for a couple of nights—on the house."

"You don't owe me nothing, ma'am," he said.

"I know, but I'd like to do something for you." Sally hadn't cleared this with John Moar, but he owed her a few favors, they had extra rooms, and what were a few meals?

"That's right generous, ma'am," said McCall. "I am kind of hard up right now. I got a bunk, but a few meals would do me right."

"Fine," she said. "Then I'll tell Shorty to expect you for dinner tomorrow night."

"Yes'm."

"I'm sure my son would like to thank you properly too."

"Yes'm."

193

She left then, marching, her back straight again, to the Hide & Skull, but without much sense of having completed thanking him. McCall was just like all the rest of these buffalo hunters: you couldn't really do anything for them. They lived in the wilderness and didn't need others.

Still, she had to get Robby to thank the man. The boy had to learn manners, but what he really needed was a stiff wallop on his backside, and with *his* size, that was something only a man could give him.

To his own surprise, McCall bathed for the second time in two days before he went to dinner the next night at the Hide & Skull.

As usual, he was staying in Mike's bunkhouse. He had dragged the trunk out that Mike kept for him and put on his suit to eat at the hotel.

He hoped she would come over to his table, perhaps even eat with him, but in his mind's eye he saw himself sitting alone in the small eating room off the saloon. Besides, she was so pretty he would hardly know what to say to her. He hadn't seen at such close range a woman as pretty and refined as her since his mother, who he had last seen twenty-odd years before. Her hair looked so blonde and evenly spun that it hardly seemed human, seemed more like something that could only exist in heaven. The vivid clarity of her blue eyes pierced him when she looked at him. Those eyes took his breath away. He liked the way she held herself, straight, as if she valued herself highly. Half the time the whores around the Hide & Skull slouched about as if they might fold in on themselves, whereas Sally wasn't going to be pushed around by anybody. He liked that in her a lot.

He had of course seen her many times over the last few months scurrying about the Hide & Skull tending to the place, and like almost every man in Hays City, he found her mysterious and enthralling. He knew about the loss of her husband, her reluctance to work in a rough buffalo country hotel, and her desire to move on farther west from what the town's casual scuttlebutt told him, but he didn't expect to get to know her, much less have her serve him a meal. Probably, whatever that meal was, it would just be something thrown together by the blacks and the Chinese in the kitchen, but McCall found himself picturing her making sure that he got the largest and freshest buffalo steak, that his bread had just been baked, and that his hominy grits were tender.

As he left the bunkhouse, he noticed how jittery he was. He felt just the way he did when he was coming up on a stand of buffalo and the wind was half with him and half against him, and it was the only way you could approach them. Few women stayed in Kansas Territory, and all those either married or quickly engaged. All McCall had ever hoped for, when he did think of another wife, was another young Indian girl. He was a fool, he told himself. That pretty lady ain't interested in you. What would such a clean and straight-backed young widow see in a smelly buffalo hunter like you?

As he walked up the street, he pulled the cool evening air deep into his lungs to steady himself, a trick Little Robe had taught him when he was first in the Rabbit Society of the Comanche. He had once had an Indian wife, seventeen when their first child was due, but she and the boy had died in the middle of a storm five years ago. He had felt awkward as he struggled to keep them both alive, feeling the pain of his helplessness more than ever before or since as he feebly ministered to them. His premature son's life had seemed to ebb between his fingers, and all his grief did nothing to stop it. Then Malla's life had drained from the bleeding from her womb that wouldn't stop. He suspected from what she said that without the baby she had little incentive to live. For two days he had simply stared at her dead body, occasionally breaking into heaving sobs that came from a part of him he had never suspected existed. It frightened him.

Never again, he had vowed upon burying the two of them in one grave. He had never before realized how much pain came along with having a family.

As he marched to the Hide & Skull, for the first time he wished he had lived differently in order to be more attractive to someone like Sally. Up to now, his life as a buffalo hunter was all he had ever thought to want. He had been hunting since before he was twenty, and he had done moderately well at it, particularly in the last few years since the railroads had come through and the demand for buffalo hides had soared. But today, as he compared himself with Sally Rawls, McCall realized what a gap separated the two of them. She always looked pretty and starched in her clean gingham dresses; half the time, like every other hunter he knew, he wore his filthy hunting clothes and lolled around the saloons without bathing or shaving.

Tonight the trousers to his outfit hung on him, for on the long walk back to Hays, the four of them hadn't found much small game, and they couldn't carry too much of what buffalo they did shoot. McCall had lost quite a bit of weight. He had tried to push the loose fabric of his trousers around behind himself, so as to make the front look as full as it should, but he suspected he had been largely unsuccessful and that he looked like what he was, an ungainly buffalo hunter.

As he walked into the hotel, his face looked like a man's who suspects he may have a great rip in the seat of his trousers. What went through his mind as he looked about for her was how *pretty* Sally Rawls was. She had such a pretty face that it made him a bit dizzy to look at it. The cunning way her blonde hair swept up around her ears awed him. She carried her head proudly, which made him admire her spunk, and her blue eyes were so clear and direct they somehow seemed to see everything in his heart, and this made him cringe.

That night he didn't see her at dinner, although he kept a sharp lookout for her. Shorty the barkeep served him in a grudging way, as if McCall was wrong to have taken her up on her offer. McCall was inclined to agree with Shorty, and decided that one meal was enough of such looking about anxiously for her while pretending he didn't care. Of course she hadn't come in to see him, he said to himself; she had left instructions he was to get his feed and that was it. McCall also thought Shorty looked funny at his clothes, and he decided that before he went into the saloon to play cards, he would go home and put on a less dandified outfit.

But as he finished, she came into the little dining room. Again he felt speechless, as he often did near people he felt stupid around, like John Moar the trader—they said he was the richest man in town—and the doctor, who used a lot of fancy words.

He rose. Greeting him coolly, she insisted that he sit and took away his empty plate. She came back with a tumbler of whiskey.

"This is a part of dinner for you, isn't it?" she said in that prissy way that both fascinated and pushed him back.

"Yes'm," he said. "I enjoy my glass."

As she set it down, she said, "My late husband Dave didn't drink."

"No'm."

She pulled a chair over and sat. "But I don't think there's a teetotaler in Hays City, is there?"

"No'm," he said, but he wanted to kick himself as he said yet another single-syllabled answer, for he saw he couldn't talk as pretty as she could. A lull fell between them.

In a sort of agony over the matter, he didn't know whether to drink the whiskey or not, much as he wanted to, for she had seemed not to approve of a man who did. How could a person think of so many things to say? he wondered. He squirmed a bit, struggling to figure out how to keep the conversation going.

An inspiration hit him. "How's the boy?"

"Robby's fine," she said. "He wants to thank you, if you have time to see him."

"Sure."

"He's upstairs. The doctor says he broke his fibula in the fall."

"His what?"

"His leg."

"Ah," he said, wondering why she hadn't said so in the first place. "I'd like to see the boy."

"When you finish your glass, perhaps?"

"Yes'm."

He finished his whiskey in between the conversational lapses, feeling deficient for not putting in more words and taking less booze. She led him upstairs.

McCall had never been upstairs at the Hide & Skull. Most of his friends in town had. They regularly used the girls who lived in the attic, who charged two to four bits for a good time. While he received his share of ribbing about his refusal to join them, McCall reckoned he just had too much of the Comanche in him. Somehow it was all right to give a father a payment of ponies for a wife, and he didn't have anything against going with a woman any number of times if she would have you, but paying to have a wife for ten minutes just didn't sit right with him. What he had been thinking was that if he did well this year, he might amble over to the Comanche tribe and see if he couldn't find himself another sixteen-year-old chief's daughter to make the trip out to the Northwest with him.

That night the upstairs hall of the Hide & Skull seemed to McCall to be a shadowy world of vague dangers. There was only one kerosene lamp on the landing and it threw its flickers feebly down the long hallway.

The boy looked lonely and mournful, but brightened at the sight of them. McCall had seen him scoot around town and the hotel. A thin, intense boy, tall for his eleven years, Robby reminded the buffalo hunter of a sickly wolf pup who keeps to the outside of the pack for fear of getting nipped by the older wolves.

Under his mother's watchful eye, Robby apologized. "I'm sorry you had to go to the trouble to save me, Mr. McCall."

"Now you thank him," she ordered her son.

"Thank you, Mr. McCall."

"That's all right, son," McCall said. He smiled at the boy, striving to make him at ease, as the lad looked as ill at ease with words as McCall felt. "I'd have done it for any lame duck."

That made the boy snicker. "You'd been out hunting?"

"I'm sure Mr. McCall has more to do than discuss

his business with you, Robby," Sally said. "Time for bed."

"Aw, Ma! It's only just dark."

"I have work to do, and you have to let your leg mend, which it won't with you squirming around."

"Yes'm."

"I can stay a few minutes," said McCall. "I'd like to talk to the boy."

For a moment she looked torn. For the first time since he had been watching her close up, she wasn't sure of herself. She looked about the room in a vague gesture of indecision, and the issue was finally decided by Robby's pleading with her. She agreed, saying she had to leave, and asked McCall not to tire Robby.

As soon as the door shut behind her, all McCall's awkwardness with words returned. He didn't know what to say to the boy, who lay in bed looking pale against the clean sheets.

Robby's eyes looked at him with a bright feverishness that unnerved him still more. It was good to see the boy comforted in clean sheets, and if his own ma had lived, McCall figured she would have made sure he had them.

But what did you say to an eleven-year-old boy who looked as embarrassed as you did?

"You were buffalo hunting, were you?" McCall asked.

"Yes sir."

"You killed that calf with your bow?"

The boy nodded, saying nothing and now hardly looking at McCall, as if he expected a scolding.

"Pretty good shot," said McCall.

Robby's face brightened. "You think so?"

McCall thought about it. "How far were you away?"

"Say from here to the stairs outside."

"Where'd you get such a strong bow?"

"Uncle John. Momma's mad at him for giving it to me."

"Mr. Moar?"

"Yeah, Momma works for him, and he's real nice to me. He gave me a Barlow once, but I lost it, and this is the second bow. He sometimes makes Momma mad 'cause he gives me things. But how am I going to learn to hunt if I don't practice?"

"Seems like a lot of people make your momma mad."

"Yeah, we're going west. She don't like it here."

"How do you like it?"

"I want to go buffalo hunting."

More comfortable than he had been with the boy's mother, he laughed at Robby's enthusiasm. "Yeah, well, so do I."

"You're grown, you can do what you want. I have to do what my momma says."

"That's right. You do."

From the silence that fell between them then, McCall gathered he had said the wrong thing. Still, he wanted to cheer the boy up. He reckoned it was hard being a boy in a town without any fellows your age. He ventured, "Maybe come the time your leg is healed, you could come help me hunt buffalo."

The boy looked up, his eyes bright. "You mean it? You'd take me with you?"

"Sure."

Robby looked downcast. "Momma says I'm too young."

"Indian boy, he comes when he's your age. Helps out. Keeps the horses, cooks, gets water, finds firewood."

"Oh, I'd do that!"

The next night McCall returned to the hotel and had

another dinner on the house. Bowing to necessity, he had asked about for a job as a shooter the last two nights at the Drum and at the Hide & Skull, but nobody seemed to be going out, or they didn't need a shooter. Though they told him this, he sensed that something was wrong with him, yet he couldn't pin it down.

Pushing a couple of his oldest friends, he found that Skinner had spread about the story of how McCall had healed Lone Wolf, the man who had escaped with McCall's horse and gun and then come back to rob him. Skinner made McCall into a figure of ridicule. Questioned, McCall admitted he had kept the Indian alive and said he hadn't figured the Indians would go so crazy. Not yet, anyway.

Much of the talk at both the Drum and the Hide & Skull concerned the fury of the Indian attacks this year, particularly the Kiowa, who seemed to have gone insane. Several wanted to send a delegation to Kansas City to see if the army would sweep the area around Hays, but nobody wanted to lose a few weeks of hunting in order to carry out the mission.

The upshot of Skinner's stories was that McCall had trouble either finding work as a shooter on anyone else's rig or borrowing the money to buy his own. Even some of the old-timers, men he had hunted with six and eight years before, got a faraway look in their eyes and said they didn't need any help now. One confided, "You might be too good at this business, McCall. Them Injuns might have a special grudge against somebody who finds their buffalo dinner as good as you do and takes away so much of it."

When he was done with dinner that night, he asked Shorty about Sally, wanting to see her again, but the barkeep told him that she was too busy to see him.

He started to leave when he remembered the boy. He climbed the stairs to the cool second floor, which again felt strange, as if he were entering a cave sheltering some hidden, spooky danger. He knew why. It was up these stairs that his buddies would climb later to join the women who lived in the attic.

Before he knocked to enter the boy's room, he paused in the empty hallway to consider what he was doing here. He hadn't had any dealings with anyone Robby's age since, well, since he was Robby's age, which was about the time the Comanche captured him after killing his folks. His adoptive father, Little Robe, had put him with the other boys, and he had learned what the Indian boys learned.

He felt a bit like a fool, coming to see the boy. It wasn't something that any of the men he buddied around with did, and the men at the Drum and downstairs in the bar would laugh and think there was something strange about his doing this.

Then he smiled. Sally might turn up, and that would make the time worth it. Besides, if he was the boy's friend, surely he would get to know his momma better, and maybe then she wouldn't look at him as if he were just another buffalo chip.

McCall ate for free at the hotel three more nights without seeing Sally, and after each meal he visited Robby, talking to the boy mostly about buffalo hunting, since this seemed his chief interest.

Without anybody saying anything to him, McCall figured that he had finished his free dinners, but still he continued to visit Robby every night.

What had started off as a ploy to get to know the boy's momma had turned into something else: he began to

like the boy and enjoy the visits. He remembered when he
had been Robby's age and in a similar position with the
Comanche. There he had felt just as lonely, for there had
been no one his age and no one who spoke English.

"She won't let me have a knife, a gun, or a bow,"
Robby complained half a dozen times in their talks.

"Maybe she thinks you ought to get a bit bigger,"
said McCall.

"You know I'm big enough, don't you?"

"Look it to me."

"I killed that calf, didn't I?"

"Yep."

"She thinks that because Pa didn't believe in guns, I
can't have one," Robby said. "But Mr. McCall, doesn't a
man have to have a gun in Kansas? Can't you tell her you
can't live here without one?"

"In my business we damn sure need them."

Toward the end of the week, Robby turned to McCall
and asked, "When are you going back out?"

"Any day now."

"How many men will you take?"

"I won't be taking any," McCall said. "I'm looking
to see if I can hire on."

He felt vaguely ashamed to admit this, for he had
talked about his wagons several times, describing to Robby
what they had to pack when they went out.

"Why aren't you taking your own wagons?"

"Run into some mean Injuns last time out," McCall
said. "I got my butt whupped."

Robby dragged out of McCall the story of Lone Wolf's
rescue, the Indian's few days with him and Skinner, and
the subsequent attacks that had cost him his buffalo hunting rig.

Till now he had been such a hero to the boy that he didn't like admitting he had failed to keep his own wagons against an Indian attack. He saw his stature diminish in the boy's eyes, although he saw as well that the boy tried politely not to show it.

"I would have killed that Indian the first night," said Robby.

"He seemed friendly enough."

"I hate the Indians. If it wasn't for them, Momma would let me go buffalo hunting."

"Indians are all right."

"No, they're not."

"Some of them are a lot nicer than some white people I've known."

"They killed my daddy."

"I heard that."

"I wish the army would kill them all."

"You got to realize that the white folks are killing the Indians' dinner, son. The buffalo is everything to the Indian."

"I don't care. Daddy didn't do anything to them."

"But other folks that came along in wagons like his did."

"I'm going to go out and kill all the buffalo and Indians I can find."

"By the time you're big enough to hunt, I don't think there will be enough buffalo for anybody to hunt."

"What? I've read there's millions of them."

"There's thousands of hunters too. With pretty powerful rifles."

"Shoot! Can't kill *all* the buffalo."

"Take the Texas herd. Half of it is already gone. When I first started following the migrations, it was as large as the other three great herds."

"If you think this, how come you hunt them?"

"I been doing it all my life. It's all I know."

"Well, I don't believe you. Nobody can kill *all* the buffalo."

"It wasn't like this when I started. I knew all the hunters in this part of the country. Today, why, there's thousands out there."

"I bet you'd kill that old Injun now, wouldn't you?" Robby asked.

"Kill? I don't know."

"But why wouldn't you?" the boy demanded. "Didn't he steal from you and then come back to rob and kill you? Next time you will, won't you?"

McCall squirmed and said nothing, for he didn't know the answer. He had asked himself the question dozens of times on the walk back to Hays, and he had never come up with a definite answer. He had respected Lone Wolf at the time, thinking the brave had a lot of spunk to be out alone looking for some damn fool thing like a white buffalo hide just because the medicine man said go. Yet McCall had kicked himself a hundred times for having given the brave the chance to come back and take his wagons. He might not have felt right about just depositing Lone Wolf back into that makeshift tepee in the middle of the snowstorm, but on the other hand, he didn't feel right about how things had turned out. His lost wagons and gear had been the result of a year and a half of hard work, and it seemed humiliating and wearisome to start all over again.

As well, McCall had difficulty answering Robby on account of his mother. He didn't want to ruin any slight chance he might have with her by changing the boy's values. From his talk with Robby, he gathered that Sally Rawls believed, like her late preacher husband Dave Rawls, that those who lived by the gun perished by it. Eastern women were sometimes like that. He didn't say so to the boy, but Dave Rawls had perished more as a result of not knowing how to handle a gun than brandishing one at the wrong time.

McCall felt like he was on thin ice during this whole situation. He had faced the raid on his wagons, taken his losses, fought Skinner when it proved necessary and trudged back to Hays on foot, some seventy-five miles, without half the hesitation he had now over what to say to the boy and how he might make some impression on Sally.

Still, he wanted to make an impression. Over the past week he had begun to realize that what he missed in his life was a wife and, yes, even children. He had even seen, with a start, that helping Lone Wolf had been a result of his need to care for someone other than himself. This notion of himself didn't stay focused in his mind for long without making him uneasy, for he had lived by and for himself over the past fifteen years except for the one-year marriage to his Comanche bride.

Through most of this time he had reckoned he'd live out his whole life this way. After all, a rolling stone gathered no moss, and wasn't life rough enough without having to look out for young'uns and a woman wanting this, that and the other thing?

His thoughts had been sparked by the boy, and his own memories of himself at that age with the Comanches suddenly came rushing back. Then he had been lonely and sure that even if the Comanches let him live, he would never fit in. His foster father, Little Robe, had been good to him and inducted him into the tribe's life in such a way that he had become a man under his teachings; he felt an urge to do for Robby what Little Robe had done for him.

207

McCall brought Robby gifts: a wooden sword he had carved, some walnuts, and an orange from Moar's General Store that had come all the way from some place down south. Neither the boy nor McCall had ever eaten an orange. McCall peeled it and they ate it together, agreeing that the stories of its miraculous flavor were correct. Robby kept the peels in a handkerchief so, as he said, he could smell them every now and then to remember what the orange's taste had been like.

But how was he to ask Sally Rawls to marry him when gossip in town had had her refusing every man who had broached the subject to her? When he played cards in the evenings, his mind wasn't on them, and he lost money he couldn't afford to lose. He found himself daydreaming about how he might get the money to give her a home. He might take the three of them along with him when they went to the Northwest Territory. It was impossible to get enough men together unless he got his own rig and went out. But how the hell was he to get his own rig when the last time it had taken him a year and a half of saving just to get one wagon? And even if he were to get enough together to ask Sally to marry him, how would he get her to listen? He thought of asking Buffalo Falla to give him some tips on how you approached a decent white woman, but the veterinarian/hunter didn't seem to be the sort who could supply such answers.

Coming down the steps from the second floor of the hotel toward the end of the first week of visiting his young friend, McCall came across Nelly, the sassiest of the Hide & Skull's whores, who called out to him, "Hey, Jack! You're not giving somebody else your trade, are you?" This question involved a long-standing joke between them.

Nelly's breasts were ballooning out of her low-cut

dress, as if she hadn't taken the time to adjust her clothing. McCall said, "Naw, Nelly, I done promised you. First time I go to pay for it, you're getting my business."

"Just remember—I'm ready to go, beau!" she said, giving him her tag line, which had become a running joke in the saloon of the Hide & Skull.

As she cawed raucously, McCall thought to himself, Nelly! Sure, she'd know what I ought to do to impress Miss Sally Rawls! Now why didn't I think of her before?

"Maybe there *is* something you can do for me," said McCall. "How much do you charge for a consultation?"

"A what?"

"To talk."

"Talk? I don't talk, I just show a man a good time."

"You want to make a buck?"

She sighed. "I guess I can learn anything, but damn, I get tired of you perverts!"

Chapter 7

"Bob, who was that lanky gimzo I saw up on the third floor just now?" John Moar, owner of the Hide & Skull, asked his barkeep.

The fat Bob asked, "Tall fellow, a little stooped over, with a black hat?"

"That's him," Moar nodded. "He doesn't dress like someone can afford to rent a room."

"That's probably Jack McCall visiting Sally's kid."

"The one rescued the boy?"

"That's him."

"How often does he go up there?"

"I seen him go by here at least once a day, Mr. Moar."

"I don't want hunters wandering all over the upstairs, Bob," said Moar. "You know that."

Moar liked the way the plump barkeep blanched a bit and shook his wattles. His help knew the boss was someone to reckon with.

"Yes sir."

"This ain't no rest home."

Bob shook his head vigorously as he reached for a glass to polish. "No sir."

211

"Pour me a glass."

Bob reached up under the counter for Moar's private jug of bonded bourbon.

Irritated, Moar thought about McCall as he stood at the bar, pulling on his thin cigar and sipping his whiskey. Just under medium height, John Moar gave the impression of being taller because of the way he carried himself. From time to time Bob glanced up at him as if worried about losing his job for not stopping McCall. This was just what John Moar wanted. He liked his help to stay a little off balance as far as he was concerned. They put out more.

About thirty, small and wiry, Moar gave the impression of being all muscle, yet his limbs were thin and he had little strength. He was just one of those men who knew how to handle himself well with others, and it showed in everything he said and did.

The great truth that John Moar had discovered about himself was that he was a natural trader. He had apparently been born one, although he had only discovered the extent of being one three years ago when he sent a few dozen hides from this camp of a town back to his brother Joseph in New York. Joseph had wired him back an order, after a few weeks, for ten thousand of the damn smelly pelts. John Moar hadn't been able to believe the wire, and had reluctantly spent fifty dollars on telegrams to confirm his brother's order. But once he understood that they held a firm order, he hired twenty hunters on speculation and had those hides on the train to Philadephia in three months. In a year, with his brother's efforts in opening up the English market, both of them were worth well over fifty thousand dollars.

Now, three years later, John Moar owned almost all of Hays City that he figured worth owning. At first he had hated the bleak Kansas plains, but as he gained wealth and

212

power over this barren land, and as being the first citizen of Hays began to mean being lord over more and more prosperity, he warmed to the place. Sure, it was hot and dusty as hell in the summer, and yes, it was colder than Buffalo, New York, in the winter, but when Moar walked down the street here, every man doffed his hat and nodded. In New York he would have had more places to throw away his money and he certainly would have enjoyed them, but he would have been a tadpole in the ocean; in Kansas he had built a kingdom, and if things continued to grow the way they had all through these hard times back East—why, when trade picked up, John Moar figured he might wind up having made himself a million dollars.

A million dollars! The very words rang like a deep voice from heaven whenever he called them to himself. *A million dollars!* A guiding voice a man could follow all his youth. With such a sum in land, hides and gold, he would be a prince back in New York. When he had started out there, he had been no more than a clerk in Mr. Bowser's wholesale grain business, doing no more than executing the trades that Mr. Bowser made, but when he returned to Manhattan, Moar wanted it to be on the same basis that he now lived in Hays City—as a man to be reckoned with.

But simultaneous with his growing wealth had come a new appreciation for this part of Kansas. He still sweltered and got caked with grime in the summer, but the mountains, sunsets and gentle swells of the land had an arresting poetry of their own. The winters still pierced the marrow of his bones no matter how much money he spent to chink his walls, but the folks here weren't the devious folks of New York. They had a directness that New Yorkers had lost. They said what they felt and minced no words, and Moar liked that. You knew where you stood with them without having to beat about the bush. Nor did they look down upon a man who had just made his money, as John Moar had seen rich customers look down upon Mr. Bowser and his girls dozens of times, even though Moar saw clearly that the genial Mr. Bowser could outthink and outtrade the lot of them.

All in all, Kansas had few things that New York didn't have, yet in the last nine months Hays City had come up with someone that New York would never have— Sally Rawls, the hostess and manager of Moar's saloon and hotel, the Hide & Skull.

On her second day in town, Moar had approached her to offer his help. She had been shy about taking it, and that shyness, compared to Nelly and her sisters, had touched him. Of course, her delicate features, downcast blue eyes and weary slump had made him doubt how valuable an employee she might make, but still she was remarkably graceful, and no matter how much rouge Nelly and Cora and Alice put on, you couldn't call them graceful. At least John Moar couldn't.

He had made it a rule of his not to sample his own girls' wares too much, figuring it lowered his dignity in town. When he did, it was mosty Nelly he sneaked into bed with him. In addition to being discreet when it counted, Nelly, in his opinion, had between her lips the tongue of Satan, and as well something else that belonged to the prince of darkness between her legs.

But no matter what tricks Nelly could do, she was no match for the grace and strength of personality of Sally, an aspect of a person John Moar particularly admired. She had the kind of looks and power that he wanted associated with him, and if she could hold up in Hays, she might be just the person to help him climb all the way to the top back in Manhattan. He decided from the beginning to move slowly and see how she handled herself before he revealed how he felt. A man couldn't pick a wife too carefully. In every trade a man wanted to make sure he didn't get damaged goods foisted off on him.

Moar had figured he needed a hostess and manager of the Hide & Skull, someone to keep the whores in line as well, and he fixed on Sally at once as the only person to fill this slot in Hays. Besides, he was likely to gain the best knowledge of her true character as an employee, as well as keep a sharp eye out for those other men who made a play for her. On the other hand, he recognized that the widow of a preacher would have objections to supervising Nelly and the other girls, so when he first offered the job, he didn't say too much except in a vague way of what he wanted, preferring to let her run out of money first.

Over the last two years Moar had found himself particularly ill suited to supervise the upstairs girls. On top of not knowing a damn thing about a woman's plumbing or temperament, his booming hide business fully occupied him. Every day now he had to inspect and buy from five hundred to three thousand hides, and arrangements had to be made to store them, get them to Kansas City and then ship them on to markets in New York, New Orleans and Philadelphia. He received and got half a dozen telegrams a day from his people east of Kansas, a fact that in itself made many in the town look upon him in awe.

Moar bided his time in approaching her, waiting till he knew she was completely down on her luck. She then told him that she might not be able to handle such work, which he understood. He told her to do her best, and they would both see.

All through these first months of her employment he had kept a firm eye on Sally, and the more he watched, the more he was sure of her. She was firm-willed enough to keep the girls in line even though she disapproved of what they were doing. She handled help expertly, and her warmth and friendliness in the dining room and saloon were putting the Hide & Skull still more ahead of the Drum. She turned out to be so honest that for once he received all the money he was due from those cheating trollops. Sally Rawls was earning him two to three times what it cost him to employ her.

He could tell that Sally still felt uneasy at the job. But six months later what it had done for business! In three months she had come to know every man in town by his last name, calling each of them Mister This and Mister That. While at first a lot of them came over just to have a chance at seeing Hays' only real lady, they stayed when they found that for the first time since the Hide & Skull had been in business, the nine girls upstairs had on clean dresses, dresses that revealed quite a curve of bosom but also enticingly hid more than flopped out. And their hair, nails and faces were clean and not done up in such garish styles. It became common knowledge that Sally was so up-to-the-minute that she had the doc look at the girls every week, although Moar still wasn't quite sure why the doctor should see a whore so often if she hadn't come down with disease. But he had learned enough about working with people in the last three years to let the most valuable of them do as they pleased.

How Sally made a go of it had impressed the hell out of Moar, as well as how Sally handled herself. Naturally, a fifth of the men who came in wanting a woman wanted her, but she made it clear without hurting their feelings that she wasn't available. Those who couldn't take no for an answer were tossed out by those who admired her and weren't allowed back in. After the first half dozen had been refused admittance, all the problems she had with discipline stopped. Or almost all.

So John Moar had pretty much made up his mind that he wanted Sally Rawls for a wife and partner. All he had to do was bide his time, be a reasonably sweet boss, and make his move when the time was ripe, after she had learned how to take orders from him. If there was one thing he knew he wouldn't be able to abide, it would be a woman who didn't know how to follow instructions.

So Moar waited to bring up the matter of the straying buffalo hunter till he caught Sally after the free lunch crowd had drifted off and before the afternoon card players settled down.

He pulled her into the deserted dining room and asked, "How come we got this hide hunter who ain't paying no freight roaming the third floor?"

John's question startled her. Sally had been occupied with Cora, who thought she was pregnant and didn't want the baby. Sally couldn't believe the practices the woman was prepared to follow to get rid of the child, and she was torn between wanting to save the child's life and wondering what sort of life she was condemning it to if she insisted that Cora have it.

"Who? What?"

When he explained, a lot fell into place for her. Robby's talk about hunting had begun to stir all over again after she thought that the accident had taught him a lesson. It also explained the shine in his eyes and the new toys he was so vague about, toys which Sally had suspected that Nelly had brought him.

"Oh, no!" she said.

"I don't want those fellows wandering around up there, Sally."

"I don't either, John. I'll stop him. I'm sorry."

"Is he a friend of yours?"

"A friend?"

"A beau, maybe?"

"A what!"

"From what I hear from Shorty and Bob, he's been seeing the boy every day for more than a week."

"A week?"

Moar nodded.

Sally didn't know what to say. She had tried to keep Robby separate from this rough world of hunters, guns, whiskey and gambling, but the boy had no father to model himself after, and he turned, naturally enough, to the rough men he saw around him. Her heart sank. What was she to do? "John, I'm sorry. I haven't known a thing about this."

"I've hired you to manage this hotel, Sally," Moar said. "I expect you to know what's going on."

She sighed, hating John's disappointed tone. "Enough, John. I'll stop it. We both agree we don't want casual traffic upstairs."

Her firm tone seemed to soften him. "Good, Sally. Frankly, you have a fine son, and I don't think as a mother you ought to allow every rascal that drifts into town to influence him."

Neither did Sally. She immediately sought out McCall, who wasn't downstairs in the saloon. At the bar, Bob told her McCall would be in tonight about six, for that was when he visited Robby.

"You knew, then?"

"The boy needs folks to talk to, Sally," Bob said. "Jack's all right."

"Just call me when he comes in. I decide who sees my son."

"Hey, no call to snap at me, Sally."

"Just call me, will you?"

"Yes, ma'am."

She caught up with the lanky buffalo hunter that night on the third floor before he could open Robby's door, and she beckoned him away down the hall. He looked somewhat sheepish, as if he had been caught doing something he shouldn't have. He wasn't wearing that ill-fitting wool suit he had worn the first night he had come to the hotel for dinner, but casual buckskins, and he looked as if a few meals had calmed some of the drawn features in his face. He looked kinder and softer than he had that first night, if a bit anxious about what she wanted, but that was all right.

She wanted a bit of privacy in which to talk to him. While her mother wouldn't have approved of a woman meeting with a man in an empty hotel room, she wasn't afraid of him, so she took him into one of the rooms on the third floor.

As for McCall, knowing from his talks with Robby that his mother didn't much approve of buffalo hunters, he had been careful about his visits. He hadn't liked sneaking about to see the boy, so he was just as glad to have it out with Sally.

The bare hotel room felt cool, but through the window the evening light still shone hot and dusty. Seeing her in this quiet room, her blonde hair swept up in a bun, her back straight and a severe look on her face, made McCall's heart jump and his breath hard to draw. An edge of wildness swept through him, as if in this lonely room he might kiss her and unbutton her starched dress and kiss her breasts and throat. But from the way her arms were interlocked across her bosom and her head was thrown back, he didn't have much hope that that was in the cards.

"What is it?"

"You've been seeing my son."

"Yep."

"For more than a week."

He nodded.

"I appreciate your saving my son's life, Mr. McCall," she said, not looking directly at him but over his shoulder, as if something about what she was doing wouldn't allow their eyes to meet. "I appreciate it more than I can ever say." Her tone of voice was so hard that he felt constrained. "He means more to me than my own life. But now that he's safe, I'd appreciate it if you would stop visiting him."

"Stop? Him and me are friends"

"He's just growing up. He doesn't have a father."

"I know. He's lonely."

"We'll be leaving soon for the West."

"I see," said McCall.

"He's going to be a lawyer or a doctor."

"He's a fine boy."

"At his age, he's very impressionable."

Her intentness began to amuse McCall. "He says he wants to be a buffalo hunter."

"Yes, and so you see the position that puts me in."

"No'm, not quite."

"I don't want him to be too beguiled by such occupations as hunting or gambling, Mr. McCall," she said.

"The boy has to make his way in the world, Miz Rawls," said McCall. "Seems to me he ought to learn all he can rather than be cooped up here around the hotel."

"He has to learn his lessons."

"The boy feels cooped up."

"What do you mean by that?"

"Miz Rawls, by luck I happened to save your boy's life," said McCall. "And—"

"And, Mr. McCall, I thank you."

"No, ma'am. I wasn't asking for thanks," he replied. "I've gotten to be friends with your boy over the last week, and it looks to me like it's time he learned how to ride a horse and shoot a gun and go hunting."

"He's going to learn how to use his brains, not skills in killing, Mr. McCall."

McCall sighed in exasperation. "Ma'am, you're making a big mistake."

"He's my son."

"Still, you—"

"I don't like saying this to you, for I'm truely grateful to you, but you leave me little choice. I forbid you to see him." After this burst out of her, she immediately seemed sorry and softened her stance. "No, that's mean of me, if he considers you his friend. But I can't have him influenced by . . . by buffalo hunters."

He heard in her voice everything he knew that farmers, bankers, folks back East and people going West seemed to find in the term buffalo hunter: a species of predatory, tick-infested, blood and dirt-covered buccaneers who would as soon skin a man of his money as a buffalo of his pelt. He had been as good as he could to the boy, and it hurt that she didn't think he would put the boy's welfare first. But in her face he saw a hardness he knew he couldn't crack.

"Me and the boy is friends," he said. "He needs a man to talk to."

"He's my son. I'm sorry. I have to do what's right."

"He needs to feel he's learning what the men around him know, or he's not going to feel right as he grows up."

This made her pause, as if he had wedged a sharp

pick through her weathered hide and touched some sensitive nerve.

"If we were going to stay here in Hays, I'd have to agree with you, Mr. McCall. But just as soon as we have enough money, we're heading for San Francisco. There he'll be raised as a good Christian boy, and not by a gang of drinking, whoring, gambling ruffians!"

With that she swept by him to the door, where she turned back to say, "And from now on, please confine yourself to the bar and dining room, unless you've paid one of the girls to come upstairs. I think you know the house's rules. Do I make myself clear?"

She looked directly at him, her blue eyes blazing with anger and energy, and he dropped his head, finding it hard to meet her cold stare.

"It ain't right, but I don't want to cause trouble. Yes, ma'am, I understand."

As the snow melted in Striking Eagle's camp, the tribe put away their indoor amusements: the moccasin game, the game of sticks and bones, and the bags of staves. It was time to begin their spring activities. The men raced ponies and bet on the results. Boys went out rabbit and squirrel hunting under the leadership of the Rabbit Leader, the man who ran the boys' Rabbit Society. The women urged the men to go hunting for fresh meat, and every day men and youths took to the trails and hills to find deer, elk, buffalo and antelope.

By the time the snows were roaring along the streams, winter-shrunk stomachs had begun to fill, and when the grasses were half a foot high, the whole tribe was in the best of spirits, for spring was always the most playful time for the Kiowa.

Once fresh meat for the tribe had been gathered,

Striking Eagle discussed the situation of the white buffalo hunters with Hoof, Left Hand and other members of the Kanasa, the Denoskin and the Big Bellies, asking that other bands of Kiowa be invited to their councils in order to help fight the enemy. At these larger meetings he asked for support of the entire Kiowa nation in setting up patrols to spot the parties of whites, who would become more numerous in warm weather.

"We must attack every one so they'll learn it's no good for them," said Striking Eagle.

As with most suggestions brought to the council, even those brought by such wise men as Hoof or those as divinely guided as Striking Eagle seemed to be, contention erupted.

"Attacking the white men is only going to arouse the bluecoats," Eagle Beak answered for the peaceful faction. "The white man needs buffalo just as we do. Let him hunt in peace."

Led by Eagle Beak, who seemed to have risen in strength and self-importance as the man married to the woman that Striking Eagle had once favored, many warriors opposed such patrols and the war parties and refused to take part no matter what the Big Bellies decided. Even Hoof, while he believed that Striking Eagle was divinely inspired in what he proposed, was cautious about committing so many of the tribe's warriors to such dangerous activity. The white men had plenty of guns and powder, and while the occasional skirmish didn't alarm them, a concentrated series of attacks such as Striking Eagle had committed at the end of winter and now proposed to continue into the spring was bound to rouse the white man to his full fury of Indian hatred. Rumors had drifted in about entire tribes farther eastward being wiped out by these invaders; did the Kiowa dare push the white ghosts too hard?

They argued for a week, and Striking Eagle was almost ready to give up the struggle, but on successive nights he had two identical dreams, each of which was so close to a repetition of his original vision that he felt *Wakan-Takan* was telling him not to abandon the path that had been given to him. Left Hand agreed with this interpretation, as did Hoof after he had taken a sweat bath, prayed and chanted for a day.

Striking Eagle attended meeting after meeting and used the new powers of persuasion that seemed to have come with his war vision to bring as many leaders and warriors as he could to his side.

For days he slept and lounged around the lodge with his wife and children. Over the past two months of patrol and attacks, he hadn't had much time with his family. Often other chiefs would drop in for a private talk about strategy and plans.

He got along much better now with Onni. They had spent the winter months together in the lodge, where they had had many opportunities to talk. After a particularly painful series of arguments in which each angrily laid out the other's shortcomings, miraculously the love that had brought them together in their youth seemed to have returned. For a month, what passed between them had the tenderness of love that seventeen-year-olds have for each other.

During these months, Striking Eagle saw Elk Woman whenever he felt restless sexually and she could sneak off. Since they had to be so careful, they didn't see each other more than once every three weeks. He felt that last summer and fall, when he had felt so much desire for her, he had been under some wicked spell, and now that the power of the amulet was gone, he controlled his movements with her. He enjoyed her, and from time to time even the waves of passion of the months before returned. What a pity she was married to Eagle Beak! A man could do worse than have a woman like her available all the time. What bothered him about this arrangement was sleeping with another man's wife, and the fact that she was Eagle Beak's, the man who opposed him in council, made it that much worse.

What he found important was leading his people. After all, his people were buffalo people. Almost everything they used in their daily life came from the buffalo: tepees, clothes, cooking utensils, moccasins, sleeping robes, saddles, weapons, and more than half their food. They faced the loss of the buffalo if his visions told him the truth. Where would buffalo people be without buffalo? He had no time for petty quarrels.

Finally the combined council of the Kiowa went along with Striking Eagle's war plans. Six permanent scout patrols of four men each were set up to report directly to Striking Eagle, who was appointed the head war chief of all the Kiowa bands.

The scouts brought word once and twice a week of nearby buffalo hunters attacking the migrating herd, so that Striking Eagle and his band of thirty-five picked warriors no sooner had a couple days of rest than they had to ride back out after white hunters.

Onni found herself happy, although with the dangerous fighting that her husband was doing, she could hardly have said why. She knew the nature of the white men he was fighting, as well as her husband's own propensity to lead the attacks, and one day he might not come back.

Her sister Willow said she was happy because she had won, that Striking Eagle was no longer interested in another woman, and Onni said she supposed Willow was right.

Onni was so happy at this time that her reaction when Willow brought the news about Eagle Beak was rather casual.

"Dead?" Onni asked.

"This morning."

"But how? I saw him last week!"

"No, you didn't. He took to his buffalo robe early last week and has been wasting away the last ten days."

"But he was so young! And he didn't look sickly."

"He's gone. They're burying him this afternoon."

"Didn't they call any shamans?"

"Elk Woman spent ten horses on three."

"Ten!"

"They have a large herd. But none of it worked."

"Well, he may be happier where he's gone," said Onni.

Willow laughed in agreement. "You don't think he'll find a woman down there to run around on him behind his back?"

They roared together with laughter.

Week after week when Striking Eagle came in from his raids with Left Hand and his closest friends, the tribe stayed up most of the night listening to the warriors tell of their exploits, thrilling the boys and making the women who overheard them either roar with laughter at how they had tricked the whites or cry along with the teller as they suffered some Kiowa death in battle.

Onni was proud of her husband and did everything she could think of to make his life easier. She didn't see much of him, but the tension that had existed between her and Lone Wolf over the past two years seemed gone; with the new name of Striking Eagle, a new serenity seemed to come to her lodge. As a family, they had achieved higher status, just below that of the Onde, as a result of his bringing in the white buffalo robe and leading successful raids. She was accorded more deference in women's ceremonies, and Onni found life with such status enjoyable. Maybe things were settled down completely. Maybe he had forgotten that he wanted another wife, and maybe Willow could help her for one more year, which would put off any question of her needing more hands around the lodge.

But when the first moon of April shone across the village, during a week's lull in the fighting, Striking Eagle made an anouncement to her.

"I'm going to take Elk Woman for a second wife, Onni."

"No!"

"Yes."

"But—"

"No buts about it. It's all settled."

"But we went through all this—it's settled the *other* way."

"Eagle Beak's dead. It doesn't befit me to have but one wife now that I'm a Kanasa and lead the tribes."

It hit her like a thunderclap. Of course! She should have seen it before! Elk Woman was free.

That was what had nagged at Onni, but she hadn't realized it when she'd heard. She had only thought in terms of her rival's bad luck, and while saying nothing to Willow, she had rejoiced that her rival now had no provider of meat.

Distraught, she tried to argue with him, cried some, and begged, but in his new life as Striking Eagle, he didn't argue or fight with her as Lone Wolf would have. At times she thought the name change accurately depicted what had happened to him, for close to half the time he didn't seem at all like her old Lone Wolf, but a stranger instead. Partly she liked this, for Striking Eagle was a greater person than Lone Wolf, but in another way he didn't have the same capacity to hear her that Lone Wolf had had. Besides, when he wasn't out fighting, he was off at council and Kanasa meetings almost every night, which she both liked and disliked. She didn't have to worry about pleasing him when he was away at night, and she didn't have to worry that he was in the bushes with another woman. But she missed him. No matter how much she enjoyed the children or her sister, there were times when she just wanted to talk to him, and when he came in to sleep after midnight, if he was interested in anything, it was in making love to her, which she accepted without protest and enjoyed.

Having made his announcement, Striking Eagle simply left the lodge, and she saw that what she wanted had no bearing on him. That demoralized her in itself and reduced her old ability to fight.

As it unfolded over the next few days, a depressed Onni had no choice about Striking Eagle's plans unless she were to leave her husband. This, Willow counseled, wouldn't be looked upon well at this point by anyone in the tribe. If she went back to her father and mother, they wouldn't understand why she had come back. But they would have mourned her behavior as they would have a death, for what other Kiowa man would want a woman who left such a good husband as the tribal leader Striking Eagle, and for no more good reason than he wanted what his lodge needed, a second wife. Her father, as feeble as he was, not only couldn't provide for her or himself and her mother,

Striking Eagle wouldn't bring him the choice cuts of meat he now did. It would be a disaster for her mother and father, and one they couldn't easily forgive.

Willow understood Onni's position fairly well and had remedies. To Willow, the tribal war leader her brother-in-law had turned into had become more and more like the man she longed to marry, and she couldn't understand how her sister couldn't give in to him on anything he wanted. Willow further told Onni she shouldn't worry. By consulting a witch woman or a shaman, she could come up with potions and charms that would keep a husband primarily interested in her rather than in a second or third wife. But Onni was dubious, certain that Elk Woman knew such things far better than she did.

Onni was left with a feeling of intense grief and no one to share it with. She cried whenever she could get away from her children, Willow and friends. No one seemed to care about her feelings. When she received congratulations from other women at the springs for her new sister-wife, inwardly she raged over each congratulation, but she didn't lash out, fearing to make a laughingstock of herself.

The very aloneness of her position after two days of grief seemed to stiffen her. She could depend on no one but herself. She saw she had to assess this situation and figure out how to survive it herself, even if she was practically incapacitated with grief. What Onni knew for certain was that this Elk Woman witch of a woman was no good for Striking Eagle, and that he was too dumb—even if he was Striking Eagle and no longer Lone Wolf—to know it. She had to protect herself and she had to protect him, because he was as much hers as one of their children. She just didn't know how to do it.

However, what shocked Onni to her foundations over

the next few days was what Willow found out about this
new freedom of Elk Woman's. Just before he had died,
Eagle Beak was a still-vigorous man of thirty-five, and
until several weeks before he had been in splendid health.
As an Onde, he had little to do but race horses, gamble
and plan horse raids on other tribes, and for the past
couple of years the Kanasa had not done much raiding.
Then, a few weeks ago, he complained of stomach pains,
and Elk Woman had brought in a shaman. Though the
shaman had given him ground roots and herbs, the pains
persisted and spread to other parts of his body. After that
the progress of the leech within him had been fast. In eight
days Eagle Beak passed from being a solidly build bear of
a man to a thin, frightened child. One afternoon, whimper-
ing with pain, he slipped away to the world below with
hardly a murmur of protest.

A large funeral had been held, and Elk Woman had
grieved by wailing for three days, giving away most of
what she owned and burying everything with him that
Eagle Beak owned, including his *Wakan* bundle.

But now that Striking Eagle wanted to marry the
widow, Onni saw the whole affair differently, and what
she saw made her afraid to say anything to even her
younger sister. She had become certain that her new sister-
wife-to-be had poisoned her old husband. To Onni it was
clear enough: Elk Woman hadn't been able to marry Striking Eagle with Eagle Beak alive and complaining, and
now that Striking Eagle was rising so fast within the tribe,
Elk Woman wanted him badly and had resorted to a
desperate measure to get him. It had worked.

The audacity left Onni gasping. Having such a monster of evil near her family, actually in her lodge helping
with the family's tasks, made her shake. She saw not only

someone coming between her and the man she loved, but a shadow of menace falling over her tepee that would snatch away everything she had, right down to all four of their souls. Her children would be blighted, Onni herself would become sickly, and whatever Striking Eagle had attained by his actions and bravery would be wiped out.

And what followed in her thoughts frightened her still more. Had her husband had something to do with Beak's death? Had the man who lived in their lodge obtained evil *Wakan* for himself? Was this the source of his new power? Was Onni herself next to receive poison from this witch, who would be in a position to drug her food with ease?

Days later, at a distance of a hundred yards and with a feeling of dread, Onni watched Striking Eagle marry Elk Woman. The ceremony was held in the center of the village before the chiefs' tepees. Ordinarily, Onni would have been expected to take part, helping to bind the new family into one unit. But she couldn't.

In some households, the two wives made a single dwelling in which two pairs of hands made light work of the chores; after this ceremony, Onni insisted that two lodges be maintained, and Elk Woman set hers up within thirty feet of Onni's.

At Willow's urging, Onni strove to keep her behavior calm, although inside she raged at what was being done to her. Everything within her felt rigid and stiff. Speaking in what she considered a natural way with almost everyone took enormous effort. She imagined everyone was snickering at her behind her back. She did not want to cook for Striking Eagle, did not want to tan hides or sew tunics and leggings for him, or allow him to creep between her legs. But Willow told her that such behavior was foolish. She would only drive her husband to spend more time with Elk Woman, just what she didn't want.

So Onni bit her tongue, lips and cheeks, and waited on him in a more attentive fashion than she ever had before. While she felt cold and removed at every moment, she remembered to smile. While she wanted to attend only to the children, she forced herself to put aside delicacies for Striking Eagle and to tell him that they would be there whenever he wanted them. He particularly liked roast buffalo hump; she traded for it twice a week so that she always had some for him. For a time, she had continued to call him Cub, her old nickname for Lone Wolf, but she changed now and called him Eagle in order to honor his new status with the tribe. She hated doing this.

As for him, Striking Eagle spent half his nights with her and half with his new wife. Striving to be fair with his time in the fashion of so many men with two tepees, he made sure he switched every night so neither would have cause to complain. Something about this rigorous routine almost cracked Onni's heart anew. Her life with him for most of their ten years hadn't been about keeping score but about loving each other. Up till a year ago, their life had been about listening and talking together. Then something had gone wrong, at about the time Lone Wolf had realized he had a chance of becoming a Kanasa.

She often sighed during the day and felt weepy. At least she had three nights a week to work on the affections of her husband, but she was certain that Elk Woman was figuring the same thing.

Life went on like this for weeks. Striking Eagle won enough battles with the white hunters to keep his war party together, but lost enough to make him fight only when the circumstances told him he had an excellent chance to win.

As May came, Onni thought long and hard about her problem. Life had become more and more unbearable. She felt that Elk Woman was winning the war of the tepees. Eagle spent somewhat more time in Elk Woman's lodge, coming to her earlier on the nights he was to spend there and leaving later in the mornings. From Onni's point of view, he took the best cuts of meat he killed to Elk Woman. But when, unable to hold back her rage, she twice confronted him with her contention, he told her he was sick of her jealousy, that he was struggling to be fair with her, and that if she didn't like what he brought, then she could go out and hunt for it herself.

She cried for two days after each of these confrontations. After the second, she knew she had to do something, but still couldn't think what.

Maybe if Elk Woman could dabble in black magic, she told herself, so could she. The audacity of her thought made her gasp a bit, but it lifted her feelings of grief enough to make her think it had promise. At least she would be doing something. She looked around the lodge for a gift and found a buffalo robe she had decorated last year that she was particularly proud of. It contained more beads and stitches than she normally had the patience to weave into a robe. She selected a large bucket too, one made from the paunch of a good-sized buffalo bull.

She waited till near noon, when it was hot and most people would be sheltered in their tepees or away from the village, and she asked Willow to watch the children.

"Where're you going with that robe?" Willow asked.

"To pick plums."

"We'll all come. That'd be fun."

"No, I want some time alone."

"Alone!" Her sister looked at her strangely. Almost nobody went berry picking alone.

"I want to think things over, sister."

Her sister cocked her head. "And what's the robe for? That's your best one."

"I may need it."

"Hot as it is today?"

Onni couldn't find another answer.

Willow looked at her with an exasperated expression. "Onni, you sure surprise me. I just don't ever understand you."

"Yes. Well, I'm off."

To mislead anyone watching, Onni first went to the spring, and although she wasn't thirsty, she drank water to make her trip there look innocent. Then she headed for the plum bushes to the north. Once she reached them, she spent an hour picking plums till she had the buffalo paunch bucket full.

She reached the tepee she was after an hour later, just before midafternoon. It always stood on the north side of the village, set up here out of sight of the rest of the tribe for so many years that no one remarked any more on such antitribal behavior. Only someone with strong *Wakan* could live in such a way, be it good or evil *Wakan*.

Onni had never before been so close to Granny Fox Face's tepee. To hear talk about the village, no one ever came within a hundred feet of it, for it was said that the air was cold around the tepee in hot weather and hot in the winter, and such power frightened everyone. She crept up on the tent from the rear, looking to see what dangers lurked about it. Standing twenty feet in back of it, Onni paused to regard its old skins and blackened smoke hole. Why would someone with such power live in such a shabby tepee, and why was Onni shivering on such a hot day?

"Come in here, child!" called a high voice from the tepee.

234

Startled, with shaking limbs, Onni walked around to the entrance and leaned down to peer into the dark interior. "How'd you know I was here?"

"Come in," said the voice. "I won't hurt you."

The voice was high-pitched and contemptuous, as if its owner had no interest in making it friendly. Maybe it would be better just to run away, Onni thought.

"No, it wouldn't," said the old woman. "You would just come back another day."

The old woman had heard her thought! Onni straightened and tried to run, but her feet were rooted to the ground. As if in a dream, again and again she willed her feet up. But they wouldn't obey, as if paralyzed by her efforts.

"Come in, child."

Onni leaned down and crawled through the hole into the tepee, which for such a bright day seemed darker than most. In the gloom she saw something that looked like a waist-high pile of skins to the left, and she stared at it, her limbs trembling.

"Sit down, child," said the voice, which came from the skins.

Obeying, Onni sat. Her heart pounded in her chest. She knew Granny Fox Face only by reputation. Even when the tribe moved, you didn't see her, for she kept her face covered with skins and fabric they had gotten years ago from the white men. Rumor had it that she had been badly burnt as a young and beautiful girl in a lover's quarrel and that since then she had lived off by herself. Her cousins and nephews set up her tepee as rapidly as they could when the tribe stopped in one place, and they refused to talk about her, all more or less acknowledging that the old woman had passed from being a mere woman to something akin to the spirits she seemed to live with. Only Old Hoof seemed to get on with her. The gossip was that he came out here to bring her tea, roots and herbs once a week.

"Give me the plums," said the old woman.

Onni could just make out a pale object that might be a wizened face in the pile of robes and fabric. She pushed the plums forward. A thin hand, reminding Onni more of a bundle of twigs than fingers and knuckles, reached out and took a plum, and then several more.

As the old woman ate, nothing appeared to menace Onni, so gradually her heart slowed and she looked around. On the walls grinned faces of animals: fox, wolf, buffalo and owl. They startled her at first. In all, twelve animals' heads were mounted there, as well as one of the white men's hats, a blond white man's scalp, and a blindingly white shirt that obviously had been taken from a white man.

The gathering of so much power in one spot made Onni's heart thud again. No wonder this tepee could defy the heat and the cold!

The old woman belched now that she had eaten a quarter of the plums.

"Give me the robe," she demanded, holding out her hand.

Onni pushed over the robe she had brought as a gift, frightened of the old woman's ability to read her mind.

Granny Fox Face first rubbed her hand all over the robe and then held it up to within six inches of her face, and she seemed to peer at a little over half the robe before she was satisfied.

"You did this decoration, didn't you?" the old woman asked.

"Yes, gran."

"But you don't do much of getting your own way, do you?" she asked, and cackled a long high laugh that confused Onni and sent a shiver up her back.

"And you want your husband back?"

"Yes, gran."

For what seemed like a long time, the old woman only regarded her silently. Onni didn't know what to do. Feeling uncomfortable, wishing she could gracefully get out of here, she noticed how loud the sounds of the insects were around her—flies, wasps, and the hum of bees.

"And you think your sister-wife killed her husband?"

"She did," said Onni. "He died too fast. She used some medicine she got from somebody—"

She cut herself off abruptly. Oh, no! Suppose she had gotten the death power from Granny Fox Face herself! Onni sat frozen. She would never leave here.

"No, she didn't get any powers from me," said Granny Fox Face. "I can't see where she got them, or if she did."

"Will you help me?"

"Tell me what you want."

"I want my husband for myself."

The old woman cackled again. "That I won't do. A woman has to learn to keep her own husband, or she isn't a woman."

Onni sighed. She had wasted her best robe and a whole bucket of plums that her sister and children would have enjoyed.

"But I will help you find out if your sister-wife killed her husband."

"You will! Did she? Didn't she?"

"Easy, daughter," said the old woman. "We have to

237

find out. Such secrets are deeply buried, and it takes work to dig them out."

So Granny Fox Face told her that if she wanted to find out what had happened between Elk Woman and Eagle Beak, she had to be the legs and hands for what Granny needed.

After a moment's reflection, Onni agreed.

"Good," screeched the old woman. She got right down to what Onni was to bring back to her: snippets of Elk Woman's hair, bundles of sage and sweetgrass, five hollow dried gourds, and six items that had belonged to the dead man, particularly his grandmother bundle, the little pouch that had contained all his *Wakan* objects.

The hair and Eagle Beak's grandmother bundle made her shiver. Onni said, "But everything of his was put with him on the hill."

"Go get them."

"No," said Onni. "I couldn't approach a dead man. Especially not to rob him." Again a shiver passed through her. "He would strangle me for robbing him."

Granny Fox Face passed her a stuffed rabbit's skin. It felt to Onni like it was full of hard twigs and stones. "Don't open that, child," the old woman said. "No matter what happens. You'll die in a whirlwind if you do."

"Yes, gran."

"Carry it with you when you go to get the six things from this foolish Onde and his spirit won't hurt you."

"Yes, gran."

"Go now."

"Yes, gran."

"And remember, don't look into that bundle, no matter what."

So Onni left and over the next few days did what she

was told to by Granny Fox Face. She felt better for doing something about her situation. The day she sneaked away from camp, she was surprised to find that even approaching Eagle Beak's burial place didn't frighten her so much with Granny's bundle thrust out before her to push away the evil spirits. A demon composed of the face of a wolf, the body of an elk and the tail of a bobcat struggled to snatch her away, but as long as she kept the bundle between it and her, it wouldn't approach closer than ten feet. Terrified, she continued on.

The place stunk of the evilness of the dead, but so much had been buried with such a rich aristocrat that she had no trouble getting the six personal items Granny wanted. Eagle Beak had begun to come apart as if he had never been more than a rotten piece of meat that was not entirely spoiled. She had to grit her teeth to pick up the man's medicine bundle, but it was worth it, for when Granny saw it, she proclaimed that Onni had done very well.

Over the following ten days, Onni brought the old woman many more items, as well as more gifts and food. Several times Willow asked her what was going on, but Onni had the sense to keep silent and put her sister off.

Finally one noon, Granny Fox Face declared that she was sure now. "I see great evil around the dead man, and also around this sister-wife of yours, daughter."

"She killed him!"

"She certainly could have. The kind of power she's using is found only at night, and thus you can't see it."

"I want to catch her. She should be expelled from the tribe, maybe killed, for what she did."

"If she did it, yes. But that's hard to show clearly, daughter. Hard and dangerous."

"I want my husband back from this witch. I don't want my children or myself to be poisoned by her."

For a long time the old woman didn't answer, which had happened frequently enough not to alarm Onni. She waited patiently. Finally Granny said, "I am too old to leave this tepee, and too old to practice many of the things that need to be done."

"I'll do them."

"I've tried to tell you, it'll be hard and dangerous."

Onni hesitated. She had been around the old woman enough to know that she meant what she said. Like every man and woman she knew, she spent plenty of time getting out of the way of spirits, good and evil, that might hurt her, the way a sparrow gets out of the way of your feet no matter what your intentions are toward him. Over the last two weeks Onni had observed many powers of spirits, and more than ever she recognized they were nothing to trifle with.

"But if I don't, such evil will destroy me," said Onni.

"Yes, child. I can see that clearly. But recognize that what you employ to aid you may damage you or one of your children."

"Yes, Granny."

"And recognize as well that you will have to show her up in some way that's clear to others, for she's now the wife of a Kanasa and a man destined to become a Big Belly."

"Yes, gran."

"She has his protection, and some of Old Hoof's, which could deflect your efforts backwards and maybe hurt you."

"But I have to! How can my children, my husband, and even I live in the shadow of a murderer?"

"Let's see what we can do," said Granny Fox Face. "Bring me her tanning knife."

"Her tanning knife?"

"Yes."

"How will I get it out of her bundles without her seeing me?"

The old woman laughed one of her high cackles. "I don't know, child. But go get it if you want me to help you!"

Chapter 8

Over the week following Sally's order that he not see Robert, McCall rose at midmorning, had a few shots of rye to clear his head, went to the Drum for the stand-up free lunch, drank four or five beers, and sat in on a poker game, during which he lost a bit more than he gained. This was unusual for him, as he played a solid game.

Except for that first night, when he bought a bottle from Bob at the Hide & Skull, he hadn't set foot in the hotel. He ate and drank at the Drum, watching his last hundred dollars dwindle.

Before that meeting with her, he had asked a dozen owners of hunting rigs if he could hunt with them, and they had for the most part given him noncommittal answers. This week he didn't even ask anyone for a position. He felt discouraged and useless, something new for a man who had lived on his own hook all his life. When he wasn't playing cards, he sat around listless at the Drum, occasionally getting up in the middle of the afternoon to walk to the window, where he would look up the street at the Hide & Skull, sigh, and sit back down.

He didn't seem to care that he lost at cards, unusual for a man who could keep himself in pocket money from the sloppy way most buffalo hunters played. He started drinking seriously at dusk, and while he never got knee-walking drunk, he had a glow on till he fell into bed at midnight. This week he didn't shave, and if there was one thing McCall had always done before, it was shave twice to three times a week. He had no energy to do anything, felt as low as a buffalo chip and couldn't figure out what was going on.

If he was listless about getting attached to a hunt or grooming himself, he wasn't about what went on within earshot. The first week he had come back to Hays, he had taken some good-natured ribbing about nursing the wolf cub who had bitten him, a reference to Lone Wolf. But during this week he fought and beat the hell out of three men who ragged him. In fact, you couldn't bring up hardly a thing around Jack McCall these days that wasn't likely to end in a fight. He was as surly as a wounded bear, and the best thing to do was to leave the son of a bitch alone. Which was just as well with McCall; he didn't want company. He told himself he didn't want anything, much less to spend an hour a day with the boy with the broken leg and his momma, but that thought would only make him uneasy and he would put it out of his mind.

Monday night, alone at his own table, he was sitting around the Drum nursing his bottle of rye when Nelly came in.

In his state, he didn't want to see even her. The sassiest of the whores from the Hide & Skull, she was the only one of them who would come into the Drum. The others were afraid of John Moar's displeasure at consorting with the competition. He remembered that she came over to the Drum on her night off. Frequently she took a table by herself, and over the course of the evening a clot of hunters would gather there. She would match them drink

for drink, and the party would get louder and more raucous. A full-figured woman with frizzly red hair, Nelly
looked most of the time as if she had just finished or was
about to begin making love to a man—which most of the
time was true.

For a long time that night McCall watched her from
his table. Mentally, he stripped her naked and made wild
love to her, then dressed her and sat her down and talked
to her, and then he wondered how come women were so
different from men.

He saw that after an hour of staring at her, she had
begun to notice it. But in his angry mood, he kept it up.

By eleven o'clock, half his bottle of rye was gone and
the party around Nelly had grown to a dozen men. She
talked about McCall's stares to the others. The men only
made polite winks and nods in acknowledgment, for McCall
had whupped too many fellows who had made fun of him
over the last week.

At midnight, Nelly rose and said, "I'm going over to
see what the son of a bitch wants."

A bit tipsy, holding her almost-empty glass in her
hand, she paraded across the room to McCall's table and
sat down.

"You want something, Jack?" she asked.

"I got something on my mind, yeah."

"Well, I always told you, you want the best, come to
Nelly. I'll show you a hell of a time."

"Remember what I said the other day?" asked McCall.
"How much do you charge for a consultation?"

"A what?"

"To talk."

"Talk? I don't talk, I just show a man a good time,"
she said. "I told you that when you asked before."

"Don't you want to make a few bits?"

"Aw, Jack, you always been too good for us girls across the street. Don't make fun of me."

She asked him for a drink, filled her glass from his bottle, then weaved her way back to her own table.

McCall watched closely, but no one laughed upon her return. That disappointed him, for he would have welcomed whipping the first one who laughed at her report of their conversation. Maybe Nelly hadn't said anything.

The next night he cleaned himself up for the first time in ten days, shaving and putting on his fanciest duds, which didn't fit any better now than they had a couple of weeks ago. McCall had come up with a plan.

That night he ate the twenty-five-cent dinner at the Hide & Skull, and then he eased into the bar. He saw Sally, and she saw him. All she gave him was a cool nod, which he returned along with a slight smile. The sight of her made his heart beat fast, and his breath grew shallow. God, she was a beautiful woman! Tonight she wore her hair up, as usual, and around her neck was a black band that set off her graceful pale neck. McCall wanted to get up and hug her, but he didn't dare move.

Like he had figured, Tuesday night was a bit slow. After things had thinned out near midnight and Sally had disappeared into the back to do whatever you did in running the place, McCall made his move. He went across the room and sat next to Nelly, who was sitting on the lap of an old codger who wasn't about to spend any fifty cents on her.

"Hey, Jack. Here you are again. Want a good time?" she asked, giving him a big smile.

"You free, Nelly?"

"Don't tell me this is my big chance?"

He grinned at her in what felt like a parody of hot lust. "Let's go."

"Well, glory be! Never thought I'd see the day when Jack McCall wanted me."

"Let's be quick," he said, afraid Sally would see them.

"In a hurry?" Nelly said, and cackled. She told the old Codger, "Gotta take a customer, Sam. Wait for me."

On the third floor Nelly knocked at a door, got a sharp shout from within, shrugged, and moved on down the dark hall.

When she found an empty room, she entered. It contained a bed, a chair, and a dresser on which stood a kerosene lamp.

"Money first, McCall. Six bits."

"Six bits!"

"Hey, don't you want a good time?"

"No, I told you last night what I wanted."

"You got the advantage of me, Jack. I don't remember much of last night. You quiet ones always got something special in mind."

In the yellow light thrown by the lantern he stared at her. He saw paint on her lips, powder smeared on her cheeks, and on her eyelashes clumps of black soot. She stood with one hand on her hip and the other outstretched for money, her voluminous breasts as usual struggling to pop out of her dress, as if too eager for play to be restrained. He sighed and pulled out his pocketbook and paid her.

"I just want to talk, Nelly."

"Talk! You come up here to talk?"

"Yeah."

"And paid me?"

"Yeah."

"You could have talked for free downstairs."

"I gotta ask you something. Private."

247

Nelly eased herself down on the bed and peered at him curiously. "What's this?"

"I got a problem."

"Yeah?"

"I want to get married."

"You what?"

He gritted his teeth and repeated himself.

"You do!"

She looked amused. "Who you fixing to ask?"

"That's what I wanted to ask you about."

The way she looked at him made him squirm. This wasn't going to work. He saw that. He had just had a damn fool notion. But he had paid. If he knew Nelly, he would never see his money again, so he might as well ask and get his money's worth.

"Married," he echoed. "To Miz Rawls."

Nelly first stared at him in astonishment, then hooted, her voice ending its laugh with a couple of screeches.

"She don't want to marry you, though."

"Damn it, I know that, Nelly."

"She ain't no buffalo you just shoot down, McCall."

"I come here and paid you to ask about it," said McCall. He wanted to bust her sassy lips and mocking eyes, but he had enough sense to know he would get in a lot of trouble with Sally and John Moar over that. He rose to leave. "You can keep the money."

"Hey, wait a minute," said Nelly, pulling herself together. "Sit down. I laughed too fast."

"I didn't come up here to be made fun of."

"Yeah, I know, and you paid me and all."

She looked as if she might laugh again. Feeling still more foolish, McCall just stared at her.

"Sit down, Jack. Maybe I can help you."

"Naw, I done made a damn fool of myself. Good-bye."

He opened the door and stepped out into the hall. Nelly caught up with him and said, "Here. Keep your money. But come in and talk."

He looked at the money, then at her serious face, then down the shadowy hall of the hotel's third floor. The lanterns threw ominous shadows into the corners and up from the stairwell. I'd rather be out in the middle of the plains than here, he thought. In a lot of ways, folks were more treacherous than a bunch of buffalo or a pack of wolves.

"Come on," she said, pulling him by the sleeve back into the room and slamming the door. He eased himself into the straight chair and looked at her. The paint on her face seemed more ridiculous, and she looked sadder and older. "You and every man in Hays, I guess, wants to marry her."

"She's mighty pretty, Nelly. Nothing against you, of course."

Nelly set her mouth into a hard line. "I know what she is. Every man in this town been wanting her since the day she got here. I'm sick to death of hearing how pretty she is."

Unsure of how to answer, McCall just nodded.

"She ain't interested in none of y'all, you know," said Nelly, looking at McCall with an expression of shrewdness.

"Of who all?"

"Of anybody in this town—or any other, for that matter," she said. "She done gave her heart to a dead man, and her soul to getting to California."

This confused McCall, and he said so.

"She's pining for that dead husband of hers, Jack,

249

that's what," said Nelly. "I ought to be mad at her, but she ain't the kind it's easy to get mad at."

"You? What for?"

"In fact, maybe you and me ought to team up," said Nelly.

"Team up?" asked McCall, more confused than ever. "What're you trying to say?"

"That's how come I give you your money back." She giggled. "I ain't never done that before, but I guess there's a first time for every whore. Before she come here, John had tried all us girls. He liked me the best." She gave McCall a smug look. "Course, he told some of the other girls the same thing, but he was telling me the truth."

"John? Mr. Moar?"

"Yeah. He's smart, Jack. Real smart. He's got more money in one bank back in Philadelphia than you and I will touch in our whole lifetimes."

"Yeah?"

"He didn't want me no more when she dropped into Hays," she said. "All he wanted was her."

The news made McCall's heart sink. "Aw, hell."

"That's what I felt too. But he ain't had no luck with her, Jack."

"None? You mean he ain't—" He stopped, unable to say it.

"Naw, every man comes into the Hide & Skull to go with a gal wants her, but she ain't been with a one of them, that I know of, including John Moar, worse luck."

"Worse luck!" said McCall, half rising from his chair. "Don't you say—" With both hands he grabbed her by her shoulders and pulled her forward.

"Calm down! I'm sorry," said Nelly. "It's just that,

if he had, he would have realized that looking like an angel don't mean you can buck like a nanny goat."

"Now I told you, Nelly, you ain't to talk about her like that."

"All right, all right," she said. Now she leaned forward. "But how'd you like it if we was to team up? You to get her, and leave the field clear for me to get him?"

All this was making McCall's head spin a bit, as if he had drunk his whiskey a bit too fast and needed to slow down.

"I'd like it, but ain't no chance of pulling that off."

"You want her, don't you?"

"Yeah, I really do."

"Then you got to go after her."

"But she don't want me. I look like a buffalo chip to her."

"Them buffalo don't want to be shot either, Jack, but you go get them, don't you?"

"That's different."

"No it ain't," she said. "If you want her, you got to go after her. That's all."

"You'll help me?"

"I done said I would."

"What do I have to do?"

"We'll take it step by step. First, though, we got to get you some clothes."

He looked down, puzzled. "What's wrong with these?" he asked. "I paid ten dollars for this suit."

"If you was teaching somebody how to shoot and they missed the buffalo, you'd tell them what they was doing wrong, wouldn't you?"

"Hell, they could see if they hit him or not."

"Not if they was blind."

251

"I ain't blind."

"Like hell you ain't. You don't wear no greasy yellow tie with a red shirt, and put on a pair of green pants to go with a brown coat."

He looked down at his clothes. "Why not?"

He didn't like the look or the sigh of exasperation she gave him. "You want to learn some of this or not? Look at John Moar. How does he dress?"

"Like a half-dead undertaker."

"Naw, he looks like a gent. Dressed quiet. White shirt, black suit, neat black tie and all."

He considered this. "Well, I didn't think it would be easy when I come to hire you. Sounds like this is going to cost me some money."

Nelly grinned. "Congratulations, McCall! You just done learned your first big lesson in courting a woman."

It put a spring in McCall's step, courting did, although he hadn't imagined how much was involved in it.

The first thing Nelly insisted that he do was buy himself some new clothes. Armed with a list from Nelly, he purchased two white shirts, a black string bow tie, a pearl-grey hat, and a light grey gaberdine suit, which he had Lang, the Chinese cook, take in for him. Then he bought a new pair of boots. He followed Nelly's instructions to the letter about keeping these new duds neat and clean.

"Think of them like you would your Sharps rifle," she instructed. "You don't let no mud get up your barrel, do you?"

"No sir."

"Well, then, you don't let no mud or dust stay on your courting clothes. It's just as important."

This didn't make a lot of sense to McCall, but she

252

had taken their arrangement more seriously than he had ever figured she would, so he felt bound to do what she said. The new clothes used up fifty dollars of his last seventy, and now he had to really scrounge for more money.

Luckily, George Malone came back into town with a big load of hides, and since he hadn't heard about McCall's foolish kindness to Indians, he advanced McCall one hundred dollars for a spell of working.

Under Nelly's supervision McCall bought two dozen lemon sour balls from Herbert's General Store, wrapped them up in some fancy tissue paper that Nelly produced, and sent them to Sally with a poem that Nelly wrote out for him.

Only in the sky, where the clouds float by,
Can I find a dream like you.
Only in heaven, where the angels sing,
Can I find an angel like you.

"Now sign it, *Your secret admirer*," said Nelly.

"What for?" McCall asked. "I paid fifteen cents for them sour balls and I want her to know it."

" 'Cause you want to make her wonder who it is."

"I can just tell her."

"It don't work as good that way."

"This is crazy, Nelly."

"Trust me, Jack. I don't tell you how to shoot buffalo."

"I'm tired of hearing that."

"Have your ways worked?"

To that he had no answer.

As well, he had to ride out into the plains and pick bunches of yellow and violet flowers. He sent the flowers over to the Hide & Skull, again with the sentiments that

Nelly wrote out for him. He got the black laundress who lived in back of Drum's to make him a dozen pralines from brown sugar and pecans. These were boxed up fancily and sent over. He wore his new suit whenever he went into the bar there, and as Nelly told him, he tipped his hat in a grave manner. He was also careful not to get drunk, for Nelly had told him that if he wanted to get drunk, he was to do it over at the Drum.

When he had been courting his Indian bride, the process had been simple. He had offered her father, Two Feather, four horses. Two Feather, no fool, told him to take the girl right then and there. They had set out that night for his camp, and the whole thing had not involved any fuss or bother. Of course, sometimes Indian weddings could be elaborate, but Two Feather didn't live close to any of the big Comanche tribes, so he could make a deal without having to go through many formal procedures.

McCall took some ribbing from the fellows in Mike's bunkhouse about his new clothes and his habit of bathing twice a week, for Mike wasn't used to anybody wanting to bathe on Wednesday *and* on the weekend. But Nelly insisted on it.

When George Malone mentioned he was going out for a short hunt, it was with relief that McCall contemplated changing back into his hunting duds to go out with him. Malone had received word that a herd was moving through just twenty miles outside of town. In the saddle, with his Sharps in the scabbard at his side, his slicker and bedroll tied on behind him, McCall figured he would once more feel at peace. He had never realized how difficult courting was. Even now, after ten days of notes and gifts, Nelly wouldn't let him tell Sally that it was him. He couldn't figure it out. Sure, you didn't get too close to a buffalo herd when you wanted to bring down a few, but sooner or later you had to shoot, or you wouldn't get a hide.

No sooner had Nelly heard that he was going out with Malone than she said, "All right, Jack, This is it."

"This is what?"

"This is when you tell her it's you."

He sighed. "I do, huh?"

"Yep. Will Mike lend you his buckboard?"

"His buckboard? I guess so. What for?"

" 'Cause you want to ask her to go for a ride."

"A ride? Where to?"

"No where to. Just a ride."

"She don't want to ride with me," he complained. "We ain't even told her I gave her that stuff. She acted like I was a buffalo chip when she did talk with me. Now I'm supposed to ask her to go for a ride and she's just going to say yes?"

"You do it my way and she will."

So he tried it Nelly's way, but it didn't make sense. He went over to the business office where Sally could be found on Wednesday mornings at ten o'clock and asked for her.

When Sally appeared, she looked him over in a strange way. "You've changed, haven't you?"

"I got me some new duds," McCall said. He felt peculiar, a little bit like this wasn't him, but he saw respect in her eyes. "I got tired of wearing my hunting clothes around town."

"The suit looks nice."

"Did you get the pralines?"

She grinned. "That was you, huh?"

"Yes'm."

"And the flowers too?"

"Yes'm."

255

She laughed outright then, and her blue eyes seemed so merry and made him so dizzy that he almost forgot what he had come for.

"Thank you," she said. "Thank you very much."

"I was wondering if you wanted to go for a ride."

"A ride?"

"Yes'm."

"Don't call me ma'am," she said. "Where? In what?"

"I got the use of Mike's buckboard."

"I couldn't go alone, Mr. McCall."

"Don't call me mister," he said, trying to adopt the same tone she had used. "My name's Jack."

As she considered this pensively, he continued, "You can bring your boy and girl if you want."

"A ride," she said. "With Robby and Eva. We haven't had a ride—just a ride—in months." She waved her hand about, indicating the town and the saloon. "Trapped here."

"It's waiting right outside."

"A ride? Will we be safe?"

"We won't go more'n five miles out, and I'm supposed to be pretty good with a Sharps."

To his surprise, Sally accepted. She called her children, and they bustled around making preparations to leave. By now Robert could hobble around on his crutch. Eva, her girl, who stayed upstairs where McCall hadn't seen her much but who was so delicate and pretty that he found himself watching her nearly as much as he did her mother, came along too.

As they left town, McCall concentrated on his driving as his three passengers delighted in getting away from the fetid air that emanated from the town's buffalo sheds. They enjoyed the breeze made by the movement of the buckboard.

They started the ride in awkward silence, not only shy around one another but also feeling strange under the glances of those in the streets. They imagined the towns-people were questioning where they were going at eleven o'clock on a Wednesday morning in the direction of Dodge in an open buckboard. After all, Dodge was two hundred miles away.

But once they cleared the last shack and bunkhouse of Hays, and the glory of a May morning on the plains unfolded across the gentle hills, they began to chatter. McCall pointed out signs of animals and hunters that he saw on the ground. He told them stories of hunts. Soon the children were caught up in his tales. Along with Sally, they asked him questions about his adventures.

It seemed that almost before they had gotten started, they were back in town again. Nelly had insisted that he leave them hungry for more.

"I'd enjoy taking you folks out again," McCall told them when they arrived back at the hotel. "I got to go on a little hunt the next few days, but right after I come back, we can go again, if you'd enjoy it."

"Yes, yes!" Robby's shouts of glee were so loud that his mother shushed him with a good-natured hug in an effort to quiet him down.

Sally asked, "And when will you come back, Mr. McCall?"

"Call me Jack."

"Jack."

"Quick. Four or five days."

"I think we'd all love it."

The two children chimed in again how much they would, and he answered, a bit amazed at how well the morning had gone, "Yes, ma'am, we'll go just as soon as I get back here. You can count on it."

"No ma'ams to me," she said with a smile, opening a dimple on her cheek so wide that McCall thought he might fall into it. "Call me Sally."

"I'll hurry back, Sally."

Over the next day, as he prepared for the hunt, he hummed and sang. He didn't want to leave Hays now, yet he was close to broke. But look what I have to come back to, he told himself. He said nothing to the fellows in the bunkhouse, but he wanted to shout, I got a chance with her!

He tried not to show it, but whenever he was in Horsemann's office, Bertram Moar, the brother of Hays City's biggest trader, felt intimidated, as he did this cheery May morning. The large envelope in his coat pocket rustled in a menacing way, as if its wad of bank notes might jump down his throat and choke him.

Bertram Moar saw that, as usual, Horsemann eyed him the way a hawk eyes a mouse. Horsmann waited for his own secretary to withdraw before coming around the massive desk to lock the office door behind Moar.

While the office was a large, expansive room, done in rich wood and buffalo hides and looking out over a green courtyard away from the bustle of Fifth Avenue, Moar still never felt at ease in it. Andrew Justice Horsmann was interested in only one thing, and that one thing rustled and crackled in Moar's pocket.

A short, fleshy man with a shrewd face, Horsmann asked expectantly, "Well?"

"Yes, sir," Moar replied quickly, reaching into his pocket for the bulky envelope to hand it to the railroad magnate.

With a smile, the pudgy Horsmann left him standing, sat behind his desk, leaned back expansively in the high-backed chair and tore open the envelope. His thick fingers swiftly began counting the clump of fifty-dollar notes.

The two Moars shipped all their hides along the Kansas Pacific Railroad, of which Horsmann was president and chief stockholder. A close relationship with Horsmann had been important to their business success, and Bertram was the one who dealt with their man in New York. As a result, not only did their hides often reach the market before their competitors, but their arrangements with him enabled them to beat their competitors' prices while giving Horsmann an opportunity to escape a number of federal and Kansas hide tariffs. After all, what wasn't recorded on paper proved difficult to tax.

While John Moar, Moar & Moar's agent in Hays City, was small and compact, almost a bantam of a man, Bertram struck most who met him as horselike. He had a horse's long, mournful face and big sad eyes, and a hank of straight black hair fell across his forehead. His large, fleshy lips gnawed constantly on a plug of tobacco.

"It all here?" Horsmann asked, halfway through his count.

"Yes, sir."

"I wouldn't want your count and my men's to be off."

"No sir, Moar & Moar wouldn't either," said Bertram Moar. "We're very grateful for the arrangement."

"Hmmm." Horsmann continued to count the money and pull on his cigar. "Sit down, Moar, and have a cigar."

Moar looked at the large humidor on the railroad magnate's desk as if he had been asked to pat a rabid dog. Horsmann made him nervous. All he wanted to do was leave.

"No, thank you, sir."

Horsmann stuffed the money into his jacket pocket. "Nonsense, Moar, take a load off and have a cigar." He pushed the container over.

Feeling he had no choice, and knowing from long dealings with Horsmann that such cordiality meant he wanted something, Moar grinned nervously, sat, and took a cigar. Most of the time, he merely brought the money in, stood while it was counted, and was dismissed. He liked that way much better.

"I want some hides, Moar," said Horsmann after he had relit his cigar.

"Hides? Of course, sir," said Moar, relieved. "How many?"

"About fifty to seventy-five. My wife wants to redo my study at home."

Moar looked around at the walls of Horsmann's office, which were covered in the brown leather of the finest buffalo. "They look good, don't they? We'll be happy to send you some. No charge."

Horsmann beamed with warm pleasure. "A man after my own heart, Moar. My wife and I thank you. There's just one thing, though."

"Sir?"

"My wife wants them in white."

"White?"

"From the white buffalo."

"White? There aren't that many, sir."

"She saw one last year at a fair."

"I haven't seen but maybe two myself in the last three years."

Horsmann seemed hardly to have heard Bertram. Moar knew this was the railroad president's usual air whenever he didn't get his way. Bertram had never found it extraordinary that Horsmann owned as many miles of tracks, hotels, farms, and buildings in New York as he did; the magnate approached every negotiation with him as if he should come out with more than the next fellow.

"She wants white, Moar."

"From what my brother tells me, the Indians take the whites, sir, before our men ever come on them." Bertram Moar expelled a pent-up breath as he saw Horsmann's expression harden. He wasn't getting anywhere by refusing Horsmann. "Well, I'll see what I can do, sir," he allowed.

"Billy Bry was in to see me last week," said Horsmann, referring to the Moars' chief competitor out of Dodge City. The Moars nearly always beat Bry on price because of their arrangement with Horsmann.

Alarmed, Moar sat up still straighter. "Billy Bry?"

"He says he can get me all the whites I want."

"Hasn't our arrangement worked out all right?"

"I'm pleased," said Horsmann. "But Billy says he can get me those hides with no trouble."

"You can't believe everything Billy Bry says, Mr. H."

"Maybe so, but Mrs. H. wants the damn things mightly strongly, Moar."

"Yes sir." Bertram thought rapidly, particularly considering that without this arrangement with Horsmann, the profitability of Moar & Moar would be cut nearly in half. Maybe worse than half if they lost the British markets to Bry, who hadn't been able to deliver to the port at anything close to the brothers' prices. And everybody said a downturn was coming in the hide business; no industry could keep booming forever in hard times. The world just wasn't made that way.

Moar got rid of his plug so he could speak more

articulately. "Well, I never said we couldn't, just that they're difficult to find."

"I've tried arguing with the little woman, Moar, but she says the house just won't look right without the hides in that room."

"Yes sir."

" A man has to keep the peace at home."

"Yes sir, he sure does," Bertram answered, trying to smile.

Horsmann gave the beleaguered look of men everywhere saddled with slightly dotty wives. Somehow Moar didn't believe Horsmann was at the mercy of any woman, but he wasn't about to call Horsmann a liar.

Moar knew enough about his brother's problems to know that finding a dozen white buffalo hides was hard, and that gathering fifty to seventy-five was nearly impossible. Not wanting to make a promise his firm couldn't keep, but seeing no way out of it, he swallowed and mumbled something about getting his brother right on it.

"And I'm going to pay you for them," Horsmann said. "Most of which I expect you to pass on to the hunters."

"Yes sir."

"Five hundred dollars each."

Stunned by the figure, Moar could only stare at him. He was lucky to get ten dollars for a single flint hide. He had heard that you could get five hundred dollars for a white, but you saw so few of them that there just wasn't any real market for them. They were more of a curiosity than an item.

Horsmann continued, "You'll do it, won't you? Pass most of it on to the hunters without taking out a big slice?"

Bertram Moar felt pushed into a corner and saw the

issue as a way of possibly squeaking out of responsibility.
"Tell you what. Moar & Moar won't take any cut at all."

Horsmann beamed in moon-faced satisfaction. "Not a dollar?"

"No sir. Give the men more incentive."

"I like that, Moar."

"Thank you, sir."

"I like that. I have to make a trip out your brother's way in about three months, Moar. How about asking him to have them for my arrival?"

"Trip? You? Out West?"

"Yes. It's a secret, sir, but we're going to expand the railroad in Kansas, and I want to plan the routes myself. Could be we'll take one on west right through Hays City."

"My God!"

"Yes."

"Through Hays!"

Horsmann boomed with laughter. "And if I decide to, what you two brothers own will be worth a lot more than it is now, won't it?"

"Yes sir! A damn sight more."

"You'll keep it quiet?"

Bertram had to laugh at the ridiculousness of the request. "Of course."

"I may even get you to do a little private investing for me."

Dizzy with the prospects, Bertram Moar rose. "Yes sir, we'd be pleased to help you any way we can."

Horsmann rose to let him out. Grinning broadly, he said, "So see that you don't let my wife down, will you? For such a sweet little lady, she has one hell of a temper."

"No sir, we won't let her down."

Chapter 9

"Eva!" shouted Sally Rawls from the open door.

Her thirteen-year-old daughter looked up guiltily, her face covered with streaks of rouge and a layer of white powder. Next to her sat Nelly, in Sally's opinion the loudest and lewdest of the upstairs girls. Nelly had obviously been teaching her angel how to apply all these enticements of Satan.

"What's that all over your face?" Sally demanded.

By Eva's side, Nelly made a grimace. "Don't scold the child, Sally," Nelly said. "It's my fault. We were playing."

"Get those marks of the devil off your face, Eva!" ordered Sally.

"It's just color, Momma," Eva said.

"A woman doesn't need paint if she's clean, Eva."

"Oh, Momma!"

"You get those colors of the devil off your face or you don't leave your room for a week, hear me?"

"Do what your momma tells you," said Nelly.

"All right, Momma," her daughter said. But the way she moved the rag over her face caused the rouge to streak, making her look to Sally more like a painted Indian than a child.

265

Had Sally not been so angry at the two of them, she might have laughed at her child's streaked face. But to Sally, what was happening to the impressionable Eva in this den of loose women was no laughing matter. The only playmates the thirteen-year-old Eva had were Cora and Nelly and Abby; much as Sally might not want her to be around these upstairs girls, there wasn't anyone else for her to play with. Her daughter couldn't sit in her room forever looking out the window and sighing over her sewing. While Robby's wish to hunt was bad enough, his soul didn't seem at stake the way Eva's did. Robby disappointed her, but she could understand his infatuation with buffalo hunters; Eva's bewitchment by the "good times" of the upstairs girls seemed more the damning mark of Satan. She had lost her daughter's confidence in the recent months since Dave's death. It was this town, Sally guessed. But not disposed to blame the town for all her ills, she had struggled over the last two months to make a better relationship with Eva, without much success.

Sally desperately wanted Eva in school and learning to sew and bake at home. Around the Hide & Skull, such lessons were almost impossible for Sally to give. She was busy from daybreak to midnight making sure the hotel ran properly and that the help didn't steal the place blind.

Eva couldn't get the paint off, and Sally sent Nelly to get hot water, alcohol and soap. Eva started crying and angrily shouted that her mother hated her, that she never had any fun and she didn't want to stay in this awful town another minute. If she had had a real mother, she said, they would have been in California by now.

Then Eva put her face in her hands and heaved loud sobs, some of which looked real, many of which looked theatrical. Sally figured that to some extent she was being thrown off the scent, so she kept her heart hardened, which wasn't easy. She didn't spend the time with Eva or Robert that she felt she should. Oh, Dave, where are you! she cried inside. How could things have come to this? Sally felt at her wit's end.

"Come here, sweetheart," she said to Eva, stretching out her arms to hug her.

Eva came to her and hugged her.

"I'm sorry, Momma."

Finally she took Eva in her arms, disregarding the smears of rouge and mascara that got on her clothes. She held her closely against her till Nelly returned, and this comforted Eva.

She cleaned Eva up and stole an hour from checking the bar's cash box so they could spend some time alone in the room they shared.

The worries spilled out of Eva: how much she missed her father, how much she hated Hays City, how lonely she was, how much she wanted other girls her age to play with, and how much she wanted her mother to love her.

"But I do love you!"

"You don't. You make me stay in my room all the time."

"But you know what this place is like."

"Of course I do. I'm not virginal."

The word caught Sally like a blow. "You're not *what*?"

"Virginal. You know. Don't look so surprised."

Holding visions in check of Eva in bed with rough buffalo hunters, Sally cautiously asked, "What do you mean?"

"I mean I'm not virginal. I already know what goes on upstairs."

"You know?"

"Yes, you might as well talk to me about it."

"What do you know?"

"I know the men go up there and lay down with the girls—Abby, Nelly, Cora and them."

"Yes, that's true. What else do you know?"

"What else is there to know?"

Such sassiness exasperated Sally, but she had to know it all. "Is that what you mean by not being virginal?"

"Yes, of course."

"Where'd you get the phrase?"

"From Cora. She said I was, but I'm not."

"How do you know?"

"Because I know what they do in bed. It's the same as I can see in the corral from the back window that the stallions do to the mares."

"That's not for you to stare at!"

"Except they don't seem to have colts. I mean Cora and Nelly don't seem to have babies even though they go up every night with so many stallions."

"Oh, Eva, Eva! I don't want you talking this way."

"But Cora says it's all the same thing—horses or men. Is she right?"

"They aren't quite the same as we are," Sally said. "You'll understand when you're older."

"Mother—you don't think I'd do what they do, do you?" Eva asked, suddenly looking shocked. "The horses or Cora?"

"No, but they aren't the best influence."

"Mother! How could you think such a thing!"

"I don't think it," Sally answered her, "but I do think you're old enough to work on a large crochet quilt."

While Eva was more interested in her mother's opinion of the women upstairs than in learning to crochet, Sally insisted that she try needlework. The devil was quick to find work for idle hands, and a crochet quilt was something she could measure every day and would keep Eva busy for months.

While Eva started working on the quilt from the yarn from her sewing box, Sally sat by their window to instruct her. Once again she puzzled over how to get out of the hell she had fallen into.

It had been a mistake, Sally told herself, to give in to McCall's invitations and go on drives with him. They had gone out on four rides.

She had been surprised at the change in the buffalo hunter. True, spring had been in the air, yellow and blue flowers appeared from her ''secret admirer'' every other day exciting her curiosity, and then came the candy all wrapped up in the fancy box. At the same time Sally *had* noticed how McCall looked handsome in his new grey suit when he had shaved and wasn't wearing that awful red and green outfit that he thought was so good-looking and was actually ludicrous.

Robert would be off his crutches soon, and he had made it clear through dozens of hints that he thought he was old enough for McCall to teach him how to ride and shoot. Oh, why can't I get them all out of here? Sally wondered. She had two hundred seventy-five dollars saved up from her pay—working at the hotel meant that her family's room and board were taken care of—but she needed nearly a thousand dollars for fares and expenses to travel to California. She sighed, thinking it just wasn't fair. It would take another two to three years saving up the money. By then, Robert would be a buffalo hunter and her daughter would be—she could hardly think the word, much less say it—a budding whore.

The next day, Sally asked Nelly not to allow her daughter to play with her rouges and powders, but Nelly argued with her.

"She wants to learn these things, Sally," Nelly maintained.

"She doesn't need them, Nelly."

"Ain't a woman made don't need to learn to look her best."

"She looks just fine."

"She'll want to get married one day."

"I managed without a jot of powder or a streak of paint."

"She ain't living in a church, you know."

"And I'm the one raising her, Nelly. Please."

"All right, she's yours," said Nelly. "But you ought to realize that little girl knows more about what goes on around here than I think *you* do."

"What does that mean?"

"Just that she keeps her eyes and ears open. Your son may not have figured it out, but she knows what the fellows pay for, and which of them's not too much trouble and which of them's a pain in the rear end."

"And how does she know this?"

"Well, think about it. She hears the girls talk, Sally. How else?"

"I've asked you to mind your manners around the children."

"And I think we all do, Sally. Don't none of us want to put the wrong ideas in the children's heads, but they're like children everywhere. They know what keyholes and chinks in the walls are."

"Nelly!"

"Wasn't you ever a child?"

Sally didn't know how to answer. It brought her back to the same dilemma she'd had from the first moment she had been approached by John Moar.

She could refuse his job and do what? Take in laundry and remain in Hays City the rest of her life? Or live in a tent on the outskirts of town with only herself to look after Eva and Robert? Instead, she chose to live and work at the hotel, where she could save her money and keep an eye on the children. But she hadn't counted on their lively curiosity about what went on here. Twice she had chased Robby away from keyholes. How many times had he spent the afternoon near one? she wondered. From the very first week, Eva had loved to sit with the upstairs girls in front of their mirrors and play with their pots of paint, powders, wigs, corsets, laces and fans.

She had thought she had done the right thing for her family in taking John Moar's offer, hard as it had been. But now she wasn't sure.

Some of Robby's resurging interest in hunting buffalo had come from their buckboard rides with Jack McCall. Where that was going, she didn't know. Nowhere, she surmised. Much as she had come to enjoy the quiet man's company, she wasn't interested in marrying a buffalo hunter and settling down in Hays City, no matter how successful he was. No more than she was interested in marrying a buffalo trader named John Moar and settling down in Hays City.

Sally couldn't help but smile, though, at Moar's reaction to her and the children taking a few wagon rides with Jack McCall. Suddenly, from being a distant employer, he had become friendly in a new way. She wasn't sure where he had gotten it, but John had hunted up an almost-new buckboard, and he insisted that if she wanted to go riding, she go with him too. For six months she had not traveled more than two hundred feet from the Hide & Skull. Now, every day she and one or both of the children were driven out into the countryside by either Jack or John. Sometimes she enjoyed their competing for her. She also enjoyed the change in scenery. True, it was a harsh landscape, but it had been made by God and looked a sight better than the hastily thrown together Hays City.

If only they could just keep riding one time, all the way to San Francisco!

Like every other buffalo man on his first visit to the Hide & Skull, Sally had started off having to teach John Moar who she was. In the beginning, he had assumed that she would be his in the same way that Nelly and Cora belonged to him and the other men of the town. But she had made sure that he knew the answer was a firm no. Since then, on that score, she had had no trouble with him.

But from time to time John did look at her in that odd way men do when they want a woman sexually, in that predatory fashion she hated. Sally was well aware that at twenty-eight she was highly attractive to men, particularly in a town that contained no more than nine women, all upstairs girls. Despite her strict ideas of how a proper woman should act, she was also shrewd enough to know that what beauty and attractiveness she had would be gone by her early thirties, and that it was this attractiveness that was a woman's primary means of attracting a husband. Over the past months, she had become enough of a realist to see that the four or five years of youth and bloom she had left should be spent carefully if she wanted to marry a man who'd support her and the children and bring her solid companionship for the rest of her years. Four or five years wasn't a lot of time when you were stuck on the plains with nothing but the dregs of frontier life. She had seen only six men over the past months who had enough money and were gentle enough for her. Three of them weren't interested, and of the three others, the two who did ask her to marry them had no wish to leave buffalo country. Sally wasn't being proud; she just knew herself.

Marrying and remaining here would be like taking a willow and putting it in the desert: she would wither and die.

To her surprise, she found that once McCall relaxed with her, she liked him quite a lot. She gathered that at first her reserve had put him off. The buffalo hunter had that same steadiness her husband Dave had had, that same way of looking at the world from slow, sardonic eyes that knew the vainness of men. McCall might not be a man of the cloth, like Dave, but he spent much of his life out on the plains. He looked on the ways of Hays men with a bit of the same eye as Dave: as if their ways were an aberration compared with how God had ordered nature and His creatures. Still, McCall played cards and drank, which she disapproved of, although her disapproval had worn down under the constant barrage of sin at the Hide & Skull.

Moar had surprised her recently. On top of taking her out for buggy rides, he had asked her to join him in his office almost every day over coffee to talk over how the hotel was doing. This was a strange departure for the man who'd told her when she started that he didn't want to know anything about the hotel, that that was why he was paying her eighty-five dollars a month—so he didn't have to learn anything about it. Of course, he had never kept to that—John constantly meddled with everything he owned—but Sally expected a man who owned so much to have ideas about how his businesses should be run, and she said little unless he stepped on her toes.

Calm now, Eva crocheted quietly by the other window. Granted, while Sally watched, she sat like an angel and demurely stitched. But get her around Nelly and Cora, and you'd think she was training to be a painted imp of Satan. Sally sighed. What was she to do?

She had told Robby several days ago that he should

get it out of his head that he was going to become Jack McCall's protégé.

"I thought you liked him, Momma," Robby had said.

"I do, son. But you're too young to be shooting and riding."

"No, I'm not. Jack says he learned when he was nine."

"His momma was different."

"He didn't have a momma. She was dead."

Though he hadn't said it, she thought she could hear in her son's voice a hidden wish that she were dead. He had moped for two days thereafter, till finally she scolded him about it. Then, while he tried to raise his spirits when she was around, Sally saw he had dropped some of his spunkiness, which wasn't what she wanted, not at all.

Was she doing the right thing? After all, what did she know about raising boys? A father would know, but Dave wasn't here. Many times, what Dave had decided had surprised her. That was the point of having two sexes, Dave had often said, so a family could see things from the different points of view that the good Lord intended.

"Come pray with Momma, Eva."

Her daughter turned the face of an angel up from her crocheting and blinked eyes so quick and vividly blue they startled Sally. "I'm truely sorry, Momma."

"Come, child."

Sally eased herself forward onto her knees. Following her mother's example, Eva rose and walked in a sedate manner to her mother's side and lowered herself. When they were both kneeling, Eva took her mother's hand.

"It won't happen again, Momma."

"Pray, child. Let me hear the Lord's Prayer."

As Eva stumbled through it, Sally cried. Surely the

Lord God wouldn't send her more hardship than she could handle, she thought. If this way was hard, then there must be some lesson God wanted her to learn.

But she felt so isolated!

Was God telling her, through Robert and Eva, that the time had come for her to put away her grief over Dave and take a new husband for herself and a father for them?

Possibly, John Moar would marry her. But she couldn't bear living in Hays City with John or any other man, as much as she had begun to feel warmth toward both John and Jack McCall.

Perplexed and confused, in a welter of conflicting, painful feelings, Sally struggled to concentrate on the Twenty-third Psalm, which Eva had slipped into.

In the crowded Drum Saloon, early afternoon was wearing into night. Jack McCall wanted out of the poker game, but he couldn't bring himself to leave.

He had seen from the beginning that the game this afternoon wasn't going to run his way after he had caught two low pairs, drew a card, and missed. A.C. Logan beat him both times with three deuces.

McCall felt weary. For the last two hours he hadn't caught any cards and his stack of chips had steadily dwindled. He kept telling himself to get out of the game, that it wasn't going to get any better, but he knew he would feel worse sitting around drinking. At least while he was playing, his mind was off what bothered him more than anything else these days: getting enough of a stake together to buy another buffalo hunting rig. Last trip out he had just barely made enough to pay off his debts to Malone, Mike and Bob. With a wagon and gear, maybe he could make enough money over three or four months to ask Sally to marry him. It all looked so far away, though. It was like stalking a deer that was five miles away. You might catch up on him, but by the time you figured out where he was and got there, the deer was likely off somewhere else. And you didn't know what would happen. Last time he had made that foolish mistake with the Indian. Maybe he just wasn't cut out to own his own business.

Riding into town from his last hunt, McCall had been shocked to see Sally and her children riding out past him in a buckboard with John Moar. The children had laughed and waved, and with all the grace he could muster, he had smiled and waved back. He had felt like running and pulling that arrogant blond bantam out of the driver's seat, beating him around the head and taking his place in the buggy, but he held himself in check. Malone and the crew had teased him the rest of the way in, saying that Moar was beating his time while he was out chasing buffalo rump. McCall had had to hold on to his saddle pommell to keep himself from knocking a couple of those grinning idiots off their horses.

That was the first time, and it seemed they went riding with Moar any time he didn't take them out. Who was going to ride the widow out today had become something the boys were betting on, which irritated McCall too. A lot seemed to irritate him these days, and he was tired of it.

"Ho! Ho!" came a shout. McCall shook himself out of his reverie to see the pot being pulled in by A.C. Logan, whose cigar was stuck in his mouth at a jaunty angle.

"Asleep at the switch, huh, McCall!" Logan shouted. "Pretty soon I'm gonna have your whole pile. Ante up, gents."

His mind a swirl, McCall put in the two bit ante. He had to pay attention. His stomach churned. He longed for a glass of whiskey, but he knew better than to drink and play. Distracted as he was by Sally, his play was bad enough; whiskey made it worse. He wouldn't stop drinking till he fell over tonight, and he didn't want another morning like the last three, when for an hour after he woke up he wished for death rather than the continued pain of his hangover. God knew what the Drum served for rye whiskey, or how many rats, toads, rusty horseshoes and buffalo livers went into making it, but hell, could it lay you out.

"Hey, Jack," came a voice to the side of McCall, and he turned to see sitting next to him the shiny dome of Skinner Kincade.

He and Skinner had spent little time in each other's company since they had come back from their defeat at the hands of Lone Wolf. McCall had heard the stories that Skinner had spread around town, stories that he was such an Indian lover it was dangerous to have him on a hunt. Those stories had made it difficult for McCall to get his last two berths.

"What the hell do you want?" asked McCall.

"Hey, McCall, the bet's to you. In this or not?" carped Logan. "Put in four bits if you are."

"Mr. Moar wants to see you," said Skinner.

"Me?" asked McCall. "What for?"

"Just said he wants to see you. Might have a job."

"Jack, put your goddamn dollar in if you're in this, damn it," said Logan.

McCall had an impulse to take his ante out of the pot as he rose to leave the game, but he knew that would start an argument. "Catch you fellows later. Where is he, Skinner?"

"In his office over at the hotel."

Wordlessly, McCall and Skinner crossed the dusty

street toward the Hide & Skull. McCall wondered what this was all about. He had taken Sally out for a buckboard ride this morning. Did Moar want to talk about their rivalry? Like many hide hunters, McCall felt both admiration and dislike of Moar. He paid low but fair prices for hides, and he paid cash on the spot. He seemed too young for such huge success, and while he didn't brag about it, his entire manner swaggered with his own cleverness and self-regard. What the hell did the upstart rooster want?

While John Moar spent more of his day down at the bustling hide office at the sheds, he had his private office next to his living suite on the second floor of the Hide & Skull, which was where Skinner and McCall went. When they were in the office, Skinner was about to turn and leave, but Moar called for him to stay.

McCall looked around. He had sold hides to Moar, but he had never been in the trader's office, for he did most of his trading down at the sheds. Out of his element, the room made him uneasy. A horsehair sofa sat sedately along one wall, the wallpaper was flocked a bright red, lace curtains rustled in the slight breeze, and the pigeon-holes in Moar's well-oiled roll-top were crammed with the slips of paper that marked an educated man.

Moar turned around in the rolling chair and pushed away from the desk. McCall saw him in a new light tonight; what struck him was the trader's youth and confidence. Moar didn't look older than thirty. His thin, hard eyes didn't blink as he stared at you. McCall hadn't paid that much attention to the man before Moar had started taking Sally out for wagon rides; what he saw in this room was money, lots of money, and money he didn't have. If this man wanted to buy Sally presents from back East, he could. If he wanted to buy her a house, he could. If he wanted to send Eva to school or Robert to study law, he could. McCall couldn't do any of these things. This bantam with the stuck-out chest was going to buy Sally just as it appeared that he bought everything else in Hays. That made McCall still more uneasy.

"Can you find white buffalo, McCall?" Moar asked.

"White buffalo?" McCall was startled by the subject.

"Like I hear from Skinner here that y'all came across last time you were out."

"Whites?" McCall asked, still thrown by the subject. "Yeah, maybe. Why?"

"I got an order from a customer back East for some," said Moar. "You willing to go after them?"

McCall felt more than uneasy now, almost cramped by this pushy fellow. He said, "They ain't all that easy to find."

"That's why I'm asking you. I hear you find buffalo better than anybody in Hays."

McCall grinned and shook his head to throw off the flattery. "No sir, I wouldn't say that."

"Better even than the redskins. That you been doing it all your life."

"Well, I have."

"That you know the movements of all the herds."

"More or less. They don't stick to the old trails like they used to, though. Too many hunters and Sharps rifles the past three years."

"I want seventy-five of them, McCall."

"Seventy-five whites! There ain't that many white buffalo on the whole continent."

"That's not what Skinner here tells me," said Moar.

"Jack, what're you talking about?" Skinner asked. "Back in the winter there, we seen dozens of them. Could have been fifty or a hundred in that herd almost run us down."

279

"We'd never find that one herd again," said McCall.

"Not even at two hundred fifty dollars a pelt?" asked Moar.

"Two hundred and fifty dollars!" McCall exclaimed. Skinner whistled in pleasure.

"Fellow back East wants a load of them, special-like."

"You got the wrong fellow," said McCall. "Get yourself somebody else to get them." He turned to leave.

"Hold on, McCall," said Moar. "You bring in just fifty, and I'm talking about paying you some twelve thousand dollars for them hides."

The figure stopped McCall. "That's a lot of money."

"Damn right."

"But there are several problems," said McCall. "One, I ain't got no rig. Two, I doubt I can find that one exact herd. I'm telling you the herds don't move right these days. And three, I don't want to take them all, which is what you're talking about. I wouldn't feel right about that."

"McCall, that's a bunch of nonsense," said Skinner.

As McCall turned to him, Moar said, "Skinner, shut up."

The tension eased. Moar continued, "I'll be glad to outfit you. I'm not asking you to find that exact herd, just one with enough whites, and you're supposed to be the best man in Kansas for that. And I'm not asking you to shoot them all, just enough for my buyer."

McCall felt tempted. Taking Moar up on his offer could cut a year or two off the time it would take him to get his own rig, which was where the profits were in this business. Shooting for other men's outfits didn't get you rich. And what Moar was offering him was a way to make one hunt give him the profits of five, an offer he found hard to resist—provided he found the elusive whites. He had strong doubts about locating them.

"You want fifty hides," said McCall. "I didn't count that whole herd, but taking that many would kill off just about all the whites."

"Then take thirty to forty," said Moar. "He'll have to take what you can get."

"I don't know," said McCall. "I'm mighty tempted, but I don't feel right about it. I think you ought to get somebody else. Skinner here looks pretty eager to go."

"Not by myself," said Skinner.

"Why not?" McCall asked.

"I couldn't never find that herd."

"No, you couldn't."

"I want to go with you, Jack," said Skinner. "I seen them before, and I want bygones to be bygones and have a whack at them with you."

McCall shook his head. "I've had enough of you, Skinner."

"Aw, come on, Jack. You know I was just funning you."

"Some fun! First you try to rob me."

"We had a misunderstanding."

"Then we get back to town and you spread a lot of lies around about me, making it hard for me to get work."

"Well, you got work now and I want him to go," said Moar, interrupting the quarrel. "I hear he's a first-class skinner. I don't mind paying for a rig, but I want somebody I can count on to look after it while you're out on the stand. He comes or it's no deal."

McCall felt torn. He had enough Indian in him to value the white buffalo as the spirit of life itself on the plains, and enough buffalo hunter in him to want to make the most fabulous load that had ever been made, as well as enough money to move on west. Maybe if he just took twenty to thirty of the hides and some brown hides at the same time, he could swing out of Hays.

"You drive a hard bargain, Moar," said McCall. "I need the money or I wouldn't take you up on it. But I'm not taking more than a third to a half of that herd."

"Aw, come on, McCall," grumbled Moar. "If I'm financing this jaunt, I want all the whites I can get once you're there."

"No sir. Get yourself another shooter."

"Half, then," said Moar. "Say six out of ten."

"No sir. I just won't."

Moar sighed and said, "You're not only the only man who can find them, but I know you won't tear them up with a lot of wild shooting, too, McCall. You drive a hard bargain, but all right."

"Another thing," McCall said. "That two hundred fifty dollars is my cut for finding them and shooting them clean. Skinner and the other fellows who haul and skin them get paid separate."

"Come on, McCall," said Moar, looking angry. "Nobody works that way. You pay them out of your share."

"That's my deal," said McCall. "I don't know that I really want this job anyway."

"So how much for them?" asked Moar.

"It's up to them," McCall said, turning to Skinner.

"These hides have to be skinned special," said Skinner. "By hand. No snatching the skin off with a horse."

"And I want you to lay them out nice and make sure they don't get ripped or turn sour," said Moar.

"How about twenty-five dollars apiece and you pay for the grub?" Skinner suggested. "I'll hire my own crew out of that."

"Fifteen and you got yourself a deal," said Moar.

"Twenty," said Skinner.

"Done and done," said Moar. "But skin them careful. I'm paying for careful, and I'm telling both of you here and now, I ain't paying a dime for sloppy. This is not your usual order for flint hides."

"For that kind of money I'll skin them buffalo with my teeth," Skinner grinned.

"One other thing," said McCall. "Everything but whites that I shoot belongs to me."

"What? Oh, all right, provided I get first crack at buying," Moar laughed. "You always bring back the best, McCall. You know I like to buy your hides."

"But you don't like to pay much for them, Mr. Moar."

"You'll get market price, and cash on the barrelhead," said Moar. He cracked his face into that strained boyish grin of his. "I've always found that cash goes a lot further than the script the big combines hand over."

"If you like it the way I outlined it, Mr. Moar, I'm ready to leave in a day or so."

"You drive as hard a bargain as I've had driven, McCall, but you're on. Draw up a list of what you need and I'll arrange it so you can draw it from the store. Skinner, line up the best you can find, but check with me before you finally hire them on."

While he showed no dissatisfaction to McCall or Skinner, John Moar was indeed unhappy with the deal he had arranged.

For an hour or so afterward, he sat at his roll-top desk, looked out the window at the dusty street and brooded over this damn Jack McCall, a scraggy buffalo hunter he and his brother could buy and sell fifty or a hundred times over. But they needed him to find this herd. John Moar knew about Jack McCall. Not only could he find buffalo when nobody else could find one for two hundred miles around Hays, but he shot them cleanly and made sure his men skinned them carefully. The man brought back real merchandise in a time when many amateur shooters brought back hides that were ripped, with half a dozen gashes in them. Ripped hides might be fine for gloves and shoes, but terrible for putting on the wall the way his brother said Horsmann intended.

McCall's arrogance and ungratefulness for this offer burned up Moar too. The man was just a scraggly buffalo hunter! For this kind of money, Moar was entitled to all the white hides on the Kansas and Texas plains.

Besides, this was the damn outlaw who had the gall to take his hostess out on buckboard rides, the little lady he had his eye on for marriage. He had been carefully biding his time, letting her see what life without his support as a husband would be like, before asking her to marry him. He had counted on her natural delicacy, one of her finer qualities, to keep her away from any of Hays City's rough lovers, and up to now, that had worked fine. She had fancy ideas of going on to San Francisco, but she would give them up when she realized how much John Moar could give her. She would find that being Mrs. John Moar of Hays City was worth a great deal more than running some dumb boarding house in San Francisco and struggling to make ends meet. All he needed to prove it to her was to let life grind her down here a bit more. Then she would be grateful for what only *he* could give.

Moar reached into the bottom drawer and took out a bottle of bonded bourbon. After stewing about McCall for another hour or so over a few shots, Moar sent word down to Bob at the bar to send Skinner up to see him the next time he came in.

* * *

Skinner appeared that night about eleven o'clock after knocking on the office door.

"You want to see me, Mr. Moar?"

"Come in, Mr. Kincade."

Skinner grinned a bit bashfully and said, "You don't have to 'mister' me, Mr. Moar. Everybody calls me Skinner. It's this head of mine."

Moar smiled as Skinner swept off his sombrero to reveal a perfectly smooth pate. The man's name fit him all right. Not a hair sprouted on his head, out of his ears, from his nose, or over his eyes, giving his face a moonish cast.

"Hairless, huh?" Moar grinned.

Skinner beamed. "That's the truth, sir. The good Lord made me smooth as a billiard ball."

"You going to do me a good job on this trip?"

"Yes sir, I plan to. I done already lined me up three fellows to go."

"How you going to pay them?"

The man looked so sly that Moar had to laugh as Skinner answered, "Well, that's my business, ain't it?"

Skinner thought he was keeping a secret. Obviously, he would make a handsome profit on the men's wages. "It sure is!" said Moar. "Just as long as I get good skins, you get paid." Now he would give this billiard ball a bit of his own medicine. "But just remember that your deal with me is to give me first-class hides. You may have to pay them for hides that I refuse."

"You're going to get first-class hides, Mr. Moar. That's what you're paying for and that's what you're going to get."

"We understand each other," said Moar. "How would you like to earn an extra twenty-five dollars a hide?"

"Sir?"

"Twenty-five dollars extra for every hide McCall brings in." Moar knew his man. He watched Skinner lick his smooth, fat lips hungrily.

"How's that?" Skinner asked.

"McCall doesn't want to bring back enough hides for me, Skinner."

Skinner gave him another sly look. "He can be peculiar, Mr. Moar."

"If you made sure that you fellows brought back, say, seventy-five to one hundred of those hides, you could earn yourself up to an extra twenty-five hundred—all for yourself."

"Just to bring back more of them white hides?"

"That's it. On top of the two hundred and fifty dollars somebody's going to get for shooting them."

"Somebody? You got me just a little confused, Mr. Moar," said Skinner. "McCall's getting the two hundred fifty dollars but he ain't going to shoot more'n twenty to forty, if I know Jack."

Pretty sure that he had his man hooked, Moar asked, "Do I have to spell it out for you, Skinner? If he don't shoot but twenty, and you and your fellows—once he's found the herd—bring back another fifty, why you get the two hundred and fifty dollars on them fifty you shot and an extra twenty-five on the whole seventy that your outfit brings in. Call it a performance bonus—but paid, let's say, only if you fellows bring in a total of fifty whites."

Skinner whistled. "That's all right! Course, we may not see any."

"All I'm saying is, don't let Mr. McCall's foolish notions keep you fellows from earning good money."

"He may refuse to let us shoot," said Skinner. "I

286

know Jack. No matter what we say to him, he can be stubborn as the meanest jackass.''

''And just how's he going to stop you fellows from shooting all you want?''

A dark cloud seemed to pass over Skinner's moon face. ''He's as stubborn as the devil when he gets his mind made up, Mr. Moar.''

''One man's going to stop the four of you?''

Skinner looked down in embarrassment. ''I guess not.''

''Don't let him buffalo you then.''

''Hell, if it comes to that, Mr. Moar, when Jack McCall finds them whites, we'll tie him up if he won't let us make our load.''

''At least one of you fellows ought to fire a Sharps pretty good, right?''

''Oh, yes sir. I do. And you're talking real money here.''

''Well, that's what I thought I was talking about with Jack McCall. I'm glad *you* see it that way.''

McCall was kept busy over the next two days. He sat down with Skinner and made a list of what the five of them would need: four of the new Sharps Big Fifties, fifty pounds of lead, two kegs of powder, two hundred pounds of beans, three sacks of flour, twenty pounds of saltback, half a dozen canteens, two water kegs, a dozen blankets, eight mules, four horses, harnesses for them all, two covered wagons, twenty knives and a grindstone to sharpen them, ten pounds of coffee—Moar cut it to five—one hundred feet of trace chain, three hundred feet of rope, and ten quarts of whiskey—Moar cut that to five too, but McCall and Skinner made it back up out of their own pockets—a Dutch oven, tin plates and cups, a cast-iron frying pan, and a big coffee pot.

As always before he set out, McCall felt excited. Finding a herd was no longer a challenge to him, but this hunt was something special. He had been watching herds longer than just about any white man in Kansas, long before the wholesale slaughter of buffalo started, and he had a better idea of the old paths of the large herds than anyone. He had seen the herd that contained the large herd of whites three times before, and he had heard of sightings from half a dozen different Indian scouts and an occasional white hunter over the years, enough to give him an idea of the usual trails that this herd took. Now that it was late spring, McCall figured they should be about midterritory, heading north for the summer to escape the Texas heat, and that if they hadn't been too spooked by other buffalo herds crossing them in places where they shouldn't, or by other hunters, he could predict within twenty miles where they should be moving. A lot of it had to do with luck. A herd could start north two weeks early because it had been a mild winter and a warm spring, in which case you missed that herd entirely if you were a week behind them.

Seventy-five hundred dollars! The words and figures swirled through him like drums and fifes playing marching music. That would be enough! Enough to ask Sally to marry him. Enough to take her and the children to where she wanted, to San Francisco. Enough for him to buy some land and horses and start his own breeding farm. McCall had had enough of Kansas and buffalo hunting and slaughter. McCall was sick to death of buffalo hides, buffalo hunters, buffalo drunks, buffalo towns, buffalo steaks, buffalo stinks, buffalo guns, and everything else associated with the hunting of buffalo. After fifteen years of killing, he wanted the chance to lay down his rifle. And thousands of others were ready to pick it up. He didn't like to have to shoot the whites to get away, but if he had to shoot a few in order to move on, he would. The most exciting thing about this hunt was that it would be his last.

Having put his order in to Moar's General Store for supplies, McCall hunted up Nelly for some advice.

He found her that evening at the bar of the Hide & Skull.

"Hey, don't you look happy!" said Nelly. "She say yes?"

"Come upstairs, beautiful?" he asked.

"Hmmm, finally getting romantic, McCall?" she asked.

"Gotta talk."

"We'll go into the dining room," she said. "Sally might spot us going upstairs. Your lady friend might get the wrong idea."

"All right."

They sat in the empty dining room. McCall stared at her for a few moments before asking, "What'd you do to yourself?"

"Nothing," said Nelly with a shy smile.

"You look different."

"You noticed?"

"Yeah. That dress isn't so low-cut. You don't have so much red paint and that powder on."

Nelly laughed loudly, then reined herself in and leaned over to whisper, "I figure if it works for her, it might work for me."

McCall shook his head. "I don't know, Nelly. Somehow you ladies are still different."

"Well, I'm trying something new," she said. "I want him, Jack. I want him real bad."

"Moar?"

"Yeah."

"You're better off without him. He doesn't think of anybody but himself."

"I know that, but I want him. He's got all that money, and it might as well be me to help him spend it as the next gal. Besides, I can see it, he's going to want to get out of this sand pit one of these years, and I don't see any other way of my getting out of here."

"I aim to quit hunting after this time out, Nelly," he said. "I want her to come with me to California."

"Hey, that's great," said Nelly. "If you can get her to leave with you, it'll leave me a clear field. I can take over her spot here at the hotel."

"But I got a problem."

"What?"

"I don't know what to say to her to make her say yes."

"What's been going on between you two?"

"Well, I done like you told me."

"Yes?"

"And you saw me take her out in the buckboard."

"And I saw John take her out in the buggy."

"Yeah," said McCall. "He's interested in her too, right?"

"I told you that."

"Yeah," said McCall. "I can't blame him."

"Just ask her, McCall. You know as well as me she wants out of this dustbox."

McCall squirmed. "But what do I say? She'll laugh at me."

"Naw."

"She will."

"Naw, she won't."

"I can't just say I got enough money, come off with me and marry me."

"Yes, you can—long as you put some sugar on it."

"Sugar? That's what I don't know about."

"You just tell her you done done right well and want to marry her and help her raise her kids."

"What's she going to say?"

"I can't tell you that."

"But she might just laugh at me."

Looking irritated at McCall, Nelly asked, "So what?"

"I just thought there might be some way of asking where she wouldn't laugh at me."

"McCall, you don't know a damn thing about women, do you?"

"If I did, I wouldn't come in here and ask for help, now would I?"

"For a big guy, I can't for the life of me see what scares you about this."

"I ain't scared!"

"Yes, you are."

"I ain't."

"You are. You're like a boy scared to get up on his first horse—afraid it'll throw him."

McCall got a sinking feeling. He'd been bluffing himself. "All right, maybe I am."

"Hey, that's all right, Jack."

"Naw, it ain't. I'm the wrong man for her if I can't even ask her."

"Is that what you'd tell the young feller who was too scared to get on his first horse?"

"Naw," said McCall. "I'd tell him to get on and try, and take his fall if he had to."

"I'm telling you the same thing."

"This is different."

"Nope, same thing."

"Is it?"

"Yep. Either you got the guts to go after what you want and take a fall if that's in the cards, or you ain't."

"I haven't thought of it that way."

"And soon as you get her out of the way, I'm going to move in on Johnny so fast he ain't going to know what struck him."

McCall grinned at her intensity. "He's what you want, huh?"

"Damn right. I done let that man play around long enough. Now I got to land him."

"He sure don't look like the settling down type, Nelly."

She looked at him with hooded, shrewd eyes. "He don't know what he is till I get through with him, McCall. I ain't making my mistake again. He'll never know what hit him, and he's going to love it."

"Good luck."

"I don't aim on needing luck."

"Alone?" Sally asked. "I can't go for a ride alone with you."

"Just to the end of town and back, then," said McCall.

Sally thought it over. McCall was dressed up in his pearl-grey suit with the white shirt and the black string tie, and with his grey felt hat and black boots he looked downright handsome. She put aside the stirrings she felt for him, the impulses to have him hold her and make love to her. She had felt such stirrings for Dave, but even though he had been her husband, she had felt ashamed of them. A preacher's wife shouldn't let such feelings run wild through her; they were more fitting for one of the black slaves or Indians dancing around a fire than a God-fearing woman who wanted to raise her family the right way.

"Let's just go for a walk," she replied.

"Fine."

"But not toward the sheds. It smells everywhere in Hays, but particularly bad there."

So they walked in the opposite direction. She could think of nothing to say, and McCall didn't seem talkative. For a while they said nothing in an awkward silence, then McCall asked how things were around the hotel. But she had the sense that he was just asking to be asking something. She told him some of the daily gossip, and then the conversation dried up.

Silently they walked on till they reached the last shacks and tents of Hays. Clumps of card players sat on wooden boxes and men bent over kettles and stood over tubs as they washed their clothes. The buffalo hunters who lived in these tents looked up curiously as they passed, making Sally feel somewhat embarrassed. Who knows what they were thinking. How sick she was of the buffalo hunter's barely concealed lust!

And whatever McCall wanted, this walk didn't feel right. It felt awkward, the way it had at first, when he had hardly known what to say. By their third wagon ride he had become—for him—almost talkative, pointing out rocks and plants and Indian signs to Robby and flowers to Eva.

"Let's turn back, Jack," Sally said at the edge of the shacks.

"Yes, ma'am."

"Yes, *ma'am*?" she queried. "As bad as that?"

He looked sheepish. "I forgot."

"You haven't called me ma'am in weeks. What's this all about?"

"Nothing. Say, ain't that Shorty Hanrahan over yonder?"

"Jack McCall, what did you drag me out here for?"

"Wasn't nothing," he said, looking still more embarrassed and stiff.

"Something's on your mind."

"No, it's not."

"Yes, it is," she said. "Spit it out."

"I was just wanting to be with you a little before I went out."

"Oh? Where're you going?"

"A hunt. I might not be back for two, three weeks. Could be even a month."

"I'll miss you," she said. She felt disappointed at his explanation, and wondered why. She searched herself, then gasped at what she saw. She had hoped this lanky man was going to ask her to marry him! No, she said to herself, I'm not marrying a buffalo hunter. I'm getting out of Hays City if it's the last thing I do.

What amazed her, though, was to see how fond she had become of Jack. In so many ways he wasn't like Dave, who had been gentle yet strong. Dave cared for his family before anything else, it being the reason he wanted to go west, where they could do better. The Civil War had left Missouri so devastated that the community could hardly support another farmer, much less a preacher. He had taken it as long as he could, then said they had to get what they could for the cabin and the little land they had and move west where things just had to be better. No place could be poorer.

Sally saw that she had become fond of Jack despite the differences between her late husband and him. Dave could talk beautifully, whether he was sermonizing as a preacher or not. In contrast, Jack spoke in single-syllable words, and used them sparsely. Dave would tell you at any time how he felt toward you; Jack could hardly talk about anybody, much less himself. Dave wouldn't own a gun, for he wanted to build a world in which guns weren't needed; Jack hardly went anywhere without one. Dave was slight and wiry and fair; Jack was tall and rangy and dark, with strong muscles from skinning buffalo and loading hides.

But was she fond enough of Jack to marry him? Sally didn't think so. In her heart lay a well of sorrow from her loss of Dave that still dominated her feelings. True, it had grown smaller, but it wasn't fair to Dave, to herself, or to another man to take him before this open wound within her had healed more. Of course, she heard a small voice inside her say, If you don't take a husband while you're young enough to attract one, you may not get one. And that one thing overrode every other consideration: Sally didn't intend on going through life alone. However terrible her grief was, the great blankness of a life of loneliness overshadowed everything else. No, she knew enough about herself to know that she wanted another husband, but one who matched her.

"I'm going to have right good luck on this trip," McCall said.

"Oh?" she asked.

He explained that he was looking for buffalo with particularly rare pelts, and that his deal with John Moar would put him further ahead then he had been before he lost his two wagons to the Indians.

"That's wonderful," she said.

"I was thinking of going away somewhere," he said.

Having walked in from the outskirts, they now were nearing the center of Hays.

"Away?"

"Away from Hays. Away from Kansas."

She felt her heart drop. "Where away? How far?"

"A long way," he replied. "Maybe as far as California."

"California! That's where Dave and I were heading."

"I know. I was wondering if you'd want to come with me."

"With you!"

"You and Eva and Robby."

For a moment she stood confused in the hot sun of noon. Around her the dilapidated shacks and cabins of Hays seemed to glide by like leering skeletons. What was she doing here? How had this come to be her life? Inside her she felt a wrench of tightness and found it hard to take a breath. Out of some tension that held no mirth, she laughed sharply, then quieted herself. "Excuse me, Jack. I'm not myself."

"I'm sorry," he said, looking dejected. "I misspoke myself."

"No!" she exclaimed. "How did you mean I was to come with you—as a passenger?"

He didn't look at her. "No, as my wife."

"Your wife."

He fairly squirmed away from her in embarrassment, making her quickly rescue him.

"Oh, Jack, that's wonderful!"

"But you don't want to."

"I—" What to say? Her loyalty to Dave, her wish for the best possible father for Eva and Robby, her deep longing to leave Hays, and her fondness for this strong, gentle man combined to leave her speechless with happiness. "What do you want to do in California?" she asked, trying to gain time.

"Anything," he said. "No, buy some land. Maybe raise horses."

"Aren't you going to miss hunting?" she asked.

"Naw, I'm sick of it."

"Sick of it?"

"Sick to death. All this"—he waved his hand around at the stores, hotel, saloons and broken-down bunkhouses— "is just going to ruin this country. Marry me, Sally. I'm going to make it big this time out, and I want to use the money for something that'll make me feel good. I want to be a father to Robby, and Eva too, but I don't know her too good. And I want you to be my wife. Maybe we can have children of our own."

"For a man who doesn't believe in talking, you've just said a mouthful."

"It's no, though, ain't it?"

"I need to think, Jack," she said, putting her hand over her eyes to shade them from the glaring sun.

"I knew it," he said. "You don't want me."

"No, Jack," she said. "I didn't say that."

"You ain't said yes."

"How long have you been thinking of this?"

He shrugged. "A few weeks, maybe a month or so."

"I haven't had any time to get used to the idea," she said. "Can't you give me a little time to mull it over?"

She saw that her answer didn't perk him up much. "Hey," she said, grabbing him by the arms and shaking him. "It's made me happy you've asked, Jack. I'm thrilled. Really."

The enthusiasm in her voice seemed to rouse him, and a smile creased his face. "Really?"

"Really."

"I'm in the running?"

"More than just in the running."

"We're leaving in the morning."

"Leaving," she echoed, feeling bleak at the mention of the word.

"When can you tell me? By tomorrow?"

"Tomorrow? I don't know if by then, but certainly by the time you get back," she said. "I'll have time to talk to the children."

"But I got a chance with you?"

"Oh, Jack, you got a good, good, good chance with me."

She liked the way his grin cracked his rugged face. "You mean it?"

"Jack, I wouldn't lie to you. I want to say yes, right now I want to say yes, but I want to think it over and make sure I'm doing the right thing both for myself and the children."

"This is going to be the fastest buffalo hunt you ever seen," he said.

"Oh, yes! Hurry back!"

"Them buffalo would be damn fools to cross me this trip. Indians too."

"Be careful, Jack. God, be careful. I wouldn't want anything to happen to you."

"You wouldn't? Does that mean a yes?"

"It means be real, real careful," she said. She gave him her biggest smile, which she saw made him dazzle with happiness.

She didn't want to tell McCall just yet, but in her heart she sung yes, yes, yes. An hour ago it wouldn't have occurred to her to *marry* him, but how he had thought of her *and* the children had struck her just right. She could be happy with Jack, really happy. She wasn't certain of it, but she was pretty sure. Of course, he wasn't Dave. No man ever would be. What counted was whether she felt right with him now, at this point in her life, and while he was off hunting, she would see.

California, a new life, and good-bye Hays City. Life could be wonderful!

"I got me three fellers who'll do as I say, Mr. Moar," Skinner told the hide trader. "Plus a helper."

"I never thought you'd have any trouble," said Moar. "I thought you were leaving this morning?"

"We're leaving in a hour," Skinner assured him. "The four of us got to talking it over. Can we have four pistols?"

"Pistols?"

"Case we have trouble with Jack."

"What? For who?"

"For me, Three-Fingers Henley, Arkansas Jones, and Charley Cook."

"Damn it, I'm furnishing rifles, Skinner. Can't the four of you handle him with them? What the hell else do you need?"

"Yes sir, I know, sir, but you can sit on a feller in a tent a lot easier with a pistol than a rifle. Besides, the only way I could get Three-Fingers to come was to agree to get him a pistol, and now the other two want one too."

"Three-Fingers," mused Moar, then grinned. "That's a good choice. And you don't want to be left out?"

"No sir. Wouldn't be a good idea."

Moar sighed and shook his head in such a way that Skinner thought he was going to say no. Three-Fingers had been particular on this point: without a pistol, he wasn't going to try to keep a Jack McCall pinned down. The son of a bitch would knock your rifle away and beat the hell out of you.

"I want all this stuff back, Skinner."

"Yes sir."

"If I don't get the wagons, the mules, the rifles, and these pistols back, I'm going to charge you for them, get me?"

"Yes sir. Then we can have them?"

He watched Moar write something on a pad of paper. "Take this to Luke at the store. He'll give you four .44s."

"And shells? A box for each of us?"

Moar sighed in that exasperated way of his and scribbled something else on the pad. "Now get out of here, and get the hell out of town and find me those white hides."

"Yes sir!"

Chapter 10

Striking Eagle and his men heard the boomings of the giant buffalo guns for five miles as they rode toward them.

"Buzzards," said Left Hand, pointing. "I've never seen so many in one spot."

"Death," answered Striking Eagle.

"And a lot of it."

After a mile or so, Striking Eagle saw they were headed for Bull Hollow, a water hole fed by an underground spring that never went dry.

The closer the band of Kiowa rode, the more uneasy the echoing boomings of the rifles and the hundreds of wheeling buzzards made Striking Eagle feel. Around him rode the best of the Kiowa fighters. This should have made him afraid of nothing and no one, but the increasing loudness of these guns grabbed his heart like a thunderstorm crashing into a tepee. When men took the thunder power of *Wakan-Takan* as theirs, as the whites did, *Wakan-Takan* arranged for the spirit of that power to crush those men.

At the hills they dismounted. They heard the rifles speak every few moments just over the other side.

"I hear at least three," said Left Hand.

"Come, Left Hand," Striking Eagle said as he began to climb.

Leaving the others to stand with the horses, Left Hand jogged to catch up with his friend. As they neared the top of the hill, the guns sounded still louder.

"How can they stand so much noise?" Left Hand asked about the white men.

"They aren't men," Striking Eagle replied. "They have no souls. They are sticks and grasses stuffed into skins."

Seeing the confusion on his friend's face, Striking Eagle knew Left Hand didn't understand. It was all right. Often Old Hoof had said something cryptic that took Striking Eagle years to puzzle through. Left Hand hadn't flown through Striking Eagle's power vision.

Just before the crest they lowered themselves to the granite rock chips and inched themselves over the ridge so as not to be seen. Lying on his stomach, peering over the rim of the hill, Striking Eagle saw around the water hole scores and scores of dead brown heaps, the corpses of buffalo, while all around the valley surrounding the water hole milled thousands upon thousands of buffalo, obviously longing to get to the water hole, but prevented by the position of the white men.

By the waterhole sat two wagons, and on the ground in front of the only opening to the waterhole lay two men. They switched rifles frequently, shooting down the leaders of the herd as they came to drink. Off to the side three other men were busily skinning the carcasses.

The evil of this scene staggered Striking Eagle so much that he almost gagged. So far, about two hundred buffalo lay dead around the passageway through the hills to the water. No meat would be used. Only the skins. And the shooters could lay here forever and fire, for no buffalo herd would leave this hole since the next water hole was twenty miles away.

Even as they watched, another five young bulls, having elected themselves leaders, moved toward the water. Nine shots brought them lifelessly to the ground.

Another few bulls selected themselves and moved forward. The herd, having smelled the water after a long, dry march across the plains, would never leave. The animals would keep coming, and as long as the whites wanted skins, they could have them.

The whole valley reeked of death. Obviously the hunters had been here for days, for the stench of rotting buffalo had filled the air with hundreds of buzzards. The birds swooped down from time to time to feed. They hopped about unless driven away by a live buffalo or the white men wanting a buffalo's pelt. The stench was enough to knock a decent man over, and the sight of so much death made Striking Eagle shake with sadness.

How could the whites do such an evil thing? Every time he saw it—and this spring he had seen dozens of groups of white shooters, although none so ruthless as these—he went through the same grief and rage. The grief came from his power journeys across the skies. He had been shown where all this killing led and he saw reflected in his brother the buffalo's slaughter the death of not only his warriors, but also of his children, his women, his children's children, and all decent life. The whites were killing no less than his entire people. A man could only throw himself heedlessly into a fight against such a foe. Here his own death had no meaning, for what was a man without his people?

As he pulled back from the rim to his warriors, he was sick at heart, for he had recognized one of the shooters below as his friend from last winter, Long Crow.

Hadn't he been taught a lesson when they burned his wagons?

With Striking Eagle were forty men and nine boys. They stood looking at him as he arrived back down the hill, trusting him to decide what to do. If he fought, one or two or four might be dead tomorrow. Yet if he chose to skip all such battles as this one, in time no Kiowa would be alive. His own death had little meaning to him just now, but who was he to decide that a father or a wife or children to these warriors would stumble around in grief for the next few months? He pulled his group away from the thunderous roar of the guns just over the hill to make camp.

Left Hand fell into step next to him. "They've killed over two hundred buffalo," he told Striking Eagle. "They're doing the same thing as we've seen before—taking the skins, leaving the meat."

"We'll talk, then attack," said Striking Eagle.

"They're good shots, with powerful guns," said Left Hand, obviously worried about attacking such efficient killers. "Especially that one shooting on the left. All around him are dead buffalo."

"That's Long Crow, the man we took the wagons from months ago," said Striking Eagle. "The man who saved me from the storm last winter."

Striking Eagle saw the curious glance Left Hand threw at him, but he volunteered nothing.

"I thought they might learn," said Left Hand, clearly amazed and a little frightened by the whites. "We took everything away from them, and here they are back."

"They're stupid," said Eagle. "They don't know what they're doing."

When Striking Eagle talked to the warriors that evening, he found that most of them also felt blunt rage. Not that their warriors hadn't slaughtered two hundred buffalo when they could, but they hadn't taken just one part of the animal. Certainly a few Kiowa might be profligate now and then if they had luck in hunting, but no Kiowa spat in *Wakan-Takan's* face by killing for skins alone.

As they talked, the guns boomed in the distance time and time again, the echoes punctuating dusk like hysterical demons, making the braves wince at every shot.

"Let's attack at dawn," Striking Eagle said, capping the long discussion. "I'll lead."

But a few warriors opposed the attack, saying that attacking such powerful guns was foolish. For hours into the night they debated, and gradually these dissenters were won over. Except for the boys, they would all ride in the attack.

No one wanted to sleep, so they built up the fire. All through the night they told each other stories of their prowess. They had Striking Eagle, the man with the most *Wakan* power among them, lead the chants and bless the paint pots before they painted themselves and their ponies.

Left Hand painted Striking Eagle with his power designs to make him strong and keep him safe: a huge eagle on his back, talons outstretched as it struck, and dozens of smaller designs on his chest, stomach, arms and legs, symbolic marks of his other victories, in order to add the strength of those times to this one.

When Left Hand had finished, Striking Eagle painted him in a similar fashion.

"You want that Crow raid on your lower back?" Eagle asked him.

"The time I dove off my horse at Staff Butte?" asked Left Hand. "Sure. I was full of power that day. I want every day to be like that one."

So Striking Eagle painted a hand pushing a crow bird

off a horse in reds and yellows on his friend's lower back, right under the larger design of the antelope, Left Hand's power animal.

By the time first light had begun to show over the hills, long stripes of blacks, whites, reds and yellows were smeared across their faces. Every man and pony on the raiding party was covered with paint that would protect and strengthen him. Designs of fighting wolves, badgers, mountain lions, eagles, buffalo, elk, antelope and foxes adorned their horses as well as their own arms, chests, backs and legs.

Before they rode out, Striking Eagle offered a prayer.

Hear us, Wakan-Takan!
We prepare to fight your enemies.
Stand by our side,
Guide each arrow,
Make steady our arms,
Deflect these enemies' bullets,
And give each Kiowa the strength of a buffalo.
Hear us, Wakan-Takan!

Hear us, Wakan-Takan!
We prepare to fight your enemies.
Make our hearts strong,
Make our eyes keen,
Open our ears,
Give our legs the firmness of treetrunks,
And give our horses strength and speed.
Hear us, Wakan-Takan!

Striking Eagle had eaten little in the past two days, part of his personal preparation for battle. He felt as thin and fluid as water. This was about the only thing he had consumed in this time. He wanted to be able to flow like air around the enemy, not bound to the earth by heavy food. He saw fear quiver in his stomach and bowels, that ball of moon water that could make a man weak. Hoof had taught him all about such moon water when he was a boy. "Fear is the warrior's constant companion," Hoof had told him over and over, just before urging him to take the next risk in his training. Hoof would tell him to speak to the fear, to acknowledge it, to put it in a special pouch in his mind, one with a tight drawstring—which Hoof had guided him in constructing—and then do what he as a warrior had to do.

Outwardly, of course, he could show no fear, for the mien of the leader of an attack had to inspire the men's confidence. This would promote their success.

When Striking Eagle led his fifteen horse fighters around the hills, all the whites were still in their bedrolls except for one, who sat beside a small fire. He looked up as they came into view in the semidarkness as if he didn't believe his own sight. He must have shouted something, for his mouth opened, but Striking Eagle could hear nothing, so loud did the hooves of the fifteen horses sound in his ear. He felt his horse pounding under him, felt the cool dawn air, felt his fear bouncing around, struggling to escape the drawstring of its pouch, and heard the shouts of his brothers. As well he heard a thousand of his ancestors shouting encouragement, and he knew that the entire Kiowa people, past and present, rode with him this morning. While few of the men who rode with him would understand this, Hoof might. For them all, he had to do his best.

The plan was to ride right through the camp, killing the whites before they could position themselves to fire, but by the time they were fifty yards away, three of the men had jumped from their bedrolls, grabbed their guns and thrown themselves behind wagon wheels. The wheels might not have offered much protection, but they made the plan of running over the whites difficult. When Striking Eagle had closed half that distance, the whites' rifles spoke, issuing little puffs of lazy clouds from their barrels. He heard a bullet or two whizz angrily by his ears, angry bees with a fatal sting. He crouched still lower and sang his own song that would deflect the whites' deadly creatures.

> Grandfather Eagle above!
> Strike with your talons
> And push away these bees.
> An eagle should eat bees.
> Eat bees today!

The rifle he had taken from Long Crow he carried in his right hand. As he rode, he wanted to use it, but he saw no clear shot and he didn't want to waste ammunition. Nearer and nearer he got to the wagons. He looked about and saw that of the men he had started with, no more than eight now rode beside him. But he dared not stop, for retreating would be more dangerous than riding on through the camp. He shouted encouragement to his fellows, who whooped and returned his shouts, and they thundered on.

As planned, they rode through the camp, shooting arrows, firing captured pistols and rifles, and throwing lances. Striking Eagle fired four careful shots, now regretting that he was using the rifle, for he could have fired a dozen arrows with his bow in this time.

He leaned down as he passed the first wagon and reined his horse in sharply to bring the animal around. Leaning down as he circled, he saw a pair of legs sticking out. The white hunter saw his wheeling shadow, turned and swung his gun up, and Striking Eagle fired and pulled his horse back. His companions had ridden on out of range of the rifles. He dashed on to catch up, again hearing angry bullets buzz past his head. He lay his body flat next to his horse's back to make a small target.

Striking Eagle heard shouts from the hill. As planned, Left Hand and twenty others came down the hill on foot, dodging from rock to bush and hole to boulder as they attempted to keep the whites too busy to fire at the horse fighters by presenting smaller, hidden targets.

Calling for his cavalry to regroup, Striking Eagle shouted instructions. Moon Face was to ride on the far end, Three-Fingers by his side, and High Shoes was to use his arrows, since the old pistol he carried misfired too many times.

Again they came through the camp, the buffalo horses galloping through the fire, knocking over cooking pots and cups. Now Striking Eagle had his short bow in his right hand, half a dozen arrows in his left, and in a few seconds he had shot them. Like most of the horse fighters, he rode on the far side of his horse so that he was shielded. But as the whites fired at pointblank range, the horses screamed as they were pulled and wheeled about.

Next to him a horse screamed in fear, and Striking Eagle turned to see Narrow Tree go down under his horse. The animal had a hole in its lung that oozed blood. Tree's leg was pinned under the writhing horse. Striking Eagle pulled up Tree from under the horse and flung him on the back of his own mount and took off toward the hill. The other horse fighters followed.

"How'd we do?" Left Hand asked him when they had come together.

"I don't know," said Striking Eagle. "Did we wound any?"

"Five men were in the camp," said Left Hand. "We think one is dead and one wounded."

"And ours?"

"So far, we've lost four horses. Wolf's Back is dead. We have two braves with wounds and Tree's leg is crushed."

"Wolf's Back?"

"Dead."

"Dead!"

"Yes."

Striking Eagle's stomach churned. "Terrible!"

"But he died in battle."

The two friends nodded together sadly. At least as consolation Wolf's Back would arrive in paradise in the full bloom of youth, not enfeebled as an old man.

The losses suffered on this first attack had been higher than he expected, and he worried that his fighters would decide that his *Wakan* power had waned. At noon two other leaders of the party met with Striking Eagle and Left Hand to talk over what to do. All morning long they had kept the whites under siege. Meanwhile, the thirsty buffalo, half-oblivious to the battle raging around them, milled forward to the water hole. By noon, neither the whites nor the Kiowa could fire at each other due to the herd of animals watering, wallowing in the mud on the banks of the large pool and wandering up and down the little hollow.

"How long will this herd be here?" Striking Eagle asked Hamana, the scout.

"I tried to ride around them, but I couldn't," said the scout. "For days."

"The whites keep shooting," said Left Hand. "Why is that?"

"You can see from the top of the far ridge," said

Hamana. "They're shooting the buffalo while they're in their camp, and the men are skinning them right there."

"The buffalo are protecting them," Left Hand noted.

Leaving his men to keep firing at the whites, Striking Eagle, Hamana and the other three leaders climbed the hill. There they could all see it. Under cover of the herd, the whites were taking the opportunity to kill still more buffalo. The thirsty buffalo didn't notice their companions dying around them; driven by a thirst composed of days without water, they pushed forward. The white men continued to shoot them down.

"We've failed to stop them," said Left Hand. "What else can we do but give up for now?"

Many others agreed with this suggestion that the attack be abandoned. They had fought hard, had lost men and horses, and could call what they had accomplished a victory, for they were pretty certain one white man was dead or dying.

"Come on, Eagle. Let's go home," said Left Hand. "I haven't seen my women for a week and a half now."

"Maybe," said Striking Eagle.

"Don't think of going back in there," said Left Hand. "You've already lost Wolf's Back. He was popular. People are going to talk about how your power is slipping."

"Maybe the same buffalo who protect them can hide us as we attack them," Striking Eagle said.

Left Hand groaned. "Come on, Eagle. We've been out here for ten days. We need to rest."

"Maybe dressed as buffalo we could move through the herd right to them?" Eagle suggested.

"What?" asked one.

"Sneak through!" said another.

"Maybe!" shouted Left Hand.

They all liked the idea and it excited them, for they

loved to trick their enemies as much as defeat them. Buffalo were such powerful creatures that they had never had much to fear, simply multiplied into ever-larger herds, so that in general they feared almost nothing strange. In fact, often they were curious over a wolf or a man or an antelope buck. While a herd might bolt and stampede over a shift in the wind, a man still might walk up to a herd if he was downwind, sometimes simply because the herd didn't care. Dressed in a wolf or buffalo skin, any warrior who knew how to bob his head like a wolf or make the little husping sounds of the buffalo could creep up on one.

"Yes, but first we need buffalo skins," said Left Hand.

It took a day for twenty of them to move out to the fringes of the giant herd, where the whites couldn't see them, kill a dozen of the midsized cows, skin them, and drag the skins back to their camp. It felt like woman work to dress the hides, but still excitement ran high. Already Left Hand and Hamana were fighting between themselves over who should get the rifles they planned to take from the whites.

While the work made him sweat in the shadeless sun, Striking Eagle prepared his hide well. Like the others, he left the head attached to the pelt. He cut the skull out of the hide and stuffed it with sagebrush. It took them two days to prepare the ten disguises, which would conceal twenty men.

On the dawn of the third day, they put on their shields, tied their quivers, knives and bows to their waists, and had the skins draped over each two-man team.

By now the herd, having drunk enough water, had thinned out some, so that moving through it was easier than they had planned as they navigated across the quarter-mile of thinly dotted clumps of buffalo. Striking Eagle felt fear and anticipation rise in him. Over the past week he had lost two warriors, and three lay wounded from the long-range guns, struck down like the buffalo. Now they would sneak up on these men, strike, and in minutes take the whites' camp.

Slowly, stealthily, with Left Hand crouched in the close dark air inside the skin with him, Striking Eagle drew closer to the whites, guided by the constantly barking guns. The sun beat down through the hot, black skin, making him sweat. The inner side of the buffalo hide stuck to his sweating flesh. The smell of freshly killed buffalo, rank with the odors of dust, blood, sour fat, urine and excrement, struck him.

The hide itself was heavy, weighing almost a hundred pounds because it hadn't yet dried, and he had to exert all his strength to keep himself in a buffalo shape, make buffalo movements and husp. But slowly, definitely, he was crossing the herd and getting closer to the whites. While he didn't dare lift his head above the herd to get a clear look, he kept moving in the direction of the shots, which became louder and louder.

He knew he was close to the camp when he heard a shot, a "hunff," and a wheeze from a nearby cow who sank to her front knees, obviously wounded. Another shot and she fell over. Her calf moved toward her in a leisurely way and nuzzled his fallen mother. When she didn't move, the calf butted her, but still the cow didn't stir.

Striking Eagle heard another gun. Two of them, as usual. The way the whites worked, he and his fighters knew, was that either one or two men shot and two or three skinned and hauled hides. Shaken by the nearness of the dying cow, who gasped frothy blood from her mouth, Striking Eagle hoped he didn't look like an attractive target. Keeping his head down to appear like a grazing cow, he moved over behind a clump of young bulls he hoped stood between him and Long Crow's line of fire.

As Striking Eagle neared them, the young bulls raised their heads and regarded him curiously. Hissing commands to Left Hand, he moved two of them backward, not wanting to excite the curiosity of the bulls. Once his curiosity was aroused, a buffalo had to investigate a thing. Sometimes a way to catch one was to present the animal with a warrior under a hide—any animal's skin—as long as the hide made movements that weren't familiar to the buffalo. At these times, their curiosity afire, a clump of buffalo would walk up to examine the strange animal. To make his kill, the brave would throw off the wolf hide, quickly fire three or four arrows, and with any luck and just a little skill bring down a fine cow or two. But as the bulls stared at him, Striking Eagle realized that the herd of bulls might just get so curious they would mash him and Left Hand in the process of trying to discover just what this strange animal was.

He looked around for the other disguised warriors, and seeing another pair under a cowskin, he made the buffalo's husping noise, expecting his men to hear it and gather according to plan.

It was Hamana who answered him and made his way toward Striking Eagle. Farther away, one more off-key husp-husp announced another warrior, and yet another revealed a fourth.

Good, he thought. Each warrior will bring one or two, we will gather, then attack. As he waited for his men, Striking Eagle felt Left Hand bump into his rear and curse. Swinging his buffalo head around, he found himself staring right into the face of a good-sized buffalo bull with his nose in the air sniffing in huge snorts. Turning, Striking Eagle hissed directions at Left Hand, then moved forward, away from the bull. When he turned back to look, the bull still stood watching him with interest, his head cocked, obviously puzzled by this strange animal with the cow smell moving away from him.

The young bull snorted and pawed the ground. Striking Eagle recognized the mating pattern of buffalo; the dumb beast thought the cow was ready to mount. Continuing to hiss directions, Striking Eagle moved on till he realized he was surrounded by six of his disguised warrior teams.

Yet behind them the young bull kept coming forward, his nose up in the air and sniffing, and in his wake came three or four more young bulls, like all buffalo, ready to follow wherever one led.

"Let's circle around," hissed Left Hand. "He thinks we're rutting. Otherwise they'll jump on us and crush us."

"All right," agreed Striking Eagle.

The twelve tried to escape from the young bulls, but their more rapid movements excited the curiosity of even more young bulls. The sounds of the shots rose louder. They were drawing closer to the whites' positions. Now they heard shouts from the white men. They couldn't be more than a few yards away. Any moment now they might be able to throw off their robes and kill at least the three skinners before they realized their enemy was nearby.

Suddenly Striking Eagle heard a curse. He turned his head, but the cumbersome buffalo skin prevented him from seeing much. He turned completely around in time to see that same snorting buffalo bull above them lurching forward to mount Left Hand in an attempt to stick it in him. Striking Eagle lay down on the ground, struggled to get free of the heavy pelt and head, unhooked his bow and cocked an arrow. As the bull again approached to mount the cursing Left Hand, he let the arrow fly. As he released the arrow, Left Hand lunged to escape and the young bull crashed forward to the ground. A lucky shot, the arrow hit the bull in the eye, sticking grotesquely out like a third horn.

With a bellow of rage, the bull backed away, his head down and his tiny feet scraping the ground. Moving backward, he crashed into the bulls following him. He turned and ran into the nearest clump of buffalo, who in turn scattered. On all sides of Striking Eagle, buffalo ran about in excitement, and the animals hit each other with a series of clashes that shook the ground.

Moaning under the buffalo disguise, Left Hand was on the ground. Striking Eagle moved on his hands and knees to his friend and pulled the pelt off him. Left Hand writhed on the ground. The other disguised Kiowa had gathered, their fake noses pushed down to the ground to ask their brother what was wrong. Crouched among them, Striking Eagle realized with a sinking hea⁺ what was going to happen: if they didn't get away fast they would either be trampled by the excited buffalo or the whites would shoot them.

"Pick him up," he ordered, as he reached down for his friend's foot. "The bull injured him."

Following his example, the others threw off their disguises and grabbed the moaning Left Hand.

"Stay crouched so the whites can't see us."

As they ran, they were almost trampled down by three different herds of excited buffalo. The whites finally shot at them; only the cover of the panicked herd protected them.

Back at camp, they counted up and examined their wounded. One man had failed to come back. Hamana announced, after a scouting foray, that this man had been trampled under his pelt and lay out on the field. Left

Hand had been knocked over by the unexpected lunge of the bull and had had the breath knocked out of him, but except for occasional wooziness, which a good night's sleep would probably cure, he seemed all right.

Striking Eagle, also shaken by the encounter with the herds, saw that the fight had gone out of his warriors. While he wanted to fight on, he knew it was wise to rest his men.

So it wasn't in complete victory that they returned to camp, but on their return, Striking Eagle insisted that they send out more scouts. He exerted all his new powers to gather another party that would be ready to fight again when the scouts brought word of another kill.

The best thing that came out of this battle was the recounting night after night before the entire tribe of how the whites had taken so many buffalo as they moved helplessly toward the water hole. It unnerved everyone, man and woman, child and old man, Onde and captive, shaman and aged grandmother. Even those who had been in Eagle Beak's peace faction were outraged. How could the whites kill so many buffalo and throw away the meat? In places on the plains, bleached buffalo bones now lay about as plentiful as grass in spring. What sort of demons were they? The spirit of the tribe united in a common cause: they had to stop these people before they destroyed the buffalo.

With enough warriors they could drive these murderers of their brother the buffalo out of their country. But given the reports of tens of hundreds of white buffalo hunters this season, where were they to find enough warriors?

Once the Kiowa had pulled out, Jack McCall and his men had no trouble filling their two wagons with skins from the dead buffalo around them.

Skinner groused about their not finding the white buffalo, but McCall insisted that it was stupid to go hauling around the countryside with two wagons almost full of hides; better to finish up their loads, get them back to Hays, and start out fresh for the whites.

The skinners with him agreed. Having buried one of their party, Peppy Smith, the helper, and with Charley having an arrow wound along the top of his shoulder and Arkansas having one in his thigh, they were happy enough to turn back.

At times they had to hitch their riding horses to pull the heavily laden wagons along, but a week later they sighted the dirty speck on the horizon that was Hays City. Jack McCall felt in wonderful spirits: he calculated that out of the eight hundred hides in the two wagons, he ought to clear three thousand dollars, enough to say to hell with looking for the white buffalo. He hadn't felt comfortable looking for them anyway. If there was one buffalo every tribe on the plains thought was theirs, it was the white buffalo. Why cause more trouble, even if he might strike it rich? He would take his chips, and if she would have him, he would put Sally and the children on a train and head west to a new life. He didn't know what he would do there, but he wouldn't have to scrabble about with mean buffalo hunters.

When they arrived in Hays, they pulled into the hide sheds first, where they unloaded the hides on the dock and had them counted and graded. McCall was pleased to see that Billy Dixon, Moar's buyer, graded their best forty pelts as beaver buffalo robes. Their fur was fine and wavy and their color was that of a beaver. Billy said they would get seventy-five dollars for these, and he added that Mr. Moar had told him to offer them top dollar on everything they brought in.

"All right!" McCall said, and the buyers from the other outfits withdrew in disgust. McCall accepted the chit, which would entitle them to nearly five thousand dollars when they presented it to Moar's hotel office, where the big money was kept in a safe.

That made McCall feel terrific. He headed for Mike's bunkhouse, where he could scrub himself well and dress in his clean clothes before he saw Sally. By midafternoon he was buying his crew and a few of the regulars drinks at the Drum.

A part of him wondered why he was at the Drum rather than across the street at the Hide & Skull, but it had something to do with wanting to finish up with his men before he saw Sally and heard her answer. It also had something to do with putting off hearing what she had to say in case she said no.

Suppose she does say no, he mused as he stood amid all the ruckus at the Drum's bar. It had been close to four weeks since they had seen each other. Anything could have happened. McCall felt his heart flutter, as it did when he was creeping up on a buffalo stand and didn't know if the herd would spook or not. He didn't like the feeling, but still, when you crept up on a herd, you didn't hurry because of how you felt, or you would never get a buffalo.

By dusk he had had a bit more whiskey than he figured he should have, and he got himself something to eat from the kitchen of the Drum. That sobered him up a bit, and he had some coffee, and by then he couldn't put off his fate much longer.

He walked out of the Drum into a soft purple dusk. Only a few figures moved through the violet gloom of the tiny town. As he pushed away from the porch of the Drum, he felt the flutter begin again. Every breath he took

319

churned his insides. He hadn't felt this nervous since the moment before he shot his first deer with Little Robe.

He crossed the street in the haze of a dream, and the lights from the windows and doors of the Hide & Skull rose to meet him like the mouth of some sparkling underwater creature baring its menacing teeth. He entered the smoky bar and looked for Sally, but he didn't see her. He pushed his way through the room, answering calls and howdies and did-you-get-anythings with a nod and a smile. Where was she?

At the bar, he ordered a beer from Bob.

"Thought you'd be in here earlier," Bob said as he set down a glass.

"Where is she, Bobby?" McCall asked.

"Putting Eva down for the night," Bob answered. "Want me to send up for her?"

McCall started to say no, not wanting to stop her from what she was doing, but he felt another overwhelming urge to get this over with. He grinned and said, "Would you, Bob?"

Bob sent Shorty up, and the wait took forever. The barroom swirled around McCall like a barrel organ. He regretted having anything to drink today, yet wondered vaguely if this rocking sickness inside had more to do with the whiskey or with her and her answer to him. For a moment he considered bolting back to the Drum, for if this swaying sickness inside was what being hooked up to Sally was like, he wanted no part of it.

Then she appeared, looking distracted and grim, pushing a lock of blonde hair back into her bun. She smiled when she saw him, but it wasn't a smile of delight. It looked forced, and plunged his stomach into a steeper slide.

"Hey," he said in greeting.

320

"Let's go outside," she said, not looking at him.

Wondering why she looked so grim, he nodded and followed her. Heads turned to watch them and he felt like a fool. Who the hell did he think he was?

On the porch of the Hide & Skull, she took both his hands in hers and said, "Yes, Jack! If you still want me, yes!"

"You mean it?" he asked, hardly aware of what he was saying because he felt so lightheaded from the heat of the day, the booze, and his anticipation.

"Yes, I mean it," she said. "I've felt so lonely without you. I didn't realize how I would feel."

"Lonely?"

"Terribly."

"We'll get married?" he asked.

"If you'll have me."

"Have you! I've been so worried that you might *not* have me."

"I wish I'd told you before. I've been terrified you wouldn't come back."

"Nothing could keep me away."

"When can we go?" she asked.

"I've got the money."

"Thank God! A good trip?"

"Real good, except that Smith got killed. Those damn Kiowa again."

"Thank God you're all right."

"Thank God *you're* all right," he answered. "Eva and Robby?"

"They're fine," she said. "Or rather, Robby *was* after he got over wanting to go with you."

"When do you want to leave?" he asked.

"Yesterday would be too late," she said. "On the next train. Let's travel to Kansas City, get someone to

321

marry us, spend a couple nights there till a train goes west, and then I don't ever want to see another buffalo skin in my whole life.''

He grinned and felt himself swell up with excitement, a combination of anticipation and worry about the future he couldn't remember feeling before. "Sounds real good to me," he said. "I'm going to try hard, Sally, to be the dang best husband ever was."

"You won't have to try," she said with a smile. "You are." She lifted one of his hands and kissed it in a demure, soft fashion that sent prickles of desire through him. "And I'm going to make you happy, Jack, as happy as a wife can make a man."

"Hey, you already have!"

"I must go."

"Already?" he asked. "I just got in."

"John Moar's been pushing me the last couple of weeks," she explained. "I have things to do. I can take some time off tomorrow."

"Quit him, quit this place, Sally."

She laughed. "When? Tonight?"

"Yes."

"No, John's been good to me."

"I don't want my wife working in a whorehouse."

She sighed. "Neither does she, but she's been running one for nigh onto a year now, and another few days isn't going to make her a whit less virtuous."

"I wish you'd quit, just walk out."

"Let me ease out of it with John, Jack," she said. "Believe me, it's better. I know John only too well."

"All right," he said, "but promise me you'll give it up in three days."

"Of course."

*   *   *

"Goddamnit, McCall, I want my hides!" shouted Moar. "The goddamn hides I sent you after."

"We looked for them, we didn't find none."

"How come you think I paid for that rig?" asked Moar.

The two stood in Moar's upstairs office at the Hide & Skull the morning after McCall had come back to Hays. Jack McCall had brought in the shed chit for the money from the hides he had unloaded at Moar's dock, but to his shock, Moar had refused to pay off on the chit, something the little man had never before been known to do. Moar had told him he would pay off, but only when McCall brought in what he had been sent out after—the white pelts.

"Hey, this isn't right. I want my money, Moar," McCall demanded.

"You ain't getting a buffalo chip from me, McCall," said Moar, "till you bring me what I hired you to bring me."

"You didn't hire me. I'm a free contractor."

"Yes, I did. Using my rifles, my wagons, my grub, and my mules."

"So what?"

"So it's my show, and I'm confiscating those hides you brought in till you either buy that rig off me or bring me what I hired you to bring."

"Confiscate?" asked McCall, confused by the big word. "What do you mean?"

"Keeping the goddamn hides, McCall, that's what I mean."

For a few moments McCall just stood there, speechless and uncertain how to handle the situation. He would have flattened the little man if the two fellows who protected Moar's office hadn't been sitting in tipped-back

323

straight chairs on either side of his desk. After considering Moar's position, McCall asked, "What do you want, Moar?"

"What I hired you for. Them white hides."

"They can't be that important."

"I got a customer that wants them, Jack. He ordered them special. I done gone to some trouble to get them, hired the man who's supposed to be the best man to find them, and you done screwed it all up. You were out there making *your* load when you ought to have been making *mine.* Now you come in here mad at *me* because I don't just say to you, 'Sure, you can use my equipment and mules for free, and anything you get yourself I'll give you top dollar for on top of that.' No sir, McCall, I might have been dumb to have hired you on, but I ain't so dumb that I got to pay you for my mistake."

"Are them hides I brung in mine or yours?" McCall asked.

"Yours—once you bring me the whites you promised me."

"Now, how do you figure this?"

"You said you'd go after those whites, and you asked me who would the brown pelts belong to that you took on this trip. I was being big-hearted and said, hell, McCall, you keep them, figuring—wrongly, I see now—that it would give you more profit and good reason to give me what I wanted. But I ain't a fool but once, McCall."

"So I got to go get the whites if I'm to collect."

"Yeah, just like we agreed."

"Goddamnit, Moar."

"Goddamnit, Jack."

McCall looked from Moar to the two big fellows who served as guards. They had come up from Texas and one of them, if not both, always kept an eye on the big iron

324

box Moar kept the gold and the bank notes in that he used to pay for hides.

"But I don't want to go back out," said McCall. "I'm quitting this business, Moar."

"Precisely why I ain't paying you, Jack."

"This ain't right."

"Tough. Next time stick to the deal you make."

"This got anything to do with Sally?"

"Sally? What the hell does she have to do with this?"

"You were riding her around in your buggy before I went out."

"So what?"

"So you figure if you can keep me out chasing what I ain't likely to find you're liable to have a better shot at her."

Moar sighed. "Listen to me, McCall, and listen good. I got a stack of telegrams in my files in which my customer is demanding those hides. My brother even tells me he's liable to come out here to pick them up himself. I'm not being personal about this. If you want to forget the load you brought in, then forget it. I'll give you shooter's wages, forty cents a hide. But it was my rig, and till my rig does what I ask, I'm not doing you any favors, get me?"

"Yeah."

"You want shooter's wages?"

"No, it wouldn't be enough."

"So go get me those white hides and make yourself a rich man."

"I don't have much choice, do I?"

Moar grinned and looked from one of his heavyset guards to the other. "Or you can jump me," he said. "I can see in your eyes you want to. But George and Sam here ain't going to let it get too far, and it's possible when they get finished with you your lady friend ain't going to find you the handsome beau she thought she figured on getting.''

As arranged, at noon McCall met Skinner and his crew at the Drum to pay them off. They were as angry as he was about not getting paid, but Arkansas summed it up for all of them: ''Hey, boys, we done shown we know how to get buffalo and whack out them Injuns. If we get him his white skins, will he pay off, Jack?''

''I ain't delivering those hides to the sheds till I see the color of his money,'' said McCall.

''All right,'' said Arkansas. ''Can we find them critters, McCall? That is, can *you* find them?''

They all looked at him wide-eyed, expectant. ''Yeah, I think so,'' he replied.

''This ain't no wild goose chase, now?''

''I got a good idea or two where they might be found—if we don't get pinned down again by the Kiowa.''

''Well, we shot our way out of them last time. They'll think twice about messing with us again,'' said Skinner. ''Let's have a drink and get our gear ready.''

''What do the rest of you say?'' McCall asked. ''Skinner can't pay you now, anyway, 'cause Moar ain't paying him or me.''

The other three men said it was just as well. If they had it they would spend it. Arkansas spoke for all of them when he said, ''Let's go, so we can come back. I'd rather get all mine in a bunch, anyway. Maybe I can do something with it when it's a lot. I get it in little dribs and drabs and I just throw it away. What I'd like to do is put it into a rig of my own.''

And so it was agreed that they would leave in three

days, and this time they would find the herd of whites, get them before they took any brown hides, and come back richer than they had ever been in their lives.

Sally could hardly sleep the night that she and Jack McCall had held hands and agreed to marry and head west.

As she lay awake, her mind a dizzying rush of images and shouts from the imagined future, she saw clearly what a major turning point this was in her life, and she couldn't peer around the corner to see what lay ahead. That night it took her three long hours to go to sleep, and then she slept fitfully, her mind full of crowded dreams. She wandered through vast canyons of purples, reds and violets, canyons filled with towering faces that called to her in voices so deep she couldn't fathom their meaning. Frustrated, she walked for miles in search of something and failed to find it.

The next morning Sally woke up drained, yet happy. It wasn't till she was out of bed, putting on her dress and struggling to decide who she could get to help Patty with tonight's dinner, that she remembered why she was so happy. She was going to marry Jack McCall! Inside her a song trilled and she laughed out loud. She went to the window and looked down at the bleak main street of Hays, in all its dusty glory. Over at the hitching post in front of the Drum stood three horses looking as if they were asleep in the yellow morning light.

Was it possible? Sally asked herself. Was she going to leave this hard, dirty corner of hell to live a normal life in some green spot?

When she met Jack at midday, she was in exultant spirits. But her heart sank when she saw the angry expression on Jack's face.

"Jack, what's the matter?" she asked.

"We can't go. Not yet."

"Can't?"

"Can't leave Hays. I got to go back out. I'm sorry."

"Out—where?" Her heart fluttered in fear. Was it over before it had begun?

"To get those white hides John Moar sent us for last time."

"But why? You made two big loads?"

"Yeah, but he won't pay." Jack told her the whole story of Moar's refusal. It wasn't fair, she told him. She would talk to John. He would listen to her, she said, but as Sally said it, she felt herself protesting inside.

With mounting dread she realized that John Moar wasn't going to help her and Jack McCall one bit in their bid to leave Hays City.

She understood the reason easily enough too. Two weeks ago John had asked Sally into his office in the evening and offered her a drink from his private stock, something Sally knew he rarely did. She refused, having no liking for spirits, and sat on the horsehair couch waiting for his discussion about the business of the hotel.

After some beating about the bush, during which Moar gave her a few compliments on her ability to manage his affairs, rare from him, he said he would like to become engaged to her. For a long time, he told her, he had thought about her as his wife. But he hadn't wanted to say anything until a decent interval had passed after her husband's death. But things seemed different now. Would she become his fiancée?

She thought she handled this proposal well, turning it aside gently as she told him how much she thought of him.

She did tell him that she had been asked by another, and was fairly sure she would marry him.

"It wouldn't be a buffalo hunter, would it?" John asked, an ugly edge to his voice.

She tried to keep her answer light by saying, "It's hard to find anyone else in Hays."

"Sally, I thought you had more sense," he said. "No buffalo hunter can give you and your children a good home."

"We're leaving Hays, John."

"Leaving? You'll be leaving?"

"That's what I expect."

For several long moments John Moar stared at her silently, and the silence was of such an edgy duration that it frightened her a bit. Then he said, "I've built quite an empire here, Sally."

She looked at him curiously, realizing that she never heard John Moar say a word about himself.

"I've lacked something," Moar had continued, smiling almost self-consciously, as if he thought he was being foolish. "A queen. An empire needs a queen. I should have realized how regal you were when I first saw you. I've regretted thinking you were in the same league as the upstairs girls."

"John, you've given me a job and helped me when it's been hard for me here," she said. "I'm grateful. But I'm ready to leave, and Jack McCall will make me a good husband."

"Jack McCall? Leave Kansas? Nonsense. Where would a buffalo hunter go?"

"We're going to California."

"Jack will never leave Kansas. What the hell will he leave with? He doesn't own a damn thing."

"He's out gathering hides now."

329

"Sally, I'll be going back East one day," John said. "And I'll be in a position to give you a lot more than an itinerant buffalo hunter can."

Somehow, she felt herself being pulled toward John, but she also felt she was being tugged in two directions by two men. Jack McCall was big and rough, even though he had always been gentle with her and the children. John Moar had the smoothness she was used to in Dave. He knew about polite society, and he controlled his destiny in a way that almost no other inhabitants of Hays City did. Sally admired this. He was a man who knew where he was going and how to get there, and having suffered from so much uncertainty over the past year, Sally felt relieved by his solid determination. If she married him, her future would be secure. John Moar would always have a destination and be rapidly approaching it.

Even if Jack would come back to Hays, she hadn't closed the door on John Moar. She told him she was virtually certain that she wanted to marry Jack, but added that John's proposal flattered her.

"Then you're not saying no."

"Well, I don't want to leave you with any hope," she said, not wanting to unduly lift his expectations.

"But you're not saying no."

"Well, I am. I guess you could say, though, that Jack and I haven't worked out all the details."

"All right. It's not much of one, but I have a chance."

"That summarizes it pretty well."

It had been left at that, except John had started to court her somewhat more overtly. The occasional buggy ride would not suffice now.

He dressed a bit more jauntily. He also insisted that she take time off from her duties. He went out of his way to take Robby to the sheds and show him how the hide business worked. He gave Eva several valuable yards of cloth so she could work on a quilt, and he allowed her to pick out of a Philadelphia catalogue any of the crochet needle sets she wanted. Several more times he asked Sally out riding, always taking along one of the children as a chaperone, and half a dozen times he ate his meals with her in the small dining room and amused her with small talk and descriptions of New York. He kept the conversation light, but underneath, she saw him at work courting her. She enjoyed the attention. He wanted her as his wife, which both flattered and worried her. John Moar wasn't the sort of man who made it comfortable for you to say no.

And now that Jack had come back to Hays, she saw John's strategy all too clearly. She went to his office, asked him to send his guards into the hall so she could talk to him, and then begged him to give Jack the money for his hides.

"Sally, this doesn't concern you," John said. "This is business."

"No, John, this has to do with what's between us."

When he pursed his lips as he decided how to answer her, she saw it as a sure sign that she had hit upon the truth.

"No," he said. "It's business. I'd do the same whether you were in this or not."

"I don't think so."

He sighed a long bushel of air and said, "Look, I don't know precisely what my motives are, Sally, and I'm not sure I care. I do have a demanding customer who wants those hides, and I'm certainly not the sort to do anyone favors if I'm not getting what I want."

"And?"

"And yes, one part of this is that I want you."

331

"I've told you I want to marry Jack."

"You also said it wasn't all worked out."

"Well, it is now."

"Sally, I want you and I'm going to fight for you."

"Please pay him. Please let us leave Hays. Please, please, I can't stand it here any longer."

"Sally, if you were married to me, you wouldn't find Hays such a burden."

"I hate it here."

"I'm leaving in a year or two, Sally," he said. "And I'm not leaving with a few thousand dollars, either, but close to a million dollars."

"A million dollars?" she asked, not quite seeing the bearing of this dizzying figure on their discussion.

"I want a queen of my empire," he said, taking her hand.

"No, I'm not her," she said, drawing her hand back.

"Yes, you are. We've worked together wonderfully here in the hotel."

"No, John. I've put my heart into doing a good job for you, but there's nothing I've done I've felt good about—I hardly approve of drinking, much less of Nelly and Cora."

"I'm not giving up," he said.

She rose to leave. "I'm giving you no hope, John. If I have to wait a year for him to come back, you should know that I'm going to marry Jack McCall."

Jack McCall planned to leave for the hunt in three days, enough time to rest, replenish his exhausted stocks of food and ammunition, and have Skinner recruit a new helper to replace the man they had lost.

In this week he spent a lot of time with his new family, and he felt still more at home with them. While

out on the hunt, a part of him had felt them to be dangerous, strange as this notion seemed now. Up to the present
he had seen a woman and children as millstones about a
man's neck, weights keeping him from maneuvering best
to keep ahead of some monster about to devour him,
whether that monster was Indians over the next hill, ban-
dits, storms, deserts so dry they burned you up, or just
time and its way of gnawing at people.

Now, as the prospective head of this little family of
four, he felt a joy he had never experienced before. He
didn't show it, but much of the same time he grew weepy
from feelings he didn't understand. This embarrassed him.
He didn't want to go on feeling like this the rest of his life,
but at the same time he felt in the grip of something more
powerful than he had felt before, as if he were being swept
off someplace like a man in a flood.

Till now Jack McCall had lived solely for himself. In
the past, he'd felt good when he got a big load of hides,
won at poker, and got drunk without too much of a
hangover. He had talked often to others about wanting his
own spread on which to raise horses, but it hadn't been
real, just something to gab about, like the saloon Martin
wanted to buy or the whorehouse Icy wanted in New
Orleans. Now, in his mind's eye, McCall saw a small
spread in a green valley with three or four shouting children mixed in with the mares, stallions and prancing colts.
These visions made him dizzy with a tense joy, as if they
couldn't come true for him, or if they did, inside such an
idyllic scene would surely be something to spoil it.

"Let's get married, Jack," Sally told him the night
before he was to leave.

"We are, just as soon as I get back."

"No, I mean now."

"Aw, Sally. I'm leaving tomorrow."

"Tonight. Buddy is a preacher."

"Hey, I thought we were going to have a nice service in Kansas City? With flowers and a real church and a real preacher?"

"I'm afraid," she said.

"Afraid of what?"

"Afraid you won't come back."

"Ha! If I don't, all the more reason not to be married to me."

"Oh, Jack!"

"I'm coming back."

"Tonight," she said. "Marry me tonight, please, Jack."

"Nothing like that, Sally," he said.

And she saw that he was smiling at her the way men did when they thought women were just having hysterical fear, nothing that a little calming wouldn't cure.

"I want to get married right," he said. "I ain't never done that before."

"I'm afraid something will happen."

"It is—I'm going to make us rich and then quit this business."

"It'll never work."

"Yes, it will. And when I get back we'll be able to get a fine start in California. I'm going to have a damn nice little stake, more money than I've ever seen in my life."

"I don't care about the money. I want to marry you and leave now. It's important to me."

"Well, it's important to me to have the money. With what you and I got right now combined we wouldn't get much farther than Kansas City."

"That's far enough."

"I'm through with Kansas. I'm carrying you clear to California."

"I don't want California as much as I want you."

"Well, I don't want to marry you if I can't take care of you right."

"It doesn't matter. I'm scared."

"It matters to me. It'll all be all right."

"No, it won't."

"It's going to work out better this way—we'll have more money."

"Not if you don't come back. Not if the Indians kill you."

"I ain't going to let them," he said, rolling his eyes in a comic way.

"Oh, Jack, don't make fun of me."

"I'm not, sweetie. I'm going to be fine."

But nothing he said could make the dread of his leaving go away. The fates might have him leave on this last trip and bring him back, but as the time for him to leave grew closer, she was certain they weren't going to give her a second chance.

Nelly felt delighted with what she had managed to engineer. To begin with, it seemed that Jack McCall, who wouldn't make that great a husband as far as she was concerned, would take Sally out of Hays City, leaving John Moar clear for her. At the same time, if she knew anything about men, this would probably leave the love-sick Johnny-boy in a needy way. Well, Momma Nelly would minister to him all the tender loving care he could take. With any luck, she might even take Sally's place as manager and hostess for the hotel, making him even more dependent on her. She had become convinced that the only way to hang on to any man was to get him to need something he thought only you could provide. She intended to come up with several somethings—some sexual, some managerial, and some as the hotel's hostess.

Before Sally had arrived, Nelly had had no idea of what John wanted in a woman. Sally hadn't even had the spot of hostess and manager of the Hide & Skull for a month when the entire picture hit Nelly so strongly it almost knocked her over. At once she saw that she hadn't aimed high enough. It had just never occurred to her how valuable John might find a single woman who combined in one package his needs for a sexual partner, a manager and a hostess. But once she saw this, she saw that the woman who managed such a combination had a lock on him. She had kicked herself scores of times for not seeing this before, and vowed that if she ever had the chance again, she was never going to lose him. Sally's departure would give her a chance.

After all, Nelly could run things just as well as Sally could. To make sure of it, she watched Sally closely to learn all she could so that when her rival left, Nelly would quickly step into her place.

And now all her efforts were paying off. While Nelly might not appear to be the lady that Sally was, she had an arrow to her quiver Sally never would: she knew what John wanted sexually and always would be more willing to give it to him than her rival. Already he never asked for any of the other girls. Nelly studied his sexual needs carefully, wanting to make sure she gave him enough of what he fancied so that he never turned to another girl. She had to hold her tongue a dozen times when the subject of Sally came up as they lay in bed; she had to bite her sharp tongue to keep it from telling John that he would never find Sally sexually satisfying, not after what Nelly knew he liked and was willing to give him. But she knew from long experience that men weren't willing to hear much truth about the women they had become infatuated with.

The Sunday night before McCall was to leave, Nelly was in a playful mood. She had washed herself well, put on her best undergarments and slipped into Moar's bedroom, which was adjacent to his office and sitting room. There she removed her dress and, wearing only her lacy underthings, she slipped into Moar's double bed. John liked this sort of play: he would come in, say he thought he heard someone in here, she would be completely buried underneath the covers suppressing her giggles, and he would look through the closets and bureaus in a loud-voiced make-believe search for the "intruder." When he found her, he would pretend to be angry. She would beg him not to harm her. He would mockingly refuse, saying she had to suffer her punishment for sneaking into his room. He then proceeded to administer the punishment, three ritualized sexual acts she had come to rather enjoy. Men!

Tonight as she lay in John's bed, Nelly heard angry voices coming through the door connected to Moar's office. Wondering what was going on, for John was normally the quietest of men, she crept out of bed to listen.

By this time, the voices had lowered. She had to press her ear against the cold wood of the door to hear.

She heard John say, "If McCall wasn't to come back, maybe there'd be something extra in it for you—say, the boss's share itself."

A rough voice answered, "Me and him's partners, Mr. Moar."

"Funny way he has of treating his partners," John said.

"What do you mean?" the rough voice asked.

Nelly dropped down to look through the keyhole and saw the bald head of Skinner Kincade.

"He cheated you out of your share two trips ago, and last load he didn't go after the pelts that could have earned you the most money of all."

"Jack has his ways."

"One of them is riding all over you."

Skinner looked uneasy, unsure of how to respond to this. "What do you mean, if he wasn't to come back?"

"It means he don't come back."

The next room was so silent for a few moments that Nelly figured they had dropped their voices, but then Skinner said, "I don't know. I done spent a lot of time with him."

"You know how much money I'm talking about?"

"No sir. I ain't never learned to count good."

"Let's say the hides I'm holding and the new load of whites are worth twenty thousand dollars, and let's say you was to take half as the boss of the outfit."

"Ten thousand dollars!"

"Ten thousand dollars."

"If Jack don't come back?"

"If Jack don't come back and a whole bunch of them white hides do."

Another silence. "I don't know. I've known Jack a long time."

"It don't seem to get you too much."

"No sir, it don't, do it?"

"If you don't want the money, forget it."

"I didn't say I didn't want it."

"Just make sure he finds those white buffalo first."

There was a loud, rough laugh. "I done already got that figured out. I damn sure couldn't never find them. Ten thousand, right?"

338

"Ten thousand."

"You wouldn't cheat me, would you?"

"Hey, ain't I always been square with every man in this town?"

"You didn't pay us this last trip."

"Damn it, we've been over that and over that!" shouted John. "You didn't bring back what I sent you for!"

"All right, all right, Mr. Moar. Take it easy."

"After all, I got my reputation as a trader to think of. I don't cheat nobody. I'll trade as sharp as I can, but I won't cheat."

"Yes sir."

Frightened, Nelly stood. She had to get out of here. If John came in and suspected she had heard this, he would be furious. She didn't know what would happen to her, but she didn't like to think of what he might do. As well, if Jack went out there with Skinner Kincade ready to shoot him, he wouldn't come back here to take Sally off.

And the consequences of that were clear. Who else would the bereaved Sally turn to but John Moar?

Damn! Damn! Damn! cursed Nelly as she sped quietly around the room gathering up her clothes.

When she had dressed, she slipped out the door into the shadowy hallway. She heard voices nearing the door to Moar's office, voices suggesting that John was seeing Skinner to the door. Frightened, her shoes in her hand, Nelly shot for the stairs, and she reached the stairwell just as she heard the door opening behind her.

Had she been seen? She didn't know. She flew downstairs and ducked into the kitchen to put on her shoes. She looked into the two dining rooms and the bar, but she didn't see Jack. Probably with Sally somewhere, Nelly thought, but then Bob told her that Sally was seeing to Cora, who was about to have her baby tonight.

Nelly went out into the warm early-summer night. Main street of Hays City lay about her like a man muttering in his sleep, a man she imagined at any moment might roll over and crush her. Shouts, music and light exploded from the Drum, and she headed across the street. There she found Jack standing at the bar with half a dozen of his cronies, talking buffalo. Without too much guffawing from the fellows with him, she managed to sidle him off to the end of the bar to tell him of the conversation she had overheard.

While she was talking, he looked up over her shoulder, and she followed his gaze to see Skinner Kincade enter the Drum and head for the two of them.

"That's him!" she hissed as Skinner approached.

"You sure of all this?" Jack asked her.

"Oh, yes, Jack."

"You ain't lying to me, now?"

"On my momma's grave, I ain't, Jack. He means to kill you."

Jack gave a laugh and a snort as Skinner closed the distance between them. "I've handled him before, and I reckon I can damn sure handle him again. Hey, Skinner-man, have a drink!"

To Nelly, Skinner bore down on them as greedily as a bullfrog coming after flies.

Skinner's eyes narrowed as he asked, "You two fixing to have a bang-up night before we pull out, Jack?"

"Naw, my new bride wouldn't understand that," said Jack. "Nelly here wants to be the bridesmaid, she's so excited about the idea of marriage."

They all laughed together as Nelly marveled over

Jack's self-control in the face of what she had just told him.

"What time you want to pull out in the morning, Jack?" asked Skinner.

"Daybreak, Skinner. You get some new boys?"

"Billy Dixon, Amos Mates, and Tom Rath."

"Doesn't Billy Dixon work for Moar?"

"He wants to go out. Says his boss wants him to see how the hides is pulled."

"They ready to roll at daybreak?"

"That's what I told them—Jack McCall will pull out at daybreak and won't wait for nobody."

"You sure know me, Skinner-man."

"We been together long enough, I ought to."

"You're really going out tomorrow?" Nelly asked Jack, a little shaken by his skillful play-acting.

"Damn right, little lady," he said. "We're going to get us some big whites, ain't we, Skinner-man?"

"That's it, boss."

"Those buffalo are going to make us rich."

"Yes sir! That they are."

And when about eleven the next morning Nelly came downstairs, she found that Jack, Skinner and their crew had indeed pulled out at dawn.

She couldn't figure it out. Why had McCall gone? Didn't he believe her? Would he come back? Did she have any chance to get John Moar, or were Skinner and his buddies going to kill Jack and ruin her chances?

Chapter 11

In the weeks after the Kiowa warriors' defeat at the hands of the whites, Striking Eagle kept scouts on the plains. What they reported alarmed him. Despite his springtime efforts to scare off the white hunters, they had come back in still larger numbers, as if attacking had strengthened them.

Striking Eagle gathered three more war parties and led them out to the attack, yet he saw that most of the warriors didn't have the heart for such extended warfare. They longed to hunt buffalo, not protect them. If they fought, they longed to fight other tribes, where taking a scalp conferred honor on a man. Killing a white ghost had no more merit than killing a buzzard.

As well, several times he and his men had spotted federal bluecoats riding through on patrol, obviously looking to keep the Indians from attacking the whites. Their presence frightened his men. Alarmed by the soldiers, Striking Eagle made sure they didn't see his warriors. Once they even had to stay secluded behind rocks on a hillside while the soldiers camped for the better part of a day not one hundred yards away. In a fight, the bluecoats weren't pinned down to their wagons and hides like the white hunters. Mounted for chase, the bluecoats would attempt to ride a war party into the ground. If they could trap a tribe of Kiowa, they would cheerfully slaughter not only every brave, but every man, woman and child of the village.

Weary from his continual efforts to gather warriors from the village and to keep those with him full of courage, Striking Eagle actually admired these bluecoat patrols. As a war leader he had no similar troops. He drew his warriors from the ranks of the tribe's hunters, whereas these white soldiers did nothing but fight, and they had no families to encumber them.

Hoof, who led many of the late-night dances and recounting of exploits that kept up the spirits of the men, looked older and older these days, as if this conflict for the buffalo was draining the life from his face. Many evenings he told them that the whites had touched powerful magic, and that it would take all the power the Kiowa had to oppose them. Whether the whites had mastered good or evil magic didn't matter: if the tribe wasn't careful, the whites could run over the Kiowa with it.

When Striking Eagle talked to Hoof about this, asking his aged mentor what they would gain by fighting the whites, Hoof declared that because the whites' power was used for evil ends, it would one day destroy the white people. He said that what the Kiowa had to do until that power did destroy them was to remain alive, make sure the buffalo remained as their support, and keep their tribe intact.

"I will die before all this happens," Hoof told him.

"No."

"Yes."

"We'll drive them out in another few weeks."

"Maybe not for years, my son. I'm training you to carry on after I'm gone."

That left Striking Eagle somewhat shaky, for he had been pressing hard with the expectation that the war with the hunters would be a matter of weeks or a few months. The idea that the strain of fighting might go on for years—decades, if Hoof's weariness was any indicator—took a lot of spirit from him, which he could ill afford to show the others.

This year the plains swarmed with the two and three-wagon teams of white hunters, and with their powerful guns, kegs of ammunition and relentless accuracy, the Kiowa could do little to stop their slaughter of buffalo. In scores of valleys across the plains, hundreds of stripped buffalo lay rotting, a stinking reminder of the savagery of the white hunters. Following Hoof's suggestion, Striking Eagle sent scouts to other bands of the Kiowa and other tribes—Comanche, Utes and Cheyenne—to ask for warriors to aid in keeping the whites from the herds. The messengers returned bearing long-winded speeches from the other chiefs that all ended up as refusals. The other leaders weren't sure how best to oppose these evil and powerful enemies.

He and Hoof talked this over for another couple of weeks, with news coming in daily of still more slaughter of buffalo. Hard as it was to believe, hundreds of more whites were out this month than last, and with still larger rifles. A single shooter, lying on his belly near a herd, might bring down as many as one hundred buffalo a day and have two or three men skinning full-time. It made a Kiowa dizzy to think about it. Even with a large herd of splendid buffalo hunting horses and a gun, a Kiowa took no more than twenty to forty buffalo a year, needing no more meat to feed the four to eight people he cared for.

Such irresponsible behavior frightened every responsible man in the tribe, much as if the whites had begun to cart off the dirt beneath their feet or break off pieces of the sky to carry away.

As Hoof and Striking Eagle reminded the cautious braves, they were buffalo people, depending on the buffalo for about two thirds of their sustenance. Buffalo bones made tools, buffalo skins were sewn into clothing and tepees, buffalo meat kept them from hunger, buffalo paunches hauled water, buffalo tail they flicked about as a fly switch, buffalo horns they drank from, buffalo hooves they boiled down for glue, buffalo teeth they drilled and strung together for decoration, buffalo tallow preserved fruit and meat for the winter, buffalo hair they plaited for twine, buffalo hamstrings they prized for bowstrings—the list was endless. Of all the animals on the plains—deer, turkey, wolf, fox, prairie dog, antelope, elk and dog—the buffalo were more numerous and gave the tribe more than any other animal. Without buffalo, Hoof preached, the Kiowa couldn't live, and Striking Eagle followed this up with another rendition of his power vision and its truth: the white man intended to kill off all the buffalo.

Still, many neighboring chiefs didn't see the situation as grimly as Striking Eagle and Hoof. They cited the old legends that said the buffalo came out of the ground in the spring and went back in the winter. Yes, the whites killed the buffalo, and yes, they wasted the meat, but surely the carcasses melted into the ground, like snow, and came back in the spring. Only a third of the Kiowa saw any compelling reason to fight; most said that it was foolish to brave the whites' long guns. Why should they do something that looked as foolish as walking off the edge of a cliff?

Caught between the daily reports of buffalo slaughter

by the white hunters and tribal indifference and confusion, Striking Eagle worried about saving his people.

Hoof came up with a solution. "We will hold a sun dance and invite all the tribes to come."

"A sun dance?" Striking Eagle asked.

"*Wakan-Takan* will talk to them at the sun dance."

"But every tribe will be going to its own."

"No, we'll have it a month before the usual season."

"It's a good idea, grandfather."

"As hosts, they'll have to listen to us."

"I'll make a big speech to the combined council."

"More," Hoof said. "You will lead it."

"Lead the sun dance?"

"Yes."

"No, I'm too old. That's for a younger man."

"It's for a man with a vision who is ready to lead his people."

Striking Eagle felt himself shrink back from the suggestion. Leading the twelve-day ceremony took all a man's strength.

"Grandfather, I'm not worthy or strong enough. It's for men nearer twenty. I'm over thirty."

"Wait, there's more."

"More?"

"And you will perform the peyote ceremony at the height of the sun dance."

"No."

"Yes, grandson."

"No, no."

"Guiding others from the other tribes who will journey with you."

"No."

"It's the only way."

"But I—died on that last journey."

347

"You may die again."

"But I came back last time. This time—I don't know. And what about our guests?"

"They may have to die too."

The suggestion made Striking Eagle grow cold all over. What would the other tribes say if their young men went on this journey with him and died? Died in such a way that they didn't come back?

"No, grandfather. It's too much for me."

"It's yours to do."

His stomach had turned cold and queasy as he remembered the feeling the peyote had given him. He remembered the hours of vomiting, the cold fear that ran in his veins instead of hot blood, the involuntary shaking of his limbs, and how cut off he had been from the others for what seemed years before he had become the eagle and flown over the world. Flying over the world, that was all right, but the thought of those other things he had gone through made him shudder.

"Not me. Others should try," he said to Hoof.

"You know how," Hoof answered. "It's better you show them the way to fly over the world."

Fear gripped Striking Eagle as he considered what the old man said. He wanted to throw up right then, feeling his stomach rebel against the peyote caps. He wanted to refuse completely, declare himself a coward or a woman, and turn his back to the idea. He wanted to take his family, leave the tribe, and go off where fighting such long-range guns didn't exist, to a place where you could hunt buffalo, trade with other tribes, and from time to time war with them in a decent manner. Before all this buffalo trouble started, before the white man arrived, you fought the Utes or the Apache till one side had wounded a few others, maybe killed one or two, and then you quit. These whites wanted to slaughter the way Death did. These whites looked like Death and grinned like Death. They smelled like Death, they sounded like Death, and they looked at you like Death—with no fear, only mockery and crazy lights in their sky-colored eyes. That too made a man's stomach sick just to think of it.

"Please, Hoof," Striking Eagle said. "Another."

"Who?"

"Big Tree," he said. "Santana. White Horse."

"But you've seen the way. They haven't."

"Yes, I have seen. But I don't want to intrude again on the picture *Wakan-Takan* has of the world."

"You're the leader of this tribe now," Hoof said in a gentle fashion. "Yes, you're afraid, son. That's all right. Fear is the warrior's companion. That is who you are—a warrior—and that is your great worth to your people."

Striking Eagle felt the old man's eyes raking through his heart. "Yes, grandfather. But I'm so afraid I don't know if I can do this."

"I know, but you will do it anyway," said Hoof.

"The others don't want to fight."

"We'll see. We have to perform our roles."

"Our roles?"

"We Kiowa are to bring the tribes together and make the right conditions for *Wakan-Takan* to talk to them."

"We are? How do you know?"

The old man didn't answer, just looked at him, and Striking Eagle realized he had protested more than he had any right to.

"I'm sorry, grandfather. But will they come?"

"The peyote-taking, something new and powerful for these tribes, will bring them. They will think this is such new power that it may save them, and it may. That you will lead it—you, who have traveled through the sky and survived—will encourage the others to tread that path.''

Over the next few days, Striking Eagle was seething with agony. Hoof might be right, but he still didn't want to lead the peyote journey, and he couldn't think of it without fear making his limbs cold.

"Ah, father,'' he said to Hoof a few days later. "I'll do this thing. I just pray I have the strength. You don't know what such a journey does to you.''

The lines in Hoof's face seemed deeper than ever, as deep as the creases in the hills, as he said, "My son, I was with you last time. I saw.'' Hoof took Striking Eagle's hands in his. "You may not come back. Those with you may not come back. I too pray you have such strength.''

Onni had followed as many of Granny Fox Face's instructions as she could, bringing in bits of Elk Woman's hair, articles of her clothing, and even scraps of food left over from her cooking pot. The old woman was attempting to discover what powers Onni's husband's other wife had taken to herself and how she had used them.

The old woman muttered and asked for more herbs: a large bundle of sweetgrass, sumac leaves, hemp, three handfuls of morning-glory seeds, white horse nettle, buttonbush and prairie sage.

Relations with Striking Eagle had settled into a wary coolness. He still spent an equal number of nights in each lodge, but Onni sensed she was losing him to the strong feelings of resentment that made her stiff with anger. Somehow Elk Woman didn't seem hampered by Onni, yet Onni felt as if the presence of her rival, not forty feet away in her own lodge, caused her to shrink back from her husband. Several times she had tried to break through her own feelings by asking Striking Eagle intense questions about his war parties, but it didn't work. Of course, a warrior might not feel comfortable talking about war with his wife, but before all this trouble had started, they had shared everything together, as far as she knew. She had lost that forever, she reckoned.

At the same time, Onni sent Willow to spy on Elk Woman. She wanted Willow to get to know her rival better, figuring that her sister would be less suspicious than she and would see more evidence of her rival's dabbling in witchcraft. If Onni could obtain evidence of witchcraft, she could ruin Elk Woman's reputation in the tribe and possibly cancel the marriage. There was little else that was seen as more evil by the tribe than secret witchcraft. So Onni's sister became friendly with Elk Woman. They cooked together, scraped hides together, and played with her children together.

They became so friendly that one day Elk Woman, passing her tent, asked Onni, "Why aren't you as friendly to me as your sister and husband? We have to live together a long time. Why not be friends?"

Yet Onni, choking on her anger, couldn't speak to her.

"Your tongue's up your nose, eh?" asked Elk Woman in the phrase that mothers used with hostile children.

Onni couldn't contain herself, replying with the curse, "May your womb shrivel into dirt!"

Elk Woman blanched and pulled back. "How dare you talk to me that way! I'm older than you and your senior."

"No, you're not! I married him first."

"Ha! *He* doesn't feel that way."

"I come first. He's been with me since we were eighteen."

"And he's just staying with you out of pity."

"No! He loves me."

"No, he loves me. He's stuck with you."

"No!"

As if possessing secret knowledge, Elk Woman smiled serenely and walked on. Onni seethed. That woman! It wasn't right! Damn Wolf, or Striking Eagle—whatever everybody called him. She didn't like his new name much more than she liked her sister-wife, for all this trouble had started just before he had changed his name.

That night she asked Willow what she had discovered in spying on Elk Woman.

"Find?"

"You were going to see if she killed Eagle Beak."

"Oh, Onni! You're not still on that."

"Yes."

"She didn't."

"How do you know?"

"We're friends. She showed me lots of things."

"What?"

Willow pointed to the amulet around her neck made of buffalo hair. "She gave me this."

Onni leaned forward. "What's that?"

Her sister giggled and whispered, "With it, I got Horse Head to follow me around for two days."

Onni remembered what a fool that young man had made of himself last week with Willow. "But how?"

"It's a secret, but I know how to get any man interested."

Onni snorted. "So do I. Go into the bushes with him."

"No, I mean to snare their eyes to the point that they can't live without looking at you."

"So you too have failed me."

"Failed you!"

"She's bewitched you with this love charm."

"Oh, Onni, you've gotten carried away by nothing."

"I'm being undermined on every side."

Willow sighed in exasperation. "There's just no talking to you, is there?"

"I guess not," Onni replied.

Over the next few days, Onni brooded over what felt like the loss of her sister too. Would it never end? Now that her husband had taken a second wife, did it mean she should drown herself?

She still brought Granny Fox Face whatever the old woman wanted, although she had begun to lose faith that the old woman could do anything for her. At her suggestion, Onni dropped into Elk Woman's stew pot several pinches of a mixture that the old woman had her grind up, a mixture of morning-glory seeds, white horse nettle and buttonbush, which the old woman said would force Elk Woman to blurt out the truth of any crimes she had committed.

When Onni reported a week later to Granny Fox Face that no blurting of crimes had occurred, the old woman merely told her to slip more of the mixture into her food. By dint of a great effort of will, Onni pretended to be friendly to her rival, keeping Elk Woman's children for her almost every day and thereby managing to put the herbs into the stew pot every day for ten days. But the only result seemed to be that Elk Woman turned redder in the face and grew even more gay, while Onni grew more despondent.

Two weeks later, Elk Woman asked, "Thank you for those spices you put into my stew pot. What were they? Both Striking Eagle and I have enjoyed them so much that we want to gather some on our own."

Elk Woman patted Onni on the cheek, and Onni felt too mortified to move from the patronizing gesture. So that hadn't worked either. She saw that nothing was likely to work, and she stopped going to Granny Fox Face. By now Onni was close to despair. Perhaps she had been wrong about Elk Woman. Perhaps she had become so blindly jealous that she had imagined that Elk Woman was evil, when really with all this spying and sneaking of herbs into stew pots Onni was the evil one. She had even had her children secretly trail Elk Woman, watch her, and tell Onni everywhere her sister-wife went in the village, hoping to discover her going to some taboo place, such as the hills where the dead were buried or the field where the owls gathered. But while the youngsters enjoyed the game of spy, Elk Woman did no more evil than any other woman.

Then, a couple of weeks before the sun dance, Onni felt a strong need to get away from the village for a few hours. Sick of the gossip and feeling that every knot of women was laughing at her, she decided to go berry picking. This gave her a good excuse to be away and didn't waste any time. Willow wanted to go too, as did the children, and while she disappointed them by saying that she wouldn't take them, she went anyway.

Carrying her two buffalo paunch buckets, she marched out of the village on a glorious day in June. Her problems back in camp melted away the farther away she strode. Getting out of the close air of the village helped, Onni realized. It gave her the perspective to see that conditions in her life had changed, and that if she didn't want to tear herself apart, she had to accept her husband's second wife. With some gaiety, she filled one buffalo paunch with plums, and had started to fill the other with blackberries when something that danced about in the shadow of the nearby cliff caught her attention. She looked more closely. Wasn't that a colt prancing about there in the entrance to the canyon? If she could trap and catch her own colt, what a coup for her! As she walked toward the colt, she saw him more clearly: six months old, with a beautiful white blaze on his forehead and chest. It backed into the canyon.

But when Onni reached the cool spot under the cliff, she was startled to find no young horse there, and not even tracks.

Puzzled, she looked about. How could she have seen it so clearly and now couldn't find any tracks? In the coolness of the shadow of the cliff a shiver of fear swept through her. Suddenly she wanted to run from this spot back into the warmth of the berryfield.

She started to leave, but her feet wouldn't lift from the ground. Around her she heard a rumbling that frightened her so much that her feet rooted still more firmly. Her stomach clenched. Onni looked up and saw the sky falling toward her. Screaming loudly, she flung herself to the right with all her force and fell onto the cool earth, where she waited for merciful death.

A loud crash, the earth she clung to rattled, then silence. For several moments she lay there without moving, waiting for more sky to fall, but around her the cool glade seemed peaceful. A blue jay sang, its song mocking her feelings of terror.

Her limbs trembling, Onni pulled herself together and sat up. She felt weak. Where she had been standing now squatted an ugly, grinning boulder as big around and tall as one of her children. Had her fear not been so great as to push her away, the stone would have crushed her. Frightened, she scrambled to her feet and backed out into the sunlight away from the cliff.

As the warmth of the sun struck her, she cried out in relief. She was alive! She shuddered all over, like a dog shaking off lake water.

She lifted her eyes to the top of the cliff and gasped,

for there she saw a demon, a creature with a long, curling tail and small, spiky horns. The demon was the size of a big dog, with a face like a man's but covered in black hair like a buffalo. It stood on its hind legs and waved its arms and tail about in anger. At once Onni saw that this demon had pushed the boulder at her and was furious that it hadn't killed her. It had lured her with the false picture of the colt and had tried to kill her!

She wanted to wring the creature's neck, but its dancing antics frightened her too much to think of chasing it. She kept backing away, and when the demon saw this, it picked up smaller rocks and threw them at her. But the creature wasn't powerful enough to fling them far and they fell many yards short.

Onni knew what this was about. Elk Woman, having discovered that Onni was trying to prove that she had murdered Eagle Beak, had captured this demon with her spells and commanded him to destroy Onni. This the creature had to do in order to be released from captivity. He was furious now because he had failed.

With exultation, she realized that she had caught Elk Woman now! She quickly found her paunches of plums and berries and hurried to camp. This time Elk Woman had gone too far. Now she had what she needed to destroy her rival!

Despite her close call, Onni was in a fever of determination. She caught sight of Striking Eagle almost as soon as she turned into the main way of the village. In the midst of an important set of Cheyenne chiefs who had just arrived, he was preparing to go into the Kanasa lodge, where they would discuss the sun dance. He could be there talking with these chiefs for days, and she couldn't spare this much time. She hurried forward.

"Eagle, I have to talk to you," she said.

A woman didn't approach a man at a time like this, and Striking Eagle looked annoyed, but she didn't care. When he heard her news, everything would be different.

"Not now," he murmured, looking at his solemn visitors.

"Please, it's important."

"I have to meet with these chiefs," he explained.

"It won't take long. I have to see you."

Knowing that she was doing the right thing, Onni persisted, and finally he broke away from his guests and came with her into their lodge. His face was full of thunder. Well, it would change when he heard her news.

She calmed herself as she began to talk, for she was tempted to rush through the events due to his being in a hurry. But it was important for him to hear it all. As she drew out the circumstances, he looked at her impatiently and asked her to hurry. She talked faster, struggling to describe how unnaturally cool it was under that cliff, how handsome the colt was, how her feet were made to root in the ground through some spell. She described the size of the boulder, the evilness of the demon and how lucky she was to be alive.

The news that she had almost been killed moved him. He cried out in anguish and took her in his arms. There she shuddered a bit and let herself sink against his warmth. She hadn't felt so relieved in months. He loved her! He believed her!

He pushed her back and said he would talk to her more when he had properly welcomed these guests.

"No, there's more!" she said.

"More?"

"The creature—the demon!"

"The demon? You told me you saw him."

He now looked resentful that she had more to say, so

she quickly blurted, "But don't you see? He was trying to kill me."

"Don't go back to that rock face."

"But *she* did it, Eagle."

"She?"

"She did, really."

He groaned. "Oh, no. You're not starting that all over again, are you?"

"She did!"

"Onni."

"She did!"

He looked disgusted and she felt herself losing him. Why wouldn't he listen?

"Yes, the demon probably threw the rock at you, but to blame your sister-wife, Onni. . . ." He looked pained. "I won't stand for it."

"She did it!"

"But you can't be sure of that," he said. "That demon was probably just wandering by and saw you."

"But why would he attack me? I didn't do anything to him."

"It's very plain. He wanted your berries," Striking Eagle said. "You promised me you wouldn't start in on her again."

"But she did it."

"No, you're just imagining things."

Onni started recounting the incident again, from the sighting of the colt, but Striking Eagle got to his feet. "No, I won't listen. I should make you apologize to Elk Woman, but I won't. Onni, this has to stop."

And he left. In despair, she complained to Willow, who reacted with the same contempt as Striking Eagle. Shocked, she said nothing to anyone else.

For the next few days Onni wandered about the vil-

lage in a dream, hardly caring whether she did her chores
or not. Willow took over the household, and even her
children seemed to back away from her. She didn't have
the strength to go after them. She didn't care about anything. Women stared at her as if she were some strange
creature, but she no longer cared. At the end of this week,
she came down with a high fever, and Willow had to bind
her to keep her in bed, where she writhed about in a
struggle to escape her bonds.

Because Onni cried out for her so much and would
have no one else, Striking Eagle hired Granny Fox Face,
the old medicine woman, to minister to her. The old
woman arrived on a sweltering June day wrapped in half a
dozen robes and quilts. As usual, no one saw her face
buried behind so many folds of cloth and hides. Granny
peered into Onni's eyes for a long time and then sat by her
side, looking just like a heap of buffalo hides. She began
to chant. Onni's fever rose. Granny chased the children
and Striking Eagle out of the lodge and started three fires.
Refusing Willow's offer of help, she made Striking Eagle
select a cousin to pick herbs.

For the next two days, Onni's condition did not improve. The fever rose and the old woman chanted day and
night. Onni screamed as demons pranced about the lodge.
The old woman kept sprinkling sage, sweetgrass and night-
shade on the fires and singing three chants over and over
to ward the demons off. She supervised all of Onni's
meals, seeing that she only got tea and a special mush she
prepared. Onni sweated so much that the old woman had
to change the robe that covered the girl four times from
one sunup to the next.

Many times Onni shouted that she had been poisoned;
each time the old woman would put her hand over Onni's

face and mouth to soothe her and then assure her that she would keep her alive.

One night the illness rose to its height. Onni burned and tossed about even more. A wild light illuminated her eyes.

"She will pass the night and live, or she will die tonight," Granny told Striking Eagle.

"No, she can't die."

"She may."

"Some demon's got her."

Contemptuously, Granny said, "Any fool can see that."

"I want her to live," said Eagle.

"Do you?"

He looked at her sharply. "She's my wife. I love her. The children and I will miss her."

"She doesn't know that."

"But it's true."

"Tell her."

"Tell her?"

"Lean down and tell her just that," said Granny. "Say it strongly and repeat it ten times."

He felt foolish doing it, but frightened as he was of the illness and of Granny, he did as she told him. When he rose to go, he said, "If she dies, I'm not giving you those two ponies we talked about." He was referring to the fee they had agreed on.

From under the hood of her many coverings, the old woman stared at him for several moments. "Do you care for this wife much?" she asked.

"Make her well."

"She feels you love your other wife and hate her."

"No."

"No matter what happens, you'll pay me my ponies," the old woman said as she turned back to her patient.

"I won't," Striking Eagle said. "You better do your best."

The old woman turned back to him. "Young man, if you don't do as you promised, this world doesn't have enough room to hide you or enough arrows to protect you. You're upset because she's ill, and that's all to the good, but get out and go gossip with that old fool Hoof."

Hardly knowing how to reply, Striking Eagle left.

Onni passed the night in a wild state, but by dawn, although weak, the old woman said she would live.

Over the next few days Onni grew stronger. She had passed through a tortuous valley filled with sharp boulders and sudden holes, a journey that had exhausted her.

She argued with Willow that she had been poisoned by Elk Woman, just as Elk Woman had poisoned Eagle Beak, the husband who stood in the way of her marrying Striking Eagle. Elk Woman wanted Striking Eagle all to herself and was now trying to kill her to get her out of the way. Willow told her that she was still ill from the fever, and that she was allowing her jealousy to mushroom into a cancerous hatred that was destroying her.

"Oh, sister, am I?" asked Onni from her sickbed.

"Elk Woman isn't evil," said Willow.

"I can't stand to see her. She makes me shudder all over."

"Onni, that's what jealousy feels like."

"But Granny Fox Face says she's evil too."

"Ha! Pay me skins and ponies and I'll say whatever you want me to."

"No, she's a good woman."

"But all medicine men have to eat and trade. And that one's crazy on top of it."

"You never played around her lodge when you were growing up."

"But I'm grown now. She hasn't got that much power."

"She made me well. Got that poison out of me!"

"Oh, Onni! There you go again!"

"Granny isn't crazy."

"As crazy as a loon that's eaten mita berries."

Onni fell silent as she considered it. "Have I been making a fool of myself, sister?"

"A big fool of yourself."

In the calm that she felt now that the fever had lifted, Onni could see this. Certainly some strong emotion raged through her, and maybe it was all just jealousy. She had fought her husband's marriage, something only a few Kiowa wives did. Maybe all she had been through was what a woman who thought she would never have to share a man went through when she learned she had to give up half her husband. A sob shook through her, but she concealed it from Willow.

"You're right, sister," said Onni. "I've been a fool."

"Oh, Onni, you love him so much. Too much. I never could love a man the way you do. It doesn't make sense to me. But it's sweet to see."

Onni smiled and reached out to clasp her sister's hand. "I don't have a lot of choice. But I'm going to listen to you and get along with her."

"Oh, Onni, you don't know what good news that is!" her sister replied. "I want so much for us all to live in peace with each other."

When Granny Fox Face, still covered with robes and hides in the midday heat, came again to see her, Onni wanted to send her away, for she was no longer sick and

Granny only reminded her of the craziness she had passed through over the last few weeks.

"I came, although you don't want to see me," said the old woman.

Onni started to protest, then fell silent as she realized that the old woman had anticipated her response.

"You're still in great danger," the old woman went on.

"I feel fine."

"I see that."

"Has my husband paid you your fee?"

"Yes."

"Good-bye then, and thank you for your help."

"Don't dismiss me so fast, young woman. I see around you great danger, and I must warn you."

"Danger? What danger?"

"I can't see that. It could be from any quarter. What's distressing is that you're mixed up in it as the agent of your own danger."

"Me?"

"The signs are strange but positive," the old woman said. "You must tread carefully or you will destroy yourself."

"What do you mean?"

"I can see no more. I had to warn you."

After repeating the warning, the old woman left. Baffled, Onni tossed about on her bed, struggling to figure out what the old woman meant. Had she put herself in a position with Elk Woman and her husband that would destroy her? But she was finished with that. Was she dying from her own overwhelming hatred of her rival?

Maybe the old woman was mad, Onni thought. Or was Elk Woman just incredibly evil and strong? If the old woman wasn't mad, it was clear that Onni had to find a method to expose her rival's evil, and soon, before she wound up following the path of Elk Woman's dead husband. She shivered at the thought.

But what would she do? And suppose it was Onni and the old woman who were mad?

In response to the dozens of messengers that Old Hoof sent to the other councils, the village gradually filled with tribesmen from neighboring Kiowa camps, as well as Cheyenne, Comanche, Utes, and Kiowa-Apache, those strange Apache who copied the manners and customs of the Kiowa and had brought peyote to Hoof from the people in Mexico.

There were thousands of warriors, women and children in the village as July neared. They had all come to take part in or observe the sun dance that Hoof and Striking Eagle had agreed on, particularly because the messengers' invitations had tantalized them. As the witnesses to his test swelled the village, the pressure Striking Eagle felt about his role in the peyote-eating increased. With more and more difficulty, he kept a calm face in deliberations and put on a smile to welcome chief after chief.

So many came this year, not only because the dance was held early—June instead of July—but because the centerpiece of the power ceremony was eating peyote. They had all heard much about eating peyote. As the strongest thing in the world, stronger even than buffalo power, such a substance commanded that a man respect it.

During the weeks before the dance, Striking Eagle, Left Hand, Old Hoof, Santana, White Horse and all the leaders of the Kiowa entertained visitors and were entertained in return. The Kiowa passed out gifts of buffalo parfleches, leggings and quivers. In turn, they received decorated buffalo robes, gourd rattles and ceremonial bows. The Kiowa fed their visitors in their tepees. In return, their visitors brought meat to their hosts, meat from buffalo they had shot on their trek across the plains. Wives visited each other, children who couldn't speak each other's language played bear-and-buffalo, and dogs from each camp chased each other endlessly through all the lodges. When they weren't gambling or racing ponies, the young men hunted buffalo, proving their bravery to each other in daring feats of horsemanship, for the ten thousand people now gathered here ate fifty buffalo a day. The weeks before a sun dance were a time of high festivity, grave talks and much foolishness—the best part of the year.

Striking Eagle had wrestled with his part in the festival. At the age of thirty-three, he didn't want to lead a sun dance.

"I'm not worthy of this attention," Striking Eagle told Hoof again as the sun dance neared.

"Tomorrow you must tell them about the peyote-eating," Hoof answered, referring to the gathered chiefs. "They need to select the young men who will eat peyote with you."

Striking Eagle sighed. Was the old man hard of hearing or just ignoring him? "I don't have the strength for this, grandfather."

"Strength? Nonsense."

"I had to die before."

"But you lived."

"They will have to die. Suppose they don't come back?"

The old man hesitated.

"You and I will bear the blame," Striking Eagle told him.

"You are our chief, Eagle. Our strongest. Who else?"

Who else indeed? The chiefs of other Kiowa bands—Santana, White Horse, Old Lone Wolf, White Wolf, Big

365

Tree and Santank—had arrived. But great as each of them was, none had eaten peyote.

The old man went on, "I don't want you to die again, but is there any way to give them the power of peyote without their eating it?"

"No."

"And will they eat it if you don't?"

"No."

"That's right. No. And hasn't it given you and your men courage all spring?"

"Yes, but we've hardly stopped the pelt hunters."

"That's why you and I have to spread peyote to the other tribes."

"Yes."

Striking Eagle understood this, but he didn't like it. He remembered clearly the letting go, welcoming dying, and the pain that had preceded it. He didn't know if he had the strength to go through it again and to struggle at the same time to get the others to go through it. Over the next few days, nothing he said could make Hoof see this, either. The old man was adamant. "It must be done," he was told. "If not you, who?"

Finally Striking Eagle had to give in. "I put myself in your hands, grandfather."

This meant that the day before any of the others began their preparations, Striking Eagle had to go into the sweat lodge with Old Hoof and his assistants. Once inside, he stripped bare and sang the chants that Hoof prescribed. He breathed as he was told to breathe, he sat as instructed, and over and over again he cleared his mind of its petty concerns so he could focus on his task: getting these other tribesmen to see what he had seen when he flew over the world.

Death, he told himself with a whisper of breath.

Death, death, death. I am going to die, and it's nothing to be afraid of. I'll be terrified, but I'll let go and live. I'll be born an eagle.

But no matter how many times he told himself he had lived through it once and would again, he still felt dread. The point of death was that you died. You ceased to be. Everything in him fought going through that.

While he focused on handling himself amid the hissing of the rocks as they were dropped into buffalo paunches filled with water, Striking Eagle, longing to be outside, pictured what was going on there. The bravest warriors were in the woods to the north picking out the center pole for the sun dance lodge. Once planted in the center, the most virtuous women would adorn it with leaves. Everywhere in the giant camp—two thousand lodges were now present, and some ten thousand people—excitement mounted as the two hundred young warriors from five tribes who would dance the sun dance prepared themselves in fifteen similar sweat lodges.

The initial four days of preparation passed. The sun dance lodges and bowers had been erected, and the sacred four arrived. The priest led the dancers and they assembled while chanting and dancing. Finally this year's most important night had arrived—the night of peyote-eating.

Heretofore Striking Eagle had told the other young chiefs of his eating peyote, but only in vague terms. He'd told them it had allowed him to fly, that he had seen marvels, and that he had seen many other tribes besides his own. Some showed an eagerness to take it. Others seemed to sense that it might be too powerful for them. Striking Eagle told them it was the strongest power he had ever touched, far stronger than the white man's gunpowder. This amazed everyone who heard it, for they all knew that for its size, except perhaps a shaman's medicine bundle, there wasn't much else that had the power of that black powder.

Hoof announced he would choose five men from each tribe's youthful dancers to eat peyote with Striking Eagle, and he would look for courage, strength and suppleness in making his choices. Much as he thought all shamans were a bit fraudulent at times, Striking Eagle had to admire this strategy. By making this dangerous practice something to vie for, the youths would eagerly eat the mushroom caps.

That big day the dancing went well, except for one Ute who screamed in the middle of the afternoon when they were doing their fourth turn around the third buffalo skull altar. The Ute youth thrashed about in a struggle to knock off the insects. As two Ute shamans ministered to the sobbing youth, the other dancers, with difficulty, kept their minds on the chants and their feet in the proper rhythms, well aware that at this point nothing should interfere with the dance. If anything did, they risked having the mountainous strength of the powers they had balanced around the lodge topple on them.

It turned out this Ute had crept away from the dancers two nights ago and slept with a Cheyenne woman who was having her monthly bleeding, a significant taboo for such a powerful time, and that giant beetles and ants had attacked him. He died that night with great welts all over his body where the teeth of the insects left their marks.

At the end of the day, Old Hoof announced his selections and led the twenty-five youths to a new tepee. One was Left Hand, Eagle's friend. Hoof and the shamans from the other tribes were placed around the edges of the tepee, and the youths were positioned in the center with Striking Eagle sitting before them. He looked like a man leading a group of singers.

Old Hoof burned plenty of sage and sweetgrass and

passed around the tobacco pipe before he told them that they were likely to have strong visions. They must attend to them, he said, for in them they would find the key to their and their tribes' lives. Of course, what he said wasn't new to them. Before any Plains youth went on a vision quest or a fast into the mountains, the shaman made some such speech. Most of them hardly listened to what he said and just stared at the three mushroom caps he had placed in their hands, wondering how something this small could create such a fuss.

After he had taken his four caps, Striking Eagle went through all the familiar states. First he felt exhilaration. All these dour people around were wonderfully gay, if they would only drop their dourness! He vomited, bringing up only bile, since he hadn't eaten in two days. Hoof brought him water and told him the others were doing well. What others? He looked up and saw the other young men, but they looked like rolls of buffalo tallow and pemmican to him, just ripe meat. They would shortly feel the dangers of eating peyote and attack him for inducing them to take it. Hoof would blame him. These ideas grew and he suffered. He lay down in a comfortable position, but fear rose again in him and he stood up and said he had to go outside. Hoof wanted to stop him, but he wandered out.

Here in the middle of the village—he realized it was after midnight now and that most of the village was exhausted by the day's events and lay sleeping—with the stars piercing him with their stares, he was struck by a fear greater than any he had ever felt in his life. He was certain he was going to die any minute. He functioned, breathed, and thought, and all this would stop because he had faith in a foolish old man who thought he could get these others to do as he wished. Wasn't his life more important than

369

this old man's foolish wishes? Fearful that he would throw himself onto an arrow or a lance if he didn't return to the peyote lodge, Striking Eagle dropped onto all fours and waddled back inside. Again he lay down, this time in a spot away from the center. He hoped someone would talk to him, which was the only thing that would prevent him from dying, and yet when one of the Comanche shamans wiped the sweat off his brow and murmured some little lullaby in that language, he knew without a doubt any moment he would die gradually.

As he lay there, something bumped him. He turned his head to look down his torso. There lay Left Hand, his friend, looking up anxiously at him.

"Eagle."

"Hand."

"I'm dying."

He felt puzzled. How could Left Hand die when he had only taken a couple of mushroom caps? Then his own fear came back to remind him. "No," he told his friend. "You just feel bad for a while."

"Yes, I'm dying."

"It will pass."

"This will never pass," said the stricken face of Left Hand. "The others too."

Striking Eagle looked up. The other youths groaned and writhed all over the lodge.

"They're dying!" shouted a Kiowa-Apache shaman at Hoof. "You've killed them!"

"No," said Hoof.

"No," said Striking Eagle. He felt shaky and weak. With enormous difficulty, he pulled himself to his feet.

Except for the stricken youths, the two dozen shamans turned to stare at him. "Even if the buzzards come and want to eat you, you have to give yourself to them."

This produced shouts of concern and fear.

"It's the only thing you can do," he told them.

A few of the oldest and wisest shamans seemed to understand such an idea, but only with difficulty could they persuade the others to go along with it.

Sitting up and attending to the others had quieted Striking Eagle. The fear was still inside him, but crouched in a corner as if it were waiting for a better time to strike. After the fevers, the sickness in the stomach and the chills, the procession began. Peyote eaters and shamans alike stared.

First the small creatures pranced into the tepee: lice, ticks, mosquitoes, gnats, mites and midges. They were soon replaced by slightly larger insects: flies, bees, wasps, beetles, doodlebugs and ants. They swaggered along in a line through the entrance hole of the tepee and danced through the air. There were about fifty to a hundred of each species, and most entered in an orderly way, but sometimes they crowded and shoved each other out of line. The men stared wide-eyed at their visitors, who came in through the entrance hole and marched upward in the air to the smoke hole. Following them flew the birds, starting with the jays, sparrows and tits, and progressing through the hawks, crows, ducks, magpies, owls, chickens, snowbirds and doves. Striking Eagle expected the buzzards to appear then, and dreaded their appearance, but at the end of this group marched the land animals, small before large.

Mice, rats, prairie dogs, muskrats, porcupine, raccoon, fox, rabbit, skunks and beaver marched in a line. Following them came dogs and wolves, ermine and coyote, deer and buffalo, then mountain lion and elk. It seemed as if all the creatures of *Wakan-Takan* were to come through the tepee tonight, and only by Striking Eagle's calming influence on the other youthful warriors were they many times able to sit still before an angry-looking mountain lion or furious wolf.

Certainly the procession had their attention, and it was obvious, to Striking Eagle anyway, that it had been sent here by *Wakan-Takan* to teach them. But teach them what?

Then in swaggered the buzzards, the final members of the procession. Striking Eagle had to put his palms on the earth floor to steady himself.

The biggest buzzard looked around the tent and cawed, "So much to eat here tonight!"

Better to run, Striking Eagle said to himself. These six, no eight, would have plenty to eat on besides me. I can be outside till they've eaten their fill.

"Eagle!" shouted Hoof. "Give yourself. Show how it's done."

Damn Hoof! He turned and saw the old man staring at him.

Damn Hoof! Easy for him to order Striking Eagle what to do!

The chief buzzard, eight feet tall, had rotted meat still stuck in its beak, and its feathers seemed covered with cobwebs and filth.

"Give him your hand," said Hoof.

Sweating, Eagle moved back.

"Your hand."

"No," Eagle answered in a small voice.

The buzzard laughed, raising its voice to a raucous caw.

Striking Eagle looked around and saw that every eye in the tepee was on him and that they all looked at his disobedience with contempt.

He had done it before. He had lived.

But I don't want to die.

I don't want to.

As if in a dream, he moved forward with his hand outstretched. The buzzard stared at it, and when he was three feet from the giant bird, it pecked forward and took off the hand in a fast snap.

Pain rushed up his arm. His hand, his right hand, that pulled the bow, held the children, was gone!

And at once he knew that the only way to get it back was to go with it. With that knowledge came laughter and he moved forward.

He offered the giant bird his other hand and forearm, and he lay down and shoved his feet at the beaks.

He shouted to the others, "Follow me! Let them eat you!"

He again felt himself being chewed and swallowed, but this time, now that he wasn't fighting it, it wasn't as painful or hard. He turned and yelled again to the others, seeing that only with reluctance were they following his lead, urged on by the attending shamans.

Of the twenty-five warriors who took the buttons with him, only nineteen followed Striking Eagle into the dozen buzzards' craws. After a long black journey through the bird, squeezed on every side by the slippery guts, like a child Striking Eagle was born again out of an eagle, and up through the smoke hole he flew to circle the lodge while he waited for the others to appear, as the nineteen did, one by one. As each flapped his new wings, amazed at his eagle power, Striking Eagle flew down to touch wing tips with his new brother and welcome him to the air. When all nineteen had come out and flew around the lodge, he led them toward the east. They had a long distance to fly before dawn.

He led them on much the same journey he had taken the time before, showing them the strange caves of the white men, the houses that walked on the water, and the huge numbers of whites who lived by the giant lakes. What impressed them were the number of whites and the foulness of their dwelling places. Where the whites crowded together, no trees grew, no brother animals sported, and no grasses waved. There was only bare dirt and hard rock. The whites seemed to live in such lonely places that they did not have *Wakan-Takan* nearby to embrace them.

In a climactic scene, they came upon a field on which all the buffalo in the world had been gathered by *Wakan-Takan,* and as the twenty man-eagles wheeled helplessly in the sky, they watched the white man with his long rods of death kill every one. Repeatedly the eagles and buffalo cried out to the white man to stop this killing, but the whites heard their cries only as foolish birds cawing and not as the angry warnings of warriors. Several swooped to attack the whites with their beaks and talons, but the whites, furious at this interruption of their slaughter, turned the guns on them. Yellow Head the Ute was brought down by a shot and fell to the earth, dead. The other eagles whirled skyward in panic. Striking Eagle pulled them back and with difficulty made them understand that they weren't strong enough at present to attack; they were being shown a vision of what was to come. Later they should fight the whites.

Not many of the eagles believed him, but he persevered in his speeches to them, fearful they would hurt themselves in these attacks. Reluctantly they went along with his argument, swooped down to pick up the dead Yellow Head with their talons, and silently beat their great wings for the return journey.

The nineteen had reacted to the journey in the way Striking Eagle had: the power to fly thrilled them, the number of whites dismayed them, and what the whites did to their brothers the buffalo shocked them. Carrying their one dead brother, passing the burden from talon to talon, the nineteen flew back to the peyote lodge with one thought: they had to unite all the horse fighters of the Plains to stop the whites, for it was obvious that the increase in buffalo hunters were merely the vanguard of a horde of whites bent on wiping the earth clean of *Wakan-Takan* before building their dead caves everywhere.

As they flew back, the eagles threw thoughts back and forth between themselves, struggling to make more sense of what they had seen.

"Can't they see that when they have wiped the earth of life, they will have destroyed themselves?" asked Red Bull the Comanche.

"They have been infected with the South Wind," answered Striking Eagle, "who everybody knows wants to have a world without creatures so it can blow about freely."

"They're like some leech, destroying the earth," said Red Bull.

"If we don't stop them, they'll kill everything that makes our land live," said Striking Eagle.

From the caws and cries around him, Striking Eagle knew every man-eagle flying with him agreed.

As the sun touched the Kiowa sky, with a great beating of wings the nineteen giant eagles flew around the peyote tepee and then down its smoke hole. The shamans and grandfathers sitting around the lodge looked up, startled and frightened by the rush of air, but as dawn broke the eagles shed their feathers and again became men.

This time Striking Eagle watched the changes within himself more closely. Death felt like pain followed by liberation. Flying through the air he had felt long and sharp, like a falling icicle. Landing back here in the tepee, he heard a raining inside himself like the falling of dozens of beads on a drumhead, as if he were filled with thousands of pebbles and grains of sand that were falling through him. Abruptly the rattling sand and pebbles within stopped. He realized he had completely returned to his everyday world, but with a sharpened sense of himself and everyone around him. He felt as if his insides had been washed clean of the clottings of filth, and that he was as ready for what the world brought as when he was a youth of eighteen.

Around him the eighteen warriors who had flown with him stirred and looked about with the same sense of wonder. Yellow Head lay slumped over, and when he was examined, he was found to be dead.

"What happened?" asked Old Hoof.

"The whites killed him," said Striking Eagle.

"How?"

Striking Eagle opened Yellow Head's deerskin tunic. There gaped a hole where a shot ball had torn through him.

The assembly gasped.

"Tell us what happened," said Old Hoof.

"What have you done?" asked the angry voice of a Ute chief. "You've killed one of our men with this dangerous power."

"We've been on a long flight," Red Bull stopped him. "We have flown over the entire world. We have much to tell you."

For two hours, the eighteen men took turns telling the shamans and grandfathers of their flight. Then they had to repeat it to the Big Bellies who had been summoned, and after that to an assembly of war captains.

Shortly a council of one hundred sat, with the war leaders, shamans, peace chiefs, grandfathers and raiding captains from the five tribes all represented.

Here the nineteen—Striking Eagle and the warriors who had flown with him—spoke as one voice. They insisted that the five tribes unite and attack the whites, for they had seen them slaughtering all the buffalo. According to Red Bull, any Indians who didn't attack the whites were as guilty of murder as the white man was.

But the vision and belligerence of the eagles didn't persuade many cautious grandfathers, Big Bellies and shamans. They knew the power of the whites. They complained of the long guns and the horse soldiers. Yes, the whites intended to kill all the buffalo—but a plan of action and action itself were two different things. Yes, this vision was powerful, but attacking the whites as the Kiowa were now doing only invited massive attacks from the bluecoat soldiers, often in the winter, when the Indians never fought. They brought up the stories of what had happened to Black Kettle and other northern chiefs who had been attacked in the harshest weather of winter. Better to keep out of the whites' way. Besides, it was foolish to think that the white man could kill all the buffalo. Sometimes the visions a man saw came from the devil, and were sent to trick a man.

"But nineteen of us saw this vision," argued Striking Eagle.

"But nineteen of you may have been snared by the devil," replied Younger Tree, the Cheyenne peace chief.

"Your own five warriors saw this vision," said Striking Eagle.

"And you want not five but all my warriors to attack with you?"

As Younger Tree said this, Striking Eagle knew how it sounded, as if he were arrogating to himself a position many a chief ten to twenty years older would have hesitated to grasp: the leader of a pan-tribal army. He had

377

never heard of such a force, and if it was put together, no one chief, not Younger Tree or Santana, could hold it together. The Indians never rode the way the whites did, in little rows, all dressed alike. Each fought separately, many times joining a war captain only to break with him a day or two later. But at the same time Striking Eagle saw so clearly, and he had to make them see too. The whites intended to kill all the buffalo, and when the buffalo were gone, so would go the Kiowa, the Comanche, the Utes, the Kiowa-Apache, the Cheyenne, and every other tribe across the Plains, for they were all *buffalo* people.

Feeling he was putting himself forward into a dangerous place politically, Striking Eagle argued strenuously for the unified attack, one led by any qualified war chief. He seemed to be carrying some weight with the council of a hundred, for they all listened as he spoke for the better part of an hour. He saw he moved them when he described life on the plains for them with, then without, the buffalo: the first picture filled them with pleasure, the second with alarm.

Then many others spoke, fear and caution uppermost in most of their hearts. While Striking Eagle understood their feelings, he knew they were a luxury against a greater truth: they fought for their very lives and those of their children and grandchildren, not as in times past when tribes skirmished over some few miles of hunting ground.

Striking Eagle only partially succeeded. But even though many of the returning eagles argued the same way as he, the cautious old men weren't swayed. The Cheyenne said they would have to have a Cheyenne council. The Comanche Many Hairs said if the whites continued to kill the buffalo, the buffalo would probably stampede through the whites' settlements and kill them all. The Kiowa-Apache said they had to go to the desert and talk to their relatives.

Other chiefs thought they should ask the whites for compensatory supplies first, as talk from the north was that the Sioux, Blackfoot and Arapaho were given free food by the whites.

What Striking Eagle won, however, was the blessing of the council of one hundred. He could establish a war party to fight these white hunters with the council's approval, and any man of the five tribes who wanted to fight with him could do so. No one would force anyone to fight, and all those who felt moved to fight could.

"This is terrific, Eagle," Left Hand said as they left the council.

"I have a stone in my heart," he replied. "I tried to tell them."

"But we'll have a huge force!"

"Our people are doomed, Hand."

Left Hand laughed. "Hey, you've gotten too serious these last months. With all the men who want to follow you, next year there won't be a white buffalo hunter within several hundred miles."

"I wish that were true."

"You'll see."

"I hope so."

Around Striking Eagle and Left Hand then crowded the eighteen who had flown with him, every man-eagle of whom, to Striking Eagle's delight, said he would stay behind when the tribes dispersed tomorrow back across the plains so they could fight with him.

Striking Eagle laughed and clasped each in turn. With these eighteen, and with the thirty others standing behind them from the visiting tribes and the fifty to one hundred he could raise from nearby Kiowa, who would be heartened and made bold by these foreign warriors, he had a small army.

*   *   *

And it was just in time. Five days after the giant assembly broke up, Kiowa scouts reported that the hunters they had beaten once before had returned to the hunt, and that this time they had found and attacked a herd of the white buffalo.

That report galloped through the village like a herd of panicked horses.

"Attacking white buffalo!"

"Twenty of them."

"I heard it was two hundred."

"Two hundred!"

"And they are killing every one, just as Striking Eagle predicted they would."

This report upset so many that Striking Eagle and his man-eagles had no trouble calling together one hundred ten warriors to mount an attack.

With such a large force, Striking Eagle was confident that this time he would smash them. This time the whites would learn. Attacking the white buffalo! If they came to hunt such *Wakan* creatures, they would get driven back or killed.

The eagle and his eagle warriors would strike!

Chapter 12

Four days after Jack McCall and Skinner Kincade left with three wagons and a crew of six to hunt white buffalo pelts for him, John Moar received a telegraph from New York. Once he had decoded it, it read:

> URGENT YOU PREPARE WELL FOR HORSMANNS VISIT. ARRIVES THREE WEEKS. FIFTY WHITE HIDES A MUST. MORE BETTER. POSSIBLE BIG PROFITS FROM NEW RAIL LINE AND LAND AND HOTEL. SUGGEST LARGE PURCHASES OF LAND. ACKNOWLEDGE RECEIPT AND ACTION. BERTRAM, MOAR & MOAR, 120 BWAY, NYC.

It took three more wires for Moar to clarify just what his brother wanted, but after he did, he became as excited as Bertram, for like his brother, he saw this as the opportunity of a lifetime.

Andrew Justice Horsemann here! The great man himself! And on a trip to choose the route for his railroad line westward! Why, the value of land in Hays should double, triple—skyrocket! It made John Moar dizzy to think of the profits. At present he and his brother's partnership owned just over a quarter of the land and buildings in Hays. At once he began to calculate how he might increase their holdings, and he made sly offers for half a dozen properties.

Over the next week he ordered from Dodge three wagons of supplies for the great man's visit, and as quietly and secretly as possible in such a tiny community he bought two large strips of land just outside town, and five more buildings.

Since Sally had announced that she was going to marry that lanky idiot of a buffalo hunter, Moar ignored her, even though he was furious with her. Defy him, would she? Let her find someone else to ride her around. She would learn. That idiot wouldn't be back if Skinner and those buffalo hunters he had taken with him had anything to do with it. She could bask in her fantasies of escaping Hays for a few weeks before they came back with some tragic story of Indian attack. Then it would dawn on her that McCall wasn't coming back, and that anyway a man with money and prospects was preferable to an itinerant buffalo hunter. Women! Where did the foolish notions that flitted into their heads come from? Such innocence was part of what he found attractive about her. But she had to learn: John Moar couldn't be beat and made a fool of.

So for the next few weeks he kept Sally at a polite arm's length, which seemed to improve things between them, for the hotel and bar were never run better. Now that the Indians attacked so many outfits, hunters spent more time in Hays waiting for bigger outfits to pull themselves together, and they spent more money at the bar and restaurant. The profits rolled in.

Once he had the date of Horsmann's arrival, he called Sally into his office and told her how he wanted to prepare the Hide & Skull for the great man's visit.

"My goodness!" she exclaimed. "We've got to get busy right away."

All four carpenters of Hays were hired to finish the porch that had only been built halfway around the building. The wagons that came back from Dodge carried cloth, new furniture, bedding, washstands, new dishes and flatware, five colors of paint, two hundred yards of red, white and blue bunting, kegs of nails, crystalware and hand tools. With the help of twenty extra men, John Moar undertook making the Hide & Skull into a more impressive building. It might not be the Drake in Chicago or the Broadway Central in New York, but he intended it to beat any whistle stop hotel Horsmann would have stayed in along his way west.

While some of the men built the porch around the side of the hotel and fixed up its dining room, others combined three rooms on the second floor into what Moar called "the presidential suite." This produced snickers from the unemployed buffalo hunters who were doing the hammering, sawing and plastering, but it impressed enough of the layabouts around town who ambled upstairs for a look-see for Moar to have to post a guard at the bottom of the stairs to keep out the curious.

John Moar pushed the carpenters, planned the menus, shouted instructions at men hanging bunting, supervised the cutting and sewing of tablecloths, insisted that the carpenters make a presidential-sized bed, sent men who had never touched a flower out onto the plains to pick hundreds, and in general fixing up Hays City to meet the most important visitor it had ever received.

And he loved every minute of it. If an election were held right then, he knew that as the town's most important and far-seeing citizen he would have been elected mayor. He liked pushing a dozen and a half things forward at one time so that everything would be ready when Horsmann arrived. While nothing in business seemed to run smoothly, still his great goal had haled within shouting distance: he would soon be able to liquidate his hide business and his holdings in town at ten to fifteen times what he had paid for them, he would pluck up Sally out of her loss of her second beau, the dumb Jack McCall, and together they would head back East.

A man could cut quite a swath through Manhattan with a million dollars, and John Moar didn't see how any power on earth could stop him from attaining his goal.

Particularly if Andrew Justice Horsmann ran the Kansas Pacific through Hays City.

Ever since she announced that she intended to marry Jack McCall, Sally Rawls found her relationship between John Moar and herself cool and strained.

For two weeks thereafter, they had had little to say to each other, but from the glances that flashed between them when they passed each other in the hall and bar, she knew that what had sprung up between them wasn't finished. She hoped it was, but she didn't like the angry turbulence she felt whenever John Moar rushed past.

That energy seemed now to be poured into readying the hotel for his important visitor's arrival. John's intensity impressed her. Dave had been brave and gentle but uninterested in power. In fact, he'd spurned it. Jack McCall she had a harder time figuring. More silent than either John Moar or Dave, a stillness hung about him that suggested strength. But John Moar the bantam exuded energy and purpose, and never more so than now. He seemed everywhere at once about the hotel. It was as if he had been sleeping for the past year in Hays as he ran his hide business and had come belatedly to grips with something he must do. Frequently he supervised the construction of the porch, every day he attended closings on real estate deals, twice a week he sent more wagons off to Dodge with long lists of foodstuffs, and it seemed every hour he was standing over the men building the large bed for the presidential suite, as if no detail could be left for carpenters to decide. At the same time a stream of runners came and went with prices and descriptions of loads of hides arriving at the sheds, and John interrupted what he was doing to huddle with these men and issue buy and ship orders.

McCall's leaving once more to hunt buffalo had depressed and angered her. She schooled herself to have patience, hoping he wasn't going to be one of those men with an eternal "one more trip" to take, and threw herself into her preparations for the great man's arrival.

It made Sally's head spin, but she found herself caught up in the town's excitement. While a strain still existed between John and her, and while she still caught a look of smoldering heat in John's eyes, he seemed so intent on making their visitor feel not only welcomed, but that he had arrived in the most prosperous and energetic town west of the Mississippi, that he seemed to have no time for her.

Strangely, Sally felt neglected, which made her ashamed of herself. Since she was going to marry Jack McCall when he came back from this hunt, why should she feel any slight from John Moar?

Because he's my boss, she told herself. It's natural that I should want to be important to him.

She didn't like that answer. The answer she also didn't like, but felt might be true, was that she was attracted to John, a man all her upbringing had trained her to abhor. She had been buffeted about by fate over the last eight years, first from the war and its terrible privations, then by the hard times afterward of Reconstruction, next by Dave's death, and then by this hell of life in Hays City. While she couldn't approve of John's selling whiskey, running a brothel and being more interested in money than saving his soul, it impressed her that John didn't allow hard times to overcome him. He had landed on his feet throughout all the troubles in the United States over the last decade, and she sensed that he would always land on his feet. A part of her wanted to nestle under the wing of all that energy and money, to be protected by it forever. Another part of her felt guilty: Jack McCall might not be rich and powerful, but he wanted first off to be her husband and a father to the children. He was a man to grow old with, whereas she sensed that if she did not prove to be either ornamental or useful to John, his loyalties might cease. Besides, she felt good with Jack in a way she didn't with her boss.

So Sally strived to put these conflicting feelings aside and stick to the hours of effort each day brought. It seemed to work. She had become, she felt, just another employee of the forty to fifty who labored to fix up, paint and clean the Hide & Skull. She smiled with a certain grimness, gave the orders he asked her to, and followed up to make sure they were carried out.

One day, just four days before Horsmann was to arrive, John called to her as she was heading into the kitchen, "I need a hostess."

"Hostess?" she asked.

It was ten in the morning and the cooks were all out back dressing buffalo and baking bread in the courtyard ovens. In John's eyes shone a tiny hot light of excitement.

"Somebody to grace my table," he said. "It won't

look right, just two of us, him and me. I want somebody
with some airs to talk to him.''

"Airs?"

"You know, interesting talk."

"Invite Nelly."

"Nelly? She only has one way of communicating
with a man."

"I wouldn't know what to say to a railroad owner."

"Yes, you would."

"No, I'll just supervise the kitchen as I have been and
keep out of sight."

"Please, Sally. Sit with us. Entertain him. Listen
good while he mouths off. You know what men like in
women."

She felt her heart sink, a feeling she often got when
John tried to talk her into doing something. She knew only
too well what he meant: flatter the man, listen open-mouthed
to whatever he had to say, and in general act the sedulous
ape. How could she be attracted to a man who made her
feel this?

"No, John, I won't be any good at it."

"You'll be better than anybody else in town, as pretty
as a flower with one of those high-neck dresses you favor.
I'll buy you half a dozen for his visit."

"Well, thank you, but it's a little late to get them."

"Naw, it ain't. I can wire Kansas City and have them
put a dozen on his train."

"John, I've worked hard to get the hotel ready for his
visit. Let's leave it like that."

"Look, I know you're going to be married—" He
stopped himself in midsentence as if respect for her for-
bade him to say more. "Anyway, there's a bonus in it for
the bride if she'll help me out. The new household may

need some extra money. And don't you owe me something?"

Sally felt caught in a swirl of conflicting claims. A part of her enjoyed seeing the hotel she had struggled so long with being spruced up. But another part of her wanted out of Hays, out of the Hide & Skull, away from the raucous girls upstairs, and shut out of the unruly air of Hays City.

"What do you want from me, John?"

"Just you to be the hostess of his visit, like they have in fancy hotels back East," he answered.

"I've never been in a hotel back East."

"Sally, I want you to sit at the table with us and talk to him," John persisted. "Keep him laughing. You can charm the skin off a lizard when you have a mind to."

His praise made her smile. He was right, he did need someone, and nobody in Hays could do it better than she could.

"Make sure that he gets good service to his room," John continued, "and make sure that they clean it right— you know these buffalo yokels, they won't change the sheets if you don't tell them to every damn day—and that what's put in front of him to eat isn't ruined by those stupid cooks in the kitchen."

John's excitement swept her along, even though misgivings nagged at her. Robby and Eva had tagged along with John on many of his supervisory trips, and the fancy decorations and new furniture were all they talked of these days.

Finally the next day she agreed to supervise and preside over the three elaborate dinners they would give the great man on his visit, one of which, the second night, would include a dozen of the town's leading citizens.

Over the next week of preparations, having thrown

herself fully into John's plans, it dawned on Sally anew how attractive being the wife or partner of a John Moar was: John didn't mind what was spent, he insisted on the best for every detail, and now that she had agreed to help, he relied on her taste regarding tablecloths, candles, flowers, food, crystal, tableware and service.

Sally found herself snapping at the girls upstairs. She ordered them not to show up downstairs at the bar during all three days of Horsmann's visit. Eventually, all nine of the girls complained in a body to John, and when John took it up with Sally, they had their biggest disagreement of the week.

"You can't keep them upstairs for three days," said John.

"You want him to see you're running a brothel?" Sally asked.

"What! I'm doing no such thing."

"They're all around the men in the bar, soliciting them and exibiting their legs and bosoms, John," Sally said. "What's he to think of the hotel?"

"But I just rent the girls rooms," he replied with mock seriousness. "It's not my fault if they use them for immoral purposes."

"You not only tolerate them, you rent them rooms at a rate that costs them half what they make."

John grinned slyly. "So what?"

"So you want me to sit at your table—to grace it, I think you put it. Having a bunch of sloppy whores hanging around your bar isn't something you'd see at the Palmer House or the Broadway Central, is it?"

"No. Maybe they could wear something more modest."

"What do you tell Mr. Horsmann they're doing here in the hotel, these blowzy women? Singing in the church choir on Sunday?"

He grinned. "And Hays don't have a church."

"Something like that."

For a few seconds John stared through her as he considered what she had said. Then he decided, "You're right. See, that's why I wanted you to be the hostess. I wouldn't have thought of this."

"I'll tell the girls to stay upstairs and that you'll make up their pay."

"Make up! Pay them for not working?"

Exasperated, she said, "Yes, pay! Why not? After all, just why are we going through this if you're not going to make money out of it?"

John looked cagey. "Well, nothing directly. He owns the railroad on which Moar & Moar ships its hides."

She sighed. "I know that, but something else is going on. So you're a customer of the man. Why are you spending a lot of money to impress a man you buy from? I don't know much about business, but that doesn't sound like any business I ever heard of."

The way John turned stone-faced told her she had put her finger on something, although she had no idea what.

"Listen, you keep those brassy tarts out of sight upstairs, Sally. Make sure they know I'll make it up to them. You know my brother and I are involved in more than just shipping hides. We aim to be big people in this country, Sally, big people. And this is the sort of man we want to have as a partner."

Without understanding much more than the visit was important, Sally nodded. If he wanted to impress the visitor, fine. She would make sure they put on a first-class show.

Andrew Justice Horsmann arrived on the spur line of the Kansas Pacific several days later. A short, portly man in his early fifties, Sally got the impression he would have preferred to have spent the visit in the comfort of his private railroad car, but he went along with John's wish for him to sleep in the new presidential suite out of politeness.

While a few snags cropped up, John and Sally's preparations paid off handsomely. The day after the great man's arrival, John had organized a nearby buffalo shoot, with several tame Indians doing riding tricks as they chased buffalo, and there was stunt-shooting by idle buffalo hunters. Horsmann was given the opportunity to bring down three buffalo from the buckboard he was driven around in.

Horsmann was a man who managed to always look grave and amused at the same time. He constantly had a cigar in his left hand and a glass near his right. On the first night, just the three of them ate in the large dining room of the hotel. French Pete served dinner in the manner Sally had made him practice over and over. Sally thought the dinner went well, with the exception of Pete's dropping a finger bowl into John Moar's lap, and bringing in tumblers when he should have brought the wineglasses they were using for brandy snifters. Horsmann laughed a lot at John's stories and Sally answered his questions about the ups and downs of life in a frontier town.

Horsmann asked John that first evening, after vague answers from Moar, "And these white hides, John, you and your brother promised. When can I expect them?"

"Hunters are out after them now."

"But are they going to bring them back?"

"Of course. Got our best people on them."

"The first and last thing my wife said about this trip was not to come back without those damn hides."

John laughed at this as if it were a particularly funny

joke and nodded as if the last word had been said on the subject. "Tell me, Mr. Horsmann," he said, changing the subject, "just how the expansion of the Kansas Pacific is going."

"Those hides," Horsmann persisted. "I'll be able to take them back with me, won't I?"

"Of course! Of course! The boys ought to be back with them any day now."

"Good. Once they're in my car, I'll feel a lot better."

Sally kicked John hard under the table and flashed him a warning frown.

John said, "Well, of course they might not get here before you leave, sir."

Horsmann nodded, tapping his cigar absently into the ashtray as if the answer had distracted him. Seeing that John wanted the subject closed, Sally opened her mouth to ask about church life in Manhattan, but Horsmann silenced her with a glance and said, "John, your brother made me a promise on those hides."

"Yes sir."

"You're not wiggling out of that promise, are you?"

"Sir!"

"In Dodge and Kansas City they told me there weren't any such creatures as the whites."

"They don't know buffalo in Dodge, sir. That's what Hays City is here for, because this is buffalo country."

Horsmann considered this, looking at John through a lazy cloud of cigar smoke. "John, do you have my hides or not?"

"Practically, sir. Not the most common animal, you understand, but the boys out here can get them for you—not the folks in Dodge, if you follow my meaning."

At times like these John exasperated Sally. She knew

what he was doing. He was promising the white hides to make Horsmann think that the hunters in Hays were so much more skillful that he would be a fool to run his rail line through Dodge City. To her, it seemed a silly way to try to impress the great man. She would have told him the truth: white buffalo were rare, there was a chance that a special group of hunters could find one or two or three, but very little chance they could find more. Wasn't Horsmann going to be disappointed when John came up empty-handed?

After the railroad magnate had mounted the stairs to the presidential suite that night, she told John so.

"Ah, he'll forget all about those dumb hides in a few weeks," said John.

"He sounded awfully particular about them," she said.

"What was I going to tell him?" John asked. "That I couldn't get them and he should try the boys in Dodge or Johnstown? I want him to know we're go-getters here in Hays."

Sally had misgivings. Lies didn't work, she felt, but maybe she knew too little about business. Maybe John knew what he was doing. He was certainly successful enough.

It was midnight, and the hotel was quiet. The banquet room, with half its candles guttered and a tablecloth stained, looked bleak now that the first night's dinner was over.

"I guess you know what you're doing," she said, turning to go upstairs to bed.

"Ah, there's just one thing, Sally," said John.

"Yes?"

"He seems to have found out about the girls anyway."

"The girls."

"The upstairs girls."

393

She smiled. "And how did that happen?"

John looked impish. "He seems to have asked a few questions."

"I see."

"When you went out to check the coffee after dinner, he told me that he would like to have a visit tonight—if she is, to quote him, 'clean, attractive, and willing to have a little fun.' "

The nod of understanding that she gave John sent a wave of sadness through her. What was it in men that made them so hungry for women other than their wives?

John went on, "Would you ask Nelly to pay him a visit?"

"Nelly?"

"Isn't she the best we got?"

"I guess."

"The doctor looked at her this week, didn't he?"

Wearily, she said, "He looks at all of them every week."

"Make sure she wears something nice, and make sure she understands she isn't to ask him for money."

"No money."

"Tell her I'll take care of her myself."

"I'm sure she'll be delighted, John."

"You being sarcastic on me again?"

"No, not really. Nelly's perfect for this."

John beamed. "Yeah, she's a great gal."

"I'll tell her you said that."

"All right. Thanks."

The next morning Nelly appeared in the kitchen at six o'clock.

Sally was at the stove making sure the biscuits were crisp and the grits creamy the way Horsmann said he liked them. She looked up and gasped at seeing Nelly's face, bruised and with welts around her cheeks and neck.

"My God, what happened to you?" asked Sally, running to her.

"Nothing," said Nelly, turning away.

"But you look terrible! Sit down."

Nelly turned away still more and said, "I don't want to trouble you. Give me some coffee."

"But what happened? When I left you last night you were going to—" Sally stopped, then continued—"to Horsmann's room."

"I just came from there."

"He did this?"

Nelly nodded.

Sally asked, "What happened?"

"I don't want to talk about it."

"Nelly Shroeder, what did he do to you?"

"Just let's drop it, Sally," she said. "It don't matter."

"We don't allow this!"

"Forget it, Sally."

"But look at you! You look as bad as that time Pig Dawkins got Abby under the bed."

"I done this for John. Let's drop it, huh?"

Horsmann arrived for breakfast at nine o'clock. He ate with John. Puzzled and disturbed, Sally had breakfast served while she stayed behind the scenes in the kitchen. Sally couldn't bear to sit at the table with the man. She saw through the door that he looked rested and much more jolly this morning than he had the day before.

"Some country out here, Moar," Sally heard Horsmann roar as she opened the door to usher French Pete in with the third plate of biscuits. "I slept wonderfully. It's this air you have out here."

John winked at Sally and laughed. "Doesn't have anything to do with the company you had, does it? We got some spirited 'company' here at the Hide & Skull."

Horsmann, waving his cigar at Sally in the doorway, roared again as if the night had awakened a long-sleeping lust for life. "Sure it does! Night riding is the best exercise a man can get!"

Sally sped from the room. Horsmann seemed to regard her, from the look and wink he had shot her way, as the madam of the establishment, and she felt ashamed. The truth was that he was right. She had to get out of the hotel. It was wrong. Women who might have been decent debased themselves. Nothing good could come from such a godless place as the Hide & Skull, and she had been a fool to think she could wallow with pigs and not get dirty.

By nightfall Sally felt calmer. Jack McCall would be back any day now. He would collect his money, they would marry, and off they would go to California. She would push this yearlong nightmare away from her. She just had to put up with this job for another few days. Horsmann was no better than any other customer of the Hide & Skull. Why should he be treated better?

That night she refused to sit at the large formal dinner, making an excuse that annoyed John.

"He likes you, Sally. Take a powder for your headache."

"No, I wouldn't be any good."

Later, after the dinner and after Horsmann had retired with a bottle of brandy to his presidential suite, John hunted her up.

"He says he'd like Nelly again," he said.

"No."

A manic grin lit up John's face. "And another gal at the same time. Some appetite for an old guy, huh?"

396

"No, John."

"How about Abby?"

"Didn't you see Nelly's face?"

"Nelly's face?"

"He beat her," Sally said. "And did something else that she won't talk about."

"What? And what do you mean she won't talk about it?"

"Some perversion, if I read it right."

"Ain't nothing serious wrong with her, is it?"

"He has unnatural appetites."

"Oh, Jesus, don't give me that preacher's daughter claptrap."

"Don't use His name with me."

"Sally, damn it, things are going great. Send him Nelly and Abby, damn it, so he can enjoy himself."

"No, I won't have them beaten."

"Aw, they're used to rough customers."

"We don't allow the roughest buffalo hunter to hit them, and the same rule should apply to him."

John's face reddened. "Just you send him two gals, Sally."

"No, I said."

"What do you mean, no? I'm not asking, I'm telling you."

"And I'm telling you no."

"Come on. You know I don't go up on the fourth floor," he said, referring to the attic where the Hide & Skull's girls had their tiny rooms.

"If you want to order them around tonight, *you* will," said Sally.

"Damn you, Sally Rawls. You're failing me at the most important time."

"You're failing me, John Moar. That man hasn't any right to do what he did to Nelly. You back me up when any common buffalo hunter wants to do something like that to a girl, but come this bloated muckamuck from New York, and he can kill the girls for all you care."

"Aw, come on. He ain't killing them."

"Did you see Nelly's face?"

"Didn't look so bad to me."

"She had a lot of powder on. Plus she can hardly walk. It's not right what he did to her."

"But this is different," said John. "The whole town is riding on this visit. He can put this town on the map."

"No, no, no," she said, unmoved by any of his entreaties. "And I'm going to tell them not to go, that it's dangerous for them. It's bad enough that they've placed their souls in jeopardy here in this house, but that they would follow the instructions of the devil—no, no, and no."

"Don't say a word to anybody else, but I think I got him to agree to put the line through here."

"The line?"

"The railway line," said John. "So that we can ship west as easy as we ship east."

"And what's that got to do with Nelly and Abby?"

He groaned. "You women never see these things, do you? He's pleased with us, that's what. He'll want to come out here again to survey his rail lines."

"Are you serious? He's going to put a rail line through here so he can come back out here to wallow around with Nelly and Abby?"

"No, no. That line can go anywhere. But he likes how we handle ourselves, that we're forward-looking and want to be prosperous, so he's going to lean our way."

Her answer was still no, and what happened afterward Sally got in bits and pieces the next day.

John had gone upstairs and called for Nelly and Abby to come out. Seeing Nelly's face without powder shocked him. When he asked her what Horsmann had done to her, she left the stairs and silently returned to her room. Abby followed.

"Hey, wait, Abby," he had cried.

Stopping her, he promised her twenty dollars if she would go to Horsmann's room for the night. She agreed to do it for thirty, although she said she had a lot of reservations.

"We need another gal too," said John.

"Another?" asked Abby.

"This is a strong man, sweetie."

"She'll get thirty too?"

John hesitated, but gave in. Abby and Cora got themselves looking spiffy and went to the presidential suite.

The next day Abby and Cora refused to come out of their tiny attic rooms. Sally went up at midmorning to take them cold biscuits, jam and coffee, and to see how they were. But she saw neither of them. In their separate cells, each hid under her blanket and told Sally to go away. As if they were children, Sally tried to coax them out, but they wouldn't remove the blankets they kept clasped over their heads.

In the dining room at lunch, Horsmann seemed again at the top of his spirits. "Such a wonderful life you have here, Johnny," he said in his characteristic roar.

"I enjoy it," John answered modestly, giving Sally a sly wink as she passed.

She looked away.

"Mrs. Rawls, you run one fine house," said Horsmann.

"I don't know when I've been better fed, better rested, and had as much healthy exercise—if you get my meaning." He gave the two of them a broad wink and a guffaw as he waved his fat cigar about.

"Now you see why I prefer Hays to New York," John said. "Out here a man can run things to suit himself. Don't have so many busybodies as you have back in New York."

As she supervised the buffalo steaks and potatoes being set out, Horsmann started in on one of his bawdy stories as if she were a part of a fraternity, and she objected by leaving the room. Through the early afternoon she heard John laughing uproariously at the stories as they sat on the porch of the hotel and sipped brandy and smoked the railroad baron's cigars.

What had she seen in John before now? she asked herself. How had she allowed herself to get so swayed by such a man? It was clear to her that he was but a nascent Horsmann, looking for money, power, and the ability to push and mold as many others to his personal tastes as he could. Miserable with herself, she saw that she needed a man like Dave, a man who lived his life with some respect and dignity for other people. A man who didn't let others push him, yet at the same time didn't feel the need to push others around.

In short, a Jack McCall.

At least she thought Jack McCall was such a man. She felt in Hays she had lost the bearings she had been so confident of with her father and then with Dave. Was she making the right decision? Maybe it was just her being here at the Hide & Skull that was making her think that way, she speculated.

And maybe I've been a fool to have wallowed with pigs.

That night was the last night that Horsmann would spend in Hays City. Sally supervised the preparations for the evening meal, but kept out of the way of both Horsmann and John. She loathed both of them. Their voices turned her stomach, and she shook with anger at the thought of sitting at the table with either of them.

After dinner, before Horsmann went upstairs, a cheery John Moar sought her out in the kitchen.

"Hey, where you been, Sally-girl?"

"I'm quitting, John," she said.

"What?"

"I'm taking the children and I'm leaving the hotel tomorrow morning," she said.

"What's going on? You can't quit now. There's breakfast and lunch tomorrow. He'll think something's gone wrong."

"Something certainly has. You're not the man I thought you were."

He looked at her with sly, hard eyes. "Don't do this, Sally. I told him you and I were thick. For a while there he wanted you."

Not sure of what she was being told, she had no answer.

"We could be thick, you know," he said. "You don't want to leave here. It's the only decent building in Hays, the only one with a roof that keeps the rain out. What are you going to do, live in a tent?"

"If I have to."

"Aw, come on. Tell me what's going on."

"No."

"Spit it out."

"John, you wouldn't understand. I'm marrying Jack McCall. I'll leave the hotel and live elsewhere till we leave for California."

"That's stupid. McCall may not be back for months. May never come back."

She felt herself waver, but pulled herself short. "He said he would be back in another week or two."

"I'm going to tell you, Sally, and I've seen a right heap more of his type than you. He don't look like the marrying type to me. A man promises a woman many a thing in the heat of the moment, if you get my meaning."

"You disgust me, John Moar. It's this in you that I despise."

His laugh sounded like a smaller version of Horsmann's guffaw. "It won't surprise me if Mr. McCall forgets all about you," he said. "It won't surprise me if you can't find a job in Hays except here with me."

"What does that mean?"

"Nothing, except do you think people are going to want to give you a decent job without asking me why you aren't with me anymore?"

"Sure."

He laughed slyly. "You don't know Hays as well as I do, then. And you don't know how much of this town I own."

"It won't be easy," she said, "but I can get by till Jack comes back."

"Till Jack comes back," he repeated, giving her a hard, mocking look.

"Good night, John."

"You aren't any better than anybody else," he said.

"I didn't say I was."

"As long as you got Mr. Jack McCall coming back, you can afford to be righteous, can't you?"

"John, let's just say good night."

"When times get hard again, you'll come back here wanting your job again, I suppose."

"Good night, John."

He laughed again. "So pack up and leave. You'll be back. Might not be for a couple of weeks, even a month or so, but mark my words, Sally-girl. You'll be back here begging me to take you back on, and it's going to be a different story then."

Chapter 13

"To the left! To the left!" shouted Skinner.

Startled, McCall wheeled, led the fast Indian ponies with his rifle sight and squeezed off a shot.

Missed! As he pumped another cartridge into the breech, the Kiowa ponies spun and rushed toward them.

"They're coming in over here!" shouted Skinner, pulling his pistol. "Get over here, Charley and Amos!"

But Charley and Amos had their own hands full on the other side of camp with the foot-braves who were trying to work their way closer by running from dead buffalo to dead buffalo.

McCall pulled his pistol and struggled to keep a rider in his sights. Whooping like triumphant wolves, the fifteen horse-braves crashed into the buffalo hunters' camp, overturning the kettle, the Dutch oven and the coffee pot and scattering dirt, clouds of dust and brands from the fire. McCall, Skinner and the other men pulled themselves back under the wagons, close together, as far out of sight as possible and at the same time trying to lean forward to shoot. The air seemed full of lances, arrows, bullets, screams and confusion. McCall knew he had hit no Indians, maybe a horse or two. The Indians moved too quickly to present good targets and rode at him so rapidly that he had had to jump back out of danger. They kept their horses between his gun and themselves.

As suddenly as the attack had begun, the Kiowa disappeared over the hill. Those behind the dead buffalo fifty yards out seemed to have melted into the ground.

"Goddamn no-good ignorant savages!" exclaimed Skinner Kincade, his face and bald head sooty with grime where sweat hadn't run rivulets through it.

Just as furious, but quieter about it, Jack McCall was as surprised as the rest of his seven men at the length of the Kiowa attacks. Normally, what an Indian couldn't snatch quickly he let go. With some difficulty, McCall and his men had managed to penetrate the huge herd of brown buffalo and bring down twenty-five of the white buffalo by the time the attacks began. For two days now they had lain under their wagons and fired their Sharps rifles at the half dozen Kiowa horse and foot attacks. Except when the Kiowa concentrated their attack, as they were right now, the fire from the big rifles kept the warriors at a safe distance.

"You know about Injuns," said Skinner. "How come they're so crazy, Jack?"

"I don't know that much about Kiowa," said McCall. "Till recently they stayed off to the west."

"I was right, wasn't I?" asked Skinner.

"About what?"

"That's your buddy out there."

"Yeah, that's Lone Wolf all right, or an Indian that looks just like him."

Skinner eyed him bitterly and shook his head to indicate what a fool he thought McCall was.

"Think your friend will keep this up long?" Amos asked McCall.

McCall snapped, "Now how the hell would I know?"

"Our herd's going to get away from us," said Skinner, referring to the giant herd drifting northward that contained the hundred or so white buffalo McCall had managed to track down. They could look down on the tail end of the big herd, which, despite all the shooting around them, still marched sedately through the valley below their camp.

"They can't stay forever," said Skinner. "We got enough firepower to keep them at a distance. Why don't a couple of us keep shooting and skinning them white buffalo while the rest of us keep the savages at bay?"

"Just keep on following the whites?" asked McCall.

"Yep."

McCall thought about it, although something about the suggestion bothered him. Upon discovering this herd a week before, they had evolved a whole new way of hunting, for they were only after specific animals, something he had never hunted before. The shooters, McCall and Skinner, rode their horses hard to get onto high ground to the side and front of the giant herd. As the herd passed or stopped for water, he and Skinner brought down as many whites as they could. Expecting the skinners to come behind with the slower wagons and strip off the pelts, McCall and Skinner would ride on ahead to shoot another half dozen whites. At night they all camped together.

"How many white hides we got now?" asked McCall.

"Maybe twenty-six, twenty-seven."

"I guess we can take another dozen or so," said McCall. Saying this increased his edginess, although he wasn't sure why.

Thereafter a strange procession made its way across the plains. McCall and Skinner slipped out of camp an hour before first light and rode ahead to catch the herd.

Come dawn, the Kiowa would attack the wagons, which would be packed and ready to move out. Having pulled up around one or a couple of dead white buffalo, the three best shooters among the skinners kept the Kiowa at bay with high-powered buffalo guns while the other three struggled to peel off the whites' pelts. Any time a dozen whooping warriors rode in too close, they would obey McCall's instructions to lead the horses by as much as two rods and were able to bring down a few of the Kiowa mounts with the heavy buffalo slugs.

Five days later found the eight-man party with fifty white buffalo hides. While McCall's people had taken only three direct hits by arrows or Indian fire, the strain of rushing to skin the animals and the fearful wariness of watching for an attack had taken their toll. They constantly peered at the horizon for signs of Kiowa and longed to be back in Hays.

"How come they don't call off the attack?" Charley Cook asked in a whisper one night. "Something unnatural about Injuns coming on and coming on like this."

The hunters sat around in the darkness, drinking cold coffee and eating cold buffalo rump, not daring to light a fire as that might blind them as well as make them easy targets. They knew Indians didn't like to attack at night no matter what the odds were, but none wanted to bet their lives on it.

"I think I've figured it," said McCall. "It's the white buffalo we're taking. They specially don't like it."

Three-Fingers hooted and said, "What the hell difference does it make?"

"Well, too bad," said Skinner. "They can take a flying leap off the moon."

"We're heading back to Hays tomorrow," said McCall.

"Doing what?" asked Skinner.

"Heading back to Hays."

"We ain't got all our load," said Skinner.

"Yes, we have," said McCall.

"Hell, I counted another fifty of them whites today," said Skinner.

"We're going to leave them for the Indians," said McCall.

"Leave, hell!" said Three-Fingers. "What have they ever left us?"

"Well, we ain't killing them. We're heading back."

"I'd like to get back as bad as the next fellow," Three-Fingers said, "but this is the best money I've ever made in my life."

Around him, Tom, Amos, Arkansas, Billy and Charley murmured agreement, and Skinner said, "Damn it, Jack, we got this method all worked out. We're bagging all we want despite the Injuns. They can't even get close to us. We can take all them whites."

"But we ain't."

"Like hell. For all we're being offered by Moar, we're damn fools not to take them."

"But we're not taking them."

"Jack, don't start no crazy stuff."

Was this it? McCall wondered upon hearing the angry belligerence in Skinner's tone. He had watched Skinner closely ever since they had left Hays for signs of what Nelly had warned him about, but Skinner had only seemed intent on bagging as many white buffalo as he could in order to earn his fee from Moar. Having heard only part of the conversation, Nelly might easily have gotten things backwards. True, Skinner seemed to be a little too chummy with Three-Fingers, Arkansas and Charley, old pals of his, but that could be just because he was paying them, was responsible for the condition of the hides, and had to keep them up to snuff.

"We all want to go on shooting whites, Jack," said Skinner.

"Naw, we got enough," said McCall.

"Aw, Jack, come on. We all stand to make a lot of money out of this," Skinner insisted. "Here we done figured out a way of keeping the Injuns off us while we get all the hides we want. Now's the time for all of us to strike it rich."

"Including yourself, McCall," put in Three-Fingers.

In the faint light from the stars, McCall saw that the six men with Skinner were on all sides of him. McCall fought to keep his fear down and his voice level. They couldn't just jump him and kill him. Rough as Skinner, Three-Fingers, Arkansas and Charley were, seven men couldn't keep that a secret.

For an hour the others argued hotly with McCall about it in hushed voices. In the distance they heard the throb of drums and shouts. The Kiowa were working themselves up to tomorrow's attack.

By nine o'clock, exhausted, they turned in, no decision reached. In the morning, when McCall awoke in the faint light, from his bedroll he saw Skinner dressed and filling his pouches with cartridges.

"Where you going?" McCall asked.

"Same place we go every day," said Skinner. "To kill me some whites."

"No," said McCall, sitting up and easing his Sharps Big Fifty across his lap in a casual gesture. "No more whites. All the brown buffalo you fellows want to skin and haul, all right. But no more whites."

"Whites, McCall," said Three-Fingers. "That's where

the money is. And if you don't want to go shoot them, I'll go with Skinner."

"Ain't none of you going," said McCall. He brought around his Sharps and continued, "I'm the boss of this outfit and I say we move on to another herd, shoot enough browns to fill our wagons, and go on in."

"What's got into you, McCall?" asked Skinner. "If we don't shoot them whites, the next man will."

"Not us," said McCall. "Maybe not him."

"So the next fellow can get rich, but not us?"

"So the whites can live. It's what's got the Indians so riled up."

"To hell with them Injuns," said Three-Fingers, and in the dim light of dawn came murmurs of agreement from the others.

"They're the last whites, the only whites," said McCall. "It ain't right to kill them all off."

"Aw, you don't know they're the last ones," said Skinner.

"Remember how much Lone Wolf wanted that white hide you shot, Skinner?" asked McCall.

"Sure! He wants these we done killed too."

"The only thing that's going to stop him is when we leave these whites, and then he may follow us for what we've taken."

"He's a bigger damn fool than I think he is, then," said Skinner, patting his rifle.

"We got to leave the rest of this herd," said McCall.

"Like hell we do."

"I been on the plains long enough to know," said McCall. "I've heard the Indians' stories. There's one big white herd and that's all, and they're going to attack until we quit."

"Bull."

McCall said, "This is the herd that creates the buffalo."

"What kind of crap is that?"

"Unbuckle that cartridge belt, Three-Fingers," said McCall. He pumped a cartridge into his rifle and drew his Colt .45 and laid it on his lap.

"Come on, McCall," said Three-Fingers. "Don't be so damn stupid. If we wait even a half a day, our herd is liable to get off somewhere where we can't never find them."

"Good."

Three-Fingers went for his horse. To put the fear of God in him, McCall aimed about a dozen feet to the left of his boots and fired, but his hammer fell on a defective cartridge and made only a little pop. Cursing, McCall pumped another slug into his gun as Three-Fingers turned.

"Shoot all you want, McCall," said Three-Fingers. "Ain't none of them shells of yours got any powder in them. I loaded them special myself."

McCall aimed his Colt at Three-Fingers' feet and pulled the trigger. The gun made the same weak pop. Three-Fingers looked a little sly and embarrassed.

"Don't think badly of us, McCall," he said. "We just got to make our way too, you know."

"We're going to shoot our whites now," said Skinner. "And they ain't going to be yours, but ours."

"If you don't help us, Jack, you can't have any part of it," Three-Fingers said. "We mean to sell them ourselves."

"I told you. We're not shooting any more whites."

"One other thing, McCall," said Skinner. "We took a kind of vote. We figure you're too strong and savvy to sit around and do nothing, so we voted to tie you up till we get back to Hays."

McCall roared, "You did what?"

The seven of them advanced on McCall with Skinner, Three-Fingers, Arkansas and Charley in the lead. Was this what Nelly had overheard? Skinner had a rope in his hand, looking as if he would throw it over McCall's head. McCall tried the Sharps again, but only got another weak pop from the shell. Then he held the rifle like a club, which made the circle of men hesitate, till Skinner encouraged them by drawing his gun.

"So help me, McCall," said Skinner. "I wouldn't want to, but I'll shoot you in the leg if you hold us up anymore. It's going to get so late we'll never get past the Injuns today." He cocked the .44 and continued, "And this has real shells, believe me." To illustrate his point, he fired at the ground, tearing up a clod of hard earth.

In the end McCall cursed them roundly and submitted to their tying his arms behind his back and his legs together. They put him in the rear of one of the wagons on the white buffalo robes.

"Suppose we get overrun by Kiowa," asked McCall, "and I'm tied up like this?"

"You going to be in a hell of a spot," said Skinner.

McCall started to argue with him again, but decided not to. It would be easier to argue with the others once Skinner and Three-Fingers went on ahead to shoot buffalo. If he protested too strenuously, he foresaw that Skinner would put more of a guard on him or figure a worse way to pull his teeth and claws.

Over the next two days, McCall spent the entire time tied up in the back of the wagon cursing the situation. Stupidly he hadn't figured that the men would side with Skinner. The hard knots chafed his wrists and the air under the canvas was stifling. His only relief was that when he called out, Billy Dixon would bring him water. He tried to talk the youthful Billy and the rarely sober Amos Mates

413

into untying him, but Billy was too frightened of Skinner and Amos. He was certain of just one thing: he didn't want to get involved between them.

In this time the little train made seven stops at places where Skinner and Three-Fingers had killed buffalo, and another eighteen white hides were added to their store. At night McCall was brought water and food. The Kiowa seemed to give the skinners less trouble and attacked the two shooters, apparently concentrating on Skinner and Three-Fingers because they had figured out the strategy of the hunters. Skinner and Three-Fingers took big, muscular Tom Rath with them the third day to stand guard as they made their buffalo stands, and when the Kiowa attacked, all three stood them off. One man with a Sharps Big Fifty and plenty of shells could hold off ten to twenty Indians, and no more than that attacked. They aimed for the horses, learning more and more how to lead them. They had to bring down three to four horses each day before they discouraged the attackers. Three-Fingers figured they had killed at least a dozen horses and two braves and wounded half a dozen men, but they dragged off their dead and wounded so fast you couldn't be sure.

From the talk that drifted into the rear of his wagon from the nightly makeshift meal, McCall gathered that after the Kiowa lost some horses each day, the attackers withdrew, and that Skinner, Tom and Three-Fingers then shot all the white buffalo they could find.

By the third day McCall was sick of the ropes, the heat, the flies, and his inactivity. Whenever Charley Cook seemed at a distance, he talked to Billy and Amos, left behind to skin the whites and guard him. He asked them about standing up for him if McCall promised Skinner that he wouldn't stop them from hunting the whites, and also

414

promised him that while he wouldn't shoot or skin them, he would cook during the day for the outfit.

But even though Billy and Amos did put in a word for him, and Tom Rath said it wasn't right for a crew to tie up its boss, Skinner would not release him.

"He's fooling you, boys," said Skinner.

"Fooling how?" asked Tom.

"I know this bastard. He says one thing, he means another. Gets loose, first thing you know he'll have a gun on us and be telling us what to do. He's a snake."

Tom said, "I don't know. I ain't never heard of Jack McCall going back on his word."

"You just ain't been out with him, Tom," said Skinner.

"But what happens when we do let him go, Skinner?" Three-Fingers asked. "The son of a bitch is going to be so snappish he'll bite our heads off."

"Maybe we won't let him go," Skinner replied. "Maybe the Indians will sneak in and take him away one night." He winked at the others. "A lot can happen before we get back to Hays."

Little chuckles of appreciation floated Skinner's way, but in the darkness he couldn't tell if he had won all the men over or not. Up till now, money had talked loudly to them all, and doubtless it would continue to shout.

Something would happen before they got back to Hays, all right. Something that would look as if Mr. Jack McCall had met up with a fatal accident. He just had to be on the alert for it.

With great difficulty Striking Eagle had rounded up a small band of the bravest warriors to come with him one night to raid the camp of the white men. But they had not been in the darkness more than thirty minutes when a towering night demon frightened them all back to the safety of the fire.

They had attacked from both sides a dozen times, tried to sneak up on the hunters, and steadfastly worked to get above them, but the buffalo guns proved too much of an advantage. Not only were they accurate up to seven or eight hundred yards on a target the size of a horse, but they drove slugs so hard that they knocked over their mounts. The bullets were designed to stop a buffalo weighing double a horse's weight.

Their attacks weren't stopping the hunters from killing the white buffalo either. The shooters rode on ahead and shot, the skinners brought up the wagons behind and skinned, and while Striking Eagle got the impression he and his men slowed them down, the hunters still diminished the white buffalo by another five or six animals every day.

Striking Eagle found none of his plans working. For more than a week now, his best warriors could not get within arrow range before the whites shot their horses out from under them. In a rage, Striking Eagle urged his men into attacks that would have been suicidal had not Left Hand held them all back.

"It has something to do with the white buffalo," Left Hand said.

"What, brother?" Striking Eagle asked.

"Men who can take so many whites are too powerful for us to take."

"No. I slept in their tepee," Eagle countered. "They're men like you and me."

"Evil power, Eagle," said Left Hand. "All of us feel it. This valley itself is torn apart by evil power."

Finally, hearing more and more rumblings of mutiny from his victory-starved warriors, Striking Eagle eased up on the attacks and decided to call for more warriors. He chose ten warriors to act as messengers, put them on the ten fastest ponies, and sent them to neighboring tribes—all those that had been to the sun dance—to describe to the most powerful chiefs what was happening to the *Wakan-Takan's* white buffalo.

Within five days, two hundred more warriors, led by Yellow Bear of the Utes, Alights-On-A-Cloud and Whirlwind of the Pawnee, Sitting Bear of the Cheyenne, Woman's Heart, Otter Belt and Red Moon of the Comanche, and Grey Leggings of the Kiowa-Apache had gathered with Striking Eagle. They were drawn by the strong *Wakan* of this area, where so many sun buffalo, as the Cheyenne called them, were present.

Most of these braves had never seen a single white buffalo, much less a herd. The sight of the remaining herd and the stories from the Kiowa of how many dozens of the *Wakan* creatures the hunters had gunned down aroused the newly arrived Indians to a revengeful fury and re-ignited Striking Eagle's own men's lust for victory.

But the tales of the powerful guns still made them cautious. They all felt caught between revenge and fear. On the one hand, the air around them shrieked that the crime of murder had to be stopped and punished. The fabric of the world had been ripped apart and must be mended, but still the powerful guns of the whites would kill them if they approached. For a day or so, small parties of the newcomers tested the hunters, only to find what the Kiowa said about the buffalo guns to be all too true.

Meanwhile, another one hundred twenty-five warriors arrived, led by Santana of the Kiowa, Bull Hump of the Cheyenne, and Walking Coyote of the Pawnee. The desert air rang all night with dances and speeches of victory, and all day the hills surrounding the hunters were lined with angry warriors. The hunters stayed near their wagons after the dozens of attacks.

One night Old Hoof arrived from the Kiowa camp, and at once he went into a huddle with the ten to fifteen leaders of the war party.

After a night's deliberations, as the most experienced shaman present, he declared, "I will prepare a charm that you may all use. With this talisman their bullets will not harm you."

Inwardly, Striking Eagle groaned. He knew that at times Old Hoof could come up with powerful charms, but what about the time he came up with the bear-taming sash, supposed to keep a bear from striking you with its powerful front paws? The bear had whapped Huncum with its enormous paw before anyone could bring the animal down. Huncum still couldn't turn his head to the left. Nevertheless, Old Hoof's charms worked well enough sometimes. Once, in exchange for a buffalo pony, Left Hand had hired him to work on his shield before a battle with the Pawnee. Hoof had hung it in the smoke from a fire, sprinkling sage and sweetgrass in the flames all night while singing those simple-minded chants of his. Left Hand had never been so strong against an enemy as in that battle. Since then, he carried the shield whenever he went into battle, and he had done better than ever before. Striking Eagle reckoned that Old Hoof's charm might encourage the warriors to attack more bravely, but he didn't suppose, as the old man claimed, it would do much to stop a bullet. Maybe all that counted was that the others would think so. After all, you couldn't win a battle without attacking fiercely.

For a night and a day and another night, Old Hoof led the several hundred warriors through a ceremony he had designed to protect them. For Hoof's sake, Striking Eagle participated. At Hoof's direction, they had managed to bring down one of the white buffalo themselves and had stripped off its hide. Each warrior who was to go into battle against the whites wore a thin neck thong made of the white's skin.

By morning, the braves felt full of *Wakan* and ready to attack, boasting to each other what they would do in battle today. Since they had the strongest possible power that *Wakan-Takan* could favor them with, they were confident that the hunters' bullets couldn't penetrate the barrier that the white buffalo had thrown around them. They could advance on the hunters without fear, for they would be invincible. *Wakan-Takan* would deflect the angry bees thrown by the whites' bullets, possibly by laying honey in the air to distract them.

Striking Eagle wasn't as certain of all this as so many of the foreign warriors, possibly because he had lived with Hoof too long. But to avoid diminishing anyone's faith, he took a strip of the hide that had been infused with *Wakan* by Old Hoof and put it around his neck too. If it got the men to attack in a rush, it was good enough, although he hoped they wouldn't do anything as foolish as walking up to the white hunters and grinning like fools. He had once heard a piece of wisdom from a Kiowa-Apache shaman that impressed him: "Trust in *Wakan-Takan*, but tie your mule."

If many warriors trusted the spirits and didn't keep their mules tied, they would die today, he thought to himself. Better I keep them from that. The only way to do that is if I'm there with them. It's only right that I be in front.

And so he stood up and said before all the other war chiefs, "Victory beckons us, brothers. I'll lead today's attack. Paint yourselves, gather your arrows and

419

your courage, and make hard your hearts. Today we take revenge for this outrage against our brother, the white buffalo!''

About the time the messengers had begun to return to Striking Eagle's war camp with parties drawn from all across the Kansas Territory, by fits and starts Skinner and his crew had taken ninety-two white buffalo hides, nearly exhausting the white herd. They had also taken a couple hundred brown pelts.

True, big Tom Rath had taken a nasty lance wound in his thigh and couldn't move around much, and an arrow that had gone through Charley's hand had probably ruined it for grasping, but better them than me, Skinner figured, elated by the success of their hunting. Not only had he paid Jack McCall back for all the indignities he had received on previous trips, but he was getting rich. He probably wouldn't need to work hard ever again, but now he could lead all the outfits he wanted to after this triumph. He couldn't figure quite how rich he'd be, but in his mind all those fifty and hundred-dollar bills that Moar had promised were piling up pretty damn high.

He saw himself in Kansas City in the best room at the Empire Hotel soaking up the good life with a couple of the house's best ladies. Every day he would drink himself a fifth of decent hooch, get them gals into bed a couple of times each, and have a cigar after every meal. After he had worn out those satisfactions, he reckoned he would put on some fancy duds and step into the saloon and play himself some cards. With a stake like he was putting together here, he'd be able to clean out quite a few dudes who didn't know as much as he did about how to make cards jump in and out of your sleeves.

Skinner felt elated. Up till now life had been tough,

but he had been learning his way up in the world. A man couldn't get ahead until he had toughened up. Skinner had, and now it was paying off. He saw clearly how John Moar had gotten to the top in Hays. It had to do with putting your boot in the other man's face when necessary. A dozen times he had smiled to himself in satisfaction. A man could go his whole life and not learn this lesson. He wouldn't have to learn it again. Trying to be the friend of Jack McCall had been about the dumbest thing he had ever done in his life.

Not only had he and his men been able to repulse the Kiowa attacks with their heavy guns, killing dozens of horses and striking braves hundreds of yards away, but, with Jack McCall tied up in the back of a wagon, they had made their way across the plains such a distance that Skinner and his men saw themselves as unbeatable, especially since over the last couple of days the Indians had slacked off. As delighted as Skinner was with the white buffalo hides, he wanted more. Their nearly empty wagons beckoned hungrily to him. If they hadn't been so pressed by Indians, they could have killed and skinned hundreds of brown as well as white hides. Shooting and skinning the few white pelts was light work physically; gathering hundreds and hundreds of brown hides would demand so much effort from the seven men that they wouldn't be able to accomplish it and keep off the Indian attacks.

McCall, even though he was tied up, bothered Skinner almost as much as the redskins did, for he was afraid of both McCall's getting loose and of letting him go. Skinner checked him every night, having to endure on each visit a storm of curses and verbal abuse from Jack. But Skinner wanted to make sure that, like an angry rattler in a gunny sack, the draw knot didn't come loose.

Skinner schooled himself to pay no attention to the

man's tongue. Every word from Jack's lips would return to him in spades.

One night Skinner came over to the wagon with the man's grub, and found McCall almost loose from his bindings.

"You think you're going to get loose, old buddy?" Skinner asked with a chuckle, giving the ropes a jerk and tightening the knots.

"I'm going to wrap a rope around your neck when I do," said McCall. "Then I'm going to yank it one hell of a lot harder."

"You ain't getting loose, Jack."

"I'm getting loose," said McCall. "You can't keep me tied up forever."

"Maybe."

"And you better be a thousand miles away when I do, you son of a bitch."

"I heard you the first fifty times, Jack," Skinner said, pulling the ropes around McCall's feet tighter.

"That's too tight, damn it."

"You'll just have to stand it, Jack. Can't have you getting loose."

"You done killed all the whites now," said McCall. "How come you're still keeping me tied up?"

"'Cause you're so riled up. 'Cause you want to beat the hell out of me."

McCall said nothing in return.

Skinner laughed mirthlessly as he drew back to leave for the campfire. "I called that right, didn't I?" he chuckled.

"Listen, Skinner, you got the whites. Let's run on back to Hays."

Skinner saw Jack's game. Back in Hays he would claim ownership of the whites. Something had to happen to Jack before that happened, but Skinner wasn't sure of what he'd do just yet.

"All in good time."

"No good time, Skinner," Jack said. "We're about to be attacked again."

"Jack, we done shot so many damn Indian ponies that if I got the same for pony skin that I get for buffalo, I'd be a still richer man."

"More than just the Kiowa. Didn't you see those warriors today?"

"Yeah, and they seen our Sharps rifles too."

"There's Utes, Pawnee, Comanche and Cheyenne out there. Maybe even a few Kiowa-Apache."

"I ain't particular. I'll shoot their horses too."

"Skinner, you've brought down too many white buffalo. It's a big deal to them. You've got every tribe in the territory massed behind those hills. Don't you see the smoke from the campfires?"

"They're a big deal to me too, Jack. Don't start that stuff again." Skinner turned and left.

He knew that he needed to do something with McCall soon, but he hadn't decided what. Keeping McCall tied up for so long, especially now that they had their white pelts, didn't sit well with Billy Dixon and Tom Rath. They didn't understand the way Charley and Arkansas and Three-Fingers did. He went back a long ways with them. The newer men didn't understand that everything was fine while the rattler was in the sack, but who wanted to stand there, open it and let him out?

As much as he wanted something to happen to McCall, Skinner couldn't just pull his gun and shoot his old partner while he was tied up. What had Moar meant by McCall's not coming back, anyway? That he was supposed to talk Jack into not coming back to Hays, or that he was to dump him in a ditch somewhere? Had Jack and he been out alone, he wouldn't have had such a problem with the situation, but with Billy and Tom around, sooner or later he would get in trouble. It would be his problem then and his alone, for Moar would deny he had had anything to do with it. While there wasn't much law outside of Kansas City in the territory, if one of these boys saw something and took it into his head to talk to a marshal or happened to spill the beans to one of McCall's friends, Skinner might find himself in a hard spot. Skinner figured there ought to be a way for McCall to have an accident that would end the whole problem. He just had to think up one.

Upon returning from a shooting spree with Three-Fingers, Skinner bawled out Charley and Arkansas, whom he'd left with the wagon, for not checking McCall's bindings.

For the next two days, Skinner checked McCall's bindings himself at least twice a day. Each time, McCall cursed him soundly and gave Skinner more reason to fear his release.

By now the white buffalo had almost thinned out completely. Skinner saw no more than another four to seven, and they were so small that it was hard to single them out as targets.

That night Three-Fingers asked the others, "Say, did you fellows see more Injuns today? They was all over here while we tried to skin that big bull you shot by the ravine."

Skinner and Charley said they had, and Charley added, "Seemed to me they wasn't the same as that bunch yesterday."

"Yeah, we seen that too," said Three-Fingers. "This new gang didn't have their hair cut off on the right side like the others."

"Jack knows about that," said Tom. "Maybe we ought to ask him."

"He says the Injuns are piling up on us," said Billy excitedly. "That the best Injun warriors in the territory are out there."

"Warriors, like hell," said Skinner in order to keep their spirits. "You can't believe much of what Jack McCall tells you. He lived too long with Injuns. He's an Injun lover and he's looking to scare us so we'll let him go." He turned to Three-Fingers. "Where's his grub?"

"Aw, Skinner, I fed him last night," Three-Fingers answered. "I'm tired of hearing what he's going to do to me when he gets loose."

"Whack him one if he opens his mouth," said Skinner. He noticed Tom and Billy looking quickly at each other, as if he had said something they didn't agree with.

"Skinner, when we going to let him go?" asked Billy.

"If you like him so much, then you get his grub, will you?"

"We got to get away from these redskins if we're going to get back to Hays," Tom put in.

"There's more and more of them," Billy added, nodding his head vigorously in agreement with Tom. "Last week we didn't see no more than forty or fifty. This week I swear I seen a couple of hundred."

"Horsefeathers," said Skinner. "You're just seeing the same Injuns coming over one hill and then riding back over another. They do that to scare you."

"McCall knows his way around this country better than any of us," said Tom. "I say we turn him loose so he can get us out of this. We're liable to ride right into more of them."

"Hey, ain't we kept them away up to now with

425

these?'' asked Skinner, patting his rifle. "And ain't I promised you a bushel more money than him? Didn't he want to go back in before we even got fifty of them white skins? Now we're going to fill the wagons with brown hides and make still more money. What the hell's the matter with you?''

The others looked around at each other silently. Then Tom said, "You got to let him go sometime, Skinner. And he's liable to take it out on *us* too.''

Skinner laughed. "Is that all that's bothering you?

Nobody answered.

"You know, a man tied up out here might have an accident,'' Skinner said. "You never know. He might get so weak tied up there, any little old thing might happen to him.''

They sat there, squatted on the ground around their cold supper without moving or speaking, as if they didn't know what to say.

"We vote to let the man go and give him his share of the catch,'' said Tom. "Even-steven with the rest of us. When we get back to Hays, we don't want no Jack McCall coming at us for what we took from him.''

"You don't get that kind of vote,'' said Skinner. "We don't need his help. We want to get away from the Injuns, right? Suppose tomorrow morning we get all packed up in one wagon, put Mr. McCall in the other, spread out before dawn, and set a couple of fires in the right places. Suppose those fires was to get the herd of brown buffalo so excited they run right over that so-called giant Injun camp over to the west. Couldn't we get miles away before they got themselves back together, if they weren't whacked out altogether? Wouldn't even Injuns have a hard time tracking us after a herd of buffalo has run over our tracks?''

They murmured agreement as he elaborated.

Later that evening, before they turned in, Skinner said to Three-Fingers, "And suppose in the stampede that Mr. McCall's wagon gets lost or turns over or gets stampeded or he falls out—I don't know. But something terrible might happen to it, don't you think?"

Three-Fingers laughed and said it sure might.

"Now, Three-Fingers, you drive one of the wagons tomorrow and don't spare the whip."

"What are you going to do?"

"I'm going to work on the tailgate to that wagon. We'll put him in that one. You hit a bump real hard and it opens, a man with his hands and feet tied good is going to have a hell of a time staying in there."

"If I'm in for a third of this load, Skinner."

"A third! A tenth."

"A quarter and you got a deal."

"Twenty percent or I drive the damn thing myself."

"You got a deal."

Chapter 14

Once more Skinner woke the men in the dark, breaking them out of their crust of sleep into moments of surprise at still being alive. Fumbling in the cold dark, they drank cold coffee and gulped down strips of cold buffalo.

They reloaded the wagons, putting all the white hides into one along with their essential supplies, and evenly distributing the several hundred brown hides in the two others. Having carried McCall, still bound, into one of the wagons with brown hides, Skinner assigned Three-Fingers to drive it. Billy was to drive the other, and Arkansas was to drive the white hides.

By full light they had moved east, each man carrying matches and oil-soaked gunny sacks. Skinner had outlined his plan: once they had crossed through the herd to the east, they were to light the dry prairie grass in a long strip east of the buffalo. With the steady east-west wind blowing, the buffalo would panic and stampede through the hills to the west right through the Indian camp. At the same time, the three wagons and the four men on horseback would strike out over the hills to the east, hoping to escape in the confusion.

Skinner felt good about his plan. With Three-Fingers

driving the wagon with the defective tailgate, once the stampede began they would find it simple work to ditch McCall. Back in Hays, he alone would deal with Moar.

As directed by Skinner, who rode up and down the line of fire setters yelling directions, the men spread out on the prairie and set fire to two miles of dry grass. In the dawn they saw no Indians, only an endless ocean of brown buffalo flowing northward between the shallow hills. The wagons set out eastward away from the flames and smoke that quickly crackled against the pale dawn.

The giant herd looked up to sniff the wind, making lowing noises as if questioning the meaning of the dark clouds of smoke. The fire spread with the wind in a westerly direction, and the herd, trapped by the semi circle of fire, looked for a way to escape through the hills to the west.

As the sun rose, its heat increased the wind. Carried northward through the natural tunnel of the valley, the fire and smoke leapt forward across the herd, singeing some of the leaders and pushing many buffalo back southward. Pressed from behind, ten thousand bulls bellowed. Five thousand calves huddled against their mothers and bleated. The cows wavered, trotting forward, jogging back, struggling to figure which direction to run in. A few strong young bulls on the east side, terrified by the flames that roared at them, bucked the tide and pressed southward through the advancing herd. Like two long railroad trains meeting each other on a single track, the herd split out sideways. Ten thousand tons of buffalo energy exploded, half stampeding east and half west.

In minutes the leaders had broken free of the circle of flames and smoke and fled east and west. From where Skinner and his men watched, they saw the smoke in front of them part where the grass had burnt completely and a tidal wave of buffalo came charging through the opening.

As buffalo did in cases of fire, no sooner had they cleared the smoke than they paused to sniff the wind to discover from which direction it blew. The thermal created by the fire had shifted the wind, however, and now it hit the lead animals as if it came from the west. The lead buffalo had little time to make up their minds, for several thousand of their brothers pressed their flanks. Even a twenty-five-hundred-pound bull could be ground under thousands of hooves if he didn't pick a direction and continue to lead.

Gathered on a little hill to the west with the wagons, Skinner, Arkansas, Billy and Three-Fingers saw the giant herd wheel toward them.

"What's happening?" asked Billy.

"They're coming this way!" said Three-Fingers.

"Goddamn," said Skinner. "Let's haul out!"

"Look how fast they're coming," shouted Arkansas from atop his wagon. "We ain't going to outrun them—not with these slow wagons."

"Leave McCall's wagon!" shouted Skinner. "Hitch its team to the one with the white hides. We'll run faster."

"No!" shouted Billy. "You can't just leave him."

Arkansas and Three-Fingers worked quickly with the harnesses, ignoring him. Their hands fumbled, for the ground shook with the thunder of the advancing herd.

"No!" shouted Billy again. "You can't leave him!" But Skinner rode up to the youth's wagon and slapped the mules with his crop. The wagon shot forward.

"Keep it moving, Billy, if you want out of this alive!" Skinner shouted.

Pausing to watch his men make the final adjustments to the harness, Skinner considered leaving the wagon with

431

its load of white hides for only a moment. No, he had worked too hard for it to leave it.

"We just ain't going to make it!" shouted Three-Fingers, looking at the herd. "Hurry up, Arkansas!"

Billy's wagon had moved a quarter-mile away. Fingers was right. The herd moved fast. In moments the buffalo would be upon them.

"Leave the wagon where it's setting. Snub those mules. Get out here with the guns!" shouted Skinner, drawing his Sharps from its scabbard and jumping off his horse. "Shoot down the lead critters."

"Do what?" asked Three-Fingers.

"Damn it, do as I say!" shouted Skinner. Waving his Big Fifty, he ordered them to follow him. He would pull the same trick the Indian had when he had saved them last year.

"Get down here!" he shouted, kneeling in the dirt and pumping a shell into his gun.

To his side, Three-Fingers and Arkansas looked as if they doubted his sanity. Skinner began to fire.

"You dumb bastard!" shouted Fingers. "You can't stop all them buffalo!"

Fingers turned and ran for Skinner's horse. Skinner yelled after him, "We *can* stop them!"

But his shout did no good, for Fingers jumped on the horse, kicked it in the belly and shot away from them. Arkansas jumped on the double-hitched wagon, picked up the reins, prepared to slap the mules with them and shouted, "Come on, Skinner! Let's outrun them!"

"You can't! Help me shoot down a barrier!"

"A what?"

Unable to explain it quickly, Skinner simply ordered him off the wagon.

In answer, Arkansas slapped the reins sharply and shouted, "Hi, mules!" The wagon shot forward.

Now that he was alone with the muleless wagon that contained McCall, Skinner wasn't as sure what to do. Suppose this trick didn't work the second time? Did his Sharps alone have enough firepower? Maybe he wasn't a good enough shot. Should he start shooting to make a blockade of buffalo or run behind the wagon?

But he had little time to reflect, for the herd now was no more than half a mile away. He would never escape unless that Indian's trick with the dead buffalo worked again.

He lay flat on the ground and stuck the Sharps in front of him and squeezed off a shot, but no animal fell. Damn, he thought as he pumped in another shell and fired. Again, no pause from the mass of brown bodies that thundered toward him. On the third shot one of the buffalo faltered no more than fifty yards in front of him. To each side more bulls were passing, galloping with the speed of a runaway freight car. The entire herd would be on him in seconds.

Remaining here and bringing down buffalo was crazy. With a shout that sounded to his own ears like that of a child who had bumped into a ghost, Skinner jumped up, left his rifle and ran backward, thinking he could take cover under the wagon, but he realized it would soon be matchsticks. As he passed the wagon, he saw through its rear gate that McCall was struggling frantically to burst out of his bindings.

"Cut me loose, Skinner!" shouted McCall.

Skinner took no time to answer, much less pause for the few seconds putting a knife to the ropes would have taken.

When he looked forward to find some natural depression of ground in which to hide, a fat pony and a big man's leg flashed in front of his face. He tried to stop himself, but ran right into the fat pony's side. He looked up and saw a club coming down at his head. Skinner tried to duck, but the club hit the side of his head. He felt arms picking him up and then the back of a pony between his legs.

In a daze, Skinner saw more Indians pulling the wagon with ropes, and behind them the buffalo came closer and closer. Suddenly he let go and everything went dark.

It took Striking Eagle and his men most of the day to collect the gear of the whites. All the rifles, shot, half-spilled kegs of lead, the Dutch oven, clothes, foodstuffs, and wood and canvas of the wagons, had been scattered across ten square miles of sagebrush.

The white hides were another matter. Old Hoof had to choose special warriors and give their white buffalo amulets another blessing before they could touch the hides, but finally they were all gathered and put into the single wagon that remained whole.

Striking Eagle and Hoof had mixed feelings. They had caught the criminals who had exterminated the herd of white buffalo, yet the herd had been destroyed, an omen of the worst possible luck for the tribe.

On the other hand, they had rescued every white hide, which was all to the good, and perhaps Hoof could propitiate the white buffalo spirit through the reverence with which the hides were handled.

Toward evening the following day, the party began its trek back to the Kiowa's main camp.

His men had found the trampled remains of four white men and captured four others: Long Crow, Shiny

Head, the boy, and the one with the mashed hand. Striking Eagle had them bound and, upon their return to the village, put into a tepee together.

McCall felt dazed and light headed. First he had been tied up by his own people for the better part of the last week, and now he was tied up by the Kiowa. Having seen the acres of tepees gathered together when they arrived, he figured he and the other three wouldn't last long. He looked around and saw that Billy and Three-Fingers appeared to be all right, but Skinner had a long gash across his bald head.

"What're they going to do with us?" asked Three-Fingers.

None of the other three answered.

"We got to make a break for it," Three-Fingers went on.

McCall laughed. "You're as tied up as I've been this past week. How you reckon to break for it?"

"Help one another. Pick these ropes loose. Scoot over here, Skinner."

"Didn't you see what I seen when we come in?" McCall asked.

"Seen?" asked Three-Fingers. "What?"

"Those poles in the center of camp."

"Poles?" breathed Three-Fingers, his eyes bulging from his scrawny face as if he had just spotted the devil's pitchfork.

Outside, it had grown dark. Drums beat and chants rose in wild rhythms.

"What's going on?" demanded Three-Fingers.

Again no one answered.

"They're going to torture us, ain't they!" he shouted. "Tell me!"

Numbed by the prospect himself, and feeling some pity, McCall nodded in a sober fashion.

Three-Fingers' face twisted up in a grimace of pain. "No," he said. "I can't stand that."

Through the translucent walls of the tepee they saw flames rise higher as the chants and shouts increased. Against the walls, shadows of dancers jumped and cavorted. Suddenly, at the opening of the tepee, a wildly painted face looked in at them, gave a piercing cry of savage delight, and withdrew. The nerves, blood and hearts of the four men froze.

The intrusion of a painted face into the tepee's entrance before giving a wild shout was repeated a dozen times over the next hour, each time startling them no matter how hard they steeled themselves. Sometime after midnight the Indians came for them.

"This is it, ain't it?" asked Three-Fingers as knives cut the ropes around their ankles.

"Yep," said McCall.

Roughly, the four were shoved out of the tepee.

Outside, a strange sight greeted them. In a circle roared eight fires, in the center of which stood six poles about ten feet high and three feet apart. Thongs hung from these poles. With Three-Fingers' screams in their ears, McCall and Skinner were shoved forward and made to stand between two poles.

Quickly, the clothes were stripped off the four of them, leaving them as naked and vulnerable as skinned squirrels.

Standing between the poles, their arms were drawn up as far as they could reach. Their right hands were tied to the stake on the right and their left hands were tied to the opposite stake. Their feet, likewise, were tied to the posts near the ground. Directly in front of them, within ten feet, were Billy and Three-Fingers in the same condition.

Thus they stood, or rather hung. Skinner and McCall faced Billy and Three-Fingers, all in tormenting suspense to learn what rite was to be performed.

The Kiowa that McCall had saved last winter, Lone Wolf, along with a number of the old men, stationed themselves near the four white men at the head of a column of about two hundred warriors. These warriors slowly moved forward, silently and in single file.

Their pace was peculiar, half walk, half shuffle, a spasmodic, nervous motion, like the artificial motion of figures in a puppet show. Each carried in one hand his knife or tomahawk, in the other a flint stone, three inches or more in length and fashioned into the shape of a sharp, pointed arrow. The head of the procession, Lone Wolf, first approached Billy and Three-Fingers. As the shuffling line passed them, two of the youngest warriors broke from the line, seized them by the hair and scalped them, then resumed their places and moved on. This operation consisted of cutting off only a portion of the skin covering the skull, about the size of a dollar. Blood flowed down their heads in profusion, ran over their faces and trickled through their beards.

Lone Wolf and the line passed McCall and Skinner without glancing at them or molesting them, marching around them again in the same order as before. Up till this time there had been silence, except yells from the two young men in the act of scalping, but now the whole party halted for a half-minute, slapped their hands on their mouths and united in an energetic war whoop. In silence the circuitous march was continued.

When they reached Billy and Three-Fingers the second time, the sharp flint arrowheads were brought into play. Each man, as he passed, gave a wild screech and brandished his tomahawk in their faces an instant, then drew the sharp point of the stone across their bodies, not cutting deep, but penetrating the flesh just far enough to cause the blood to ooze out in great crimson gouts. By the time the entire two hundred had passed, Billy and Three-Fingers presented an awful spectacle that left McCall feeling weak and dizzy.

They had left him and Skinner unharmed. Nevertheless, McCall regarded it as a matter of certainty that soon they would be subjected to similar tortures. He would have been devoutly thankful then could he have been permitted to choose his own mode of being put to death. He could not say how many times they circled around, halting to sound their war whoop and going through the same demoniac exercise, but the Indians persisted in their hellish work till every inch of the bodies of Billy and Three-Fingers was hacked, mangled and covered with clotted blood. It would have been a relief to McCall, much more to them, could they have only died, but he saw that the object of the tormentors was to drain the fountain of their lives by slow degrees.

In the process of this torture, there occurred an intermission of a quarter of an hour. During this period, some Indians threw themselves on the ground and lit their pipes, others collected in little groups, but all of them laughed, shouted and pointed their fingers at the prisoners, as if taunting them as cowards and criminals.

Billy uttered not a word, but his sobs and cries were those that only the most intense agony can wring from the human soul. On the contrary, the prayers of Three-Fingers were unceasing. Constantly he exclaimed, "Oh Jesus, have mercy on me! Oh Father in heaven, strike me! Lord Jesus, come and put me out of my pain!"

McCall hung his head and closed his eyes to shut out this sickening scene, but he wasn't allowed to do this. Several warriors sprang up and drew McCall's and Skinner's heads back violently, compelling them, however unwillingly, to stare directly at the writhing sufferers.

At the end of about two hours came the last act. The warriors halted on their last round in the form of a semicircle, and two of them moved out from the center, striking into a war dance, raising their war song, advancing, receding, now moving to the right, now to the left, occupying ten minutes in proceeding as many paces. Finally they reached their victims and for some time danced before them this hellish dance. Then they drew their hatchets suddenly and sent the bright blades crashing through their victims' skulls.

Their bodies were cut down and thrown aside upon the ground.

McCall and Skinner anticipated that they would suffer the same fate and stiffened themselves to meet it. To McCall's astonishment, however, they were unbound, taken in charge by guards, re-dressed in their hunting shirts and leggings and pushed toward the tepee in which they had earlier been kept.

As McCall moved off, he turned his head to take a last look at Billy and Three-Fingers. He saw that the Indian dogs had already gathered around the corpses and were lapping the blood from their innumerable wounds.

"God have mercy on their souls," said Skinner.

"Pray for yourself, Mr. Kincade," said McCall. "Our turn is next."

"I'm going to run for it. I'm going to make them kill me quickly."

"No! Don't!"

With a leap Skinner jumped forward. To his credit,

he got twenty feet before fifteen braves brought him to the ground. He was carried back amid a sea of grins to the spot where McCall had quietly stopped.

Striking Eagle gave orders, and Skinner's right leg was placed between two logs. Before Skinner or McCall could say or do anything, a large rock was hammered down once on the knee, breaking it with a crack and making Skinner scream loudly. With his leg dragging uselessly, Skinner uttered pitiful moans and was dragged toward the tepee. Between his guards, McCall walked back.

They were left alone. McCall straightened out the shattered knee of the moaning man and tried to soothe him. He found food and water in pots by the fireplace and gave some to Skinner.

"Hurts," said Skinner. "Hurts, hurts, hurts."

"Yeah, looks like it does."

"What'd they do that for?" Skinner's face was awash with sweat from the pain.

"You fool. Because you ran."

Without answering, Skinner lay gasping in pain. A movement behind them startled McCall, who turned to see if they were now to be dragged back to the three poles for their turn. In the light of dawn, he saw Lone Wolf enter, but a different-looking Lone Wolf from the man they had rescued last winter. Instinctively McCall backed away, knowing that Lone Wolf was the leader here, that he had killed Billy and Three-Fingers, and that he would start in next on him. This man had the lean, hard look of a man with a purpose, not the look of a young man interested in his pleasures. The man they had rescued had looked as if life was to be enjoyed; this one looked as if it was a contest he had to win at all costs.

"Hello, Lone Wolf," said McCall, struggling to keep up that front of bravery Indians cared so much for.

"I'm no longer called that name. I'm called Striking Eagle."

McCall nodded, willing to call him anything.

"Sit," said Striking Eagle.

McCall sat and Striking Eagle squatted across from him. To their side lay Skinner, gasping and moaning. Striking Eagle looked over at the moon-faced white man with disdain.

"It's old Lone Wolf!" gasped Skinner. "Remember how we helped you out last winter?"

Ignoring Skinner, Striking Eagle asked McCall in a combination of Kiowan, English and signs, "Why were you tied up, Crow?"

"Tied up?"

"My braves found you bound hand and foot near this one."

"We had a disagreement, him and me."

"What disagreement?"

"This one wanted too much gold."

"Why have you fought with me, Crow Man?"

"I haven't fought with you. Your braves attacked me. We've just been trying to make our load."

"You've been killing our brothers. Then you went too far. You killed the white buffalo."

"Yes."

"All of them."

"Not all," said McCall. "It's not right to kill all. We just wanted a few skins."

"We've collected almost a hundred white buffalo hides from your killing," said Striking Eagle.

"Yes."

"I don't think there are six whites left."

441

"No, I guess not."

"Old Hoof says when the whites are gone, the Kiowa will go. That we will all die off as a people."

McCall didn't answer. He had heard such stories from the Comanche, Cheyenne and the Utes, and he could only nod. For the tribes, such an event as the death of the white herd would be experienced as a disaster the equivalent of a volcano erupting in a white man's city, or a fire that destroys an entire town, or a plague. They would feel wiped out and unable to function as a people if the power of their animal, the buffalo, was slaughtered out of existence.

In his halting Kiowan, McCall said, "I didn't want to take all the hides, Striking Eagle."

"But you took them."

"No, that's why I was tied up."

"What?"

"I led this hunt. I tried to stop them, but these others wouldn't listen. They wanted them all. To keep me from interfering, they tied me up, just as you found me."

For a long time Striking Eagle just looked at McCall as if he could discover the truth with an unblinking gaze. "You just want to save your life with this story," he finally said. "But you are both to die making noises like an animal who has no courage, not like men."

McCall shrugged. "It's a good day to die, Striking Eagle."

Striking Eagle smiled. "Are you braver than the others?"

"No, but it's a good day to die. Better to die young than an old man in bed."

"I didn't think the white men had courage."

"We'll find out, won't we?"

"You saved my life, and I'm grateful."

"And I respect the big whites, Striking Eagle. I told

you I lived with the Comanches when I was young. Remember?''

Striking Eagle nodded.

''My new father married the year after I arrived at the Comanche camp, and my new stepmother decided that I should be her personal slave rather than my stepfather's son.''

Striking Eagle looked at him as if he didn't believe him and asked, ''Who was this stepfather?''

''Little Robe.''

''Old Hoof has talked of him. And then?''

''He was a fool over her and went along with the plan. She made life so hard for me that I spent six months looking for a way to escape. I found a way to go one spring day and left. I was no more than twelve. On the way back to what I thought was my people I got caught in an April blizzard, something like the storm we found you in. I got lost and I was ready to give up and die. I lay down in the snow next to a large rock and I found the rock was warm. As I remember, I had a kind of fever then and thought the warm rock was my momma. All I know is I hugged that big animal for what must have been two days, could have been longer, covered by snow and expecting to be crushed or eaten or the animal to leave. One morning the sky was blue and clear. I had to roll out of the way quick when the animal got to its feet.''

''What kind of animal?''

''It was a big buffalo cow with a dead calf. A big white buffalo cow with a dead white buffalo calf by her side. I reckon she thought I was her calf, for she hadn't moved with me wiggling up next to her. Since then I've had a soft spot in my heart for whites, as few of them as there are. I don't have any trouble understanding that they protect the Kiowa. They saved my life.''

443

Striking Eagle responded with a proverb. *"When the white buffalo no longer graze, the Kiowa will starve."*

"Yes," said McCall. "That could be."

"They're gone, and so are you. You'll live today," said Striking Eagle as he rose to leave. "We have more guests coming. Tonight will be your time."

"Yes," said McCall as the Indian chief left.

Skinner reached feverishly for McCall. "What was all that Indian jabber, McCall? Notice I didn't say anything to interfere with your play. Did you make a deal with him?"

McCall laughed. "No deal. Just jabber, Mr. Kincade."

"You didn't figure a way out?"

"No. If I were you, I'd spend my day praying."

In answer, Skinner groaned. "Why me? I'm just a poor old buffalo skinner that never had no luck at all. Never, never, never. God, you ain't never given me nothing, and may the devil take you down when you go."

McCall laughed. "Is that your prayer? You figure that's going to help you?"

"My leg, McCall," said Skinner. "I can't see straight for the pain. Comes in waves."

"You'll forget the pain quick enough."

"I will?"

"About ten minutes after they string us up, it's going to seem like a mosquito bite."

They were fed and watered once during the day. Half a dozen times McCall managed to pull up the dewcloth of the tepee to see that what Striking Eagle had told him was true. All day, fresh, cheerful arrivals rode into camp for the evening's festivities, processions of braves on horses followed by women pulling travoises on which were heaped bundles of tepees and children.

Night settled, several hours flew by, and the opening flap was pushed aside. Striking Eagle himself came in with two pots of water and food.

"Thanks, Striking Eagle," said McCall.

The chief sat down across from him. From under his shirt he drew a knife, a pouch of water, and a cloth that was tied up. He reached over and cut the hobble and bindings off McCall.

"What's this?" asked Skinner in a whisper. "Is it time?" His face glistened with sweat in the dim light from the fires that shone through the tepee.

In Kiowa, Striking Eagle said, "You can escape in a few minutes, friend Crow."

"Escape?" asked McCall.

"I don't think you will get far, but I will give you that."

"Escape? How escape?"

Striking Eagle nodded toward the back of the tepee. "Under the dewcloth. When you hear the shouts of the corn dance at its height. Then all eyes will be on Left Hand and his dancers. You'll have an hour in the darkness before you are missed."

"They'll be right after me."

"They'll be right after you."

"And my friend?"

"You'll be caught quickly enough. With your friend to burden you, you'll be caught more quickly still."

"Thank you, Striking Eagle."

"You gave me a chance last year. I give you one now."

McCall nodded as Striking Eagle rose and left.

"What's he say, Jack?" asked Skinner in a croak. "When are they coming for us?"

Mentioning nothing to Skinner about escape, McCall said, "In about two hours, Skinner. Two hours."

"Oh, God. My knee is worse. I wish it was over."

"Not long now."

"Two hours to live! Only two hours!"

McCall didn't want to leave Skinner to this torture. Still, he could figure no way to take the man with him, not with a broken leg. McCall figured he himself had maybe one chance in ten of getting away, maybe less. Struggling to help a big man like Skinner who couldn't walk would make it impossible.

"What was all that jabber about, McCall?"

"He wanted to know if we'd seen any more white buffalo, Skinner."

"White buffalo? What did he want to know about them for?"

McCall sighed. "You still don't know, do you?"

"Know what?"

"That's what all this is about, Skinner."

"What?"

"Striking Eagle got half a dozen tribes to come help him because we killed off so many white buffalo."

"What the hell for? God knows he's got enough buffalo meat on the hoof out there to last him and his people several lifetimes."

McCall shook his head with exasperation. "I tried to tell you. The white buffalo are sacred to them."

"What kind of hogwash is that? Meat tastes the same as a brown buffalo."

"You still don't see it, do you?"

"See what?"

"That in all likelihood you wouldn't be here with your broke kneecap if you'd left them whites alone."

"Horsefeathers."

"You tell yourself that when they string you up."

* * *

Near midnight, when the corn dance was at its height, McCall lay down and carefully pulled up the dewcloth to peer outside.

"What you see, McCall?" hissed Skinner in the gloom that was only lit by the distant firelight that came through the tepee.

"They sound excited," said Skinner. "They coming now?"

"Ain't nobody back here."

"What!" exclaimed Skinner. "Let's run for—aw, shit. I forgot about my leg. Is that a knife you got? Where'd you find that?"

"Laying behind the robes over there."

"What a break!"

"Not much to do with it, though, is there?"

"You ain't going out there, are you?"

"I'm thinking about it."

"You ain't going to leave me, are you?"

"How you going to make it with that leg?"

"I can walk."

"You can't walk."

"I'll hop."

"You can't even stand."

"Yes, I can!"

"No." McCall turned to peer again under the dewcloth. He saw that he had to go quickly if he was going to make it. Once they had ceremonially harvested the dancers who represented the ears of corn, the dance was nearly over.

Behind him, McCall heard a shuffling. He turned, and in the gloom he could see Skinner struggling on his hands and his good-leg in an effort to get to his feet. McCall held his breath as he watched Skinner release his hands from the earth and, with a cry of pain, teeter for long seconds before he toppled over.

"I can't stand!"

"Yeah, I know."

"Take me with you, McCall!"

"Good-bye, Skinner."

"Don't leave me!"

McCall hesitated. Even though Skinner had bound him for a week, stolen his hides, and probably had planned to kill him, as Nelly had said, McCall didn't want to leave a fellow white man to the fate the Kiowa planned for him before their Comanche and Cheyenne guests. But how could he help this crippled creature escape?

Skinner pleaded, "I'll do anything for you if you get me out of here."

"Hell, man," McCall said, shaking his head and looking away. "I'm not likely to get more than two tepees away. I'm likely to be sitting next to you in five minutes with *two* broken legs."

McCall heard the shouting as the corn dance began to ebb. Not liking it, he said, "I'm sorry, Skinner. Good-bye."

"Oh, God, McCall—don't leave me!"

"Good-bye, Skinner."

McCall turned back and raised the dewflap again. The next time he heard shouting, he'd slide out. Near him he felt something slither, and turned his head to the left to see Skinner's sweating face not six inches from his.

"What do you see?" Skinner asked softly.

"Right now, nobody."

"If you carry my right side, I can make it," Skinner whispered.

McCall knew Skinner was wrong. He needed to be able to crouch low and slide from the shadow of one tepee to another effortlessly. The more he studied the shadowy backways he would have take, the less he thought of his

448

chances. With Skinner as a burden, he wouldn't be nearly agile enough to dodge so many Indians.

"So long," said McCall.

He pushed himself out of the tepee, but his legs didn't clear, caught in Skinner's iron grip.

"Goddamnit, let go!" hissed McCall, kicking at Skinner.

Kicking did little good, for the man had clamped McCall's legs around his chest and held on with a grip like a bear's.

"No! Take me with you."

McCall tried to kick free again, but couldn't. Half turning, he rolled toward the tepee and back under the wall to confront Skinner's moon face.

"I'm going to cut the hell out of you if you don't let go," he told Skinner.

His voice hoarse with desperation, Skinner said, "Cut or take me with you."

"You dumb son of a bitch, there's no way I can make it with you."

"If I don't make it, you don't make it, Jack."

McCall reached down and put the knife's blade against Skinner's throat. "Let go my legs, Skinner."

"No."

"I'll kill you."

In the dim light, McCall thought he saw Skinner smile. "Better you than them. I ain't letting go."

Drawing his fist holding the knife back, McCall punched Skinner on the side of his head with his knuckles, but the man merely ducked his head, and McCall felt his hand scrape painfully against the man's skull.

"I ain't letting go, McCall. Hit all you want."

"Don't be stupid!"

"I ain't letting go!"

449

Steeling himself, McCall slashed across Skinner's throat with his knife, felt the resistance of a hard knot of gristle, and heard, rather than saw, through a gasp and a gurgle, the effect of the knife on his partner's throat. In seconds, Skinner had relaxed his grip on McCall's legs. Not giving himself time to feel anything about what he had done, McCall quickly scooted under the tepee's edge and crawled toward the back of the next tepee.

Keeping to the shadows, he made it past the rear of a dozen tepees before he paused. Once he heard voices and six braves came rushing toward him, but he pressed himself to the ground and they didn't see him. Another time he stumbled over a couple of bodies, but they merely giggled and grunted, and he realized it was a brave and his lover and moved quickly away. Finally he found himself on the back row of tepees, a good distance from the shouting and the fires. He was next to a picketed herd of ponies. He looked around but saw no sentries. Were they all at the dance?

Lowering himself to the ground, he slid into the herd. He felt the horses that he passed for the size of muscles and calluses around the mouth: he wanted a strong pony who was well broken, not some yearling that had never accepted a rider. Locating one, he cut a piece of rawhide off the picket line and fashioned a halter.

Around him the horses pulled away in newfound freedom. He knew they would begin to scatter shortly, the one thing that would both alert the Kiowa that he had escaped and yet make it more difficult for them to pursue him. With the haltered horse in his wake, he moved through the herd away from the camp, cutting picket lines as he went.

When he reached the herd's back edge, he kept bent over and walked quickly, not daring to climb up and be

450

seen, pulling his mount behind him. Minutes later he was surrounded by darkness. Behind him he heard shouts and turned to see the merriment of the camp, but he didn't think they saw him. He mounted and turned his horse's head away from the camp and urged the pony forward.

Right now he wasn't as interested in going in the right direction—back to Hays—as putting distance between himself and the Kiowa.

Shortly his eyes adjusted to the weak starlight and he increased the speed of the horse. When the ground became rocky he pulled the horse toward the hills. With any luck, the hard surface would slow down the Kiowa's attempts to track him.

When he reached the top of a hill, he turned back to look. The Kiowa village in the valley below was lit up by the fires, and he saw Indian youths running throughout it struggling to catch their ponies. At one end he saw braves gathering. One of them was pointing in a direction several degrees south of him, but nevertheless in his general direction, as if someone might have seen his escape.

He concluded that he wouldn't have much time. Weak from the events of the day and exhausted from lack of sleep, he turned his pony and rode down the hill.

The Kiowa were among the best trackers on the plains. If he was to survive, he had to put as much distance between himself and them as he could before dawn. He had no illusions about his chances: next to none. This was Kiowa country and they numbered in the hundreds, and in addition he noticed as his horse picked its way that it seemed lame in the right front hoof.

As he got off the pony in the darkness to check its hoof for a stone, he prayed that was all it was. A man on foot against the Kiowa wouldn't last till noon tomorrow.

451

Chapter 15

Every young warrior wanted to ride after McCall, and if he didn't have a good war horse, he borrowed one. Tracking down the captive who had killed his shiny-headed companion, stolen a horse and robbed the Kiowa of their rites before the assembled guests would provide a glorious day out on the plains, and each warrior wanted to be the man to kill him. They figured they should pick up Long Crow Man's trail early and run him down before the day was out.

Striking Eagle stayed behind to meet with the war leaders of the other tribes. Led by Left Hand, excited and voluble, one hundred fifty warriors set out an hour before dawn.

By midmorning, Old Hoof had turned his attention to the problem of the white hides that he had had the bravest of the warriors gather from where they had fallen out of the white man's wagon.

These hides sat now in one tepee off a bit from the village, guarded by six husky warriors. On this morning Hoof approached the lodge slowly, concentrating on every step, struggling to make the power within that lodge accept him as he sung a variety of power chants to protect himself. He didn't like this. He didn't like it at all, no matter how much of an honor it was. As he approached the entrance, he felt the power within. His own skin grew warm while the blood underneath it ran cold. His limbs trembled, and all his skill at dealing with his own fears seemed to have abandoned him. He felt more like a child before a growling dog than one of the most experienced shamans of the six gathered tribes.

As he stared at the piles of hides, sweat burst out under his arms and inside his thighs. He knew he had one of the trickiest jobs a shaman had ever received, handling so much power in a safe way. Just being in the same place with so much *Wakan* made him tremble. He worked carefully. A man could forget a syllable on a chant and cause his entire tribe to be crushed by the forces he had unleashed.

Inside the tepee he chanted for another couple of hours, struggling to tame the white pelts' awesome power and allow the situation itself to dictate what he should do. What Hoof wanted, and hardly dared ask for, was to strike down the curse the tribe now lived under from the death of the white buffalo. The future of his entire people depended on it, but he didn't think his buffalo power was strong enough to redirect all the power in this lodge. He simply had to try, however, even if the white buffalo destroyed him. What else had he trained himself for all his life?

Gradually one action became clear. The first thing to do was show the hides respect by proper handling, which meant making them into the best robes that the tribe's women were capable of producing. Meanwhile, he could chant and pray with the other shamans in an effort to discover what they must do with such sacred objects as the tanned and decorated robes.

Later that afternoon he appointed a crier to walk slowly through the camp with a message: "Women are wanted to clean and dress the hides of Grandfather White Buffalo. Hoof the shaman asks it. Only women who are honorable, virtuous, and free of all sin. Much merit comes to those whose hands can bear such a task.''

By dusk a crowd had gathered a safe distance from the tepee that contained the piles of white hides. Hoof had chanted to himself since midmorning, asking *Wakan-Takan* for guidance.

When Onni heard the crier, she decided to join the women to work on the hides. She wanted to show the responsible women of the tribe how virtuous she was and how much she belonged to their ranks. She had only recently recovered from her terrible sickness and hoped that through this she could show herself, if not others, that she was a fit wife to Striking Eagle, one of the greatest warriors ever of the Kiowa. She had convinced herself that she had to stop acting like a ninny, although the thought of working within the critical sight of older women on such dangerous pelts made her want to take the children and go plum picking.

Her sister Willow shrank from Onni's invitation to join her, frightened of such awesome power and proclaiming that she was too young, raw, and unclean to even look at a white hide. On top of that, Grandfather Hoof had asked for ''women,'' not ''girls,'' which was all she, Willow, was.

Onni gathered with the other women before the special tepee. Her sister's words were still ringing in her ears. Was she clean enough? Was she woman enough? Was she liable to sicken and curl into a dying ball of pain because she was not enough woman to touch these powerful pelts?

''Where is the other wife of Striking Eagle?'' asked Hoof as he reviewed the crowd of women who had answered his call. Onni's heart sank as Elk Woman and the wives of several other chiefs were sent for. In front of all these women, Old Hoof would choose Elk Woman over Onni because she was older or more powerful or her family had been Onde, aristocratic. The tongues of women all around the village would wag night and day at Onni's humiliation. Why had she thrust herself forward? She would have turned and walked away now, except that would have looked worse.

A little out of breath, Elk Woman and the other half dozen wives made a hurried arrival. Hoof told them that as the wives of strong chiefs, they were expected to take part in the work of turning the white hides into well-tanned robes.

Elk Woman said, "But one from our family is here." She pointed at Onni.

"Two may work," said Hoof. "Striking Eagle is a powerful warrior, and all his wives are full of power."

"I must take care of Striking Eagle and his guests," Elk Woman said. "And someone must bring those who work food and water, and care for their children. That's how I will serve."

"Others may do such work," said Hoof.

"I'm not worthy," said Elk Woman. "Allow me to serve in this humble way."

And when it was proper, Elk Woman left, leaving Onni with the other senior women of the Kiowa. Onni's heart sang. All the women saw that in Striking Eagle's family, Onni was regarded as the first wife.

When Hoof outlined what needed to be done with the hides, Onni thought she could do it well, for her thin hands were as skilled with chisel, adze, rasp, squeegee and awl as any woman's.

As Hoof had instructed, the young men of the tribe made a bower out of poles, branches and leaves to work under. By nightfall, in the light of fires and torches, the women started their task.

Two hundred women bent over the hundred pelts, two women to a hide. Old Hoof said they were to take shifts to eat and sleep. No team was to let its hide out of sight till the task was completed and the green hides had become finely tanned and richly decorated robes.

Working with Teema, a pleasant young woman, they used buffalo leg bone chisels to gouge from the underside of the hide the scraps of flesh and fat that remained from the white hunter's hasty stripping. This took them till far into the night.

Next they scalped the underside of the hide with a short adze, a flint blade right-angled into a handle. They took turns, one holding the hide and the other pulling the adze. Gradually, carefully, they planed the hide to an even thickness, a job that took them till midmorning the next day, for the importance of their task demanded great care. The power of the white buffalo might strike them with lightning or sickness if they dropped their attention and punched an inadvertent hole in the pelt.

To brain the hide, they dressed it with a paste of fat, cooked buffalo brains and liver, using two rounded stones to work in the greasy blend. Onni and Teema didn't talk much, and neither did the other women under the long bower. Hoof and the shamans roved through the makeshift lodge chanting and singing, and Onni and Teema gathered that the shamans were keeping the force of the white buffalo in control through their prayers.

In the middle of the night, one of White Horse's wives began to sob and moan in pain. She was covered with boils, and when questioned by Hoof, the truth came out. The woman confessed she had gone into the bushes with another warrior last summer. Although she was unclean, she hadn't dared not to work on the white pelts. Hoof sent her back to her family and told her to beg her husband's forgiveness. For a long time silence gripped the bower. Not even the furtive whispers of partners slithered through the gloom.

When the skin was thoroughly oiled, Onni and Teema laid it out in the sun. The sun's warmth would work the paste into the pelt even more.

They worked without stop for a day, a night, another day under the pressure of not making a mistake. It had exhausted Onni. Teema had taken a long break this morning and had even gotten some sleep back in her own lodge. As they watched their hide's progress under the sun—they didn't dare leave it—Teema urged Onni to spend the night back in her own lodge with her family, promising to keep vigil over the hide. After all, she said, the next step was easy: soaking the hide in warm water and then drying it with long strokes of the squeegee.

Grateful, Onni took her suggestion. Tonight was Striking Eagle's night in her tepee, and she hadn't seen him or the children for far too long.

Back at her lodge, her tepee had an eerie, desolated air and was uncharacteristically empty. Hearing laughter from Elk Woman's tepee, she strode over to it. When she reached the entrance flap, she paused in the dusk and listened. She heard Willow, her own children, Elk Woman's children, Elk Woman and Striking Eagle talking and joking in a jolly fashion. How happy they all sounded together, a collection of hoots and squeals that made Onni's stomach knot. She had never heard them all together before like this, her entire family without her. She didn't want to join them either, for she didn't believe she could be as happy as they were while she was in their company, and they would quickly see something was wrong with her.

Oh, what was she thinking? What rot! Wasn't she the first wife of Striking Eagle and the wife dressing the white pelts?

Putting her fears aside, she pushed aside the flap of Elk Woman's tepee and entered. Although she was greeted effusively by everyone—her children especially—the festive tone of the evening never rose to the pitch she had heard while standing outside, although she tried several times to make things as jolly.

What all this meant to Onni as she trudged back to the bower the next morning was that she might try to tell herself she was the first wife of the family, but all she really did was drag it down. When she was with them, none of them felt as good as they did when she was away. She wanted to cry. It wasn't right. They had been as jolly a year ago when it had been just her as the family's mother. Now that Elk Woman was there, she had no place.

In a dispirited mood, Onni relieved Teema, who thanked her and went back to her family. Down the length of the sun-dappled bower, one hundred twenty-five women bent over similar tasks as she grained the gorgeous hide to give it a uniform smoothness. While she worked, she reflected about her life over the past months.

Why should she feel so bad? She might have failed in her efforts to prove Elk Woman had murdered her husband and tried to murder her, but hadn't she succeeded in showing everyone that she was Striking Eagle's first wife? Just now her sister-witch-wife was in her tepee preparing food, having piously told Onni last night that she need not worry about Striking Eagle as she, Elk Woman, would feed him well in her absence at the white hide tanning.

The way she had said that, with such a smirk, had made Onni feel as if something awful would happen to her while she worked here, and that feeling wouldn't leave her. Somehow being here and working on the huge white robe didn't feel much like an honor when Elk Woman was back in the bosom of her family, where she could come and go freely in both tepees and take over the hearts of Onni's family. Why didn't anything work out right when it involved Elk Woman?

If Elk Woman had been here tanning the white bull's hide instead of Onni, Onni was certain that somehow Elk Woman would have taken advantage of that too. Onni didn't know exactly how, but she would have. Somehow Elk Woman would have shown herself to be more virtuous than Onni, more of an Onde woman. Somehow Elk Woman had won once more. No matter what Onni did or accomplished, Elk Woman would always win, and Onni sensed the sloppy-faced witch wouldn't rest till she had destroyed her.

And just why wasn't Elk Woman here? Onni asked herself. Now that she thought of it, giving up this honor wasn't like Elk Woman. How strange that she didn't want to show Onni up by tanning hides! Did it mean that she was back in camp cooking up mischief? That she had maneuvered Onni out of the way for a specific reason? Or that—Onni gasped as she thought it—she was too unclean to risk touching the hides?

No, that couldn't be.

But maybe it was. After all, Granny Fox Face had said she was evil. If she had killed Eagle Beak with some witch's potion, wouldn't she be terrified of touching the white bull's hide?

Well, it might explain why she wasn't here, but it

didn't help Onni at all. Elk Woman had exploited not working on the hides to her own advantage.

What a pity Elk Woman hadn't been more ambitious! How much Onni would have liked the white buffalo to punish her! Then she sighed as she worked with her adze. If Elk Woman *were* here, then Onni wouldn't have worked on the hides, and the rest of camp wouldn't have seen how important she, Onni, was.

Still, better to get rid of Elk Woman.

She grinned. There was still time. How could she get Elk Woman here?

Pleased with her thoughts, Onni said to Teema when her partner returned, "My sister-wife is afraid to come here."

Her friend looked up at her with troubled eyes. "Oh, Onni, don't start in again on Elk Woman! A person gets tired of hearing a dog bark."

Determined to make every effort, Onni shifted tactics, smiled, and said in a strong voice, "A woman married to Striking Eagle risks offending the spirit of the great whites if she doesn't help prepare its hides."

Down the long row of silent women, a couple of heads looked up at her statement. They had for the most part obeyed Hoof's injunctions about speaking softly but had relieved the pressure of silence by continually whispering to their partners. Onni smiled broadly at them and said, "I'll yield my place to her. I have served. Our husband, Striking Eagle, is a powerful chief, and all his wives deserve a chance to bring him honor."

"But she said she didn't want to," said one of the matrons on the far side of the bower.

"She was generous," said Onni, rising. "I'm giving up my place to her." She turned to all the women. "After

461

all, I'm the younger of the two of us, and the second wife. It's not right for so much to fall to me.''

Murmurs of approval ran up and down the long rows of kneeling women as they all turned to look at her. From the background, Old Hoof came forward.

"Onni, are your hands tired?" he asked.

She regretted standing and wanted to sit again. She hadn't counted on facing the old man with the strong eyes.

"No, grandfather," she said. "*Wakan-Takan* has spoken to me."

Hoof looked at her sharply. "Watch whose name you call on, young woman."

Trembling, she said as firmly as she could, "I've been spoken to, grandfather."

"Spoken to."

"Yes. Clearly."

"And what was said?"

"That I was to yield my place to my sister-wife, Elk Woman."

"Yield your place? Here?"

"Yes, that I am the younger of us, and that I have usurped her honor as first wife by being here."

Old Hoof peered at Onni with a creased brow as if struggling to penetrate her meaning. "This is the woman you've fought with for a year?"

"Yes, grandfather."

"A change of heart?" he asked suspiciously.

Onni bowed her head and nodded in a humble fashion. "Yes, grandfather. The power of this bull is great."

For moments, no one said anything, as if the entire long bower held its collective breath. It was suspicious, Onni knew, but no one could argue with the power of the white buffalo. And who would think she was lying? What woman would give up such an honor, something to tell her children and grandchildren about, to another? And would the white buffalo be able to strike her down if she was away from its side?

"Ask Elk Woman to come," said Grandfather Hoof to his crier, who jumped up and trotted off to camp.

Onni simply stood there, neither working on the hide nor moving away. A few minutes later Elk Woman appeared, looking bewildered.

"This one gives up her place at the tanning for you," said Hoof.

"I'm not worthy," said Elk Woman, and Onni saw the woman's dark eyes flash hatred in her direction.

Onni said nothing.

"It's a great gift she's handing you," said Hoof. "Does the first wife of Striking Eagle refuse to work on the white spirit's pelt?"

"No, not refuse," said Elk Woman. "This one standing here in such humility still wants me to leave what she regards as only her family, despite her husband's choice of me as his wife. This one standing here in the fashion of an innocent calf still thinks I had something to do with my late husband's death. She won't let it go, grandfather."

"This one wants to make peace in your family and offers you a gift," said Hoof in a gentle tone. "Peace in the lodge of our greatest warriors, particularly in such hard times, isn't something to be lightly turned aside."

"Yes, grandfather," said Elk Woman, bowing her head.

"What do you say now to her gift?"

When Elk Woman didn't answer, Hoof asked again, "Well, what do you say?"

"Whatever you think, grandfather," said Elk Woman.

"I think you should accept with a grateful heart."

So it was agreed. Elk Woman took Onni's place

across from Teema, and Onni lingered in the bower only a few moments, feeling sad at leaving such an important place for such mundane tasks as cooking and shouting at children. It had felt good to be one with the Onde women of the tribe.

From what Onni saw over the next couple of days as she visited the bower, Elk Woman's spirit seemed to thrive on the work of tanning the pelt of the great white bull, despite her being an unclean person. Elk Woman and Teema, having stretched a sinew between two trees and draped the hide over it, seized an end in each hand and seesawed the hide back and forth over the sharp edge of the sinew, soft-tanning it. Already some of the women were building smokehouses in which they would cure the robes for half a day. Now in the center of the other women, laughing and trading jokes with Teema, Elk Woman appeared more hearty than ever. Onni brought her food and water, and she thought her sister-wife's cheeks had become more rosy and that her whole being had inflated with a surge of power, as if something of the great spirit of the white bull had flowed into her.

On the third day of Elk Woman's work, Onni saw a further change. While Elk Woman had eaten little of the food she had left the day before, Onni thought the rosiness in her cheeks had increased. Elk Woman worked with a heartiness Onni had never seen in the woman. Onni put on as gay a face as she could force, but inside, her spirits wailed. Elk Woman was too much for her. She was unbeatable.

She started to say something mean, but checked herself. She just put the cold buffalo, the paunch of water, and the water lily tuber mush she had brought on the ground next to Elk Woman and backed away. The look of hatred that Elk Woman flashed at her jolted Onni. With all she had been through over the past year, never had so much hatred been directed at her. A little shaken, Onni tottered backward and scurried to the safety of her lodge. What would life with Elk Woman be like from now on?

At daybreak the next morning, Onni was shaken awake by Willow. Striking Eagle was pulling a robe about his shoulders against the chill of dawn.

"What is it?" Onni asked, assuming that Striking Eagle had risen early and wanted something to eat.

"It's Elk Woman," hissed her sister, not wanting to wake the children. "They said come quick!"

At that hour the bower seemed deserted. Then, with a shock, Onni realized that over a hundred women lay about the dirt floor unconscious. Hoof, his crier, Stomach Wind and half a dozen assistants stood looking uneasily over the scene as Willow, Onni, Striking Eagle and others from the village trotted up. Of the one hundred twenty-five women who should have been busily at work tanning the hides, all were bowed over their tasks, asleep—or worse.

Onni gasped again as she saw on the ground directly in front of Grandfather Hoof a terrible sight. The great robe she had worked on seemed wrapped around a carcass of meat the size of four or five dogs, as if it had been struggling with this new flesh to remake itself into a white bull. From the head of the robe a hand and arm shot out, capped by rigid, extended fingers. She knew that hand.

With a start, Onni shouted, "Elk Woman!"

"Yes."

"My God! What happened?"

More blood than she believed could come from one human body ran over the edges of the white robe, staining the cleanness that Onni and Teema had worked so hard to achieve. The meat, bones and flesh within the white robe looked to be little more than a bloody mess of twisted flesh.

Hoof shook his head sadly. "This one had filthy hands. The white bull crushed her."

In a daze, Onni asked, "And these other women? Are they dead too?"

"He didn't want them to watch. He put them to sleep. We haven't yet been able to rouse them."

"But what happened to her?"

"Sometime during the night the robe seems to have wrapped itself around her and crushed her to death."

"Crushed her!"

"See the blood?" Hoof asked. He pointed out that so much had gushed from the dead woman's body that it had spread out in a pool almost two paces around the white pelt.

Onni shuddered and felt dizzy. While she had fought for months to prove that Elk Woman had murdered Eagle Beak, some part of her hadn't quite believed herself. Had she been right all along? Hardly realizing what she was saying, she blurted, "She did kill him."

"Onni, leave the dead alone," said Striking Eagle, who looked bleak with grief when she turned to look at him.

Hoof gave a sad shake of his head. "Kill him? You mean Eagle Beak?"

"Yes, grandfather," said Onni in a small voice.

"We'll never know," he said. "All I'll say for sure is that she did something so evil that she had no business putting her hands on the white hide."

"She looked all right the first couple of days," said Striking Eagle from behind Onni. Onni turned again to watch her husband.

"Yes, I saw her," said Hoof. "She fought its power. At the time I wondered what she was doing. For a while

466

she was successful. But evil cannot long oppose such power.''

Almost in a whisper, Striking Eagle asked, "Evil? Hoof, was she truly evil?''

"My son, look for yourself."

Striking Eagle squatted down to peer. He reached out a hand to touch the outstretched hand of Elk Woman, but Hoof grabbed it.

"No, son. Don't touch her."

"She was my wife."

"She, this robe, and all this bloody earth must be taken away and burned. Don't besmirch yourself."

When the other women awoke, it was all Hoof could do to keep them working, but work they must. If they quit now, they would anger the entire herd of white buffalo. The buffalo might rise and trample the tribe into the dust. Not even Hoof dared touch Elk Woman or the hide, much less remove her from her shroud. He had men slide long poles under her and take her out a mile from the village, where she was placed on a pile of brush. Some earth was shoveled up, placed in old skins and taken to the same spot. The brush was lit, and as it burned, more brush was thrown on the pile. It took a day, but only a few bones remained when they were finished. Hoof had the site covered with a large pile of rocks and made sure signs were left on top of the pile that warned passersby that this spot was permeated with the most evil *Wakan* possible.

When the rest of the robes were cured and completely decorated, Hoof sent one to the chief shaman of the five tribes that had helped Striking Eagle rescue the pelts from the white hunters. As power objects to be added to the grandmother bundles, they would bring each tribe as much prosperity as these troubled times permitted. The rest of the hides were used as the centerpiece of an elaborate purification rite that took Hoof and his assistants ten days to perform. Then they were taken to a high hill where, covered by an elaborate tower of boulders and rocks, they were left as thanks to *Wakan-Takan* for giving the six tribes life and buffalo.

Onni had made up her mind to say nothing about Elk Woman to Striking Eagle till he brought it up, for Willow had told her the worst thing she could do was crow about how right she had been.

The next night Striking Eagle asked Willow to keep an eye on the children and took Onni for a walk away from their lodge. Cooking fires burned quietly, children ran about in glee, and warriors trotted in from the hunt. Onni felt life in the village was good.

"She must have been very evil," said Striking Eagle.

Startled, Onni replied, "Yes."

"I feel differently about her now," he said. "I think she bewitched me."

"Bewitched you?"

"She did once, but I thought it was over."

"When do you mean?"

"Before we were married. I thought I married her out of my own will, but when I saw her dead, I could tell from my relief that she had done it a second time."

From the tone in his voice, she felt it was safe to touch him, and she slid her arm around his waist. He pressed her against him. They had reached the outskirts of the village. She was a bit frightened by the dark beyond the cooking fires, and she shivered. But Striking Eagle would protect her, and they hadn't been alone like this in a very long time. The feeling harked back to the times before they were married.

"Thank you, little flower."

"Thanks—for what?" she asked.

"For saving us."

She laughed nervously. "Have I?"

"I was angry at you for making me stick to my youthful promise."

She didn't say anything, hardly knowing what to say. It just felt good to have that tone back in his voice, the one that said the two of them had something special that no one else could ever share. She realized that this was what she had been fighting for.

"In time she would have destroyed you," he said, "and I think me too, not to speak of the children."

As much as Onni longed to gloat, she held her tongue. Willow had stressed how much she must not tell him that she had been right.

He went on, "Every time I think I might have lost you and the children, I know what a fool I've been."

She squeezed against him more tightly.

"I don't want to make promises to you I can't keep," he said.

"Maybe I've been the one who's been foolish, Striking Eagle," she said. It was hard to say this, but she pushed it out. "Maybe I've been too much a girl at heart, not a woman. I should have seen how important to our people you were becoming and made sure you had everything a successful warrior needs, including enough hands to make the robes and leggings you need as gifts."

In the dark, she felt his muscles relax. She wanted to give him something to make him feel good and happy with her forever. She needed to sacrifice something.

"I love my sister," she said.

"I love Willow too."

"You might take her."

"Take her?"

"You look at her sometimes. She looks at you. I could live with her."

"You mean marry Willow?"

"Yes."

"I can't believe you're saying this."

"You'd like her, wouldn't you?"

"Uh, yes."

"Then I mean it. Daddy would take five horses."

"Five horses!"

From the sound of his laughter, Onni knew she had proposed a good thing. She only hoped that Willow wouldn't try to take her place in Striking Eagle's heart.

But, as she had told herself a dozen times over in the past two days of considering this, it was up to her to keep her man. If I handle myself with Eagle right, Onni thought, no matter how many wives he has, no woman can take my place in his heart. I'm a woman now, and I'm the first wife of the most important warrior of the Kiowa. I have to deal with this the way any strong Kiowa woman would. I have to make sure no woman pushes me from my place— whether she's wife, sister, loose woman, or witch. It's part of woman's work.

She slipped her hand into her husband's, and he squeezed it and bent to kiss her. As they paused and he pulled her against him, a thrill shot through her. As she felt his lips on her, she heard the chirping of crickets and the rustle of small night creatures. As they kissed again, she felt him respond to her and she felt herself opening to him for the first time in months. She abandoned herself to his embrace. After a while, he led her away from the path into a little grove of bushes, and shortly they were lost together in the timeless embrace of bodies.

Chapter 16

The five men stood stiffly in front of the low dwelling that was half tent and half shack.

"Go on," said Joe Bob to Squint, who carried the cloth-wrapped bundle. "We come with you now. Get it over with."

Squint sighed and knocked at the nailed-together planks that served as the door to the makeshift shack.

When Sally Rawls appeared, Squint and the other four took off their hats, and he said, "Miz Rawls, begging your pardon, ma'am, but we done brought back Mr. McCall's things seeing as how you and him was fixing to get married."

Sally's hand went to her throat in alarm. "His things?"

"Yes'm." Squint held out the package, which she only stared at. Finally Squint set it down on the small porch.

"Where's Jack?" she asked.

The men averted their eyes.

"Where is he?" she asked again "He's dead, isn't he?"

Squint nodded a couple of times in a vague manner.

"No, no," she said, shaking her head sadly.

The dour men still seemed unable to say or do anything.

"Open it," she said stiffly, and after Squint had squatted next to the stoop and done so, she nodded and said, "Those don't look like his."

"Yes'm, they do," said Squint. "This hide vest is what Jack always wore out hunting. And this is his mashed up rifle and hat."

"But that hat's—so crushed."

"Yes'm."

"Maybe he escaped," she said.

"No, ma'am," said Squint. "We buried all them fellows, although you couldn't hardly tell one from another."

"Couldn't tell. . . ."

In a whisper, Squint said, "Injuns, ma'am."

"No!"

"Yes'm. Seems like the men the Injuns didn't kill when they raided the wagons they took back to their campsite."

"And Jack?"

"Looked like he was one of them they took back."

"What happened?"

"It don't do to tell, Miz Sally."

"What did they do? I want to know."

"Let me just say you couldn't hardly tell one from another by the time they got through with them."

"Did he suffer?"

"I reckon. For a while, anyway."

For a week Sally didn't believe it. Often she found herself at the front door of the stifling shack looking westward, expecting to see McCall's tall frame lurching down the empty street. Every time she caught herself, she felt foolish as well as miserable and threw herself back into her work.

God help her, she was learning the hard way the

472

lessons in humility. Dave Rawls had always said that learning humility was one of life's main purposes. She had left the hotel a few weeks before, lived off her meager savings, and felt especially virtuous and proud of standing up to John Moar. For a third of her savings, she had bought a dwelling that was more tent than shack from the partner of a hunter who had never returned from a hunt. Although it seemed terribly expensive, she was assured that she could sell it for more than she had invested in it when she moved to the west. She doubted it, seeing no reason for anyone not to go another quarter of a mile on farther into the scrub and throw up his own canvas-covered shack for much less.

For two weeks, away from the hotel and expecting Jack to return shortly, she had felt wonderful. But for the first time, now that she was preparing to leave it, she felt fond of Hays City. If you didn't blink, its citizens would treat you honestly, particularly if you had endured with them the heat of their summers and the freezing winters. The inhabitants of Hays had their own hard charm, and she would miss some of the town's characters—Seesaw, Bob, Squint, and Shorty Hanrahan.

By the third week she was worried, for Jack had not returned. But she kept it to herself. Her money was running low. It amazed her how much things cost when you weren't taking whatever you needed from the hotel's larder. She thought the men on the street eyed her with more speculation in their hard glances than they had when she had been established as the manager of the Hide & Skull. She felt they were examining her to discover the chinks in her armor, and their looks frightened her. Knotting up her courage, she spent money she couldn't really afford to at Moar's General Store for a .32 pistol. She practiced with it close enough to town so that every man knew she kept it in the shack.

Jack McCall still hadn't returned by the fifth week. There were rumors from returning buffalo hunters that he and his companions must be dead or they would have come across his outfit. Of course, there was nothing new to this. At least twice a month an outfit failed to return, and its remains were later found scattered across half a valley where the Indians had dropped what they tired of carrying.

Then Squint and his crew had turned up with their news of Jack's death, devastating her. First Dave, now Jack. Grief-stricken, she felt still more vulnerable in the canvas shack with the two children. She had no idea what to do when her dwindling money ran out.

Knowing how fast they were becoming destitute, Robert found work clerking in Hanrahan's Store, but was fired for stealing cartridges that he sullenly claimed he hadn't. She didn't know what to believe. The next day he announced he was going buffalo hunting. Sally, of course, refused to allow it. They had an argument that lasted two days and left them with little to say to each other for the next few weeks. She saw the future clearly. One day Robert would run off with a buffalo hunting team, and he would either be killed or roughened up into one of those hard, aged men of twenty-five who hung around the Drum and the Hide & Skull waiting for outfits that needed an extra man.

At the same time, Eva grew sulky and refused to help around the shack. Twice she had to be fetched from the hotel where she was visiting with the upstairs girls.

Sally felt she was drowning. She visited each of the ten stores in Hays and not one had work for her. She supposed that this was partly due to John Moar's either having an interest in them or their owners being afraid of him. This town would grind her down till she was like the dust in its streets. A part of her longed to let go and stop fighting. Why not simply become Moar's woman and live easily? Why not take a man, like the girls upstairs at the hotel took men, and at least survive? If she didn't marry Moar, she could pick out a successful trader or hunter and marry or make an arrangement with him. But each time she considered actually making a commercial arrangement of her affections, something inside rebelled, and she hung on for another few days hoping things would change.

Surely it was better to get ground into dust than have no respect for myself, she thought over and over. But, she wondered, am I being so righteous that I'm destroying myself? Maybe I'm no more than a prissy preacher's daughter who's been fed a lot of hog's swill as a girl. Maybe life's got nothing to do with how Daddy and Dave saw it. Maybe I ought to let go and live the way most of the world lives.

When she got down to her last five dollars, Sally had a much clearer sense of how the upstairs girls at the hotel had gotten into their style of life. She had fought hard and she was losing, she told herself, and not everyone had so much fight in them.

One blisteringly hot day in late July, John Moar turned up at the front of the shack with his wide-brimmed black hat in his hand. She just stood in the door looking at him and wondering dully, What now?

"Aren't you going to invite me in?" he asked.

"What do you want, John?"

"To apologize," he said in a self-mocking manner that seemed a shadow of his usual arrogant self.

"Apologize?"

"I'm sorry I acted like such an ass."

Somewhat disarmed, Sally moved back and John entered the hot shack.

"You've done very well with nothing," he said as he looked around at the shack's one room.

"Thank you."

"May I sit?"

She gestured vaguely toward one of the straight chairs at the plain table. Was he here to rub her nose in her misery?

He said, "You're not making this any easier."

"Making what easier?"

"My apologies."

"I have a lot to do."

"No, you don't."

For several long moments they just stared at each other. She dropped her eyes as she felt something jump in her. For all that she hated in John Moar, she loved his constancy and his ability to make in this desert an oasis of sorts. She certainly admired his ability to lay out his course and stick to it.

Tears rose in her, for her fate stared at her with his black hat twisting in his hand and a hangdog look on his face. It would be hard, but learning to love this man wouldn't be impossible.

"I was under a lot of pressure when Horsmann was here," said John. "I said things to you I shouldn't have."

"This doesn't sound like the John I know."

"I missed you, Sally."

"Missed me? You miss someone?"

He seemed to take a great interest in picking lint off his hat. "For the first time."

"I'm flattered."

"Well, you ought to be. Things aren't the same at the hotel without you."

"I'm glad to hear it."

"I've thought about it, and if you'll accept my apology, I'd like to start fresh with you."

"Start fresh?"

"Your job," he said. "Nelly's not too good at it. I'd make it worth your while."

A smile came to her lips and she laughed. John wasn't after her as a woman, only as an employee. She could hardly stop laughing.

He looked puzzled. "What did I say?"

"Nothing. It's not you. I'm sorry. It's Hays," she said, shivering in the heat. "Sometimes it gets to me."

"I know it does," he said. He nodded in a way that told her he didn't understand but was chalking it up to the strangeness of women.

"Yes," she said. "I'd love to have my old job back."

"You would!"

"Yes, I would."

The grin that broke across his face delighted her. "I shouldn't have bullied you," he said. "I get a little addle-headed sometimes," he went on, sheepish. "Makes me do stupid things. Let's try working together again."

She noticed that this statement of his made her a little lightheaded. The heat seemed to swarm through her. Sweat had made her body wet and her dress clung to her back. To counteract her lightheadedness, she nodded and stuck out her hand like a man to seal the agreement, saying, "Fine, let's try it once more."

For the third time on the same day, Sally forced herself to keep away from the hotel's front door.

She had been back at the Hide & Skull two weeks now, and the hotel was just getting back to what she considered normal. In her absence, the cooks had gone back to serving fried buffalo steak three times a day instead of varying the fare with roasts, chops, bread, vegetables and stews. The girls upstairs hadn't seen Doc during her absence; Sally got him over right away. She had the Chinese clean all the rooms on the second floor, even made them take the mattresses and bedclothes out in the sun to bake out their mustiness.

Except for Nelly, who had occupied her spot during her absence and who had been demoted by John from manager to just one of the girls upstairs, everyone at the hotel seemed glad to see her. The receipts from the bar and the dining room almost doubled from the first day she was back. Nelly sulked, saying little, and Sally tried to be thoughtful and give her few direct orders, certain that Nelly was angry and would flout them. Give her time, Sally thought. After she's used to my being back, we'll have ourselves a little heart-to-heart talk.

That talk came two weeks after Sally's return. Nelly had been drinking too heavily the night before and had gone to sleep while entertaining a customer. Angry, he'd tried to wake her up. She grew sick and threw up. The next afternoon, when Sally figured Nelly ought to be feeling somewhat recovered yet still remorseful, she chased the other girls out of the top floor and sat down on Nelly's bed to get things straight with her.

"You and I were friends once," she told Nelly, who looked puffy and bruised about the face. Had her customer beaten her? Very likely.

"We wasn't never friends," said Nelly. "You done took John from me. He's all I ever wanted."

So that was it! "I haven't taken him. I don't sleep with him. I know you have."

"That's just it!" said Nelly. "You make out like

you're something so special. It ain't fair. It makes him
chase you. I bet if you was to spend a couple of nights
with him he'd know what he's got with me."

"I don't doubt it," said Sally.

Nelly glowered at her. "There you go! You're such
sweet britches, ain't you? But you still want him, don't
you?"

"John?"

"Yeah, John."

"I don't know. He might not want me."

"Oh, he wants you, all right."

"Maybe."

"Did you like Jack McCall?"

Sally felt herself tighten. She didn't want to discuss
Jack with anyone, particularly not with Nelly.

"Oh, don't give me that injured stuff," said Nelly.
"No thanks to our Johnny, he didn't come back."

"What?"

"Oh, didn't he tell you?"

Sally's heart skipped a beat. Nelly was about to di-
vulge something important that she had been too naive to
see right in front of her face. "Tell me what?"

"How he made sure that Jack wouldn't come back to
take you off. How he planted Skinner Kincade and them
men of his to make sure Jack didn't come back."

"Didn't come back?"

"Kill him if they had to."

"No! You don't know that."

"Yes. Yes, I do know that. There's some things you
learn in a man's bedroom you don't learn sashaying about
as Miss Prissy."

"John wouldn't."

Nelly laughed a spiteful guffaw. "Wouldn't he? You
ask him."

479

Sally rose. She hadn't accomplished what she had come up here to do—straighten out Nelly—but she wasn't interested in that now. She wasn't sure what to do. Was there no end to the horrors Hays City had for her? Could John have done such a thing?

She found her hand on the doorknob before she drew herself up short and turned back to Nelly. "What did you hear, exactly?"

"I already said too much," she said. "Don't go saying nothing to John about me. He'd kill me."

"I want to know what you heard."

"Overheard," said Nelly. "I overheard it."

"What was it?"

"I done said too much already."

Sally advanced on her menacingly. "Look, I'm going to get the two of you together and get this straight. Now if you're afraid of him, I can understand that, but I want the truth, you hear me?"

She must have frightened Nelly, for the girl nodded in a quick, sober fashion and told the story of what she had heard at the door to John's office the night before Skinner and Jack had left for the last hunt.

John kill Jack? Sally thought in astonishment. Where was she, in hell?

"But don't say nothing to John about me, Sally," pleaded Nelly. "He'll kill me, he finds out."

Numb, hardly knowing what she was saying, Sally asked, "You're not lying?"

"No, I swear it."

"I know you want him. You might have made this up just to sour me on him."

"No, I didn't. I swear it."

"How do I know that?"

"Oh, Jesus, don't tell him, Sally, please. He'd kill me for sure. It just came out of me."

"Then you better tell me the truth or I get the two of you together."

"Sally, I swear it on my little child's grave, all I told you is the truth."

"Little child?"

"I had a baby once. It died."

In the August heat, the air felt as thick as sand. Sally sat on the bed and picked up Nelly's sweaty hand.

"Tell me the truth, Nelly."

"I did. I did, I did, I did."

"All right, don't worry. I won't say anything."

Sally left. The world spun as she clunked down the stairs, her legs trembling and about to toss her forward. Could she get to her room without meeting anyone? She crept along the cool halls quickly, keeping near the walls with the vague hope she could melt into the plaster. Would Hays never stop springing surprises on her? To think she had considered marrying the man! As bad as her situation was, that would have made it worse. Of course, it was still possible Nelly was lying. She was mean enough to lie, and if not that, stupid enough to mix up whatever she had heard. But Sally didn't really believe Nelly had gotten it wrong. Nelly's fear of John Moar was too genuine, and Sally's sense of things told her Nelly wasn't smart enough to have orchestrated such an elaborate lie.

Inside her room Sally locked the door behind her. At the window a faint, hot breeze stirred the gauzy curtains, bringing in the usual stench of the hide sheds. While she had nearly always hated Hays and its stink of death, she realized the killing of buffalo the town depended on was a part of its life as a butcher to the nation. She also knew that one day she would leave, just as eventually you left a butcher's shop.

Now she threw herself on her bed. She would never leave! This town was so permeated with death that no real life lived here. Maybe she had died in that attack on the wagon train with Dave and hadn't been good enough to go to heaven with him. This whole town was an elaborate arrangement in hell, designed especially to torture her. She let herself cry, but no tears came, only sobs as hot and dry as the foul-smelling breeze that was all the relief Hays ever gave you. She wanted to rise up and fling herself against the walls of this room like a fly against a windowpane, till she had beaten herself to death. But she couldn't move.

Oh, God, she pleaded, how long does eternity in hell last? What if I can't stand it?

But you have to, came the answer. That's the point of hell. No matter how much you flail about, you only hurt yourself worse.

If that day was terrible, things went downhill over the next couple of weeks.

After a day of telling those who came up to her room that she was too ill to come out, she went back to work.

She put on a brave face and said nothing to Moar, but in her heart, hatred of him blossomed. When at lunch he bragged about some particularly good land purchase or deal he had made with a buffalo hunter, she would nod stiffly and think, This man plotted to kill the man I planned to marry!

She saw that till now she had never understood hatred, but now Sally understood murder. When someone did something to you that was horrible and irreversible, you had almost a duty to yourself to right things by killing that person. The notion made her tremble, as did the size of her rage. She had never believed she was capable of such hatred.

The only thing that saved his life, Sally saw, was that it had been the Indians who had killed Jack, if she was to believe Squint and his crew. John's plan hadn't had time to work. In any event, Skinner and the rest of the killers had suffered similar fates. It made Sally shudder to think what she would have done had Skinner come back with the others with some made-up story of what had befallen Jack. Her visions were of her killing Skinner and John Moar with a pistol, or maybe better, a shotgun. She would have carefully learned how to use one and just as carefully killed them when they weren't looking to make sure she left them a bloody mess.

Things might have stood like this forever, but what grew along with her hatred was her knowledge that she had to confront John at some point. She smiled and smiled and John thought they never got along better. She was left with just enough doubt from Nelly's confession to feel guilty that she might be condemning an innocent man. She had to confront him, and in such a way that he would be forced to tell her the truth. But how?

That problem she turned over for weeks. It obsessed her. She would have to rope Nelly into confronting John, but the girl might—in fact, probably would—lie. John too would then lie with a smile, and Sally would be left thinking what had happened never had. Whatever she came up with, it must force the truth out of both of them.

To cap off her problems, Robert—she could hardly call the tall youth Robby anymore—had killed four of Mr. Billings' scrawny cows when he was out target-shooting with John's pistol, which he had snitched along with some ammunition. She had to pay for the cows, the ammunition, and the gun, for Robert had broken its hammer. When she remonstrated him, he was nasty with her, and she could do little except give him a tongue-lashing, about which he seemed indifferent. She was losing him to Hays, of that she was certain. Within a few months he would start spending time in the saloon. Before she knew it he would be off on a buffalo hunt, and the mock flirtations with the girls upstairs would turn into the real thing.

At the same time, Eva looked down on her mother still more, and Sally seemed to have lost the will needed to keep her daughter separate from the gangrene that flowed through Hays City. Eva and John spent a lot of time together, with John explaining the hide business to her and letting her do his books. John said she had a great aptitude for business. When Sally tried to deflect his influence over her daughter, Eva fought back.

"You're just jealous of me, Momma," she said.

"Jealous, child!"

"I'm not a child. Uncle John says I understand the business better than anyone except Sonny."

"Sonny?"

"The new buyer at the sheds."

"Oh, yes. You're too young to be learning such things."

"You're too prissy, Momma," Eva responded, looking her mother right in the eye as if daring her to say anything in return.

"Maybe so."

"You think Uncle John wants you, don't you?"

Sally felt too dispirited to fight with her daughter. "I don't know."

"Well, he doesn't. He's probably going to marry me."

"You!"

"Yes, when I'm a couple of years older."

484

"Well, you can still take my breath away, Eva."

"So, I'd appreciate it if you'd leave him alone, Mother. If you chase him, it will just make things more difficult for both of us."

"Eva, Eva!"

"No, Mother. I'm a young woman now, and I have to make my way in the world."

"You're just fourteen!"

"Only for a little while," her daughter answered. "I'm going to play my cards well. All I ask is that you not knock them off the table."

Jack McCall limped into Hays City on a brilliant day in mid-July. His boots were worn through, his shirt was falling off in tatters, and his thigh had a terrible arrow wound, but he was alive and moved under his own power.

He collapsed on the outskirts of Hays and was picked up by several men and carried to the Hide & Skull, where Sally swooned upon seeing him and had to be helped into a chair. Then, despite his filthy condition, Sally hugged him. He could hardly stand the excitement of it and passed out twice. He was quickly given a couple of belts of rye and pressed for his story by the excited crowd, but Sally saw he was in no condition for this and ordered the cooks to boil water for a bath. She cleaned him, put him into bed and sent for the doctor.

For four days she hardly left his side and nursed him with buffalo broth, dry biscuits and weak tea. By the fifth day he could dress and sit in a chair, and they talked.

He told her of his capture and of riding across the plains with the Kiowa hot on his trail and of the dozen times when he thought they would catch him. His stolen horse had failed him and he had had to run into the mountains, where the Indians had to leave their horses behind and come after him on foot if they were to catch him. That had at least made the chase even and it had enabled him to finally evade recapture.

She told him what Nelly had told her about Skinner.

"Yeah, Moar sent Skinner and them after me," McCall confirmed. "I didn't figure Skinner would have help from the others. I was stupid. I figured I had handled him before and I could again, but I overestimated my ability."

"Oh, Jack, I thought you were dead!"

"A dozen times the past two months, I thought I was too."

"Are—are our plans still good?"

"Our plans?" he asked with a grin.

"You know."

"Know what?"

"Don't tease me," she said. "I've been through hell since I thought you were dead."

"I'm sorry. Thinking of you, coming back here, that's what kept me alive through all that walking—leaving with you and getting out of Hays City." He shook his head bitterly. "They're just going to kill off all the buffalo."

Sally couldn't see what difference that would make, but since it seemed important to him, she said nothing. She just felt full and content now that Jack had come back. If only they could get out of Hays, out of Kansas, she would never ask God for anything else for the rest of her life.

"When can we leave?" she asked.

"Just as soon as I clear my account with Mr. Moar."

"Account?"

"He owes me for that first load, and I figure something for those hides that those idiots he hired stole from me."

"Let's just go, Jack. Let's not fool with John."

"Not fool with him? I figure he owes me about fifteen thousand dollars. He's going to pay up."

"No," she said. "He might—"

"Listen, if we don't get the money from him, how are we going to go west?" he asked. "You got anything saved?"

"Two hundred dollars."

"That won't hardly get us out of Kansas. There's four of us, you know."

The sureness in his voice eased her. No man since Dave had talked like this to her. But she was worried about John. He had guards, and he didn't part with anything he didn't have to.

She tried to explain this to Jack, who said, "Let's see what he has to say."

Still feeling a little shaky from his ordeal and further unnerved by the glare of the half dozen employees standing around, McCall found Moar in a sour mood when he located him at the hide sheds.

Having heard McCall's request for the profits from the first load and the whites he claimed Skinner lost, Moar said, "I don't think I owe you a goddamn thing, McCall."

"You know damn well you do."

Moar glared at him as he asked, "Where's my wagons and gear? My mules and horses you took out?"

"Scattered all across Kansas, if I know the Kiowa."

"You bring them back and I'll talk to you."

"I was bringing them back when your men tied me up and kept me from coming back."

"My men! Tied you up! What the hell you talking about?"

"I think you know. You put them up to going after the rest of the whites, and that's what riled up the Kiowa.

You put them up to dumping me someplace so you could get out of paying me for the hides.''

"That's the biggest pile of bullshit I ever heard. I lost a lot of money because you didn't bring me back those hides you promised.''

"You owe me three thousand dollars for the first load I brought in and another twelve thousand for the whites your haulers and clerks kept me from bringing in with their elbows.''

Around them, Moar's men snickered, and a couple punched each other in the ribs.

"I got work to do, McCall,'' said Moar. "Get out of here.''

"I ain't going anywhere till I get my money, Moar.''

Moar backed away and said to a couple of his men on the platform, "George! Petey! Get this stinking buffalo skinner out of my shed!''

George and Petey, who worked as Moar's guards whenever he had money around, and three others who worked in the sheds as haulers, advanced on McCall. He looked around for an advantage, but saw none. As he turned to leave, three of them grabbed his arms.

"What you want us to do with him, Mr. Moar?'' asked the huge man named George.

"The son of a bitch is trespassing,'' said Moar. "Throw him in the street. Make sure he understands I don't want to see his ugly face again.''

McCall tried to escape, but no matter how hard he wiggled, the five pairs of arms that spent their days moving around two-hundred-pound bales of hides held him pinned.

"You done picked on the wrong feller now, Jack,'' said the grinning George, who stood over six feet tall and weighed nearly a sixth of a ton.

The others whooped as they rushed McCall down the little flight of stairs. Before he knew what had happened, they flung him across the dirt road into the ditch full of the stinking water from the hide-cleaning operation.

George sauntered over to stand above the sprawled-out McCall. Grinning, he asked, "You had enough, Jack? Or you want us to drum this lesson into you?"

From the ditch, McCall asked, "What lesson? That five of you can toss me in a ditch? Hell, I knew that before."

George laughed again. "Then why'd you come around here bothering the boss, bull chip?"

Though he was furious, McCall hid his anger behind a rueful smile. "You got a point, George. Your surely got a point there."

George smiled. "Sure I do."

Later, back in the center of town, McCall looked up Sally.

"What happened to you?" she asked. "God you stink."

"I run into your boss."

"What happened?"

After he told her, she asked, "Are you hurt?"

"Just my pride."

"And we can't leave Hays?"

"Not till I get my money."

"Not much chance of that."

"Sally?"

"Yes?"

"You still care for me?"

"Care? Of course!"

"You're sure, now."

"Of course I'm sure."

"Will you marry me?"

"Oh, yes, Jack! Oh, yes!"

"Will you leave with me? You and the children?"

"Oh, there's nothing I want more! But how can we? We haven't got the money."

"You got faith in me?"

She gave him a puzzled look. "Yes, I think so."

"Let's take the train to Kansas City tomorrow morning. It's the last one for ten days, isn't it?"

"Yes. There's nothing I'd like better, but what do we live on?"

"You don't say nothing to nobody," McCall said. "You don't even tell your children. Just put a few things into a carpetbag and be on the train to Kansas City at eight tomorrow morning."

"Not tell the children?"

"Not till, say, seven o'clock tomorrow, and caution them then not to say anything or dress special. It might get back to the wrong person. Get them to pack at the last minute."

"All right, I can do that."

"Good. You got a gun?"

"A gun?"

"A pistol."

"Jack—why?"

"Never mind. You got one? You told me you had bought one."

"Yes."

"Good. Give it to me."

"Jack, what're you going to do?"

"Get us our money."

"How?"

"Take it."

"No, Jack. You'll get hurt."

"I don't think so."

"What're you going to do?"

490

"Better you don't know. Just promise me that all of you will be on that train no matter what."

"Be careful," she said. "I lost you once. I don't know if I could live through it again."

McCall gave her his biggest grin of reassurance, although he wasn't feeling all that sure of himself. Getting his money would be tricky and dangerous, and he had to make sure he was well out of town after he got it in his hands.

"Just promise me you'll be on the train. I'll fight through a pack of devils to get there if you promise me that."

"Oh God, Jack, whatever you say."

McCall packed that night, putting everything he really needed to take west in a small carpetbag. There wasn't much, and there was plenty of room left over for fifteen thousand dollars in bank notes.

The next morning he awoke before dawn and dressed quietly, leaving without waking Sam, an old friend who had let him stay in his shack.

By six-thirty he was in back of the Hide & Skull. He entered the kitchen from the back door. The blacks and the Chinese man were fixing breakfast.

"No ready yet," said the Chinese with a frown.

"Just coffee," said McCall.

"No ready," said the Chinese.

"Well, supposing I sit here quiet in the corner till it's ready?" asked McCall, who proceeded to sit.

When the Chinese looked up a few minutes later to give him coffee, he had disappeared. The Chinese shrugged at the blacks and drank the coffee himself, figuring that McCall got tired of waiting and had wandered back outside.

McCall had slipped into the main part of the quiet hotel. Nobody was in the dining room, the saloon, or the

491

reception hall, except for the sleeping desk clerk, who was slumped back in his chair.

McCall crept up the stairs to the second floor to Moar's office and living quarters. The long hallway was deserted. Quietly he tried the door to Moar's office, but it was locked. Opening his carpetbag, he took out the .32 pistol, checked its load, and pushed it into his belt. It wasn't too powerful, but it ought to do. From the sheath at his waist he took his stubby skinning knife and quietly pushed at the edge of the door till he had sprung the lock. Then he silently opened the door and entered the room.

He must have made some noise then, for as he entered, George was rousing himself from sleep in the club chair in the corner.

"McCall!" George exclaimed, reaching for the shotgun leaning against the wall.

Before he had reached it, McCall had the .32 Colt drawn, cocked and aimed at the big man.

"Just pull that hand back real easy, George," McCall instructed.

"You're dumb," said George. "I thought you learned your lesson yesterday."

"Where's he keep his money?"

"What money?"

"All the cash he pays for hides."

"I don't know."

McCall walked up to him, eased the hammer down on the brass shell, and then for emphasis cocked the hammer on the Colt again with an ominous click.

"Don't play around with me, George. I'm not happy after yesterday's lesson."

George stared at the muzzle of the gun as if it were a rattler not two feet away that was poised to strike. "All

492

right, all right," he whispered, as if not wanting to scare the snake. "In the safe."

Easing around to scan at the room, McCall saw a small safe squatting in the corner.

"How do you get in it?"

"What?" asked George, who seemed more fascinated by what he saw in the dark muzzle of the Colt.

"Wake up, you son of a bitch, or you're going to come to in hell," said McCall, waving the pistol to arouse George.

"Key," croaked George. "Mr. Moar has a key."

Another glance told McCall that George was right. In the center of the safe was a brass plate with a keyhole, and without it he would never open the safe before the eight a.m. train pulled out.

"Where's Moar?"

George's eyes glanced to the left. "Bedroom."

"Where's he keep that key?"

"His neck," said George.

"Goddamnit," said McCall.

"He's locked in there."

"Alone?"

"That whore's in there with him."

"What whore?"

"Nelly."

"We're going in."

"We?"

"You're going to wake him up and get him to unlock the door."

"Not me. He'll kill me."

"If you don't, I'll do it for him." McCall again eased the hammer down on the cartridge and re-cocked the Colt. For added emphasis he pressed the cocked gun's cold muzzle against George's temple. George's eyes strained ninety degrees in their sockets to look at the gun's cylinder.

Whispering in order not to startle McCall, George said, "Just watch yourself, Jack. Your finger might slip."

"Just move across the room real easy, George, and I'll try to hold myself steady. But remember, my gun stays on your temple or it goes off."

"Yes sir," whispered George.

As slowly as crabs on a cold dawn the two moved noiselessly across the room to the door. George knocked, but there was no response.

"He might have gone downstairs," whispered George.

"Just knock louder," whispered McCall back. "Tell him you got an urgent wire from New York."

This ruse worked.

"You want what?" Moar's voice asked through the door.

Under the prodding of McCall's gun, George repeated the story. As the bolt was being thrown back, they heard the hide trader curse his loss of sleep and the entire telegraph system of the United States.

McCall yanked the door back as soon as it was unlocked to keep Moar from barricading himself in. He got the drop on both Moar and George.

"You son of a bitch," Moar shouted at George, who backed against the wall away from the outburst. "I left you out here to guard things."

"The man can't stay awake," said McCall.

"And you!" Moar said. "What the hell are you doing in here? Didn't we learn you a damn thing yesterday?"

"No sir," said McCall. "Just that if I was going to get what's coming to me I had to take it myself. Open that safe and pay me what's mine."

"I'm not opening my safe for you," said Moar.

"Besides, you won't get five miles out of town before my men run you down."

"Just open the goddamn safe, Moar," said McCall, "before I open you up with this Colt."

Moar looked angry enough to forget prudence and jump him. A shot now would draw everybody in the hotel here and McCall would never get his money. McCall threw a left hook across Moar's face, hitting his cheek and throwing him to the floor.

"You didn't have no call to do that," said Moar as he pulled himself to his feet.

"You didn't have no call to toss me in the ditch yesterday," McCall countered. "Now open that safe or I take that key off your neck and open it myself."

"All right," said Moar. He went over to the safe and knelt in front of it.

McCall heard the tumblers click, saw the door swing open, and figured out what Moar was doing just as he was wheeling around with a little derringer. He scrambled to the side out of the way. The derringer went off and George ran to the wall for the shotgun.

McCall pushed a chair at Moar, hitting him in the groin and forcing him to the floor behind the sofa. With his Colt in front of him, he spun to find George had wheeled the twelve-gauge shotgun up—McCall was a second behind him.

In back of George, though, he saw Nelly bringing down a full whiskey bottle onto George's head. The shotgun's muzzle dropped, and both barrels of it went off, tearing a hole a foot and a half across in the sofa Moar was crouched behind.

"Don't shoot me, you fool!" shouted Moar.

George toppled to the floor like a felled tree.

Figuring Moar had held on to the derringer, McCall

sprang forward and pushed the sofa over onto Moar. The hide trader was pinned beneath it.

McCall had to hurry. That shotgun blast would bring people here in minutes. Pulling the sofa upright, he turned Moar over. Keeping his knee in the small man's back, he ripped off Moar's nightshirt and tied his hands and feet. He reached into the safe and pulled out five stacks of fifty-dollar bills. He riffled them, trying to figure how many bills were in each stack, but he didn't have time to count them. He took out another couple of bundles for good measure. They would have to do. Having stuffed them in the carpetbag, he stood.

Across the room stood Nelly, naked, the neck of a broken whiskey bottle in her hand. She was gazing down at George, who was still unconscious. She quietly beckoned to McCall with one hand and held a finger to her lips with the other, indicating that he should move quietly. He stepped over the struggling, cursing Moar toward her.

Still beckoning him, she backed into the bedroom, drew him in and closed the door.

"They didn't see me, did they?" she asked.

"He?"

"George or John?"

Puzzled, he answered, "I don't know."

"I don't think so. Whack me one, McCall, and tie me up."

"What?"

"As a favor. I want them to find me tied up and bruised, so he'll know how loyal I am."

"Christ, Nelly."

"Just do it! You're getting out of town, aren't you? I only helped you so he wouldn't drag *her* back here. Slap me so hard across the cheek it'll bruise."

McCall thought he heard the voices of men gathering outside. He wanted to race to the station.

"I can't hit you."

"Hit me, damn it!"

"Jesus."

"Just do it!"

She picked up his hand and pushed it toward her face. In the end he did whack her with his hand, and he tied her up with a couple of Moar's neckties. As he finished, he heard several men coming down the hallway.

He stepped out of Moar's bedroom door into the hallway to face them. "Where was that gun blast from?" McCall asked, rushing by them as if he were hunting for it.

"Thought it was down there," answered one man, looking puzzled.

"Naw, I heard it from up here," McCall claimed, pointing toward the ceiling as he ran toward the stairwell. But he headed down, not up, the stairs.

When he hit the street, he looked at his watch and found that he had four minutes to go before the train pulled out. He untied the first horse he saw, a heaving mare who looked as if her rider had just dismounted, and was about to swing into the saddle when he heard a shout behind him.

"Hey, fellow, that's my horse!"

McCall mounted anyway and wheeled to say, "You'll find her down at the station!"

When he reached the station, he saw the train had just cleared the platform on its way to Kansas City. Digging his heels into the horse's flanks, he shot on. The train picked up speed and he urged the horse forward. He drew abreast of the train, gathered the carpetbag in one hand and pulled himself onto the back porch of the caboose with an awkward thud.

As he opened the door of the caboose, the brakeman looked up from his breakfast and said, "Hey, you can't come in here."

Flashing him a grin, McCall strode forward past him. "It ain't you I'm taking this trip with, ace. Just you shovel in your grub."

Having to clamber over half a dozen flatbed cars with their mountainous bales of buffalo hides, he found Sally, Robby and Eva in the seventh car forward.

Facing forward, their backs slumped, the three of them looked mournful till Eva, sensing someone was behind her, turned, spied him, and squealed, "Momma!"

Sally looked up and her face seemed to shake all over. When she stood up, he saw she had tears in her eyes.

"I didn't think you would come!" Sally cried.

McCall answered, "I told you nothing would keep me from making this train."

McCall dropped the carpetbag and took her in his arms and gave her a long, hard squeeze.

He had her now, and a whole family, and a new life somewhere farther west. He was going to make sure she was never too far out of his sight and that he never lost her, not for the rest of his life.

AFTERWARD

In 1867, a year or so before white hunters began to kill the American buffalo in a systematic way, historians believe fifty million bison roamed the American plains from Mexico to Canada in four great herds.

During the six years from 1868 to 1874, they were slaughtered close to extinction.

In 1872, when General Philip Sheridan heard that the Texas state legislature was drawing up a bill to save the survivors of the buffalo herds, he left his regional military headquarters at San Antonio and rushed to address a joint assembly of the House and Senate at Austin.

During his speech, Sheridan said, "Instead of stopping the buffalo hunters you ought to give them a hearty, unanimous vote of thanks, and appropriate a sufficient sum of money to strike and present to each one a medal of bronze, with a dead buffalo on one side and a discouraged Indian on the other. These men have done in the last two years, and will do in the next year, more to settle the vexed Indian question than the entire regular army has done in the past thirty years. They are destroying the Indians' commissary; and it is a well-known fact that an army losing its base of supplies is placed at a great disadvantage. Send them powder and lead, if you will; but for the sake of a lasting peace, let them kill, skin, and sell until the buffaloes are exterminated. Then your prairies can be covered with speckled cattle and the festive cowboy, who follows the hunter as a second forerunner of an advanced civilization.''

Sheridan's advice was heeded. The lawmakers put the bill aside, and for the next three years the great herds of buffalo moved through a sleet storm of lead.

All the Plains Indians, including of course the Kiowa, who had thrived for centuries on a bountiful supply of buffalo, suddenly found their larders bare. Some struggled along on muskrats, gophers, rabbits and grass. A few survived by butchering their once-prized horses and mules. Conditioned since childhood to buffalo meat and their existence as nomadic hunters, so strongly did they love their way of life that the Plains Indians resisted changing these ways even if it meant starving. One winter twenty-nine Cree were reduced to three survivors "on account of starvation and consequent cannibalism." The sudden elimination of Montana buffalo in 1883-84 resulted in six hundred deaths by famine among the Blackfoot.

The passing of the giant herds brought the Indian way of life to an end. Plains Cree who had been aloof and arrogant in their former dealings with whites eventually besieged every trading post and settlement with piteous requests for food.

Ultimately the entire Plains Indian culture shifted and fell apart. This shift and dissolution might have taken decades, even centuries, in the normal course of tribal development and the arrival of the white man, but with the disappearance of the buffalo it took less than two years.

Within that time most tribesmen had to abandon their nomadic way of life as hunters and become farmers. They